THE PARASITES

Books by Daphne Du Maurier published by Robert Bentley, Inc. in cloth-bound library editions.

Frenchman's Creek
Hungry Hill
The Loving Spirit
Mary Anne
My Cousin Rachel
The Parasites

DAPHNE DU MAURIER

The Parasites

1971
ROBERT BENTLEY, INC.
872 Massachusetts Avenue
Cambridge, Massachusetts 02139

This edition published by arrangement
with Doubleday & Company, Inc.

Library of Congress Catalog Card Number 72-184728
ISBN 0-8376-0410-9

First published, 1950, in the United States

Manufactured in the United States of America

For whom the caps fit

MENABILLY

SPRING, 1949

PARASITES

ANIMAL parasites are invertebrate animals which have taken up their abode in or upon the living bodies of other animals. . . .

From a broad biological outlook parasitism is a negative reaction to the struggle for existence, and always implies a mode of life that is nearer the line of least resistance. . . .

Occasional parasites are to be distinguished from permanent parasites. Among the former are the bedbug and the leech, which usually abandon their host when they have obtained their object.

In the embryo stage they are migratory, moving from host to host, or to a free life before becoming mature. . . .

Amongst the latter are the so-called fish lice, which, with piercing mouth organs and elaborate clinging apparatus, remain in the same host always, and are amongst the most degenerate parasites known. . . .

Parasites affect their hosts by feeding upon their living tissues or cells, and the intensity of the effect upon the hosts ranges from the slightest local injury to complete destruction.

The Encyclopedia Britannica

THE PARASITES

CHAPTER ONE

IT WAS Charles who called us the parasites. The way he said it was surprising, and sudden; he was one of those quiet, reserved sort of men, not given to talking much or stating his opinion, unless upon the most ordinary facts of day by day, so that his outburst, coming as it did towards the end of the long wet Sunday afternoon, when we had none of us done anything but read the papers and yawn and stretch before the fire, had the force of an explosion. We were all sitting in the long low room at Farthings, darker than usual because of the rain, and the french windows gave very little light, chopped as they were in small square panes that added to the beauty of the house from without, but inside had all the appearance of prison bars, oddly depressing.

The grandfather clock in the corner ticked slowly and unevenly; now and again it gave a little cough, hesitating momentarily, like an old man with asthma, then ploughed on again with quiet insistence. The fire in the basket grate had sunk rather low, the mixture of coke and coal had caked in a solid lump, giving no warmth, and the logs that had been flung carelessly on top earlier in the afternoon smouldered in dull fashion, needing the bellows to coax them into life. The papers were strewn about the floor, and the empty cardboard covers of gramophone records were amongst them, along with a cushion that had fallen from the sofa. These things may have added to Charles's irritation. He was an orderly man, with a methodical mind, and looking back now with the realization that his mind was at that

1

time labouring under heavy strain, that he had in fact reached a point where it was imperative that he should make up his mind about the future and come to a decision, it is understandable to see that these little things, the untidiness of the room, the casual careless sprawling atmosphere of the whole house that pervaded when Maria came for the week end, and which he had endured now for so many months and years, acted as the first spark to fan the boiling resentment into flame.

Maria lay, as she always lay, stretched out upon the sofa. Her eyes were closed, her usual defence against attack from any quarter, so that people who did not know her thought she slept, that she was tired after a long week in London, that she needed rest.

Her right hand, with Niall's ring upon the third finger, drooped in weary fashion over the side of the sofa, the finger tips touching the floor. Charles must have seen it from where he sat, in his deep arm-chair, opposite the sofa; and although he had seen and known the ring for as long as he had known Maria, accepting it in the first place as he would have done any personal belonging of hers dating possibly from childhood days, like a comb, a bracelet, worn from routine without sentiment; yet the sight of it now, the pale aquamarine stone, clinging tightly to the third finger, so valueless and paltry compared to the sapphire engagement ring that he himself had given her, and the wedding ring, too, both of which she was always leaving about on the washbasin and forgetting, may have served as further fuel to his smouldering anger.

He, too, would know that Maria was not sleeping. The play she had been reading was thrown aside—the pages were already crumpled and one of them torn, the puppy had been allowed to play with it—and there was a smear of a sticky sweet dropped by one of the children on the cover. During the next week or so the play would be returned to the owner, with the usual note from Maria scribbled in her careless handwriting or typed on the indifferent machine she had bought at a junk sale years ago, "Much as I liked your play, which I found extremely interesting and which I am sure will be a great success, I don't somehow feel that I should be quite right or really what you want in the part of Rita. . . ." And the owner, though disappointed, would be flattered and say to his friends, "She liked it enormously, yes indeed," and think of her ever afterwards with regard, almost with affection.

But now the play lay on the floor, scrapped and forgotten with the

Sunday papers, and whether any thought of it passed through Maria's mind as she lay on the sofa, with her eyes closed, Charles would never know. He had no answer to that, or to any of her thoughts, and the smile that hovered a moment at the corner of her mouth and went as swiftly—it happened now, in her pretence of sleep—had no connection with him, or with his feelings, or with their life together. It was remote; the smile of someone he had never known. But Niall knew. Niall was sitting hunched on the window seat with his knees drawn up, staring at nothing; and even from there he had caught the smile, and guessed the reason.

"The black dinner dress," he said, apparently without reason, "tightly cut, revealing every curve. Doesn't it just show what sort of man he must be? Did you get beyond page five? I didn't."

"Page four," said Maria, her eyes still closed, her voice coming from a lost world. "The dress slips, a little further on, betraying a white shoulder. I skipped to see. I think he must be a little man with pince-nez, going rather thin on top, and too many gold fillings."

"Kind to children," said Niall.

"Dresses up as Father Christmas," went on Maria, "but they're never fooled because he's not careful enough about hitching up his trousers; they will show under the red gown."

"He went to France last summer for his holiday."

"That's where he got the idea; he watched a woman across the dining room at the hotel; nothing happened, of course. But he couldn't take his eyes off her bosom."

"Now it's out of his system he feels better."

"The dog doesn't, though. He was sick on the lawn just now, under the cedar tree. He's eaten up page nine."

The movement from the armchair, as Charles changed his position and straightened out the sports page of the Sunday Times, should have warned them of irritation, but they took no notice.

Only Celia, intuitive as always to approaching storm, raised her head from her workbasket and flashed the warning glance which was disregarded. Had the three of us been by ourselves she would have joined in also, from force of habit, from amusement; because this was something we had always done, from childhood days, from the beginning. But she was a guest, a visitor, and it was Charles's house. She felt instinctively that Charles disliked the tone of banter between Niall and Maria, which he did not share; and the silly mockery of

3

the author whose tangled play lay on the floor, discarded by the puppy, seemed to him cheap and not particularly funny.

In a moment, Celia thought, watching Niall straighten up and stretch his arms, Niall will wander to the piano, and yawn, and frown, and stare at the keyboard with that tense look of concentration that means in reality he is thinking of nothing at all, or merely what there would be for supper, or whether there was another packet of cigarettes up in his bedroom; and he will begin to play, softly at first, whistling under his breath, as he had always done since he was twelve years old, on those old prim upright French pianos; and Maria, without opening her eyes, would stretch also, and put her arms under her head, and hum softly, under her breath, in tune to Niall. At first he would lead, and she would follow, and then Maria would break away into a different song, a different melody, and it would be Niall who caught the pattern and come ghosting after her in repetition.

And Celia thought that she must in some way, however clumsily, prevent Niall's going to the piano. Not because Charles would dislike the music; but because it would be yet another of those unnecessary pointers to the fact, from which he must suffer, year in, year out, that Niall alone, before husband, sister, children, knew what went on in the closed shell that was Maria's mind.

Celia put down her workbasket—week ends at Farthings were generally spent in mending the children's socks; poor Polly couldn't keep pace with them, and of course nobody asked Maria—and swiftly, before Niall could settle himself at the piano—he was already straddling the stool and opening the lid—she said to Charles, "We none of us seem to do the acrostic nowadays. There was a time when we all had our heads buried in dictionaries and encyclopedias, and things. What is the first upright today, Charles, in the acrostic?"

There was a moment's pause, and then Charles said:

"I haven't looked at the acrostic. A word of nine letters in the crossword caught my attention."

"Oh, what was that?"

"An invertebrate animal preying upon the body of another animal."

Niall struck the first chord on the piano.

"A parasite," he said.

Then the explosion came. Charles threw down his paper on the floor and got up from his chair. We saw that his face was white and tense, and his mouth a thin hard line. He had never looked like this before.

4

"Correct," he said, "a parasite. And that's what you are, the three of you. Parasites. The whole bunch. You always have been and you always will be. Nothing can change you. You are doubly, triply parasitic. First because you've traded ever since childhood on that seed of talent you had the luck to inherit from your fantastic forebears; secondly, because you've none of you done a stroke of ordinary honest work in your lives but batten upon us, the fool public who allow you to exist; and thirdly, because you prey upon each other, the three of you, living in a world of fantasy that you have created for yourselves and which bears no relation to anything in heaven or on earth."

He stood there, staring down at us, and for a moment none of us said anything. It was painful, embarrassing, not a time for laughter. The attack was far too personal. Maria opened her eyes now and lay back against the cushion, watching Charles, an odd self-conscious expression upon her face, like a child uncertain of punishment who has been caught out in misdemeanour. Niall remained rooted to the piano, looking at nothing and at no one. Celia folded her hands in her lap and waited, passive and expectant, for the next blow. She wished she had not taken off her glasses when she put aside the workbasket; she felt naked now without them. They served as a defence.

"What do you mean?" said Maria. "How do we live in a world of fantasy?"

She spoke in her puzzled voice, the voice that went with wide-eyed innocence—Niall and Celia recognised the note at once—and so perhaps did Charles, who possibly was deceived no longer, not after years of marriage.

He rose to the bait, gladly, like a voracious fish.

"You have never lived anywhere else," he said, "and you are not an individual at all, you're just a hotchpotch of every character you've ever acted. Your mood and your personality change with each new part that comes along. There is no such woman as Maria, there never has been. Even your children know it. And that's why they are fascinated by you, for two days only, and then go running up to the nursery to Polly, because Polly is real, and genuine, and alive."

These are things, thought Celia, that men and women say to each other in bedrooms. Not in drawing rooms, not on Sunday afternoons, and please, Maria, don't answer him back, don't whip up his anger more, because it is obvious now that he has been unhappy for a long

5

while, and none of us knew, or understood; it has been boiling up for months, for years. . . . She plunged into the battle to forestall Maria. She must guard both Niall and Maria from attack, as she had always done.

"I do understand what you mean, Charles," she said. "Maria does alter, of course, with different parts, but then she used to do that when we were children; she was always being somebody else. But it's not fair to say she doesn't work. You know how she works, you've been to rehearsals, or you used to, at one time—it's her life, it's her profession, everything goes into it—you must admit that."

Charles laughed, and Maria knew from the sound of the laugh that Celia had not made things any better, only worse.

Once Maria could have dealt with that laugh, she would have got up from the sofa and put her arm round Charles, and said, "Don't be such an old silly. What's bitten you, my darling?" and she would have led him off to the farm buildings and feigned an interest in some old tractor, or a bin of corn, or fallen slates from an outhouse, anything to preserve the serenity of their being together; but nowadays, it was different, these things did not work any more, and surely now, thought Maria, at this late hour, he is not going to start being jealous of Niall; it would be too silly, too futile; he must know that Niall is like another part of me and always has been. I have never let it interfere with my marriage, my work, or with anything; it hasn't hurt Charles, it hasn't hurt anyone, it is just that Niall and I, Niall and I . . . And then her thoughts lost themselves in a tangled web and she felt suddenly frightened, like a child in a dark room.

"Work?" said Charles. "You can call it work, if you like. A circus dog, trained as a puppy, jumps for a biscuit, and then jumps automatically for the rest of its life when the lights go on in the tent and the people clap."

What a pity, thought Niall, that Charles has never talked in this way before. We might have been friends. I perfectly understand his point of view. This is the kind of conversation that I like having when everyone else is rather tight and I am perfectly sober and it's about half-past four in the morning; but now, in Charles's own house, it's somehow all wrong, and rather terrible, like a priest for whom one has a great respect suddenly taking his trousers off in church.

"But the people enjoy watching the dog," he said swiftly, trying to divert Charles. "That's why they go to the circus, for distraction.

Maria supplies the same drug in the theatre, and I give it in large doses to all the errand boys who whistle my songs. I think you've got hold of the wrong word. We're pedlars, hawking our wares—not parasites."

Charles looked across the room at Niall seated at the piano, and here it comes, boys and girls, thought Niall, this is what I've been waiting for all my life, a real slashing blow beneath the belt; how tragic that it has to come from dear old Charles.

"You . . . ?" There was a world of scorn in his voice, of contempt, of bitter pent-up jealousy.

"What about me?" said Niall, and just as a house loses all charm from without when the shutters are drawn, the light went away from his expressive face, leaving it blank and impersonal.

"You're a freak," said Charles, "and you have the intelligence to realise it, which must be singularly unpleasant for you."

Oh no . . . no . . . thought Celia, this is the worst yet, and why did it have to happen today, this afternoon? This is all my fault for asking about the acrostic. I should have suggested a good walk across the park and through the woods before tea.

Maria got up from the sofa and threw a log onto the fire, and she wondered what would be the best thing to do; whether to make a gigantic foolish joke, or to whip round and scream and have a tearing scene to clear the air, so that the attention would focus on her and away from Niall, an old childhood trick that had worked well when they were little and Niall had been in trouble with Pappy, or Mama, or old Truda. Or whether it would not be best to get out of the house, and away, and up in the car to London, and forget that this disastrous Sunday had ever happened? She would soon forget, she forgot everything, nothing stayed in her mind for very long. It was Niall himself who saved the situation. He closed the lid of the piano, and went over to the window, and stood watching the trees at the end of the lawn.

It was that still, quiet moment before dark that comes at the close of a short winter's day. The rain had stopped, too late now to matter. The trees were lovely, and forlorn, massed together, where the woods began, and the old dead naked branch of a fir twisted a grotesque arm into the sky. A dank starling grubbed for worms in the wet grass. These were the things Niall knew and loved and watched when he was alone; they were the things he would have drawn had he known how to draw, the things he would have painted had he known how to paint, the things he would have woven into music had the sounds that came into his head, day in, day out, gone out again as symphonies. But that never happened. The sounds went out as jingles, as catchpenny tunes, whistled by errand boys at street corners, sung by giggling shopgirls for a fortnight and forgotten, the pitiful, cheap nonsense that was his single claim to fame. No genius, no real power was his; only a small seed of inherited talent that enabled him to spin out one tune after another, without effort, without even inclination, and thereby reap a fortune, which he did not want.

"You're so right," he said to Charles, "so absolutely and entirely right. I am a freak." And for a moment he looked haunted, as he had looked many years ago as a little boy when Mama ignored him, and to show that he did not care would run to the hotel window that looked out over the Paris street and spit on the heads of passers-by; then he was haunted no longer, he ran his fingers through his hair and smiled.

"You win, Charles," he said, "the parasites are defeated. But if I remember my biology aright, in the long run the hosts they prey upon die too." He went over to the piano again and sat down.

"Never mind," he said, "you've given me an idea for another worthless song." He struck the favourite chords of his favourite key, smiling still at Charles.

"Let's all prey upon each other,
Let's all feed upon ourselves,"

he sang softly, and the sensuous dancing rhythm of the foolish song broke into the tense, disastrous atmosphere of the dark drawing room like the sudden laughter of a child.

Charles turned on his heel and went out of the room.

And the three of us were left alone.

CHAPTER TWO

PEOPLE always gossiped about us, even as children. We created a strange sort of hostility wherever we went. In those days, during and after the first World War, when other children were well-mannered and conventional, we were ill-disciplined and wild. Those dreadful Delaneys . . . Maria was disliked because she imitated everyone, and not always behind their backs. She had the uncanny knack of exaggerating some little fault or idiosyncrasy, the shrug of a person's head, the turn of a shoulder, the inflection in a voice, and her unfortunate victim would be aware of this, aware of Maria's large blue eyes that looked so innocent, so full of dreams, and which were in reality pondering diabolical mischief.

Niall was disliked not so much because of what he said, but more for what he did not say. A shy, taciturn child, with a sullen expression like a Slav, his silence was full of meaning. The grown-up individual meeting him for the first time would feel summed-up and judged, and definitely discarded. Glances would pass between Niall and Maria to show that this was so, and later, not even out of earshot, would come the sounds of ridicule and laughter.

Celia was tolerated because she had inherited, by a stroke of fortune, the charm of both her parents and none of their failings. She had Pappy's large generous heart, without his emotional extravagance, and Mama's grace of manner, with none of Mama's power for destruction. Even her talent for drawing—which did not develop in strength until later—was a kindly quality. Her sketches were never caricatures, as

9

Maria's would have been; nor were they twisted to the bitterness that Niall would have given them. Her fault, as a child, was a fault common to all youngest children: a propensity to weep, to whine, to clamber on people's knees and seek indulgence. And because she had neither Maria's grace nor beauty but was a stout, heavy little girl with red cheeks and mousy hair, the adult was soon bored, wishing to push her away like a clinging dog, whereupon Celia's eyes would fill with tears and the adult feel ashamed.

We were too greatly indulged; a shocking thing. We were permitted to eat rich food, drink wine, stay up to all hours, roam about London and Paris on our own, or whatever other city we happened to be living in at the time; so from an early age we were cosmopolitan in outlook, belonging to no particular country, with a smattering of several languages, none of which we ever learnt to speak with fluency.

Our relationship to each other was such a muddled thing that it was small wonder no one reached the truth of it correctly. We were illegitimate, they said; we were adopted; we were little skeletons from Pappy's and Mama's respective cupboards, and maybe there was truth in this; we were waifs they had found abandoned in the gutter; we were orphans; we were the spawn of kings. And why did Maria have Pappy's Irish blue eyes and Pappy's blond hair, yet move with someone else's lissom grace? And why was Niall dark and lithe and small, with Mama's white texture of skin, yet carry the high cheekbones of a stranger? And why did Celia sometimes pout like Maria, and sulk like Niall, if they were no relation to each other?

When we were little the whole business puzzled us ourselves, and we would ask questions, and then forget again, and after all, we thought, it did not really matter very much because from the very beginning of time none of us remembered anything or anyone else; Pappy was our father, and Mama was our mother, and we three belonged to both of them.

The truth was simple, once learnt and understood.

When Pappy was singing in Vienna, before the first war, he fell in love with a little Viennese actress who had no voice at all but was allowed to speak one line in the second act of an indifferent operetta because she was very naughty and very lovely and everybody adored her. Perhaps Pappy married her, none of us have really known or cared; but after they had been together a year Maria was born and the little Viennese actress died.

Meanwhile, Mama was dancing in London and in Paris, already breaking away from the ballet in which she had trained, and becoming that unique, unforgettable personality who filled the theatre of whatever city she happened to visit: Mama, whose every move was poetry, whose every gesture a note in music, and who had no partner ever upon the dim-lit, eerie stage, but always danced alone. Someone was Niall's father. A pianist, old Truda used to say, whom she permitted once to live with her in secret and make love to her for a few weeks only, and then she sent him away because someone told her that he had T.B. and it was catching.

"And she didn't catch T.B. at all," Truda told us in her dry fashion, sniffing in that disapproving way of hers, "she had my boy instead, and never forgave him for it."

"My boy" was Niall, of course, whom Truda, as Mama's dresser, took into her charge at once. She washed him and dressed him, and put on his napkins, and gave him his bottle, and did everything for him that Mama should have done: while Mama danced alone, and smiled her secret individual smile, and forgot all about the pianist who had disappeared out of her life, whether to die of T.B. or not she neither knew nor cared.

And then they met in London, Pappy and Mama, when Pappy was singing at the Albert Hall and Mama was dancing at Covent Garden. Their encounter was a thing of rapture that could only happen to those two, never to others, Truda said, with a world of perception rising suddenly in her blunt voice. They fell in love instantly and married, and the marriage brought ecstatic happiness to the pair of them, and possibly despair, too, at times—no one enquired into that— and it also brought Celia, the first legitimate offspring of both.

So there we were, the three of us, related and not related, one of us a stepsister, another a stepbrother, and the third half sister to each; no one could devise a greater mix-up had they done it deliberately. And only a year or so in age between us all, so that there had never been a life that any of us could remember but the life we had known together.

"No good will come of it," Truda would say, either in the one of many dingy hotel sitting rooms that would be serving us as temporary nursery-schoolroom, or in some other top-floor room in a furnished house which Mama and Pappy would have taken for the duration of some season or tour. "No good will come of this mixture of race and mixture of blood. You're bad for each other and always will be; you'll destroy yourselves somehow," she used to say after one of us had been especially naughty and wild, and she would fall back upon proverbs and maxims that meant nothing at all but had a sinister sound to them, like "You can't touch pitch without being defiled" and "Birds of a feather may flock together, but the weakest goes to the wall." She could do nothing with Maria. Maria defied her always. "You are eldest," she said, "why don't you set the right example?" And straightway Maria would mock her, pulling her mouth into the set thin lines of Truda's mouth, jutting out her chin and exaggerating the wobble, thrusting the right shoulder a little before the left.

"I'll tell your Pappy of you," said Truda, and there would be grumbles and groans and mutterings all day; but when Pappy came to see us nothing happened but an immediate riot, and even greater tomfoolery, and then we would all three be taken to the drawing room and set to caper and show off and play wild bears upon the floor, to the boredom no doubt of the visitors who had come to gaze upon Mama.

Even worse would follow, not for us, of course, but for the visitors, when, if we were staying in a hotel, Pappy would permit us to run about the corridors, knock on doors, change people's shoes outside their bedrooms, ring bells, peep through banisters and make monkey faces. Complaints were useless. No manager cared to lose the patronage of Pappy and Mama, who by their very presence brought prestige to an apartment or hotel, whatever city it should be, whatever country. Because now, of course, their names were billed together, they shared a programme, the performance that they gave was a dual affair, and they would take a theatre for a season, for two or three months perhaps at a time.

"Have you heard him sing?" "Have you seen her dance?" And in every city there would be the discussion as to which of them was the greater artist, which was the master, whose were the brains, who led, who followed, how the whole thing was planned.

André, who was Pappy's valet, said it was Pappy. That Pappy did everything, Pappy arranged each detail down to the final curtain, and where Mama should place herself, how she should look, what she should wear. Truda, always loyal to Mama and at loggerheads with André, said Pappy had no hand in it, he did only what Mama ordered him to do, that Mama was a genius and Pappy only a brilliant amateur.

Which was the real truth we, the three children, never discovered, nor did we care. We knew only that Pappy was the most wonderful man that had ever lived and, to our prejudiced ears, the greatest singer; and that no one, since the beginning of time, had moved and danced like Mama.

These things added to our arrogance as children. As babies, we heard the thunder of applause. We went about, from country to country, like little pages in the train of royalty; flattery hummed about us in the air; before us and within us was the continual excitement of success.

We never knew the ordinary placid routine of child life, the settled home, the humdrum day by day. For if yesterday we were in London, tomorrow would be Paris, and the after-tomorrow, Rome.

There were always new sounds, new faces, bustle, and turmoil; and in each and every city was that mainspring of our lives, the theatre. Sometimes a gold and gaudy opera house, sometimes a drab and shoddy barrack, but wherever it was the place was ours for the little space of time we borrowed it, forever different, yet unchangingly familiar. That dusty, musty theatre smell, how it still haunts each one of us in turn, and Maria at least will never shake it free. That swing door with the bar across it, the cold passage, those hollow-sounding stairs, and the descent to the abyss. Those notices upon the walls that no one ever reads, that prowling cat with tail erect who mews and vanishes, the rusty fire bucket into which someone throws the stub of a cigarette. The first sight of it would always be the same, no matter in what city or what country. The posters, sometimes black-printed, sometimes red, with Pappy's and Mama's names upon them, and the photographs, always of Mama, never of Pappy—this was a superstition of them both—hanging by the entrance.

We would arrive en famille in two cars. Pappy and Mama and the three of us, with Truda and André, and whatever dog or cat or bird that temporarily possessed us, and whatever friend or hanger-on who was in favour. Then the assault began.

The Delaneys had arrived. Order had departed. Chaos reigned.

We poured from the hired cars with whoops of triumph like an Indian tribe. The foreign manager, smiling, obsequious, bowed us welcome, but with a look of apprehension in his eyes at the sight of the animals and birds and, above all, the romping children.

"Welcome to Monsieur Delaney, welcome to Madame," he began,

flinching at the parrot cage and the sudden bursting of a cracker under his nose, and as he began his conventional speech of introduction his shrinking form would melt, would almost disappear under Pappy's thundering clap upon the shoulder. "Here we are, my dear fellow, here we are," said Pappy, his hat on one side, his overcoat hanging from his shoulder like a cape; "you see us bursting with health and vigour like the ancient Greeks. Be careful of that case. It contains a Gurkha knife. . . . Have you a small court or yard where we could put the rabbits? The children refuse to be parted from the rabbits." And the manager, swamped by Pappy's laugh and Pappy's flow of conversation, intimidated possibly by Pappy's height—he was six foot four—turned like a beast of burden into the dark precincts of his theatre, with a rabbit cage under one arm and a bundle of walking sticks, clubs, and Eastern knives under the other.

"Leave everything to me, my dear fellow," said Pappy happily, "you will have nothing to do. Leave everything to me. First and most important, what room do you propose to offer to Madame?"

"The best, Monsieur Delaney, but naturally, the best," replied the manager, stepping on a puppy's tail, and when he had sorted himself from the confusion, and had given directions for the various items of luggage and livestock to be placed in the passages pending their final destination, he led us down to the dressing room nearest to the stage.

But Mama and Truda were already in possession. They were putting mirrors in the passage, moving dressing tables outside the door, and tearing curtains from their rods.

"I can't use any of this. All this must go," announced Mama.

"Certainly, my darling. Whatever you wish. Our friend will see to that," said Pappy, turning to the manager, clapping him again upon the shoulder. "That you should be comfortable, my darling, is our first concern." The manager stammered, apologised, lied, promised Mama the world, and she turned her cold dark eyes upon him and said, "You understand, I suppose, that I must have all this by to-morrow morning? I cannot rehearse unless the curtains in my dressing room are blue. No enamel jugs or basins. All must be earthenwear."

"Yes, madame."

He listened, with sinking heart, to her list of absolute necessities, and then, when she had finished, as a reward, she smiled; the smile that came so seldom, but, when she gave it, promised the spoils of paradise.

Then the three of us, who had listened to the conversation with bright eyes, turned with shouts of triumph to the pass door beside the stage. "Catch me, Niall. You can't catch me," called Maria, and, running through the pass door and the passage beyond, she ran down into the murky stalls. She vaulted across the back of one of them, tearing a slit in the cushion, and with Niall in pursuit she ran in and out of the line of stalls, throwing aside the dust sheets, leaving them to trail upon the floor. The curtain on the stage was raised, and the manager, one eye on Pappy, the other on us, stood mute and helpless.

"Wait for me, wait for me," cried Celia; and, hampered by her plump body and her short legs, she would inevitably fall. The fall was followed by a wail of anguish, penetrating to the dressing room behind.

"See to Baby, Truda," Mama must have said, cool and composed, knowing that if the child had been crushed beneath the great chandelier of the theatre it would only mean one less to take around, and, throwing the contents of yet another valise upon the floor for Truda to sort and tidy after she had retrieved either the living body or the corpse of Celia, Mama would move on to the stage to damn it, to condemn it as unfit for human beings, even as she had condemned the dressing room.

"Pappy, Mama, look at me—look at me," shouted Maria, now standing in the front row of the gallery, poised on one leg upon the rail; and Pappy and Mama, engaged in heated conversation upon the stage with several men who were either carpenters, electricians, allies of the manager, or possibly all three things at once, took not the slightest notice of her imminent doom. "I see you, my darling, I see you," said Pappy, continuing his conversation, never looking at the gallery at all.

So much for the first assault. Carpenters were sullen, electricians exhausted, managers and their assistants despairing, cleaners blasphemous. Not so the Delaneys. Heated, happy, clamouring for supper, we drove away triumphant. And our performance would be repeated in whatever hotel, in whichever suite, we happened to be staying.

At ten o'clock that evening, blown out by a four-course meal taken side by side with Pappy and Mama in the restaurant, and served by shuddering waiters who loathed the sight of us and loved our parents, Pappy in particular, we were still jumping and turning somersaults upon our beds. Jugs of water would be upset upon the floor, cake crumbs, smuggled from the restaurant, spilt and strewn upon the sheets, and Maria, ringleader of every folly, would suggest to Niall a keyhole expedition along the corridor, to watch the other visitors to the hotel undress.

We stole along in our night clothes. Maria, her fair hair short and curling like a boy's, wearing her own nightgown tucked into a pair of Niall's striped pyjamas, with Niall slopping along behind in Truda's bedroom slippers, because he had been unable to find his own. Celia, trailing a stuffed monkey, brought up the rear.

"First peep to me. I thought of it," said Maria, pushing Niall away from the closed door, and, kneeling down, she put one eye to the keyhole while Niall and Celia watched in fascination.

"It's an old man," she whispered, "taking off his vest," but before she could continue her description, she was whipped off the floor by Truda, who had stolen upon us unseen.

"No, you don't, miss," said Truda, "you may take that road one day, but not while you are in my charge," and down came the heavy hand upon Maria's delectable bottom, and up went Maria's fist into Truda's buttoned, disapproving face. Wriggling, protesting, we were dragged back to our beds, and sprawled upon them, exhausted from our day, to sleep like puppies. In the morning only we were brought up to the value of silence. Pappy and Mama must never be disturbed. Whether in an apartment, in a hotel, or in a furnished house, we spoke in whispers and walked tiptoe in the early hours. To this day, we none of us rise early in the morning. We lie abed until the sun is high. The habit is ingrained within us. This, then, was our one rule of discipline, with another stricter still. The rule of silence in the theatre at rehearsal. No scampering then along the corridors. No jumping over stalls. We sat like dumb things in some far corner, in the circle, probably, or, if in Paris, in one of those loges behind the stalls.

Celia, the only one of us to care for dolls and toys, would have two or three with her upon the floor and, with an eye to the movement on the stage, set them in motion.

The bear was Pappy, full-chested, tall, his hand upon his heart; the Japanese geisha, her black hair in a topknot as Mama wore hers when she was rehearsing, bowed and curtseyed and stood upon one leg. When she became tired of this, Celia played house; the chairs in the loge were shops, were apartments, and in a little whispering under-current, too faint to be heard upon the stage, Celia held converse with her toys.

Maria, even in those days, threw herself into the ardour of rehearsal even as Pappy did, even as Mama. From the back of the stalls or from the circle she would enact the whole of the performance in dumb show, taking up her stance, if possible, before a mirror.

In this fashion she could watch herself, as well as Pappy or Mama upon the stage, and this made a double excitement; she was a singer, she was a dancer, she was a shadow moving among other shadows, the stalls shrouded in their dust sheets were her audience, and the pitchy blackness of the empty theatre sheltered her, caressed her, found no fault with anything she did. Losing herself in silent ecstasy, she threw her arms out to the mirror, like Narcissus to his pool, and her own image smiled at her and wept at her, but all the while one fragment of her brain watched and criticised, noted the manner in which Pappy threw his voice so that the last soft whisper of his song reached her where she stood.

It came, surely without effort, with the greatest ease, that last high note, and he would stand there a moment, a half-smile on his lips, on the opening night of a performance, and then gesture with his hand as if to say, "Take it—it's yours." After which he walked away into the wings, loping with that great easy stride of his, his shoulders and his back proclaiming, "I really can't be bothered to sing any more tonight," and as he did this the applause would come, a deafening clamour, bringing him back, with a shrug, smothering a yawn, to sing again. The people would shout for him, "Delaney! Delaney!" laughing, delighted, adoring the fact that anyone paid for his services could apparently treat them with such contempt and care so little for applause. And they never knew, as Maria knew, as Niall and Celia knew, that these smiles, these walks into the wings, these gestures with his hands, were timed and practised, an integrate part of his performance.

"Once again," he would say during the rehearsal, and old Sullivan, the conductor who went with us always, on every tour, wherever we went, waited a moment, his baton poised, holding the orchestra—and then into it again they went, the last verse of the song, and the same inflections were repeated, the same gestures, while away back in the circle, on tiptoe in the darkness, stood Maria, a flickering shadow moving across the surface of the mirror.

"That's all—thank you," and old Sullivan would take out his handkerchief and mop his brow and polish his pince-nez, while Pappy crossed the stage to speak to Mama, who had been to the coiffeur, or to the dressmaker's, or to a masseuse—Mama never rehearsed in the morning, and she would be wearing a new fur cape around her shoulders, or a new little feathered hat, and as soon as she appeared there would be a different feeling in the theatre, a sense of strain, stimulating and somehow sapping; the aura that Mama brought with her, always, wherever she went.

Sullivan replaced his pince-nez, straightened himself in his seat, and Niall, who had been crouching beside the first violin trying to read the score, fascinated by those illegible figures that meant less than nothing, his ears humming still with that last final twang upon the strings, would glance up, aware of Mama at once, guilty for no reason except that he felt she did not like him to sit amongst the orchestra. He heard her voice saying something to Pappy about the intolerable draught upon the stage, something must be done about it before she rehearsed that afternoon, and the whisper of the scent she wore, elusive, gentle, wafted down to him as he crouched by the first violin, and he longed suddenly, with a pain in his heart that was bewildering, to be the theatre cat that had found its way onto the stage and was standing now beside Mama, arching his back and purring, rubbing his sleek head against her feet.

"Hullo, Minet, Minet," said Mama, and she stooped and picked up the fawning cat, and now his head was tucked inside the wide dark collar of her fur cape, and she was stroking him, whispering to him, and the cat and the fur cape were one, they were blotted against each other, and Niall on sudden impulse leant over to the piano in the orchestra and clamped both his hands upon the keys, fierce and loud, in a hideous discord of sound.

"Niall?" She came to the footlights and looked down upon him, her voice no longer gentle, but hard and cold, and "How dare you do that? Come up on the stage, instantly," and old Sullivan, apologetic, lifted him over the head of the first violin and set him down upon the stage before Mama.

She did nothing to him, the slap he would have welcomed never came. She turned, ignoring him; and now she was speaking to Pappy, arranging some detail for the rehearsal that afternoon, and Truda was by his side, brushing his coat that had become crumpled and dusty from kneeling beside the first violin, while dancing through the pass door into the wings came Maria and Celia, with smeary finger marks upon their faces and cobwebs in their hair.

CHAPTER THREE

NIALL stopped playing the piano when Charles went out of the room.

"I've got that queer feeling," he said, "that I used to have as a child, and I haven't had for years. That all this has happened before."

"I have it often," said Maria. "It comes suddenly, like a ghost touching you, and then it goes again, leaving you rather sick."

"I believe there's an explanation for it," said Celia. "One's sub-conscious thinks ahead a fraction before one's brain, or vice versa, or something. It doesn't really matter."

She reached out once more for the workbasket, and took the sock with the hole in it in her hand, and looked at it.

"When Charles called us parasites he was thinking of me," she said. "He was thinking how I come down here every week end and never leave him alone with Maria. When he goes into the schoolroom I'm there playing with the children, breaking into their routine with Polly, taking them for walks when they should be resting, or telling them stories when they ought to be learning lessons. The other Saturday he found me in the kitchen showing Mrs. Banks how to do a soufflé, and yesterday morning I was in the shrubbery with a pair of clippers, clearing the brambles. He can't get rid of me, he can't shake himself clear. It has happened all my life, this business of clinging to people, of getting too fond of them."

She threaded the needle and began to darn the sock. It was worn and rubbed and rather smelly from the little boy's foot, and she thought of the many times she had done this, always for Maria's children, never for a child of her own, and how up to now it had not mattered too deeply, but this afternoon the whole scheme of things was altered. She could never come to Farthings again with the same lightness of heart because Charles had called her a parasite.

"It was not you," said Maria, "it was me. Charles is devoted to you. He loves having you about the house. I have always told you he picked the wrong one."

She lay down again on the sofa, sideways this time so that she could see the fire, and the hot white ash from the smouldering wood curled and fell away through the bars to the dead stuff below.

"He should never have married me," she said. "He should have married someone who likes the things he likes, the country in the winter, riding, going to Point to Points, having couples to dinner and playing bridge afterwards. It has never been any good to him, this mixed-up life, me in London, working, coming down only at week ends. I pretended we were happy, but we haven't been happy for a long while."

Niall closed the lid of the piano and stood up.

"That's absurd," he said abruptly. "You adore him, you know that perfectly. And he adores you. You would both have parted years ago if it had not been so."

Maria shook her head.

"He doesn't really love me," she said, "he only loves the idea he once had of me. He tries to keep it in front of him always, like the memory of a dead person. I do the same with him. When he fell in love with me I was playing in that revival of Mary Rose. I've forgotten how long it ran, two or three months, wasn't it? But all the time I thought of him as Simon. He was Simon to me; and when we became engaged I went on being Mary Rose. I looked at him with her eyes, and with her understanding, and he thought it was the real me, and that's why he loved me, and why we married. The whole thing was an illusion."

And even now, she thought, gazing into the fire, as I say these things to Niall and Celia, who understand, I'm still acting. I'm looking at myself, I'm seeing a person called Maria lying on a sofa and losing the love of her husband, and I'm sad for that poor lonely soul, I want to weep for her; but me, the real me, is making faces in the corner.

"There's only one parasite," said Niall. "Don't flatter yourselves he was blowing off at either of you."

He went over to the window.

"Charles is a man of action," said Niall, "a man of purpose. He possesses authority, he has bred children, he has fought in wars. I respect him more than anyone I have ever known. Sometimes I've wanted to be like him, to be that sort of man. God knows I've envied him—for many things. Just now he called me a freak, and he was right. But I'm even more of a parasite than a freak. All my life I've run away from things, from anger, from danger, and, above all, from loneliness. That's why I write songs, as a sort of bluff to the world. That's why I cling to you."

He threw away his cigarette, looking across the room towards Maria.

"We're all getting morbid," said Celia restlessly. "This introspection doesn't do us any good. And it's nonsense saying you're afraid of being lonely. You love being alone. Look at those mad places you go and bury yourself in from time to time. That leaky boat . . ."

She heard her voice becoming fretful, the voice of the child Celia who called, "Don't leave me behind. Wait for me, Niall, Maria. Wait for me. . . ."

"Being alone has nothing to do with loneliness," said Niall. "Surely you've learnt that by this time."

From the dining room we could hear the sound of the tea trolley being laid. Mrs. Banks was alone. She trod heavily, and, being hamfisted, she jingled and clattered the cups. Celia wondered whether she should go and help, half rising, then sank back again as she heard the brisk, cheerful voice of Polly saying, "Let me give you a hand, Mrs. Banks. No, children, don't finger the cakes."

For the first time Celia dreaded the communal tea. The children chattering about their walk, and what they had done, Miss Pollard—Polly—smiling behind the teapot, her healthy attractive face dusted with powder for the occasion—Sunday tea—the powder a shade too pale for her complexion, and her conversation, "Now, children, tell Aunt Celia what you saw out of the window, such an enormous bird, we wondered what it was—don't drink too fast, dear—more tea, Uncle Niall?" always rather nervous when Niall was present, colouring a little—she never knew where she was with Niall; and today of all days Niall would be difficult, and Maria more bored and silent than usual, and Charles, if he were present, grim and taciturn behind the monstrous cup that Maria had once given him for Christmas. No, today of all days, communal tea was something to be avoided. Maria must have had the same thought.

"Tell Polly we won't be coming in to tea," she said; "get a tray and we three will have ours in here. I can't face the racket."

"What about Charles?" said Celia.

"He won't want any. I heard him go out through the garden door. He's gone for a walk."

The rain had come on again, a melancholy drizzle, pattering thinly against the prison panes.

"I always hated them," said Maria. "They take away the light. Little, ugly squares."

"Lutyens," said Niall. "He always did it."

"They're right for this sort of house," said Celia. "You see them dozens of times in *Country Life*, generally in Hampshire. The Honourable Mrs. Ronald Harringway—that sort of name."

"Twin beds," said Maria, "the kind they push together to look like a double. And the electric light, disguised, comes from the wall above."

"Pink guest towels," said Niall, "and exquisitely clean, but the spare room is always cold and faces north. There's a very efficient house-maid who has been with Mrs. Ronald Harringway for years."

"But she will put the hot-water bottles in too early, and they're tepid when you go to bed," said Maria.

"Miss Compton Collier comes down once a year and photographs the border," said Celia, "masses of lupins, very stiff."

"And corgis, with their tongues out, panting on the lawn, while Mrs. Ronald Harringway snips at the roses," said Niall.

The handle turned, and Polly put her head round the corner of the door.

"All in the dark?" she said brightly. "It's not very cheerful, is it?"

She flicked on the main switch by the door, flooding the room with light. No one said anything. Her complexion was glowing and fresh after her brisk walk with the children in the rain, and the three of us were haggard in comparison.

"Tea's ready," she said. "I've just been giving Mrs. Banks a hand. The children have such an appetite after their walk, bless them. Mummy looks tired."

She stared critically at Maria, her manner a strange mixture of concern and disapproval. The children stood beside her, saying nothing.

"Mummy should have come for a walk with us, shouldn't she?" said Polly. "Then she would have lost her London look. Never mind,

Mummy shall have a big slice of that lovely cake. Come, children."

She nodded, and smiled, and went back into the dining room.

"I don't want any cake," whispered Maria. "If it's the same as the kind we had last time I shall be sick. I hate it."

"Can I eat your slice? I won't tell," said the boy.

"Yes," said Maria.

The children ran out of the room.

"Uncle Niall would prefer brandy, neat," said Niall.

He went into the dining room with Celia, and together they fetched a tea tray, and a second tray of drinks, and then came back into the drawing room, closing the door behind them, shutting off the domestic sounds of Polly and the children.

Niall turned off the light; the comforting darkness enveloped us again. We were alone, and quiet, and undisturbed.

"It wasn't like that for us," said Niall, "all bright, and clean, and purged, and commonplace. Plastic toys. Things that go in and out."

"Perhaps it was," said Maria, "perhaps we don't remember."

"I do remember," said Niall, "I remember everything. That's the trouble. I remember much too much."

Maria poured a spoonful of brandy into her tea, and into Niall's cup also.

"I hate the schoolroom here," she said. "That's why I never go to it. It's prison again, like the windows of this room."

"You can't say that," said Celia. "It's the best room in the house. Due south. Gets all the sun."

"That's not what I mean," said Maria. "It's self-conscious, pleased with itself. It says, 'Aren't I a nice room, children? Come on, play, be happy.' And down those poor little things used to squat, on shiny blue linoleum, with great lumps of plasticine. Truda never gave us plasticine."

"We never needed it," said Celia. "We were always dressing up."

"The children could dress up in my clothes if they wanted to," said Maria.

"You haven't any hats," said Niall. "It's no fun dressing up unless you have hats. Dozens and dozens of them, all piled at the top of a wardrobe, just out of reach, so that you have to get on a chair." He poured another spoonful of brandy into his teacup.

"Mama had a crimson velvet cape," said Celia. "I can see it now. It fitted around her hips, swathed, I believe you'd call it, and a great belt of fur round the bottom. When I dressed up in it the whole thing touched the ground."

"You were supposed to be Morgan le Fay," said Maria. "It was so stupid of you to put on the red cape for Morgan le Fay. I told you at the time it was not right. You were obstinate, you would not listen. You started to cry. I nearly hit you."

"You didn't hit her because of that," said Niall. "You hit her because you wanted the red cape for yourself as Guinevere. Don't you remember we had the book on the floor beside us and were copying the Dulac pictures? Guinevere had a long red gown and golden plaits. I put my grey jersey back to front for Lancelot, and some long grey socks of Pappy's on my arms to look like chain mail."

"The bed was very big," said Maria, "simply enormous. Larger than any bed I've ever seen."

"What are you talking about?" asked Celia.

"Mama's bed," said Maria, "in that room where we were dressing up. It was in that apartment we had in Paris. There were pictures of Chinese people round the walls. I've always looked for a bed as big as that and never found one. How very queer."

"I wonder what made you think of that suddenly?" said Celia.

"I don't know," said Maria. "Was that the side door I heard just now? Perhaps it's Charles." We all listened. We heard nothing.

"Yes, it was a big bed," said Celia. "I slept in it once, that time I pinched my finger so badly in the lift. I slept in the middle, and Pappy and Mama on either side."

"Did you really?" said Maria, curious. "Just the sort of thing you would do. Were you embarrassed?"

"No. Why should I be embarrassed? It was warm and nice. You forget, those things were easy for me. I belonged to both of them."

Niall pushed his cup back on the tray.

"What a bloody thing to say," he said, and he got up and lit another cigarette.

"Well, it's true," said Celia, surprised. "How silly you are."

Maria drank her tea slowly. She held the cup in both hands.

"I wonder if we see them with the same eyes," she said thoughtfully. "Pappy and Mama, I mean. And the days that were. And being children, and growing up, and everything we did."

"No," said Niall, "we all have a different angle."

"If we pooled our thoughts there would be a picture," said Celia, "but it would be distorted. Like this day, for instance. We shall, each of us, see it differently when it's over."

The room had grown quite dark, but the coming night outside seemed grey in contrast. We could still see the shadowy shape of huddled trees shivering under the listless rain. A bent twig from the jasmine creeper growing against the walls of the house scratched the leaded pane of the french window. We none of us spoke for a long while.

"I wonder," said Maria at last, "what Charles really meant when he called us parasites."

The drawing room felt cold, suddenly chill, without the curtains drawn. The fire had sunk too low. The children and Polly, who sat round the table in the brightly lit dining room across the hall, belonged to another world.

"In a way," said Maria, "it was as though he envied us."

"It was not envy," said Celia, "it was pity."

Niall opened the window and looked out across the lawn. In the far corner, by the children's swing, stood a weeping willow, which in the summer made an arbour cool and leafy, the foliage twined and interlaced, blotting the hard glare of the sun. Now it stood white and brittle in the sombre darkness of December, and the branches were thin, like the bleached bones of a skeleton. As Niall watched, a breath of wind came with the spitting rain and stirred the branches of the weeping willow, so that they bowed and swayed, sweeping the ground. And it was no longer a lone tree that stood there, outlined against the evergreens, but the wraith of a woman who stood poised against a painted back cloth for one brief moment only, and then came dancing towards him across a shadowed stage.

CHAPTER FOUR

ON THE last night of the season Pappy and Mama would hold a party on the stage. We would be dressed for the occasion. Maria and Celia in chiffon frocks, with cords slashed through the waist, and Niall in a sailor suit, the blouse of which always felt too big so that it sagged.

"Stand still, will you, child?" Truda would scold. "How can I ever get you ready in time unless you stand still?" And she would tug and pull at the rags in Maria's hair, and then brush the hair itself with a stiff hard brush until it stood up around Maria's head like a golden halo.

"Anyone that didn't know you would think you an angel," she muttered, "but I know better. I could tell them a thing or two. Now then, don't wriggle. Do you want to go somewhere?" Maria looked at herself in the wardrobe mirror; the door was half open, moving slightly, so that the reflection of Maria moved with it. Her cheeks were flushed, her eyes were sparkling, and the wave of excitement that had been growing all the day swept upwards now to her throat, so that she felt like choking. But she had grown lately, and the dress that had fitted her so well a few months back was tight across the shoulders and too short.

"I can't wear this," she said, "it's babyish."

"You'll wear what your Mama says you're to wear, or you'll go to bed," said Truda. "Now, where's my boy?"

My boy was standing in his vest and pants, shivering, beside the washbasin. Truda seized him and, soaping the flannel in the scalding lathery water, rubbed at his neck and ears.

"Where all the dirt comes from I don't know," she said. "What's the matter with you, are you cold?"

Niall shook his head, but he went on trembling, and his teeth chattered.

"It's excitement, that's what it is," said Truda; "most children of your age would be in bed and asleep by now. It's nothing but foolishness, this dragging you off to the theatre, and they'll be sorry for it one of these days. Hurry up, Celia; if you go on sitting in there much longer, you'll be all night. Haven't you finished? Coming, madam, coming . . ." And with a little click of exasperation she dropped the flannel into the basin and left Niall standing there, the soapy water trickling down his neck.

"We're off, Truda," called Mama. "If you bring the children along after the interval it will be time enough."

She stood for a moment in the doorway, cool and detached, and she was dragging long white gloves onto her hands. Her smooth dark hair was parted in the middle, as always, with a low knot at the nape of her neck. Tonight she wore the collar of pearls round her neck, because of the party afterwards, and pearl earrings.

"What a lovely dress," said Maria. "It's new, isn't it?"

And she ran forward to finger it, forgetting her own dissatisfaction, and Mama smiled, opening her cloak to show the hanging folds.

"Yes, it's new," she said, and she turned so that it swung round her beneath the cloak which was black velvet, and her scent was with us as she turned.

"Let me kiss you," said Maria. "Let me kiss you and pretend you are a queen."

Mama bent, but for a second only, so that Maria caught no more than a fold of velvet.

"What's the matter with Niall?" asked Mama. "Why does he look so white?"

"I think he feels sick," said Maria. "He always does before a party."

"If he feels sick he can't come to the theatre," said Mama, and she looked at Niall, and then, hearing Pappy call her from the corridor beyond, she turned, wrapping her cloak round her, and went out of the room, leaving her scent with us, stroking the air.

We listened to the sounds of departure, the voices and murmurs of grown-up people, so different from our own chatter and our own laughter. Mama was explaining something to Pappy, and Pappy was speaking to the chauffeur, and André was running down into the hall with a coat Pappy had forgotten—they were getting into the car; we could hear the engine starting, and the slam of the door.

"They've gone," said Maria, and then, for no reason, the excitement died within her and was gone. She felt lonely suddenly, and sad, and because of it she went across to where Niall stood shivering by the washbasin and began to pull his hair.

"Now then, you two, none of that," scolded Truda, coming back into the room, and, bending over Niall, she peered into his ears. Niall was bent in two, undignified, a thing he hated, and he was glad Pappy had not come with Mama to say good-bye, magnificent in his evening clothes, with a carnation in his buttonhole.

"Now, keep quiet, the three of you, while I get myself dressed," said Truda, and she went to the wardrobe in the passage where she kept her clothes, and took down her stuffy black dress that she wore when she was changed.

Already there was a sense of finality about the apartment. Tomorrow we were leaving, and it would be ours no longer. Other people would come and live there, or it would stand empty, perhaps, for several weeks. André was packing Pappy's suits in the long trunk, the chest of drawers and the wardrobe stood wide open, there were rows of shoes and button boots upon the floor.

He was talking in French to the little dark maid who had been hired with the apartment and who was folding Mama's things into sheet after sheet of tissue paper. Tissue paper was everywhere, strewn about the room. He was laughing and talking in rapid French to the little maid, who smiled and looked demure.

"That's his trouble," Truda would say. "He can't leave the girls alone." She always had her knife into André.

Presently they went away, off down the corridor into the kitchen for some supper, where Truda joined them. There was a goodly smell of cheese and garlic, and their voices came droning steadily from the half-open kitchen door.

Celia went and sat in the empty salon and looked about her. The books and photographs were packed, and all the personal possessions. There was nothing left but the bare furniture belonging to the owners of the apartment. The stiff sofa, the gilt chairs, the polished table.

On the wall was a picture of a woman in a swing, her petticoats show-ing, and a shoe falling from her foot, while a young man pushed the swing from behind. It was strange to think of the woman sitting there in the swing being pushed by the young man, day in, day out, month after month, year after year, ever since the picture was painted, and that after this night there would be no one to look at them, they would have to swing alone in the empty room.

"We are going away," said Celia aloud. "How will you like that? I don't suppose we shall ever come here again." And the woman went on smiling her fatuous smile, kicking her shoe into the air.

Back in the bedroom Maria was changing feverishly. She had taken off her party frock and hidden it in the dirty-clothes basket, and she was dressing up in the velvet suit that she had worn for fancy dress at the New Year. It was a page's costume, hired at great expense, and Truda had packed it in a dress box, tied and labelled, ready to return to the shop. There was a striped doublet and short puffy trunks, and a pair of long silk hose, and best of all a cape that was worn thrown back from the shoulders. Round the waist was a sling, and stuck into it a painted dagger.

The suit fitted perfectly, and as Maria stared at herself in the glass all her excitement returned. She was happy, nothing mattered, and she was not Maria any longer, a dull little girl in a stupid party frock. She was a page, and her name was Edouard. She paced up and down the room, talking to herself, stabbing the air with her dagger.

In the bathroom Niall was trying to be sick. He heaved and spat, but nothing happened, and still the pain at the pit of his stomach would not go away. He wondered miserably why it always had to happen, this feeling sick on great occasions. His birthday morning, Christmas, first nights, last nights, going to the sea, everything was spoilt by feeling sick.

On an ordinary day, when it would not have mattered, he never felt sick at all. He straightened himself and sighed, and then, coming out of the bathroom, he stood in the passage a moment, wondering what to do. He could hear Truda and André talking in the kitchen. He turned and went into Mama's bedroom. André had switched off the lights, all except one, which was by the mirror on the dressing table. Niall went and stood before the dressing table. The little bottles and lotions were still there—the maid had not packed them yet—and there was face powder spilt on the tortoise-shell tray. Mama's shawl was lying on the stool as she had thrown it after dressing. Niall picked it up and smelt it, and then put it round his shoulders. He sat down on the stool and began to finger the things on the tray. Then he noticed that Mama had forgotten to put on one of her earrings. It lay there, a round white pearl, amongst the powder. He was sure she had worn it when she came into their bedroom to say good-bye. Perhaps it had fallen off when Pappy called and she had not noticed, and André, or the maid, had seen it lying on the floor and put it back on the dressing table.

Niall decided to take it and give it to her, and surely she would be pleased and say, "How thoughtful of you," and smile. He took the pearl in his hand, and as he did so he had a strange uncontrollable longing to put the pearl in his mouth. He did so. He rolled his tongue around it, and it was cool and smooth and nice. How peaceful it was in the quiet bedroom. He did not feel sick any more. And then suddenly he heard Truda calling down the passage, "Niall—Niall—where's that boy?" and the sound startled him so that he jumped, and as he jumped his teeth bit into the pearl; it crunched horribly. In a panic he spat out the fragments into his hand, stared at them a moment, then flung them under the protecting valance of the bed. He crouched beside the bed, his heart beating, as Truda came into the room, switching on the light.

"Niall?" she called. "Niall?"

He did not answer. She went out again, calling for the others. He crept out from beside the bed and tiptoed down the passage to the bathroom and went inside, locking the door behind him.

Truda was in a bad mood as she took us to the theatre in the car.

"There's too much to see to, that's the truth of it," she said. "I can't have eyes everywhere in my head. What with packing up, and getting you children dressed, and now this caper on top of everything else—that girl never put the earring on the dressing table, I'll be bound. She has hidden it somewhere, to sell, knowing your Mama and all of us are off tomorrow—— Put the window down a bit, Maria, it's stifling in the car. You're sitting very still, muffled up in your party cloak. Don't say you feel sick too. Are you all right now, Niall?"

She went on talking, half to us, half to herself. Maria, her cheeks pink and her hands sweaty, wondered when Truda would discover that under her party cloak she was not wearing the frock at all, but the page's suit. She did not care, she would not change now, it was too late; even if she were punished, it would not matter. She bounced about on the little seat facing the driver, her mouth stubborn.

Niall felt for the comfort of Truda's hand under the rug.

"All right, my boy?" she said.

"Yes, thank you," said Niall.

They would never find the crushed pearl under the bed, and if they did they would think that the maid had trodden on it. Tomorrow they would be gone and everything would be forgotten.

It was only a few minutes now to the theatre, along the wide boulevard amongst the hooting taxis and the glittering lights, where the people jostled one another, chattering. And so into the foyer where there would be more people, a babble of sound, everyone talking excitedly, greeting their friends because it was the interval. Then as Truda whispered something to the ouvreuse, pushing us into the loge, and we stared about us, the bell would go outside in the foyer and the people come crowding in to take their seats, with the clamour dying away into a hush, as Sullivan in the orchestra paused and waited, his baton in the air.

The curtains parted, caught up at the sides as if by magic, and we were looking at a deep wood, where the trees were crowded close together; but there was a clearing in the centre of the wood, and in the centre of the clearing was a pool.

Although she had touched the trees many times and knew them to be painted, and had stared down at the pool and seen it to be cloth, not even shining, Celia was deceived again.

She echoed the little "Ah!" that came from the audience as they watched the figure rise slowly from beside the pool, the hair loose upon her shoulders, the hands folded, and although her reason told her that the figure was Mama, it was only Mama pretending, and of course her real things were lying in the dressing room behind the stage, the fear came to her, not for the first time, that she might be mistaken, that there was no dressing room behind the stage, no comfort of familiar things, no Pappy waiting until it was his time to come and sing; but only this figure, this person who was Mama and not Mama. She glanced at Maria beside her for reassurance; and Maria was moving, even as Mama moved, her head inclined a little on one side, her hands unfolding, and Truda was poking Maria in the back and whispering, "Ssh—keep still."

Maria started; she had not realised she was copying Mama.

She was thinking of the chalk lines on the stage, the ones on the bare boards before they laid the cloth. When Mama rehearsed she had chalk lines drawn in squares across the stage, and she would practise her steps from one square to another, over and over again. Maria had watched her many times.

It was the second square where she was moving now, and in a moment she would glide down to the third, and fourth, and fifth, and then the turn would come, and the backward glance and the movement of her hands following the glance. Maria knew all the steps. She wished she were a shadow, on the stage, beside Mama.

There was once a leaf blowing before the wind, thought Niall. The first leaf falling from a tree in autumn. And then it was caught, and tossed, and blown with the dust, and you never saw it again, it vanished and was lost. There were ripples on the sea, and they went, and they never came back. There was a water lily in a pool, closed and green, and then it unfolded, waxen and white, and the water lily was Mama's hands, opening, and it was the music rising and falling and losing itself, to echo in the woods. If only it would never stop, the music never die away into silence, but go on like this forever and ever, the fluttering leaf, the ripple across the water. Presently she was back again beside the pool, and she was sinking down to it, her hands were folding, were closing, the trees were crowding in upon her, it was dark —and suddenly it was finished, it was over. The curtains came ripping across the stage, tearing the silence, and all the peace was gone with the senseless fury of applause.

Hand upon hand, like silly waving fans, all clapping together, and heads nodding, and mouths smiling. Truda and Celia and Maria clapping with the rest, flushed and happy.

"Go on, then, clap your Mama," said Truda, but he shook his head, frowning, and looked down at the floor, at his black laced shoes beneath his white sailor trousers. An old man with a pointed beard leant over from the next loge, laughing, and said, "Qu'est-ce qu'il a, le petit?" And for once Truda did not help. She laughed back at the old man.

"He's shy, that's what it is," she said.

It was hot and stuffy in the loge; our throats were parched with thirst and with excitement. We wanted to buy sucettes on a stick and suck them, but Truda would not let us.

"You don't know what they're made of," she said.

And still Maria clung to her party cloak, pretending she was cold, and deliberately, when Truda's back was turned, she put out her tongue at a fat woman covered with jewels, who was surveying her through a lorgnette.

"*Oui, les petits Delaneys,*" the woman said to her companion, who turned to look at us, and we stared straight through them, pretending we had not heard.

It was funny, thought Niall, that he never minded clapping Pappy; he had a different feeling entirely when Pappy came on the stage to sing. He looked so tall and confident, and somehow powerful; he reminded Niall of the lions in the Jardin d'Acclimatation. He had such a tawny look about him.

Pappy started with the serious songs, of course, and just as Maria had remembered the chalk lines on the stage when Mama danced, so Niall thought back to rehearsal, and to Pappy going over the notes of music, phrase by phrase.

He wished sometimes that Pappy would sing certain songs a little faster, or perhaps it was the fault of the music, the music was too slow. Hurry on, there, he thought impatiently, hurry on. . . .

Pappy always kept the well-known songs, the favourites, for the end of his programme, for the encores.

Celia dreaded these because too often they were sad.

> "*In summertime on Bredon*
> *The bells they sound so clear . . .*"

It began so hopefully, and with such confidence, and then that terrible last verse, the churchyard; she could feel the snow under her feet, and hear the bell tolling. She knew she would cry. It was such a relief to her when he did not sing it, but chose instead "O Mary, at thy window be."

She saw herself at the window, looking out, and Pappy riding by, waving his hand and smiling.

All the songs were personal; she could never disassociate herself from any of them.

> "*See the mountains kiss high heaven,*
> *And the waves clasp one another;*
> *No sister flower would be forgiven*
> *If it disdained its brothers . . .*"

That was herself and Niall. If she disdained Niall she would never be forgiven. She did not know what disdain meant, but something terrible.

"O moon of my delight that knows no waine."

Celia felt the corners of her lips quiver. Why must Pappy do it? What did he do to his voice to make it so unhappy?

"How oft, hereafter, searching shall she look
Through this same garden after me—in vain."

And it was Celia, looking everywhere for Pappy, and never finding him. She could see the garden, full of dead leaves, like the Bois in autumn.

Now it was all over, all finished, the applause went on and on, and people were shouting, and Pappy and Mama were standing before the parted curtain, bowing to the audience, and bowing to each other, and Pappy was coming forward to make a speech, just as Truda hurried us through the pass door to the stage, before the crush, before the people started filing out into the street.

As we stood in the wings, Pappy had just finished speaking, and Mama was burying her face in the bouquet that had been handed up to her by Sullivan from the orchestra—there were several bouquets, one a great basket of ribbons, so silly when we were leaving Paris in the morning. Mama would never be able to pack it.

Now the curtains came together for the last time, the clapping and the cheering died away. Pappy and Mama stopped smiling and bowing to each other, and Pappy turned with a roar of anger to the stage manager at his elbow.

"The lights—the lights—God in heaven, what had happened to the lights?" he shouted, and Mama brushed past us, white, unsmiling, shrugging her shoulders in exasperation.

We were too well trained to question her. We recognised crisis when we saw it. We slipped away to the back of the stage, and Truda let us go without a word.

Soon we forgot everything in the bustle and turmoil about us.

In Paris the stage hands were a law unto themselves, like the porters at Calais. Agile as monkeys, skilful as jugglers, they shifted the props out of the way, backstage, screaming to one another as they did so, "Hop-la," while one little man with a beret, his face streaming with

3 5

perspiration, directed them, cursing at the top of his voice, flooding the air with garlic.

The waiters from the Meurice pushed past them with trays of glasses and plates of creamed chicken; André had appeared from nowhere, and was pulling bottle after bottle of champagne from a busted crate, and too early, too soon, came the first guest through the pass door, but it did not matter. It was only Mrs. Sullivan, wife of the conductor, in a hideous purple cape. She advanced towards us, smiling, trying to seem at ease. We ran away from her, leaving her alone on the stage amongst the waiters, the three of us hysterical at the sight of the purple cape, and we went to find Pappy in his dressing room. He waved his hand, laughing at the sight of us, his rage about the lights forgotten; and in a moment he had lifted Celia on high, right above his head, so that by holding up her hands she could touch the ceiling. He carried her like this down the stairs, and down the passage, with Maria and Niall clinging to his coat-tails; it was exciting, it was gay, and we were happy. We came to the door of Mama's dressing room, and we heard her say to Truda, "But if she put it on the tray of my dressing table it must be there now," and Truda answered, "It is not there, madam. I looked myself, I looked everywhere."

Mama was standing before the long mirror, dressed once more in the new dress she had worn earlier in the evening. The collar of pearls clasped her neck, but she wore no earrings.

"What is wrong, my darling, what is all the fuss? Aren't you ready? People are arriving," said Pappy.

"One of my earrings is missing," said Mama. "Truda thinks that girl must have stolen it. I dropped it back in the apartment. You must do something. You must ring up the police."

She had the cold, angry face that spelt trouble, the face that sent servants flying, stage managers running for their lives, and ourselves to whatever distant room we might possess.

Pappy alone showed not the smallest sign of discomposure.

"That's all right," he said easily. "You look better without earrings. They were too large, anyway. They spoilt the effect of the collar." He smiled across the room at her, and we could see her smile in answer, wavering an instant. Then she caught sight of Niall, standing white and dumb, behind Pappy in the doorway.

"Did you take it?" she said suddenly, with sure and fearful instinct.

There was a moment's pause, a pause that to the three of us lasted half a lifetime.

"No, Mama," said Niall.

Celia felt her heart begin to thump under her frock. Let something happen, she prayed, let everything be all right. Let no one be angry any more, let everybody love everybody else.

"Are you telling the truth, Niall?" asked Mama.

"Yes, Mama," said Niall.

Maria flashed a look at him. He was lying, of course. It was Niall who had taken the earring, and lost it, probably, or thrown it away. As he stood there, forlorn and lonely in his sailor suit, his face expressionless, giving nothing away, Maria felt a wild and desperate longing rise within her to scream, to push all the grown-up people away. What did it matter if the earring was lost? No one must hurt Niall, no one must touch Niall. No one but herself, ever.

She stepped in front of him, throwing off her party cloak.

"Look at me," she said. "Look what I'm wearing." And she stood there dressed as a page. She began to laugh and clap her hands, pirouetting round the dressing room, and, still laughing, she ran out of the door and through the wings on to the stage, where all the people were arriving.

"Well, God bless my soul," said Pappy, "what a monkey," and he started to laugh, and his laugh was infectious. When Pappy laughed, no one could go on being angry.

He put out his hand to Mama.

"Come on, my darling, you look lovely," he said. "Come on, and help me control these brats of children," and, still laughing, he drew her after him onto the stage, and we were all of us engulfed amongst a crowd of people.

We ate creamed chicken, we ate meringues, we ate chocolate éclairs, and we drank champagne. Everyone pointed to Maria and said how lovely she was, how talented; they praised her to her face as she swaggered in her cape. And Celia was lovely, too, was sweet, was ravissante, and Niall was a knowing one, a deep one, a numéro.

We were all lovely, we were all clever, there had never been such children. Pappy smiled down at us, approving, a glass of champagne in one hand, and Mama, more beautiful than she had ever been, caressed our heads as we ran past her, laughing.

There was no yesterday and no tomorrow; fear had been slung aside and shame forgotten. We were all together—Pappy and Mama; Maria and Niall and Celia—we were all happy, with so many people looking at us, we were all enjoying ourselves. It was a game that we played, a game that we understood.

We were the Delaneys. And we were giving a party.

CHAPTER FIVE

"I WONDER if their marriage was really a success," said Maria.

"Whose marriage?"

"Pappy and Mama's."

Niall got up and started to draw the curtains. The mystery had gone now from the garden; there was nothing strange about the darkness any more. Evening had settled in, and it was raining fast.

"They are both dead and gone. Let's forget them," he said.

He crossed the room and switched on the lamp beside the piano.

"How can you, of all people, say that?" said Celia, pushing her glasses back on her forehead. "You think more about the past than either Maria or me."

"All the more reason for forgetting," said Niall, and he began to droon upon the piano, no melody, no song with a beginning or an end. It went on without interruption, like the sound of someone humming in a room upstairs.

"Of course their marriage was a success," said Celia. "Pappy adored Mama, we all three know that."

"Adoring a person does not necessarily mean you're happy," said Maria.

"It generally means you're miserable," said Niall.

Celia shrugged her shoulders and went on darning the children's socks.

"Anyway, Pappy was never the same after she died," she said.

"Nor were any of us," said Niall. "Let's change the subject."

Maria sat cross-legged on the sofa and stared into the fire.

"Why should we change the subject?" she said. "I know it was terrible for you, but it was just as bad for Celia and for me. Even if she was not my mother, she was the only one I had ever known and I loved her. Besides, it's good for us to delve into the past. It straightens things out."

She looked suddenly forlorn, there alone upon the sofa, with her legs tucked under her and her hair rumpled. Niall laughed.

"What does it straighten out?" he said.

"I see Maria's point," interrupted Celia. "It brings our own lives into focus, and heaven knows, after what Charles said about us just now, it's time we did that."

"Nonsense," said Niall, "wondering whether Pappy and Mama's marriage was successful doesn't help us to decide why Maria's has suddenly become a flop."

"Who says it's a flop?" said Maria.

"You've sat there hinting it for the past hour," said Niall.

"Oh, don't start that sort of thing," said Celia wearily. "I never can decide which is the more irritating, when you two agree or disagree. If you must play the piano, Niall, play something real. I hate that drooning, I always did."

"I won't play at all if it's a nuisance," said Niall.

"Oh, go on, don't take any notice of her," said Maria. "You know I like it. It helps me to think."

She lay back again upon the sofa, her hands behind her head.

"How much do you two really remember about that summer holiday in Brittany?" she asked.

Niall did not answer, but his playing turned to discords, harsh and unpleasant.

"It was very thundery," said Celia, "one of the most thundery summers we ever had. And I learnt to swim. Pappy taught me to with infinite patience. He never looked his best in a bathing suit, poor darling, he was much too big."

But, she was thinking, surely the only real thing we remember was the climax. Did not that overshadow all the rest?

"I played cricket on the sands with those frightful boys from the hotel," said Niall surprisingly. "They would use a hard ball and I hated it. But I thought it best to practise because of going to school

40

in September. I was much better at jumping. I beat them hollow at jumping."

What, in God's name, was Maria up to, raking back the past? What good could it possibly do? What use was it to anyone?

"We were discussing earlier on about us all having different angles on the same thing," went on Maria. "Niall said we saw things from a separate viewpoint. I think he is right. You say that summer was thundery, Celia. I don't remember a single storm. It was hot and fine, day after day. No wonder nobody knows the real truth about the life of Christ. Those men who wrote the Gospels all told a different story." She yawned and settled a cushion behind her back. "I wonder what age I ought to tell the cihldren the facts of life," she said inconsequently.

"You are the last person to do that," said Niall. "You would make it sound much too exciting. Leave it to Polly. She will model little figures in plasticine and demonstrate."

"What about Caroline?" said Maria. "She's long past the plasticine stage. The headmistress of that school will have to tell her."

"I believe nowadays they do it very well in schools," said Celia seriously. "They make it clean, and bright, and unemotional."

"What? Drawings on blackboards?" asked Maria.

"Yes, I think so. I'm not sure."

"Wouldn't that be rather rude, though? Like those awful chalked figures on the front at Brighton, with 'Tom goes with Molly' scrawled underneath."

"Oh well . . . Perhaps it's not on blackboards. Perhaps it's things in bottles. Embryos," said Celia.

"That's much worse," said Niall. "I couldn't bear to see an embryo. Sex is tricky enough, without embryos."

"I didn't know you found it so," said Celia, "or Maria, for that matter. But anyway, we're wandering from the point. I don't know what sex has got to do with that summer holiday in Brittany."

"No," said Maria, "you wouldn't."

Celia wound up the darning wool on the card and put it back in the basket with the socks.

"It would be much more important, Maria," she said severely, "if instead of worrying about whether to teach the children the facts of life you taught yourself how to darn their socks."

"Give her a drink, Niall," said Maria wearily. "She's going to start that preaching, spinster thing. So boring."

Niall poured out a drink for Maria, and for himself and Celia.

Then he wandered to the piano. He put his glass down on the ledge beside the keys. He was whistling something under his breath.

"What were the words?" he said. "I can't remember the words."

He began to play very quietly, and with the tune the three of us swung back into the past.

"Au clair de la lune,
Mon ami Pierrot,
Prête-moi ta plume,
Pour écrire un mot.
Ma chandelle est morte,
Je n'ai plus de feu
Ouvre-moi ta porte,
Pour l'amour de Dieu."

Maria sang softly in her clear child's voice; she was the only one to remember the words.

"You used to play it, Niall," she said, "in that funny little stiff drawing room of the villa, while the rest of us sat out on the verandah. You played it over and over again. What started you?"

"I don't know," said Niall, "I can't remember."

"Pappy would sing it," said Celia, "after we had gone to bed. We had nets, because of mosquitoes. Mama used to lie in a long chair, in that white frock; she used to have a fly whisk in her hand which she used as a fan."

"It did thunder, I remember now," said Maria. "The whole of the lawn would be flooded in five minutes. We ran up from the beach with our frocks over our heads. There were sea fogs too. That light-house."

"That man who wanted to write a ballet for Mama and never understood that she despised ballet, that she did her own individual form of dancing—what was his name?" asked Celia.

"Michel Something-or-other," said Niall. "He was always looking at Mama."

"Michel Laforge," said Maria, "and he was not always looking at Mama."

We remembered the house too clearly and too well. It stood back a little from the cliffs, which were steep and dangerous. A path wound down through the gardens to the sea. There were rocks and pools, and curious dark cold caves, through which the sun filtered slowly like a torch's beam. Wild flowers grew upon the cliffs. Sea pinks, and thrift, and celandine . . .

CHAPTER SIX

WHEN the weather was thick the foghorns used to sound throughout the day and night. There was a little cluster of islands about three miles offshore; they were uninhabited, rock-bound, and dangerous. Beyond them was the lighthouse. The foghorn sounded from there. In the day it was only a minor irritant; we soon grew used to it. But at night it was different. The muffled boom was like a threat, coming with ominous regularity. We would wake in the small hours after a preceding day that had been clear and warm with no hint of fog, and suddenly in the stillness of the summer night the thing that had wakened us would sound again, moaning and persistent. We tried to picture it as something friendly, a mechanical device worked by the lighthouse keeper, some sort of engine or machine that could be turned by hand. But it was useless. The lighthouse could never be reached, the sea was too rough, the rocky islands were denied us. And the voice of the foghorn remained the voice of doom.

Pappy and Mama changed their room to the spare room at the back of the villa because Mama could not bear to wake up and hear the foghorn in the night. The spare room had no view. It looked out upon a piece of kitchen garden and the road leading to the village. Mama was more than usually tired that summer. The season had been a long one. We had been in London all the winter, and had gone to Rome for Easter, and then on to Paris for May, June, and July. Plans were being made for another long tour in the autumn, to America and Canada. There was talk of Niall going to school, and possibly

Maria too. We were all growing too fast, we were all getting out of hand. Maria was as tall as Mama, which was not saying much, perhaps, for Mama was small, but when Maria leapt from rock to rock down on the shore, or stood for a moment poised on a ledge before diving, Pappy said she had become a woman overnight and none of us had realised it. We were all depressed when he said this, Maria most of all. She had no wish to be a woman. It was a word she hated, anyway. It sounded like someone old, like Truda; it sounded like a very dull person, Mrs. Sullivan, perhaps, shopping in Oxford Street and carrying parcels.

We sat round the table on the verandah, sipping cider through straws, discussing it.

"We ought to take something to stunt our growth," said Maria. "Gin or brandy."

"It's too late," said Niall. "Even if we bribed André or someone to get us gin from the village, it wouldn't work. Look at your legs."

Maria stretched out her long legs from under the table. They were brown and smooth, and golden silky hairs ran down the centre of them. She began to laugh suddenly.

"What's the matter?" said Niall.

"You know when we were playing vingt-et-un the other evening after supper," she said, "and Pappy made us laugh so much telling us about his young days in Vienna, and Mama had gone to bed early with a headache, and Michel came and joined us from the hotel?"

"Yes," said Celia. "He was very unlucky at vingt-et-un. He lost all his counters to me and Pappy."

"Well," said Maria, "guess what he did? He kept stroking my legs under the table. I got such giggles, I was afraid you would see."

"Rather cheek," said Niall, "but I should think he's the sort of man who likes stroking things. He always makes a fuss of the cats here, haven't you noticed?"

"Yes," said Celia, "so he does. I think he's very affected, and I'm sure Pappy does too. I don't think Pappy likes him."

"He's really Mama's friend," said Niall; "they're always having talks about this ballet he wants to write for her, for the autumn tour. They went on and on about it yesterday afternoon. What did you do when he stroked your legs? Kick out under the table?"

Maria shook her head and sipped comfortably at her cider.

"No," she said, "I liked it. It was rather a nice feeling."

Celia stared at her in surprise and looked down at her own plump legs. She never tanned properly like Maria.

"Is it?" she said. "I should have thought it was silly." She leant forward and stroked her own leg and then stroked Maria's.

"It's not the same, you doing it," said Maria. "That's dull. The whole point is to have someone doing it who you don't know very well. Like Michel."

"Oh, I see," said Celia. She was puzzled.

Niall felt in his pocket for a sucette. It was lime and very bitter. He sucked it thoughtfully. It was being a strange sort of summer. They none of them played the games they used to play. Catholics and Huguenots, English and Irish, explorers up the Amazon. There was always something else to do. Maria would wander off on her own, or become friendly with grown-up people from the hotel like this boring Michel, who must be quite thirty anyway, and Celia had started a new, irritating business of wanting to be good at swimming. She took things up with such enthusiasm, concentrating hard on her strokes, counting loudly, and then jumping up in the water and calling out, "How many strokes that time? Was it better? Do watch, someone."

No one wanted to watch, but Pappy would glance up with an indulgent smile and answer back, "Very good. Keep at it. I'll come and show you directly."

Once, thought Niall, we would be together, Maria choosing the game, saying who was to be who, what were their names, which was to be the enemy. And now it was changing, the thing of pretending to be other people. That was what Pappy meant about us all growing up, about Maria becoming a woman. Soon we won't be children any more. We shall be like Them.

The future held no security with this talk about the American tour, taking only Celia, with school for himself and Maria. Niall threw away the bitter end of his lime sucette and went indoors to the sitting room. It was cool and quiet inside; the shutters were all down. He went over to the piano and gently lifted the lid. It was only this summer that he had discovered how simple it was to find a combination of notes, turn them into chords, and make sense from them. When the others were down on the beach, bathing or lying in the sun, he would come into the empty house and do this. We wondered why people bothered to learn the piano properly, read music, weary their brains with things called croches, and quavers, and semi-quavers, when it was the simplest thing in the world to find the right sound of something that you had heard once, and play it straight off upon the piano.

Already he knew all Pappy's songs. You could change the meaning of them, too, by the alteration of the notes; you could turn quite a bright, jolly song into something sad by putting in or omitting one single chord, and by making the melody run, as it were, downhill. He could think of no other way of expressing it. Perhaps if he went to school somebody would teach him properly, give him lessons. Meanwhile, there was endless fascination in this private method of exploring. It was, in a way, as much fun as the old games of pretence with Maria and Celia, possibly even better, because he could choose his own sounds, whereas in the games he had to play whatever game Maria proposed.

> "Au clair de la lune,
> Mon ami Pierrot,
> Prête-moi ta plume,
> Pour écrire un mot.
> Ma chandelle est morte,
> Je n'ai plus de feu
> Ouvre-moi ta porte,
> Pour l'amour de Dieu."

Pappy used to sing this for a final encore very often. The simpler the song, the wilder became the audience. They would scream, and wave handkerchiefs, and stamp with their feet—just because he did nothing at all but stand perfectly still on the stage and sing a little simple song that everybody had learnt in their cradle. It was the voice going soft that did it—you got the same effect with a muted string on a fiddle. And, more exciting still, you could get the same sadness out of "Mon ami Pierrot" by changing the notes around; the melody was the same and the general sense, but by changing the chords, the note of despair became sharper. It was even more exciting to play the melody to a different time.

Pappy used to sing every word for its own value, and that was why it came over so well and with such grace—

> "Au clair de la lune . . ."

But if you changed that, if you started with emphasis on the "Au" and then ran on and emphasised again on "lune," breaking the "lune" into two, it became a dance rhythm and was altogether different. The pathos was gone; nobody need be sad any more. Celia would not have to cry. Niall would not have that awful feeling that swept over him at times of being terribly unhappy for no reason.

Au clair beat—beat—de la lu—beat—beat—ne
Mon ami—beat—beat—Pierrot
(ding-a-dong-and a ding-a-dinga-dong)

Yes, of course, that was the answer. It was gay, it was fun. Pappy ought to sing it in this fashion. Niall repeated the song over and over again, making the new beats come in at the most surprising places, and he began to whistle the song against the timing of the beats. Suddenly, he did not know how it was, but it came to him that he was no longer alone in the room. Someone had come in through the door that led into the hall behind him. He had at once a furtive feeling of guilt, of shame. He stopped playing; he turned round upon the stool. Mama was standing in the doorway, watching him. For a moment they looked at one another. Mama hesitated, then she shut the door and came towards him and stood beside the piano.

"What made you play like that?" she said.

Niall watched her eyes. She was not angry, he saw that at once, and he was relieved. Nor was she smiling. She looked tired rather, strange.

"I don't know," he said. "I felt I wanted to. It just—happened."

She stood there looking down at him, and he realized, sitting upon the stool, that Truda was right about her after all. He had never noticed it before, but she was not tall, she was smaller than Maria. She was wearing that loose peignoir that she generally wore at breakfast, or in her room, and straw sandals without heels.

"I had a headache," she said. "I was lying down in my room upstairs, and I heard you."

It was queer, thought Niall, that she had not rung the bell for Truda or someone to come and tell him to stop. Or even thumped on the floor. As a rule, if they made too much noise and she was resting, she always did this.

"I'm awfully sorry," he said, "I didn't know. I thought everyone was out. The others were on the verandah a while ago, but they went off, to the beach, I think."

Mama did not seem to be listening. It was as though she were thinking of something else.

"Go on," she said, "do it again."

"Oh no," said Niall quickly, "I can't play properly."

"Yes, you can," she said.

Niall stared at her. Had her headache turned her queer? Was she all right? And she was smiling now, not a mocking smile, but kind.

He swallowed hard and turned once more to the piano and began to play. But now his hands stumbled and slipped, the sounds were false.

"It's no use," he said, "I can't."

Then she did a surprising thing. She sat down on the stool beside him; she put her left arm round his shoulder and her right hand on the keys next to his two hands.

"Come on," she said, "we'll play together."

And she took up the pace and the rhythm of the song where he had left it; she turned the song into a dancing, happy song, as he had done. He was so surprised, so startled, that he could not think at all. Perhaps Mama was sleepwalking, or had taken a pill for her headache that had driven her mad, like Ophelia in *Hamlet*. It seemed to him that it could not be true, Mama sitting like this beside him at the piano, with her arm in the peignoir round his shoulders.

She stopped and looked at him.

"What's the matter?" she said. "Don't you want to play any more?"

It must have been true that she had been resting because there was no powder on her face like there usually was, or lip stuff. Her face was not "done," as Maria would have said. It was just her face. The skin was soft and smooth, and there were little lines at the corners of her eyes that did not show as a rule, and at the corners of her mouth. He wondered why it was that she should seem so much prettier when she looked like this, so much kinder. Not a person to be afraid of any more. She was suddenly not like a grown-up person. She was young, like himself, like Maria. . . .

"Don't you want to play?" she repeated.

"Yes . . ." he said. "Oh yes . . ." And now he was not nervous. The feeling of nervousness went away; he was happy at last, happier than he had ever been, and his hands were no longer false, no longer clumsy.

> "Ma chandelle est morte,
> Je n'ai plus de feu."

And Mama was playing with him and singing too—Mama who never sang with Pappy.

Outside, through the shuttered window leading to the verandah, the foghorn sounded for the first time that afternoon; it boomed deeply. Once, twice, and then again.

Niall went on playing, with Mama beside him, quicker and louder than before.

> "Ouvre-moi ta porte,
> Pour l'amour de Dieu."

Down over the rocks, by the deepest pool, Maria was lying on her tummy, watching her own reflection. She found she could make tears come into her eyes without the slightest effort. She did not even have to pinch herself, or squeeze her eyes. She just pretended she was sad, and the tears came. You said words to yourself that sounded sad, and the thing happened.

"Never more . . . never more . . ." she murmured, and the face that stared back at her from the pool was tear-stained with grief. There were pieces from the Bible that were good to say too, not for crying, but just to say.

> "How beautiful are thy feet with shoes, O prince's daughter."

Was that the Bible? Well, anyway, it was from something. There were so many lovely things to say. She wanted to string them all together in a hopeless jumble.

> "Now seems it more than ever rich to die,
> To cease upon the midnight with no pain . . ."

She turned over on her side, shutting her eyes, listening to her own voice talking.

> "To-morrow, and to-morrow, and to-morrow . . ."

It was warm and lovely, lying there beside the pool. It should be summer always. Never anything but summer, and the sun and the splashing sound of waves, restful and lazy.

"Hullo, water nymph," said a voice.

She looked up and blinked. It was Michel. She wondered how he had discovered her. She was so well hidden by the overhanging rock. "Hullo," she said.

He came down and sat beside her. He wore bathing trunks, with a towel round his waist. Maria wondered idly why it was that men could go about with their top half bare and women could not. Because of being fat, she supposed. She was not fat yet, thank goodness, but Truda made her cover her top half this summer for some silly reason. She was getting too big to run around like that, Truda said.

"I've been looking for you everywhere," said Michel, a note of reproach in his voice.

"Have you?" said Maria. "I'm sorry. I thought you were talking to Pappy, or Mama."

Michel laughed. "Do you think I would be with them if there was the slightest chance of being with you?" he said.

Maria stared at him. Well, really . . . He was grown-up, he was their friend, wasn't he? Grown-up people generally preferred being together. She did not say anything. There was nothing to say.

"You know, Maria," he went on, "I'm going to miss you terribly when I go back to Paris."

"Are you?" said Maria. She lay back against the rock and shut her eyes. How hot it was, really to hot to bathe. Too hot to do anything but lie against the rock.

"Yes," he said. "Won't you miss me?"

Maria thought a moment. If she said no he would be offended. Perhaps she would miss him a little. He was tall and nice and rather good-looking, after all. And he had been very good-natured playing tennis, and looking with her for starfish.

"I expect I shall," she said politely. "Yes, I'm sure I shall miss you very much."

He leant over and began to stroke her legs as he had done at vingt-et-un. It was queer, she thought. Why was he so mad on this business of stroking legs? At vingt-et-un it had been nice, oddly exciting, chiefly because the others were all there and did not know, and she had an instinctive feeling that Pappy would have been angry, which was fun. Now that she and Michel were alone she did not like it so much. It was rather silly, as Celia said. But again, if she moved her legs away, he would be offended. Suddenly she thought of an excuse.

"Heavens, it's hot," she said. "I simply must have a swim to get cool."

She stood up and dived into the deep pool. He sat there on the rock, watching her. He looked rather annoyed. Maria pretended not to notice.

"Come in, too, it's lovely," she said, shaking the water out of her hair.

"No, thank you," he said, "I've had my swim."

He leant back against the rock and lit a cigarette.

Maria swam around, watching him from the pool. When he sat slumped, lighting his cigarette, he looked nice. The top of his head, bent, was fair, and his neck a deep brown. But when he smiled, his teeth were rather too big, and that spoilt everything. She wondered if men were ever nice altogether, hair, eyes, nose, mouth, legs, arms, or if there was always something that would be irritating, putting off. She kicked her legs, and splashed, and then dived again, showing off, because she knew she dived well. Michel went on smoking his cigarette. Presently Maria climbed out of the pool and, picking up her towel, she dried herself in the sun. She felt fresh and cool after her swim.

"I wonder where the others are," she said.

"Never mind the others, come and sit down," he said.

The way he said it, almost like an order, and patting the rock beside him, surprised Maria. Generally, if anyone ordered her to do anything, she refused, instinctively. Her nature was to disobey rules on principle. But when Michel spoke like this she realised that she liked it. It was much better than his soft voice saying he would miss her. Then he looked a fool. Now he did not look a fool at all. She spread her wet towel on the rock to dry, and sat down beside him. She shut her eyes and leant back against the rock. This time he did not speak, nor did he touch her legs. He reached out for her hand and held it.

It was nice to have her hand held, peaceful and strangely comforting. And the feel of his shoulder, just touching hers, was comforting too. Yet, thought Maria, if Pappy came and saw us sitting here, and looked down over the rock, I should feel embarrassed, ashamed. I should quickly take my hand away and pretend Michel had not touched it at all. I wonder whether that's why it is so nice. I wonder if I like it just because it's something Pappy would not let me do.

Away in the distance, the foghorn sounded from the rocky islands across the bay. . . .

Celia heard it, and frowned, and turned her head towards the sea, but the mist was coming down fast, and already the islands were hidden. She could not see them any more.

Boom . . . There it was again, doleful and persistent. She simply could not forget it, once it had begun. She stood back, surveying the house she had made. It was a lovely shape, with shells for windows, and trailing paths of seaweed from the front door to the gate. The doors and gate had been difficult to find, she was so particular about the exact shape of the stones. There was a bridge, too, and a tunnel. The tunnel went right underneath the garden to the house. It was sickening to think that the sea would come up and destroy the house she had taken such pains to make. Seep it away, little by little. It just showed how useless it was to make things that did not last. Drawing was different. If you drew a picture you could put it away in a drawer, and look at it again, and it would always be there whenever you wanted it.

It would be nice to have a model of the sand house, and to keep it always so that when they were home again, wherever home should be next time, Paris or London or some other place, the sand house would be a possession, something to treasure with all the other things she hoarded, she never quite knew why, but in case . . . In case of what, Truda asked? Just in case, Celia answered. There were shells, and smooth green stones, and pressed flowers, and stubs of pencils, even little old bits of stick, picked up in the Bois, or in Hyde Park, and carried back to the hotel or the apartment.

"No, no, you mustn't throw that away," she used to say.

Because once she had chosen an object it must remain, forever; it was a treasure, it was something to be loved.

Boom . . . The wretched foghorn sounded again.

"Look, Pappy," she called out, "come and look at the dear little house I've made, just for you and me."

He did not answer. She turned round and ran to the place where he had been sitting. He was not there any more. His coat and his book and his field glasses were gone. He must have got up while she had been building the sand house, and gone back to the house. She had been alone on the beach perhaps for ages, and she had never known. The foghorn sounded again, and the mist came nearer, closing in upon her.

She was swept in sudden panic. She picked up her spade and ran.

"Pappy," she called, "Pappy, where are you?"

Nobody answered. She could not see the cliffs. She could not see the house. They had all gone, they had all deserted her. She was alone, she had nothing left but her wooden spade.

She went on running, forgetting she was no longer a little girl, but would soon be eleven, and as she ran she panted under her breath, "Pappy . . . Pappy . . . Truda . . . Niall, don't leave me. No one must ever leave me," and all the while the pursuing foghorn was booming in her ears.

He came suddenly, out of the mist, just by the garden gate that led to the house, Pappy in his old blue coat and white sun hat, and he bent down and lifted her from the ground.

"Hullo, my old silly," he said. "What's the matter?"

But nothing mattered. She had found him. She was safe.

CHAPTER SEVEN

THE last days of August had come and gone, and September was upon us. Soon, in a week or ten days, the inevitable packing up would begin again, and we would be saying good-bye to the villa. There would be the sadness of last walks, last swims, last sleeping in beds that had become familiar. We would make all sorts of promises to the *cuisinière*, and to the daily *femme de chambre*, saying, "We'll be back again next year," knowing in our hearts that it would not be so. We never took the same villa twice. Next year it would be the Riviera, perhaps, or Italy, and the cliffs and the sea of Brittany would become no more than a memory.

Maria and Celia shared a room, with Niall in the little dressing room adjoining, the door open between the two so that we could all talk to each other. But somehow, this summer we did not play the old noisy, romping games of a year ago. We no longer chased each other in pyjamas about the room and jumped across the beds.

Maria would be drowsy and yawning in the mornings. "Don't talk, anyone, I'm making up a dream," and she used to tie a handkerchief round her eyes so that the sun could not waken her.

Niall was not drowsy in the morning, but he would sit on the end of his bed, which was underneath the window, and stare out across the garden to the sea and the rocky islands. Even on the calmest day the sea was never still around the lighthouse. There was always a white surf breaking on the rocks, and a long thin line of curling foam. Truda would come in with his breakfast, coffee and croissants, and golden honey.

"What's my boy dreaming of now?" she used to say, to be met with the inevitable answer, "Nothing!"

"You are all growing up too fast, that's what it is," she would reply, as though growing was somehow a disease that had come upon us, though in some fashion shameful, awaking disapproval.

"Come on now, none of that shamming sleep. I know you're foxing," she said to Maria, dragging back the curtains with a jerk, flooding the room with sunshine.

"I don't want any breakfast. Go away, Truda."

"That's the latest, is it? Don't want your breakfast. You'll be glad enough of breakfast once you get to school, my girl. No lying in bed then. And no dancing in the evening, or other nonsense."

And Niall, glad of his breakfast and the warm melting croissant, wondered why it was that Truda, whom he loved, should have, in spite of this, such a talent for arousing irritation.

Let Maria lie and dream if she wanted to; let Niall crouch by the open window. We did no harm by this; we did not attack the world of grown-up people.

Grown-up people . . . How suddenly would it happen, the final plunge into their world? Did it really come about overnight, as Pappy said, between sleeping and waking? A day would come, a day like any other day, and, looking over your shoulder, you would see the shadow of the child that was, receding; and there would be no going back, no possibility of recapturing the shadow. You had to go on; you had to step forward into the future, however much you dreaded the thought, however much you were afraid.

"Oh God, put back Thy universe and give me yesterday!"

Pappy quoted it, joking, at lunch time, and Niall, looking round, thought this moment already belonged to the past, it is over and done with. In a minute we shall be pushing back the chairs and going onto the verandah, and it can never, never happen again. Pappy at the end of the table, the sleeves of his shirt rolled above his elbows, his old yellow cardigan with the hole in it thrown open, unbuttoned, his blue eyes, so like Maria's, laughing across at Mama.

Mama drinking her coffee and smiling back, cool and detached. She was always cool when other people were hot, wearing a mauve frock and a long chiffon scarf round her shoulders. Mama will never look quite like this again because soon she will have finished her coffee and put the cup back again on the saucer, and she will be saying to Pappy, "Have you finished? Shall we go?" the way she always did, feeling for her scarf, twisting it round her neck, and as she moves from the dining room to the verandah she will be moving from the past into the future, thought Niall, she will be entering another life.

Maria wore a blue sweater over her bathing dress that matched the colour of her eyes, and her fair hair was still wet from her morning swim. She had been snipping at it with nail scissors to make it shorter.

Celia's fair was in two tight plaits that made her face seem rounder and plumper than ever, and as she bit on a chocolate the expression of her face changed suddenly, became pensive; she had bitten on a stopping, the stopping had come out.

There will never be a photograph of this, thought Niall, never a photograph of the five of us together, round the table, holding the moment, smiling and being happy.

"Well, shall we go?" Mama rose from the table; the spell was broken. But I can hold it, said Niall to himself, I can hold it if I don't speak to anyone, if nobody speaks to me, and he followed Mama onto the verandah in silence, watching her pat the cushions into place on the long chair, while Pappy opened her sunshade and tucked the coverlet round her legs to keep away mosquitoes. Maria had already sauntered off in the direction of the beach, and Celia was at the back of the house somewhere, calling to Truda about the stopping in her tooth.

"I don't know which grows up faster, this lad or Maria," said Pappy, and he put his hand on Niall's shoulder, smiling; and then wandered down the steps into the garden, to lie full-length on his back with his hands under his head, and an old panama hat over his face.

"You shall come for a walk with me presently," said Mama to Niall, and the moment at the table that he had wished to hold throughout the afternoon was thrown away upon the instant. It had become a thing of no account, and he wondered why only a few minutes ago he had given it so much importance.

"I'll leave you to rest," he said, and then, instead of going into the drawing room to play the piano as had become his custom, he ran round the back of the house to the kitchen garden where the garden boy kept his bicycle, and he jumped upon the saddle and steered it out into the road. He grasped the hot shiny handle bars of the machine, and his naked feet in sand shoes felt strong and free as they touched the pedals. He rode fast and furious along the twisting sandy road, and the dust blew in his face, and he did not mind.

Back in the house Celia was showing her gaping tooth to Truda, and Truda was packing into it a little hard wedge of tooth paste.

"You'll have to wait now until we get to London," she said, "these French dentists are no good. Be sure to remember and bite on the left side. Where's Maria?"

"I don't know," said Celia. "I think she went for a walk."

"What she wants to go off walking for in this hot weather, I can't think," said Truda, "but I can make a pretty shrewd guess she won't walk alone. Don't pull at the tooth, Celia. Let it be."

"It feels funny."

"Of course it feels funny. It will feel funnier still if you let that piece of tooth paste slip and you bite on the nerve. You and Niall had better run off and join Maria, and see she doesn't get into mischief. It's a good thing we're going back to England next week."

"Why is it a good thing?"

"That's none of your business."

How just like Truda to start hinting things and not follow them up. Celia fingered the iron that Truda was busy heating.

"Maria is old enough to take care of herself," she said. "We can't any of us come to harm, can we, now we can swim? We don't go out far."

"I don't mind what Maria does in the water," said Truda. "It's what she does out of it that worries me. It's not healthy for a young girl of her age to be so free and easy with a gentleman like that Mr. Laforge. I wonder your Pappy allows it."

The iron was very hot. Celia nearly burnt her fingers.

"I've always said we'll have trouble with Maria," said Truda.

She pulled Mama's nightdress out of the pile of washed linen and began ironing it, smoothing it gently up and down. The smell of the hot iron and the steaming ironing board filled the small room. Although the window was wide open there was no air at all.

"You're in a bad mood, Truda," said Celia.

"I'm not in a bad mood," answered Truda, "but I soon will be if you keep fingering everything."

"Why should we have trouble with Maria?" asked Celia.

"Because none of us knows what blood she has in her," said Truda, "but if it's what I suspect, then she's going to lead us all a dance."

Celia thought about Maria's blood. Yes, it was brighter than either her own or Niall's. When Maria cut her foot bathing the other day, the blood spurted very scarlet, in a little bubble.

"She'll run after them, and they'll run after her," said Truda.

"Who will?" asked Celia.

"The men," said Truda.

There was a brown mark on the ironing board where the iron had scorched the cloth. Celia looked out of the window, as though she expected to see Maria dancing along the cliffs pursued by a great company.

"You can't go against the blood," Truda went on. "It will out, however careful you are. Maria may be your Pappy's girl and have your Pappy's talent when it comes to acting, but she's her mother's girl, too, and what I've heard of the mother is best left unsaid."

Up and down the nightgown went the savage iron.

Celia wondered if Maria's mother had had bright scarlet blood as well.

"You've all three been brought up just the same," said Truda, "and you're all three as different as chalk from cheese. And why? Because of the different blood."

How horrid Truda was, thought Celia; why must she go on and on about blood?

"There's Niall," said Truda. "There's my boy. He's his father all over again, the same pale face, same small bones, and now he's found out what he can do to a piano he'll never leave it. What does your Mama think about it? That's what I'd like to know. What has been going on in her mind all these past weeks as she hears him play? If it takes me back across the years, what does it do to her?"

Celia gazed thoughtfully at the plain lined face of Truda, the grey thin hair screwed back over the temples behind the bony forehead.

"Are you very old, Truda?" she asked. "Are you ninety?"

"Bless my soul," said Truda, "what will you be saying next?"

She lifted the nightgown from the board, and the garment that had been limp and crumpled was now fine and smooth, ready to put on.

"I've seen some strange things in my life, but I'm not ninety yet," she answered.

"Which of us do you love best?" said Celia, but the answer came back as it always did, "I love you all the same, but I shan't love you at all if you will keep fingering my ironing board."

How they put you off, the grown people, with their back answers, their evasion of awkward questions.

"If the others go to school I'll be the only one," said Celia. "You'll have to love me the best then, and so will Pappy and Mama."

She suddenly saw herself getting a threefold measure of attention, and the thought was a new one to her. She had not considered it before. She tiptoed behind Truda and, to plague her, tied her apron bow into a triple knot.

"Too much love is bad," said Truda. "It's as bad one way as too little is the other. And if you go through life asking for too much you'll be disappointed. What are you doing to my apron?"

But Celia backed away, laughing.

"You're all three greedy for affection," said Truda. "That's something you've all inherited, along with your other talents. And where it will lead you I don't know, but I wonder sometimes."

She tested the back of the iron with her horny fingernails.

"Anyway, my boy has made up for lost time these last few weeks," she said. "If ever anyone was hungry, he was, poor mite. I only hope she keeps it up. If she does he'll grow up a real man and not a dreamer. But she'll have to keep it up. Maybe she will. Maybe it's come at just the right time for her, now she's reached the difficult years."

"When was Niall hungry?" asked Celia. "And what are the difficult years?"

"Ask me no questions, and I'll tell you no lies," said Truda, suddenly impatient. "Now run along, can't you? Get out into the fresh air."

She twisted Celia's plaits into a topknot on the top of her head to keep her cool, and tucked her short cotton frock into her knickers.

"Be off with you," she said, patting her fat behind. But Celia did not want to go out into the fresh air. It was not fresh, either. It was much too hot. She wanted to stay in the house and draw.

She ran along the passage to her room to find some paper. There was a block tucked away at the back of the cupboard that she had brought from Paris, and her favourite pencils, the yellow ones, Kohinoor. She found her knife and began to sharpen one out of the window; it flaked off in clean strips, revealing the sharp lead, and the smell was good. The murmur of voices floated up to her from the verandah below. Pappy must have finished his sleep. He was sitting on one of the wicker chairs talking to Mama.

". . . you can't start them too young, in my opinion," he was saying, "and those dramatic schools are useless. I wouldn't give a damn for any of them. Let her learn her job the hard way, the same as I did myself, and you, too, my darling, if it comes to that. She won't come to any harm."

Mama must have said something in reply, but her voice was soft and low, it did not carry up to the window like Pappy's voice.

"Who says so? Truda?" Pappy answered. "Nonsense, you tell Truda to mind her own business. She's a barren old woman with a nasty mind. Maria won't go astray, she's got her head screwed on too well. If it was Celia, now . . ."

His voice sank lower, difficult to hear, hidden by the scraping noise of his chair on the verandah. Celia paused and looked at her pencil.

"If it was Celia, now . . ." What had Pappy been going to say?

She listened hard, but she could only catch scraps of the conversation, little indistinct words and phrases that made no pattern.

"All three of them, for that matter," Pappy's voice droned on. "The name alone will carry them through, if nothing else does. They've got the spark all right, but possibly nothing more than the spark. Anyway, we shan't live to see it. . . . No, probably not first-class. He'll never have the confidence unless you can give him that. He's your responsibility, my darling. What did you say? . . . Oh, time alone will tell, when it comes to that—it's the same for us, isn't it? Where would you be without me, or me without you, my darling? Of course, he clings, so do they, so do you and I. . . . There are only two things that matter in the whole world; you've taught me that, perhaps we've taught each other—if everything else fails, work remains. We can instil that into the three of them, if nothing else. . . ."

Celia moved away from the window. That was the worst of grown-up people. They started something, and you thought they might be going to say something special, like "Celia is the nicest of the three," or "Celia will be very pretty when she slims down a bit," but they never did. They got sidetracked onto other things. She sat down on the floor, her block on her knees, and began to draw.

Never anything big. Always little things. Always little men and women living in small houses, where they could never be lost, and where nothing could ever happen like a fire or an earthquake, and as she drew she talked to herself for company. The afternoon went by, and still she went on drawing, her legs tucked under her, her tongue

61

between her teeth, and when it happened—the thing she was to remember all her life—when it came, the shouting and the screaming, the terrible sound of it rang in her ears like a summons from another world.

As Maria turned out of the garden gate she looked to right and to left, undecided which way to go. To the right led to the beach, and to the rocks; to the left was the path to the cliffs, and to the hotel.

It was very hot, the hottest day of the year. The sun beat down on her bare head, but she did not mind. She never had to wear a hat in case of sunstroke, like Celia, and even if she had gone walking naked the sun would not blister her. She was brown and firm, she was browner even than Niall with his dark hair. She shut her eyes and stretched out her arms, and it was as though a great wave of heat came up out of the ground and touched her; there was a smell of earth, and moss, and hot geranium coming from the villa garden just behind her, and in front of her the smell of the sea itself, dancing and glittering under the sky.

She had her happy feeling. The happy feeling that came suddenly and swept right through her, for no reason. It travelled from the pit of her tummy right up to her throat, nearly choking her, and she never knew why it came, what brought it, or where it went, for it would vanish as swiftly as it began, leaving her breathless, enquiring, still happy but without the ecstasy. It came, it went; and she went down the right-hand path to the beach, the hot sand burning her naked feet, and as she walked she hummed to herself, and she moved in time to the tune that she was humming.

> "Who's wonderful, who's marvellous,
>   Miss Annabelle Lee,
> Who's kissable, who's lovable,
>   Just wait and you'll see . . ."

They played it every Saturday evening at the hotel when they had the dances; they had played it last night. The little jerky dance band, consisting of a pianist and a drummer, imported down from Quimper for the evening, who played too fast and to the inevitable quick French time, possessed, for all their faults, a sort of magic. The windows of the hotel would be wide open, and if you stood outside and listened, with the people from the village, you could see the silly stiff figures of the English visitors bobbing past in evening dress.

Maria had gone once. Pappy had taken her. She had worn the blue frock she wore every evening at the house for supper, with her ordinary house shoes and a coral necklace, and Niall and Celia had peeped through the windows and made monkey faces at her. It had not been much fun. Pappy danced too slowly, and kept going round and round the same way, making her giddy. And those idiot English boys were rotten, treading on her feet, clutching her waist and pulling up her dress at the back so that her knickers showed. It was only Michel who was any good at all, and he did not come until halfway through, until nearly the end, because he had been with some other people in a café in the village.

When he danced he held you the right way, and his body did the things that your body did, not swaying, not bending stupidly, but moving against the beats. Niall did the same thing on the piano, he played tunes against the beats. So few people understood the way to play, the way to dance.

It was better really to dance alone. Better to listen a moment outside, and let the music come to you, and laugh with the village people, and smell the harsh French tobacco, and the garlic, and then to slip away into the darkness and move to your own time.

"Who's kissable, who's lovable,
Miss Annabelle Lee . . ."

Better to dance alone, as she was doing now, under the hot sun, to the sound of her own humming, her hands plucking the air, feeling for invisible strings, and her toes digging the soft sand. The tide was out. Away in the distance an old peasant woman, with a basket on her arm, stripped the rocks for seaweed, a strange humped figure, outlined against the sky.

The sardine boats were returning to port. They followed one another like battleships, in line astern, painted all colours, their blue nets drying in the sun. Maria wished she could be with them. She wished suddenly, and with passion, to be a fisherman, burnt black with wind and sea, dressed in red sailcloth trousers and wearing clogs.

She had watched them once with Pappy. They had walked to the little port and stood on the end of the quay, and the men had stood laughing and joking with one another, standing waist-deep in fish. The

63

fish slid from their bronzed rough hands onto the wet decks of the boats, and the fish were slimy, and fat, the scales glistening. The men talked to each other in the Breton patois, and one of them kept looking up and laughing at Maria, and she had laughed back at him.

Yes, that would be it, that would be the thing. To be a fisherman, smelling of the sea, your lips caked with salt and your hands stinking of the slimy fish, and then to walk back along the cobbled quay with your feet in clogs, and go and sit in a little café and drink raw harsh cider, deep brown in colour, a bitter brew, and smoke rank tobacco, and spit, and listen to the wheezy, tinkling phonograph behind the bar.

> "Parlez-moi d'amour,
> Redites-moi des choses tendres.
> Votre beau discours,
> Mon coeur n'est pas las de l'entendre."

The disk would be cracked and old, the woman screeching at the top of her voice, but it would not matter.

Maria was a fisherman, her cap tilted over one eye, laughing with her comrades, lurching along a cobbled quay, and as she jumped down the steep crevice of rock to the inlet below she remembered that she must stop being a fisherman and become Maria again once more, Maria at the appointed tryst-place, who had come to say good-bye to Michel, the man who loved her.

He was waiting there, sitting against their usual slab of rock, smoking a cigarette. His face was drawn and pale, and he looked unhappy. Oh dear, it was going to be one of those days. . . .

"You've been a long time," he said, accusing her.

"Sorry," said Maria. "We finished lunch late."

It was not true, but it did not matter. To appease him she sat down beside him and took his arm and put her head against his shoulder.

"I heard you singing," he said, still reproachful, "as if you were happy. Don't you realise I'm going tomorrow, we may never see one another again?"

"I couldn't help singing," she said. "It was such a lovely day. But I'm sad, really. I promise you I'm sad."

She turned her face away so he could not see her smile. It would be dreadful to hurt his feelings, but really, when his face was long and grave as it was now, and his eyes watery, it was so silly, like a complaining sheep.

64

When he put his arms round her and kissed her it was better because then she did not have to look at him. She could shut her eyes and concentrate upon the kissing, which was warm and pleasant and very comforting. Even that did not seem to please him today. He sighed, and groaned, and kept harping on the business of their never seeing one another again.

"We shall see you in Paris, or in London," she said. "Of course we shall meet again, especially if you are going to do some work for Mama."

"Oh, that," he said, shrugging his shoulders. "That won't come to anything. Your Mama is even more difficult than you. She nods her head, she smiles, she says, 'Yes, how interesting, how clever, we must discuss it,' but that is all. Never anything more. There is no getting anywhere with her. Even this tour they talk of to America, she and Mr. Delaney, will anything come of it? I wonder. I very much wonder."

There was a periwinkle stuck to the rock beside Maria. She tore it off and began to prod at it with her nail. It vanished instantly to its lair beneath the shell. She took another and prodded him. It was fascinating, the way they scuttled back into the darkness. Presently Michel stood up and looked around him. The sound of the sea was nearer now. The tide was coming in.

"There's no one in sight," he said. "The beach is quite deserted."

Maria yawned and stretched herself. It was time really to have another bathe, but perhaps Michel would think her heartless to suggest it. She glanced idly over the rocks to the gaping cave under the cliff. She had explored it once, with Niall. It travelled quite a long way, and then the roof sloped suddenly, descended, shelving to their heads, and a cold trickle of water fell onto their shoulders.

She looked up and saw that Michel was watching her.

"I see you are looking at the cave too," he said. "Have you the same thoughts that I have?"

"I don't know what you are thinking," said Maria. "I was just remembering how dark it was in there. I went once, with Niall."

"Come again," said Michel. "Come with me."

"What for?" said Maria. "There's nothing up there. It's very dull."

"Come with me," repeated Michel. "This is the last time we shall be together. I want to say good-bye."

Maria stood up, scratching her ankle. Something must have bitten her, there was a little red spot. She looked over her shoulder at the advancing sea. There was still some way for it to come. It broke with a surging roar on the farther rocks, and somewhere it struck a funnel, throwing a cloud of spray into the air.

"Why go into the cave?" said Maria. "Why not say good-bye out here? It's warm and nice; it will be gloomy in the cave."

"No," he said, "in the cave it will be quiet and still."

She looked at him standing on the ledge of rock beside her, and she thought how tall he looked suddenly, as tall as Pappy. And he did not have his sheep's face any more. He looked confident and strong. Yet something inside her whispered, "I wouldn't go into the cave, stay in the open, much better stay in the open."

She looked back over her shoulder, at the rocks she knew, and the boisterous sea sparkling in the sun, and then down to the cave across the narrow spit of sand. The mouth of the cave looked mysterious suddenly, inviting. Perhaps it was not gloomy after all, but quiet and still, as Michel promised her, and perhaps the path of it did not end abruptly with a sloping roof, as she remembered, but on to something else, another cave, another secret cavern.

Michel put his hand out to her, smiling, and she took it and held it fast, and followed him into the cave.

When they came out and started scrambling over the rocks for home it was Michel who saw the people first, crowded into a huddle on the cliff edge, and he pointed, saying, "Look—over there, something's happened, something's wrong," and Maria followed his pointing finger and saw Pappy, she saw Truda, she saw Niall, and a feeling of guilt swept over her, a feeling of panic, and with it a new stricken sense of apprehension, and without glancing at Michel she started to run towards the base of the cliff, her heart thumping in her side. . . .

Niall wheeled the bicycle through the side gate into the kitchen garden, and left it propped against the hedge. The boy to whom it belonged was bending over the vegetables at the far end. Niall could see the top of his beret bobbing up and down, and the steady scraping sound of the hoe. The boy had probably never even noticed that his bicycle had been taken. Niall walked through the house and onto the verandah. Although the sun had worked round to the opposite side of the house and no longer shone direct upon the verandah, there was still the heavy, drowsy atmosphere of after-lunch.

André had not come to take the coffee cups away. They were still lying on the round table, where the ash had dropped from Pappy's cigar. Pappy must have been sitting on the verandah talking to Mama, his panama hat was lying on one of the chairs, beside a fly whisk and yesterday's *Echo de Paris*.

Now he had wandered off again, and Mama was lying on the long chair alone. Niall came and stood beside her. She was asleep. She had her left hand up to her face and was resting upon it.

Once he would have been shy had he come upon her suddenly like this, sleeping. He would have tiptoed away, fearful that she might wake and stare up at him and frown and say, "What are you doing?" Now he was not shy any more. He had the feeling inside of him that he would never be shy of her again. Since that afternoon, only a few weeks back, when she had come into the drawing room and found him playing the piano, something seemed to have happened. He did not know what it was, nor did he think about it much. All he knew was that the queer pain of anxiety that had been a part of him for as long as he could remember had gone away. It used to be with him always, in some form or other. So that waking in the morning and getting up and facing the day brought fear with it and apprehension. And to counteract this he had to invent for himself stupid superstitions. "If I tie my right shoelace tighter than my left, the day will be all right," he used to say to himself, or he would have to touch some object on the mantelpiece and turn it round facing another way, because if this was omitted something would happen. He did not know what the something was, but in some queer way it was connected with Mama. Either that she might be angry, or suddenly unwell, or face him with an accusation. So that really it used to be better if she were out of the house and at the theatre, because then there would be a sense of freedom for him.

Now everything was changed. All since that afternoon at the piano. The strain and anxiety had left him. It must mean that Pappy was right about him, that he was growing up, the same as Maria.

He looked down at Mama as she lay sleeping in her chair, and he noticed how white her hand was, resting against her face. The blue stone of the ring that Pappy had given her was the same colour as the vein that ran down the back of her hand. There were shadows, like smudges, under her eyes, and two hollows in her cheeks, and he saw for the first time that where her dark hair swept back from her forehead there were white streaks.

It must be nice for her to lie there, sleeping in the long chair. No worries about the theatre, no plans about the future, no talking and arguing about the American tour. Just peace, and forgetfulness, and a quiet slipping away into nothing. He sat down on the step of the verandah and watched her sleeping, watched her hand touching her face, and the chiffon scarf round her shoulders, and he thought to himself, I shall remember this always. When I'm an old man of eighty-nine, staggering on crutches, I shall remember this.

From inside the drawing room, from the stiff little gold French clock on the mantelpiece, came the whirring sound of four o'clock, to break the stillness.

The sound of it woke Mama. She opened her eyes, and looked at Niall, and smiled.

"Hullo," she said.

"Hullo," he answered.

"You look like a little watchdog sitting there," she said.

She put her hands up to her hair, patting it, and loosened the chiffon scarf. She reached for her bag that was lying on the table beside her, and took out a mirror and a powder puff, and began to powder her nose. A piece of fluff from the powder puff stayed on the corner of her chin, and she did not notice it.

"Heavens, I'm tired," she said.

"Why don't you go on sleeping?" said Niall. "It doesn't matter a bit about the walk. We can always walk another day."

"No," she said, "I'd like to walk. A walk will do me good."

She put her hand out to him so that he could help her from the chair. He took hold of it and pulled her up, and the action of doing this made him feel older than he had ever felt before, as though he were grown up, as though he were a man, like Pappy.

"We'll go along the cliffs," she said. "We'll pick wild flowers."

"Do you want me to carry a coat for you?" he said. "Or your bag?"

"I don't want anything. I'll just wear my scarf," she said, and she draped it round her hair and round her throat, the way she did, motoring, when the wind blew. They went out of the house and onto the cliffs. The tide had turned, the sea was coming in, surging and breaking on the rocks below. There was no one but themselves walking on the cliffs. Niall was glad. Sometimes, when they walked, the English visitors to the hotel would be walking, too, and would turn and stare at them, nudging each other.

"That's her—look, quick, before she sees you," Niall would hear them say, and he and Mama would have to pass on, pretending not to hear. Mama would walk straight ahead, treading another world, and no one ever dared come up to her. Pappy was different, he was easy game. He would hear the murmur "Delaney" and would look up and smile, and then they would be upon him, asking for his autograph. Today there was no one, and it was very hot and still.

They had not gone far when Mama said, "It's no use, I shall have to sit down. You go on. Don't mind about me."

She looked white and tired. She sat down in a little hollow in the cliff where there were some soft tussocks of straggling grass.

"I'll stay with you," said Niall, "I'd rather."

For a while she did not say anything. She stared out across the sea at the little islands where the lighthouse stood. Then she put out her hand to him, but she did not turn and smile. She went on staring at the lighthouse.

"I'm not very well," she said. "I haven't been well for quite a while. I keep getting an odd sort of pain."

Niall did not know what to say. He kept hold of her hand.

"That's why I lie about so much and rest," she said. "It's not really a headache at all."

A dragonfly came and settled on her knee. Niall brushed it off.

"Why doesn't Pappy send for the doctor?" he asked.

"Pappy doesn't know," she said. "I haven't told him."

What a strange thing to say, thought Niall. He always imagined she told Pappy everything.

"You see, I know what it is," she said. "There's something gone wrong inside. It's that sort of pain. If I told Pappy he would make me see a doctor, and the doctor would say I must have an operation."

"But it would make you better," said Niall. "It would take away the pain."

"Perhaps," she said, "I don't know. All I know is that it would do something to me, and I should never dance again."

Never dance again. He could not imagine the theatre without Mama. He could not imagine Pappy going down every evening, singing his songs alone, and her not being there. Why, she was the core of the whole thing, the centre, the inspiration. Sometimes Pappy had not been able to sing because of laryngitis or a cold. Voices were tricky things. But it had never mattered very much, Mama had always gone down to the theatre. She had never failed. It just meant she had to alter the programme about a little, and rearrange her dances. The people came just the same. They loved Pappy, of course; they loved his personality, they loved his songs, but it was really Mama they came to see.

"Never dance again?" said Niall. "But what would happen? What would everybody do?"

"Nothing would happen," she said. "The theatre is a funny world, you know. They forget one very soon."

He went on holding her hand, twisting the ring with the blue stone, and it seemed to him that by doing this he comforted her in some strange fashion and enabled her to talk.

"It's me," she said. "It's my whole life. Nothing else matters. It never has done."

"I know," he said, "I understand."

He knew that she was talking about her dancing, and that she was trying to tell him that this was the reason why so many things about her were different from other women, other mothers. This was why so often in the past she had been cold and angry and unkind. No, she had never been cold, never angry, never unkind. That was not what he meant at all. It was just that when he was a little boy he had expected too much, and hoped for things that did not happen. Now all that was finished and done with. Now he was older. Now he understood.

"It's queer how a woman is made," she said. "There is something deep inside that can't be explained. Doctors think they know all about it, but they don't really. It's the thing that gives life—whether it's dancing, or making love, or having babies—it's the same as the creative force in a man, but men have it always. It can't be destroyed. With us, it's different. It lasts only a little while, then goes. It flickers, and dies, and you can't do anything about it. You have to watch it go. And once it's gone there's nothing left. Nothing at all. . . ."

Niall went on twisting and turning her ring. The blue stone flickered and gleamed in the sun. He could think of nothing to say to her.

"It does not matter to a lot of women," she said, "but it matters to me."

The last of the fishing boats had gone into the harbour, and a little breeze of cool air blew towards the land for the first time. The wind was changing with the turn of the tide. The breeze played with the chiffon scarf she wore, lifting it gently. It ruffled Niall's hair.

"Men don't understand," she said, "not men like Pappy. They're sweet and thoughtful, and wrap rugs round one, and fetch one things, but they're puzzled just the same. They think one is just a woman being nervy. They have their own courage and their own vitality, and they haven't an answer."

"Pappy isn't very courageous," said Niall. "He makes an awful fuss when he hurts himself. If he has the smallest cut he goes to Truda to get a plaster."

"That's different," she said. "I wasn't really thinking about that sort of courage." She smiled and patted his knee.

"I've been talking a lot of nonsense, haven't I?" she said.

"No," said Niall. "No."

He was afraid that she would stop, or that she would tell him it was time to go, that they must go and find the others.

"I like you talking to me," he said. "I like it very much."

"Do you?" she said. "I wonder why."

Once more she was looking out across the sea towards the islands.

"How old are you?" she said. "I always forget."

"Nearly thirteen," he said.

"You used to be such an odd little boy," she said. "Never demonstrative like Maria or Celia. I never thought you cared twopence for me or for anyone."

Niall did not answer. He picked a daisy and turned it in his fingers.

"You're so much nicer this summer," she said, "so much easier to understand."

He went on twiddling the daisy and picking off the petals one by one.

"Perhaps you'll write music for me one day," she said. "Perhaps you'll write something that I can turn into a dance. We'll work on it together, and you shall come down to the theatre with me and conduct for me instead of Sullivan. It would be fun, wouldn't it? Would you like to do that when you're a man?"

He looked at her a moment, then turned away his head.

"It's the only thing in the world I want to do," he said.

She laughed, she patted him again upon the knee.

"Come on," she said, "it's getting cool. It's time we went home and had some tea."

She stood up. She tightened the chiffon scarf round her hair and throat.

"Look at those pinks," she said. "How lovely they are growing there beneath the ledge. Let's pick them. I'll put them in water and stand them in the little vase beside my bed."

She bent down and began to gather the pinks.

"Look, there are some more," she said, "higher up there, to the left. Can you reach them for me?"

He scrambled up the cliff and reached for the pinks, holding onto the loose tussocks of grass. It was rather slippery, but his sand shoes held. He had about six pinks in his hand when it happened.

He heard her call out suddenly, "Oh, Niall, quick . . ." and, turning, he saw her slip beneath the ledge where she was stooping to gather the pinks. She put out her hand to save herself, but the stones and the grass came away in her hand and fell with her. She went on slipping in the loose earth and stones. Niall tried to scramble after her, but his foot struck a boulder, and it went rolling down the side of the cliff, crashing to the shore below. He saw then that if there was further movement in the sliding earth of the cliff face she would fall, too, like the boulder, down to the rocks, fifty, sixty feet below.

"Stay there," he called. "Stay quite still. Hold onto that little ledge there by your hand. I'll get help."

She looked up at him. She tried to turn her head.

"Don't leave me," she called. "Please don't leave me."

"I must," he said, "I must get help."

He looked over his shoulder. Beyond, with their backs to him, were two figures walking, a man and a woman. He shouted. They did not hear. He shouted again. This time they heard. They turned and stood still. He waved his arms, shouting at the top of his voice. They began to run.

Suddenly she said, "Niall, the stones are slipping. I'm going to fall."

He knelt on the ledge of cliff and stretched out his hands. He could not reach her. He saw the earth crumble and loosen beside her, but she did not fall because her scarf had caught in a great jagged piece of stone above her head. The scarf did not tear. It was twisted round her throat, and it held fast to the stone.

"It's all right," said Niall. "People are coming. It's all right."

She could not answer because of the twisted scarf. She could not answer because the scarf was twisting itself and getting tighter and tighter round her throat, held fast by the jagged stone.

And that was how it happened. That is why all three of us will always remember the crowd of people coming to the cliff's edge, and the sound of that Frenchwoman screaming and turning and running away. Always the sound of screaming, always the sound of running feet.

CHAPTER EIGHT

IT WAS a mistake to separate us. We should have stayed together. Once a family breaks up and splits, they never come together again. Not in the old way. If there had been a settled home to which we could have gone, it would have been different. Children need a settled home, a place that smells familiar. A life that goes on, with the same toys, the same walks, the same faces day after day. Where, wet or fine, existence can be a pattern, a routine. We had no pattern. Not after Mama died.

"It was all right for Maria," said Celia. "Maria was allowed to go and act. She was doing the thing she wanted to do."

"I did not want to play Juliet," said Maria. "I hated Juliet. And they would not let me wear my own hair because it was too short. I had to have that awful flaxen wig. It didn't fit."

"Yes, but you had a lot of fun," said Celia. "You wrote those letters to me, so funny they were. I have them still—I found them the other day. There was one about Niall running away from school and coming to find you in Liverpool."

"If we had had a settled home I should have run away even more often than I did," said Niall. "As it was, I ran away four times. But there was nowhere to run to. They sent me back from Liverpool. And Pappy being in Australia, it was hopeless."

"It was Celia that had the good time," said Maria. "No proper lessons, travelling all over the place, being with Pappy all the time."

"I don't know," said Celia. "It wasn't always easy. When I think of

Australia nowadays, all I remember is the lavatory in the hotel at Melbourne, and shutting myself up in it and crying."

"What were you crying about?" asked Maria.

"It was because of Pappy," said Celia. "It was because of Pappy's face when he talked to Truda one evening in the sitting room. They didn't know I was listening at the door. He said I was the only thing left in the world, and Truda said it would spoil my life. You remember that sour flat way she had of talking. 'You'll spoil her life,' she said. I can hear her now."

"Why did you never write and tell us that?" said Niall. "Those letters you wrote from Australia were affected and silly, talking about the parties you had been to with some governor. And there was one with a priggish P.S. 'I hope you are getting on with your music.' My music . . . Don't fool yourself. You weren't the only one to lock yourself up in a lavatory. I didn't cry though. That was the difference."

"We were all crying then," said Maria, "each one of us in our separate way. The ferry to Birkenhead. Backwards and forwards in the ferry from Liverpool to Birkenhead."

"Who are you talking about?" said Niall.

"Myself," said Maria. "They were so cliquy at the theatre. They none of them liked me. They thought I had been given the job because of Pappy."

"You probably had," said Niall.

"I know," said Maria. "Maybe that was why I was crying. I remember the smoke from the ferry blowing in my face."

"That's why your face was dirty when I found you," said Niall, "but you never told me you had been crying."

"When I saw you I forgot all about it," said Maria. "Your funny white face, and the mackintosh much too long for you."

She smiled across the room at him, and he laughed back at her, and it must have been then, Celia thought, that the bond between them strengthened, never to break. It must have been then, when Niall was a fugitive from the school he hated, and Maria was alone in Liverpool, pretending to be happy.

It had been a shock, Maria remembered, to discover that acting, after all, was not so easy. She had gone off in the beginning with that touring company with such confidence, and little by little the confidence was broken. No one was really impressed by her. No one was even interested. The face that drew tears from her own mirror did not

7 5

draw tears from other people. The Maria who had stood alone before a looking glass with her arms outstretched, saying "Romeo—Romeo," to no one, found it hard to say the same words before the company when she was asked to for the first time. Opening a door, even, and crossing the stage required hard work and concentration. There came a queer sort of fear in the pit of her stomach that people would laugh at her, and it was a fear she had never known in her life before. It meant a new kind of pretence. She must pretend, from this moment onwards, all her life, that she did not mind what anyone said to her, or about her. It had to be smothered down, inside. They must never know. And by *they*, she meant the rest of the company, the producer, the manager, the critics, the audience. All the people in the new world to whom she must keep up the pretence.

"You're hard-boiled for a youngster," someone said. "You don't give a damn, do you?" And Maria laughed and shook her head.

"Of course I don't. Why should I?" And she went off singing down the passage, and she heard the stage manager say, "The trouble with that kid is she needs her bottom smacked."

So much was anticlimax. She would work hard, she would do what she felt instinctively to be right, and a kind of excitement would come over her, a feeling of power as she heard her voice saying certain lines, so that when the rehearsal of the scene was over, she would swagger a little, her hands in the pockets of her jacket, and think, They will come up to me now and say, "That was wonderful, Maria."

She would wait by the side of the stage, combing her hair, peeping into the little cracked hand mirror of the bag Truda had given her before she had come away on tour, and she would go on waiting, and nobody would say anything at all. The others were whispering in a group. Were they whispering about her? One of them threw back his head and roared with laughter. It was nothing to do with her at all. It was about some other play, some show they had all been in together. And then the producer came up from the stalls and said, "Right. We'll break for lunch now. Two o'clock, everybody." Maria waited a moment; surely he would turn to her and say something. Surely he would say, "Maria, that was brilliant."

He was talking over his shoulder to the stage manager; he was lighting a cigarette. Then he saw her. He came over to the side of the stage where she was standing.

"That wasn't so good as yesterday, Maria. You're forcing it. Not worried, are you?"

"No."

"Oh, I thought you looked worried. Well, run along and get some lunch."

Worried . . . She had not been worried at all. She had been happy, excited, thinking only of the part. But she was worried now. The happy feeling had gone. All the confidence drained away. She could feel it seeping into her shoes, and she pulled the scarf round her neck and buttoned up her coat. She was not lunching with anyone. The day before, someone had said something about lunching all together at the Cat and Fiddle, but nothing seemed to have come of it. They had all gone off their different ways. She could either go back to the dreary digs or buy a sausage roll somewhere, and a cup of coffee.

She walked alone down the passage and up the stairs to the stage door, and as she walked she heard footsteps just ahead of her. It was those two who had been laughing a little while ago on the stage.

"Oh well," the voice was saying, "the whole thing is rank favouritism, of course. She only got in because of her name. Delaney fixed it all up before he went off to Australia."

"Just shows what influence can do," said the other. "We sweat and toil for years, and she slips in by the back door."

Maria stood still and waited. After a moment she heard the swinging of the door to the street. She waited until they would have crossed the street and turned the corner. She gave them time, and then passed through the swing door after them. But they were still standing there, talking. When they saw her they broke off, looking awkward. Perhaps they were wondering if she had heard what they had said.

"Hullo," said one of them. "Are you coming along to lunch?"

"I can't today," said Maria. "I'm lunching with a friend of my father's who's come up to see the play. I've got to meet him at the Adelphi."

She waved her hand and went off singing, and she continued singing all the way to the Adelphi because the other people must be fooled too, that man driving the lorry, that woman there crossing the road.

And to show off to the world, to show off even to herself, she went pushing in through the doors of the Adelphi, to the ladies' cloakroom, so that she could say with safety during the afternoon that she had been there. When you lie, she told herself, there must always be truth in the lie. She tidied herself and used the powder in the bowl and filled her compact with the powder when the woman was wiping the basin, and she put sixpence in the little glass jar.

"Why don't you leave your coat? It's warm in the restaurant," said the woman, and "No, thank you," smiled Maria, "I'm having a very quick lunch," and she swept out of the ladies' room and through the swing doors, and thank heavens nobody had seen her. She was afraid one of the porters might say, "What are you doing here? You can't use this place like a station lavatory."

She walked down a side street and went into a teashop and had five buns, stale ones, and a cup of tea, and all the time she kept thinking of the sort of lunch she would have had if there had really been a friend of Pappy's at the Adelphi. Or the lunch she would have had with Pappy himself at the Savoy. The waiters buzzing round, smiling, and people coming up and talking to them, and Pappy saying, "This is my daughter. She's just gone on the stage."

But Pappy was with Celia in Australia, and Maria was in Liverpool, in a teashop, eating a stale bun, and she was only there anyway because Pappy had fixed it. She was only there because she was Delaney's daughter.

I hate them, thought Maria. Oh God, how I hate them. And her hatred was a seething, angry thing against the whole world, because it seemed to her suddenly a different world from the one she wanted, where everyone was friendly and happy and holding out their arms to her, Maria. . . . She went back to the theatre late, on purpose, hoping the producer would find fault with her, so that she could be scolded, but he was late, everyone was late, and because of this they started right away rehearsing a scene in which she did not appear.

She went and sat by herself at the back of the stalls.

At four o'clock the producer happened to look round. He saw her sitting there, and he said, "Maria, there's really no need for you to wait. I shan't want you again. Go and have a rest before this evening."

Did someone snigger? Was someone making a joke about her in the corner over there?

"Thank you," she said. "I'll go then. I've got some shopping to do."

And she went out again into the street, leaving them all behind her in the theatre. That was when she caught the bus to the ferry. And she went backwards and forwards on the ferry. Somehow, now it did not matter any more how she looked, or who should see her. The wind blew, and it was cold, and she tried first one side of the deck and then the other, but the wind blew all the time, and she was crying. Backwards and forwards, between Birkenhead and Liverpool, and all the while the hard, clear-cut voice of that woman rang in her ears, "She only got in because of her name."

Now it was getting dark, the lights were creeping up on Mersey-side. It was thick and murky.

If I went on for the rest of my life on this boat they would not miss me back at the theatre, thought Maria. They would get someone else to play my part, anyone, it wouldn't matter.

She walked down the gangway, onto the quay, and caught another bus, and then along the street to her lodgings, and she realised now that she was tired and very hungry, and she hoped with a sort of passion that there might be meat to eat, hot meat, and that there would be a brightness to the fire. She went into the house, and the landlady was coming down the stairs with a lamp in her hand, and she said:

"There's a young gentleman come, dear. He's in the sitting room. He says he's come to stay. You never told me there would be two of you."

Maria stared at her. She did not understand.

"A gentleman? I don't know anyone. What's his name?"

And she opened the door of the sitting room, and he was standing there in a mackintosh much too big for him, his face very pale, and his hair lank and unbrushed, falling over his face.

"Hullo," he said, anxious, half smiling, and uncertain, "I've run away. I just got into a train. I've run away."

"Niall . . ." she said. "Oh, Niall . . ." And she ran to him and put her arms round him, and they stood there hugging each other and laughing. Nothing mattered any more. The silly ferry was forgotten, and the long exhausting day, and the voice of the woman at the theatre.

"You came to see me act, didn't you?" she said. "You ran away from school and you came all this way to see me act. Oh, Niall, it's all such fun. . . . Oh, Niall, I'm so happy."

She turned to the landlady.

"It's my stepbrother," she said. "He can have that room next to mine. He's very quiet. He'll be no trouble. And I'm sure he's hungry, very, very hungry. Oh, Niall."

She was laughing again, pulling his shoulders, dragging him to the warm fire.

"Is it all right?" said Niall. "Can I stay?"

How queer, thought Maria, his voice is breaking. It's not gentle any more. It's all creaky and funny, and he's got a hole in the heel of his sock.

"All right," said the landlady. "If you've got the money for your room, you can stay."

Niall turned to Maria.

"That's the awful thing," he said. "I haven't any money. My fare took the lot."

"I'll pay," said Maria. "Don't worry. I'll pay."

The woman looked doubtful.

"Run away from school?" she said. "That's against the law, isn't it? We'll have the police here."

"They can't track me," said Niall swiftly. "I threw away my cap. Look, I bought this awful thing instead."

He drew a tweed cap out of his mackintosh pocket. He put it on his head. It was much too big. It came down over his ears. Maria burst out laughing.

"Oh, it's lovely," she said. "You look so funny."

He stood there grinning, a small white face under an enormous common cap. The woman's mouth twitched.

"Oh well," she said, "I suppose you can stay. Bacon and eggs for two, then. And I've a rice pudding on the boil."

She went out of the room, leaving them alone together. They began to laugh again. They laughed so much that they could hardly stand.

"Why are we laughing?" said Niall.

"I don't know," said Maria, "I don't know."

He stared at her. She was laughing so much that she was crying.

"Tell me about school," she said. "Is this new one worse than the last? Are the boys beastly?"

"It's no worse," he said. "They're all the same."

"Why, then?" she said. "What happened? You've got to tell me."

"There's nothing to tell," he said. "Nothing at all."

He wondered how long the landlady would be with the eggs and bacon. He was very hungry. He had not eaten anything for a long while. It was no use Maria asking questions. He was tired, too, now that the journey was over. And the clock on the sitting-room mantelpiece reminded him of the metronome on the piano of the music room at school.

Once again he was sitting at the upright piano, and the metronome was swinging to and fro. Mr. Wilson pushed back his glasses and shrugged his shoulders.

"You know, Delaney, you'll have to do better than this."

Niall had not answered. He had sat there, stiff as a ramrod.

"I've had letters from your stepfather, and so has the headmaster," said Mr. Wilson. "In each letter your stepfather makes a great point of demanding that you have 'individual tuition,' as he calls it, with your music. He says you have talent. And I am supposed to further that talent. So far, I can't discover any signs of it."

Niall sat silent. If Mr. Wilson would continue talking, the hour of the lesson would pass. And it would be over then until the next time. Niall would not have to play the piano the way Mr. Wilson expected him to play.

"Unless you can do better than this, I shall have to write to your stepfather and tell him that it's sheer waste of money, paying for music lessons," said Mr. Wilson. "You don't seem to grasp the basic theory of it. Not only is it a waste of your stepfather's money, but it's a waste of my time."

The metronome swung to and fro. Mr. Wilson did not seem to notice it. Now that would make a tune in itself, thought Niall. If you once arranged your chords and got the tick of the metronome between the chords, you could get dancing time, irritating and monotonous, perhaps, but then there might be a kind of fascination in it for all that, if you kept working in the inevitable tick-tock, tick-tock. . . .

"Haven't you anything to say?" said Mr. Wilson.

"It's my hands, sir," said Niall. "I can't make my hands do what I want them to do. They slip all over the place."

"You don't practise," said Mr. Wilson. "You don't follow the exercises I set you. Look at this, and this. Page after page of simple little five-finger exercises that a child could do."

He struck the pages with his pencil.

"It's not good enough, Delaney," he said. "You're just bone idle. I shall have to write to your stepfather."

"He's in Australia."

"All the more reason to write then. Prevent him from pouring his money down the drain. Individual tuition. No amount of individual tuition is ever going to teach you to play the piano. You're not even fond of music."

Soon it will be over, thought Niall. Soon it will be over, four o'clock will strike, and he will get up and stop the metronome, because he will want to go off for his tea. That long, droopy, idiotic moustache will be wet at the ends with tea. He will drink it sweet, with a lot of milk in it.

"I understand," said Mr. Wilson, "that your mother was very fond of music. She had great hopes for you. She talked of your future to your stepfather shortly before she died. That was the reason your stepfather made such a great point of this individual tuition."

Set Mr. Wilson's voice against the tick of the metronome, set his droning, searing voice against the steady tick-tock, and you might get something with that. You could get the chords, too, if nobody was listening. The chords would come crashing in and splitting up the sound, and it would be like splitting Mr. Wilson's skull open with an axe.

"Now, then, one more effort, Delaney, please. Try the Haydn sonata."

He did not want to try the Haydn sonata; he did not want to touch the filthy upright piano. All he wanted was to be away from the music room, away from the school, back again in the theatre with Mama, Pappy, Maria, and Celia. Sitting in the darkness, and the curtain rising, and old Sullivan leaning forward, his baton raised. Mama was dead. Pappy and Celia were in Australia. Maria remained. He thought of the picture postcard that was in his pocket, and of Maria's careless, scrawling handwriting. Maria remained. That's why he walked out of the place, with seventeen and sixpence in his pocket, and had got on a train and found his way to Liverpool. Maria remained.

The landlady came into the sitting room with the eggs and bacon. There was a great rice pudding with a burnt brown top. They held their breath to stop themselves from laughing. She went out of the room again, treading heavily.

"I can't eat it," whispered Niall, "not even when I'm starving."

"I know," said Maria, "nor can I. We'll put it on the fire."

They messed their plates to look as if they had eaten some of the rice, and then they scraped the rest out of the dish onto the fire. It turned black. It did not burn. It just stayed in the fire, a black mass, limp and soggy against the coals.

"What shall we do?" said Niall. "She'll come in to put more coal on the fire, and she'll find it."

He tried to scrape some of the rice away from the coal with a poker. The poker got sticky, too, and covered with black rice.

"We'll put it in our pockets," said Maria. "Look, the paper there. We'll scrape it off the coals with the paper and put it in our pockets. Then on the way to the theatre we'll throw it in the gutter."

They worked feverishly against time, filling their pockets with the smouldering, sodden rice.

"You'll tell me if I'm bad, won't you?" said Maria suddenly.

"What do you mean?" said Niall.

"At the theatre, if I'm bad in my part," said Maria.

"Of course," said Niall, "but you won't be bad. You couldn't be bad in anything."

He crammed the remains of the pudding into the cloth cap that was too big for him.

"Couldn't I?" said Maria. "Are you sure?"

She looked at him standing there, lanky and pale, his pockets and the frightful cap bulging with rice pudding.

"Oh, Niall," she said, "I'm glad you came, more glad than anything on earth."

They went into the street. It was raining, and they had borrowed the landlady's umbrella. They held it between them, and the gusty wind blew it about like a metronome. Niall went on telling Maria about Mr. Wilson. Mr. Wilson did not seem important any more. He was nothing but a pathetic old man with a drooping moustache.

"Has he a nickname?" asked Maria. "Surely all masters have a nickname?"

"We call him Long Chops," said Niall, "but that's nothing to do with his moustache. It's to do with something else."

"I meant to tell you," said Maria, "our landlady's name is Florrie Rogers."

"What of it?" said Niall.

"Well, it's awfully funny," said Maria.

They emptied their rice pudding into the gutter outside the theatre.

"Here's the money for your seat," said Maria. "You'll be very early. You'll have to sit and wait for ages."

"I don't mind," said Niall. "I'll stand in the foyer and see if people come in with rice pudding on their shoes. Besides, I shan't be lonely. It's like coming home."

"What's like coming home?" said Maria.

"Being in the theatre," he said, "and being with you. Knowing that when the curtain goes up one of us is there."

"You'd better give me the umbrella," she said. "It would look silly for you to walk into the foyer carrying an umbrella."

She took it from him and smiled.

"What a bore," she said. "You've grown as tall as me."

"I don't think I've grown," said Niall. "I think it's you who have grown smaller in some way."

"No," said Maria. "It's you that's grown. And your voice has gone all cracked and queer. It's nicer. I like it."

She pushed against the stage door with the end of the wet umbrella.

"You had better wait here for me afterwards," she said. "The man is awfully strict about letting people in. If anyone asks who you are, say you are waiting for Miss Delaney."

"I could pretend I wanted your autograph," said Niall.

"Yes," said Maria. "Pretend that anyway."

It's queer, she thought as she swung through the door, this morning I was unhappy and nervous and I hated the theatre. Now I'm happy. Now I'm not nervous any more. And I love the theatre, I love it more than anything. She clattered down the stone stairs, singing, trailing the wet umbrella. And Niall, sitting in a corner seat in the front of the upper circle, talking to no one, felt a strange warmth steal over him and hold him as he watched the members of the orchestra come in and take their places.

Because, although they had told him at school that he did not like music and that he could not play the piano, already there was something whispering in his head, a snatch of melody, half heard and half forgotten; and it was all mixed up with that first violin there tuning his fiddle, and the hot, musty, draughty smell of the theatre itself, and the knowledge that someone he knew and loved, like Mama once, like Maria now, was sitting before a mirror in a dressing room at the back of the stage, putting make-up on her face.

CHAPTER NINE

"THEY came and fetched you, didn't they?" said Celia. "You did not have long together."

"We had two days," said Maria.

Two days . . . It was always like that, forever afterwards, throughout the years. Niall turning up sometime, somewhere, and being with her. Never for very long. Only for snatches of time. She could never remember where they went, or what they did, or what happened; the only thing she knew was that they were always happy.

Being irritable, being tired, and all the endless worries of problems and plans, none of this mattered any more when he was with her. He brought with him always a funny kind of peace, and with the peace a strange sense of stimulation. So that when she was with Niall she was rested and excited, both at once.

Never a day passed that she did not think of him at some moment. I must tell Niall that, he would laugh, he would understand. And weeks would pass and she would not see him. Then, suddenly, for no reason and without warning, he would turn up. She would return, exhausted, perhaps, after a long rehearsal, or having had a row with someone, or the day having gone against her for no reason, and Niall would be sitting there, deep in the armchair, saying nothing, looking up at her and smiling. Her hair needed doing, there would be no powder on her face, and she would be wearing a dress she hated anyway and must give away, but these things would be forgotten in a moment because Niall was there and Niall was part of her and it was like being alone.

"It was Pappy's fault," said Celia. "The headmaster cabled to Pappy and told him Niall had run away, and Pappy cabled back, saying, 'Try the Theatre Royal, Liverpool.' Truda guessed you would have gone to Maria."

"That was the only unkind action I ever knew Pappy to do in all his life," said Niall.

"He hated doing it," said Celia. "He called Truda into the sitting room—we were in Melbourne at the time; there was a heat wave—and he said to Truda, 'The boy's bolted. What the devil am I to do?'"

Celia remembered how they had to have the fans on all the time. There was one above the door and another at the far end of the room to make a draught. There was an idea that if you shut the windows and drew the curtains but kept the fans on full blast, the room kept cool. It was not true. It made the room hotter. Pappy sat about all day in pyjamas, drinking ginger ale.

"My darling," he said to Celia, "I shall have to give up. I can't cope any longer. I hate these people and I hate the country. And anyway, my voice is going. I shall have to give up."

He always said this. It did not mean anything. It was part of the ritual of a farewell tour. Only a few months back they had been in New York in a snowstorm, and he had said the same things about America and Americans. His voice was always going. He was never going to sing again. He was not going to sing that night.

"Ring up the theatre, my darling," he would say. "Tell them I'm not going down tonight. I'm very ill. I'm starting a nervous breakdown."

"Yes, Pappy," she said, but of course she took no notice at all. She went on drawing imaginary people in her sketchbook, and Pappy went on drinking ginger ale.

The cable came, she remembered, in the middle of the afternoon, and Pappy burst out laughing at first, and threw the piece of paper across the table to Celia.

"Good for Niall," he said. "I would never have thought he had the guts to do it."

But she had been anxious at once. She had visions of Niall lying in a ditch somewhere, murdered, or else he had been beaten, beaten unjustly by a brute of a headmaster, or perhaps stoned by the other boys.

"We must tell Truda at once," she said. "Truda will know what to do."

And Pappy had just laughed. He had gone on drinking his ginger ale and rocking with laughter.

"What's the betting he turns up here in six weeks' time?" he said. "Good for Niall. I never did think much of that damn school, anyway."

But Truda knew at once that Niall had gone to Maria.

"He'll be at Liverpool," she said firmly, putting on the thin firm mouth that both Celia and Pappy knew too well. "You must cable the school that they'll find him at the theatre in Liverpool. That's where Maria is this week. I've got a list of dates in my room."

"Why should he go to Liverpool?" said Pappy. "No, God, if I were a boy and had to run away from school, I'm damned if I should run to a place like Liverpool."

"It's Maria," said Truda. "He'll always go to Maria, now his mother's gone. I know him. I know him better than anyone."

Celia glanced at Pappy. The mention of Mama always did something to him. He stopped laughing and drinking ginger ale. He looked heavily at Truda, and his body seemed to sag, so that he looked older, suddenly, and tired.

"Well, I don't know," he said. "It's beyond me. What am I expected to do about it over here, the other side of the ruddy globe? André!"

And he shouted for André, for André, too, must be told about it, about Niall's running away, and not only André, but the waiter when the waiter came, and the chambermaid, and of course everyone down at the theatre. He would make a wonderful story, exaggerated but good to tell, about his bright boy of a stepson running away from school.

"It's no good calling for André," said Truda, her mouth tight. "What you've got to do is to tell the school to get in touch with that theatre in Liverpool. They must fetch him away. That's where he is, in Liverpool."

"Let him stay, then," said Pappy, "if he's happy there. He might get a job with the orchestra, playing the piano."

"His mother wanted him to go to school," said Truda. "The theatre is no place for a boy of his age. He has to have his schooling. You know that."

Pappy looked across at Celia and pulled a face.

"I suppose we have to do what she tells us," he said. "Run down and get me a cable form, my darling."

And Celia went downstairs to the reception desk in the hall of the hotel, and all the time she kept thinking of Niall running to Maria in Liverpool. Niall was her brother, not Maria's. Why did Niall have to run to Maria? And anyway, why couldn't they all be here together? Why was everything so different, so insecure, that had once been permanent and solid? She went upstairs with the cable form, and through the half-open door she heard Truda talking to Pappy.

"I've wanted to speak my mind for some time," she was saying. "Now that I've spoken about the boy I can speak about Celia too. It's not right, Mr. Delaney, dragging her around from place to place like this. She should be having a proper education and mixing with other children. It was different when she was a little girl and her mother was alive and the three of them were together. But she's a growing girl now. She needs the companionship of other girls her own age."

Pappy had turned round and was facing Truda. Celia, watching through the half-open door, saw the lost, frightened expression in his eyes.

"I know," he said, "but what am I to do? She's all I have left. I can't let her go. If I ever let her go I shall crack up. If she ever leaves me I shall go to pieces."

"It's spoiling her life," said Truda, "I'm warning you. It's spoiling her life. You're giving her too much responsibility. You're trying to put an old head on her shoulders. She'll suffer for it. Not you, Mr. Delaney. She'll suffer for it."

"Haven't I suffered?" said Pappy, and he went on looking at Truda with that terrible lost look in his eyes. Then he pulled himself together; he poured out another glass of ginger ale.

"She's seeing the world," he said. "The child is seeing the world, and that's an education in itself. Better than anything she would get in a school. I tell you what we'll do, Truda. We'll advertise for a governess. That's the answer. A good, all-round governess. And we'll look round for some other girls to come and have tea. That's it. We'll ask some children to tea."

He smiled, then he patted Truda on the shoulder.

"Don't worry, Truda. I'll arrange something. And I'll send the cable to the school. I'll tell that headmaster chap to look for the boy in Liverpool. You're right, of course. He mustn't hang about a theatre. All right for Maria, she has a job of work to do. No good for the boy. That's all right. Don't worry, Truda."

Celia waited a moment and then went into the sitting room.

"Here's your cable form," she said. They both turned and looked at her, and nobody said anything, and there was not a sound except the whirring of the fans.

Celia went away down the passage, and locked herself in the lavatory, and instead of reading the book she kept there, she sat down on the seat and began to cry. She kept seeing Pappy with his lost face, saying to Truda, "I can't let her go. If she ever goes I shall crack up. If she ever leaves me I shall go to pieces."

And she would never leave him, never. But how was he spoiling her life? What did Truda mean? Was she missing something? Was she? The things that other girls did at school, like playing hockey, writing notes and hiding them, laughing, pushing each other over? She had no wish to do any of those things. She just wanted to stay with Pappy. But if only one of the others could be with her, if only Niall or Maria could be there, too, so that there was someone young . . .

"How did Niall get back?" said Celia. "Did one of the masters arrive from the school and take him away? I've forgotten."

"They sent the padre," said Niall, "the chap who used to take the services in the chapel. He had sandy hair and used to make us laugh. He loved the theatre. That's why the head beak sent him. He wasn't a fool, he knew what he was doing."

"He took us out to tea before you caught the train," said Maria, "and he kept telling us funny stories all through tea so that we had no time to think."

Many years later, in London, he had come to see her at the theatre. He had been in front and had sent a note round asking if he could pay his respects to her, and she had said yes, very bored, wondering who on earth it was going to be. She was tired, she wanted to get away early; and as soon as he appeared she recognised him, the round-faced padre with the sandy hair, but it was not sandy any more, it was white. Niall was not in London. And they had sat there in her dressing room, talking about Niall, and she forgot she was tired.

"He bought us chocolates at the teashop," said Niall, "an enormous box with a scarlet ribbon. You tore off the ribbon at once and put it in your hair. It looked wonderful."

"Showing off," said Celia. "I bet she was showing off. She hoped the padre would fall in love with her and let Niall stay."

"You're jealous," said Maria. "You're still jealous after all these years. You wish that you had been with us up in Liverpool."

Niall was hungry in the night. He had always been one of those boys who were hungry at the wrong times. A good breakfast or a heavy lunch was wasted upon him. He would eat nothing. And then suddenly, at three in the afternoon, or at three in the morning, he would want a kipper, or a great plate of sausages. He would be so hungry that he would want to eat the doorknobs.

"We crept downstairs to the larder, do you remember?" said Maria. "The kitchen smelt of cat and Mrs. Rogers. Her shoes were in the fender."

"Strapped ones," said Niall, "bursting at the seams. They stank."

"There was some cheese," said Maria, "and half a loaf of bread, and a jar of paste. We took it up to my bedroom, and you came and lay on my bed in your vest and drawers because you hadn't any pyjamas."

Niall had been cold. He was always a cold boy. Always shivering, his feet like blocks of ice. Often since he had lain beside her, cold and shivering, and she had to put blankets on the bed, or rugs, once even a great heavy carpet, because of Niall's being cold. Dragging a carpet between them, hysterical, choking with laughter, and heaving it on a bed.

"There was a Bible on the table beside the bed," said Niall. "We lit two candles and read it together. We did that thing of opening it at random and whatever we saw had to be a symbol of the future."

"I do it still," said Maria. "I'm always doing it. I do it before a first night. But it never works. The last time it was, 'And he that gathereth the ashes of the heifer shall wash his clothes.' It just didn't mean a thing."

"You can cheat a bit," said Niall. "If you open the last half of the Bible it's the New Testament. The New Testament is better. You get things like 'There shall be no more fear.'"

"I wonder what you got that night in Liverpool?" said Celia. "I don't suppose you remember, either of you."

Maria shook her head.

"I don't know," she said. "It's too long ago."

Niall said nothing. He remembered. He could see again the flickering greasy candles in the green china candlestick, one of the candles much shorter than the other, with a blob of grease at the top beside the wick. And Maria putting a blanket round his shoulders because of the cold, tucking it round his middle, and she herself warm and cozy in flowered pyjamas, girl's pyjamas that did up at the side, and they had to speak in whispers because of Mrs. Rogers in the room next door. He was eating bread and paste, with the cheese on top of the paste, and they opened the Bible, and it was the Song of Solomon, and the verse was "I am my beloved's, and my beloved is mine: he feedeth among the lilies."

"That's you," said Maria, "but you aren't among the lilies. You are sitting here in bed with me, eating bread and paste."

She began to laugh and she had to stuff her handkerchief in her mouth because of Mrs. Rogers. Niall pretended to laugh with her, but in reality his mind did a somersault and jumped ahead. He saw Maria dancing through the years, living for the moment, caring for no one much and for nothing in particular, troubles slipping from her shoulders, soon forgotten; and he himself trailing after her like a distant shadow, always a step or two behind, always a little in the dark. It was midnight and she was warm, and tomorrow was another day. But tomorrow, thought Niall, something will happen. They will trace me from the school, and I shall have to go back again.

And he was right. The padre came. It was useless, protesting. He had no money; Maria could not keep him. So back he went again, the padre lighting up a pipe in the corner of the smoking carriage, and Niall leant from the window, waving, watching Maria, who stood at the far end of the platform, with the scarlet ribbon from the chocolate box tied round her hair.

There were tears in her eyes when she kissed him good-bye, but she would brush them away so soon, too soon, directly she left the platform.

"It must have been great fun," said Celia. "I wish I hadn't missed all that. And, Maria, even if the others were sniffy about you, you must have been good. Otherwise you wouldn't be where you are now."

"That's just it," said Maria. "Where am I now?"

Niall knew what she meant, but Celia was puzzled.

"Really," she said, "whatever more can you want? You've reached the top. You're popular; everyone rushes to whatever play you happen to be in."

"Yes, I know that," said Maria, "but am I really good?"

Celia stared back at her, nonplussed.

"Why, surely," she said, "you must be. I've never seen you bad.

Some things are better than others, but that's bound to happen. Of course you're good. Don't be such an idiot."

"Oh well," said Maria, "I can't explain. You don't understand."

She forgot most things in life, but not all. The little whispers, the careless innuendoes clung. She could not brush them off. Influence, she does it by influence. Someone else said that later. She does not do a stroke of work. She slipped in by the back door. It was the name. It was the name that did it. The whole thing was luck. Luck from start to finish. She landed that first big part in London because she set her cap at You-Know-Who, and he was mad about her. . . . It lasted quite a time, but of course . . . What she does is clever, but it's monkey cleverness. No one could call it acting. She's inherited Delaney's charm, and she has a photographic memory and a box of tricks. Nothing more to it than that, they say. They say . . . They say . . . They say . . .

"You see," said Maria slowly, "no one is ever honest with a person like me. No one really tells me the truth."

"I'm honest," said Niall. "I tell you the truth."

"Oh, you," sighed Maria. "You're different."

She looked across at him, at his queer expressionless dark eyes, his lanky hair, his narrow mouth with the jutting underlip; there was no part of him she did not know, no part of him she did not love, but what had that to do with her acting? Or had it everything to do with it? Were the two things hopelessly mixed? Niall was the reflection in the mirror, to whom she danced and gestured as a child. Niall was the scapegoat, bearing all her sins.

"What you really mean," said Niall, "is that we're none of us first-class. Not the way Pappy was, or Mama. And that's one of the things Charles was getting at when he called us parasites. We've fooled most people with our individual antics, but we know the truth, the three of us, inside."

And he was standing in the shop in Bond Street, Keith Prowse, looking for a record. A record of Pappy singing an old French song. He could not remember the title, but there was the line about "le cor."

"*Que j'aime le sond du cor, le soir, au fond du bois . . .*"

Some line like that. He knew the record well. It had "Plasir d'amour" on the other side. No one, ever, had sung those songs as Pappy had sung them. But the silly fool of a girl hunting through the lists stared at him blankly.

"It's not listed. It must be a very old one. I don't think it's recorded any more."

As she spoke the door of one of the little rooms leading off the passage opened. One of the rooms where people tried out records, and Niall heard the jigging rhythm of one of his own songs played rather indifferently by a second-rate band. A man in the shop passed at that moment and recognised Niall and smiled, nodding his head in the direction of the little room.

"Good afternoon, Mr. Delaney. You must be getting tired of hearing that one. I'm almost tired of it myself."

The girl behind the counter looked at him curiously, and Niall's song seemed to grow louder and louder, filling the shop with sound. He had made some excuse, and left the shop hurriedly, and walked away.

"The trouble is you're both of you ungrateful for success," said Celia. "You had it too young. It came to you, Maria, when you were barely twenty, in that roaring success at the Haymarket, and I was sitting at home in that house in St. John's Wood, looking after Pappy."

"You loved looking after Pappy," said Maria. "You know you did."

"He was drinking too much," said Celia. "You never noticed, or if you did, it never worried you. I had the awful thing of watching him go to the sideboard. And Truda was not with us. Truda was in hospital at the time with that ulcered leg."

"You made too much of it," said Niall. "Pappy never got unpleasantly drunk. He never actually fell down or anything. He used to be rather funny. He always recited. Yards and yards of poetry. Nobody minded. And he sang better than ever."

"I minded," said Celia. "When you've loved someone all your life, and you've looked after them, and you see them gradually slip away, and the best in them run to waste, you mind then."

"It was because he wasn't singing," said Maria. "He knew it was the beginning of the end, and it did something to him. When I begin getting old I shall probably drink too."

"No, you won't," said Niall. "You're too conceited. You care too much about your figure and your face."

"I don't care," said Maria. "I don't have to, thank goodness."

"You will one day," said Niall.

Maria looked at him sullenly.

"All right," she said, "go on. Say something else unpleasant. And anyway, we all know what you were up to that winter."

"Yes," said Celia. "That was another thing. Poor Pappy, he was very worried about you, Niall. It really was rather shocking."

"Nonsense," said Niall.

"You were only just eighteen," said Celia. "It caused an awful lot of talk."

"You mean Pappy talked," said Niall. "He always talked. It was the breath of life to him."

"Well, he was very upset," said Celia. "He never forgave that woman."

"People always say 'that woman' when they dislike a person," said Maria. "What reason had you to dislike poor old Freada? Actually, she was a very good sort. She was very good for Niall. She did him no harm at all, quite the reverse. And anyway, she was an old friend of Pappy's and Mama's."

"Perhaps that was why Pappy was angry," said Niall.

"Did you ever ask Freada?" said Maria.

"God, no," answered Niall.

"How funny men are. I would have done," said Maria.

"It all began at that awful party," said Celia. "It was a horrible evening. I shall never forget it. That awful party at the Green Park, or whatever the hotel was called. Pappy would give the party for Maria, after the first night at the Haymarket."

"It wasn't an awful party," said Maria. "It was a wonderful party."

"Of course it was wonderful for you," said Celia. "You had just made a big success. It wasn't wonderful for me. Pappy got tight at the party and couldn't get the car to start afterwards, and there was all that snow."

"Snow everywhere," said Niall. "It amazed me that anyone came to the party at all, let alone the play. It was inches thick all up the Haymarket. I know, because I spent most of the evening walking up and down. I couldn't go in the theatre and watch. I was too nervous for Maria."

"Nerves, don't talk to me of nerves," said Maria. "My hands and my feet and my tummy got colder and colder through the day. I went and said a prayer in St. Martin's in the Fields."

94

"Once you got on the stage you were all right," said Celia.

"I was not all right," said Niall, "walking up and down the Haymarket with chattering teeth. I might have caught pneumonia."

Maria looked across at him. She was still a little sullen, still a little resentful.

"Well, your evening ended up all right, didn't it?" she said.

"If it ended the way it did, it was your fault," said Niall.

"Oh, go on," said Maria. "Blame everything on me."

Celia had not been listening. She was still thinking of the car that would not start, and Pappy bending down, doing things to the handle.

"If you come to think of it," she said, "it was a queer sort of evening for all of us."

CHAPTER TEN

WHEN Maria woke that morning she could see the flakes of snow falling outside the window. The curtains were pulled aside—she never slept with them drawn—and the snow was falling sideways, slanting to the left, so that if she looked at it for long something happened to her eyes and she felt giddy. She closed them again, but she knew she would not sleep any more. The Day had come. The dreaded Day.

Perhaps if it went on snowing for several hours the traffic would be stopped by the evening, and no one would be able to get anywhere, and all the theatres would have to close. A message would be sent to the company that, owing to the weather, the first night had been postponed.

She lay sideways in bed, her knees tucked up to her chin. She could pretend to be ill, of course. She could just lie there in bed all day and people would come in and she would pretend to be in a trance. The most frightful thing has happened. Maria Delaney, who was to play the young lead at the Haymarket, has been suddenly stricken with paralysis in the night. She can't hear, she can't speak, she can't move as much as a finger. It is the most terrible tragedy. Because she was brilliant. We all had such high hopes of her. She was going to do wonderful things, and now she will never act again. She will lie forevermore with that wistful, sweet, lost look in her eyes, and we shall all have to tiptoe to her bed and take her flowers. . . .

Poor, lovely, brilliant Maria Delaney.

There was a knock on her door, and the heavy-footed housemaid, Edith, burst into the room with her breakfast.

"Lovely weather," she said, dumping the tray beside the bed. "The snow came over my ankles when I opened the back door. Someone will have to shovel it away for the tradesmen, but it won't be me."

Maria did not answer. She kept her eyes closed. She hated Edith.

"You won't find many turning out to the theatre this weather," said Edith. "It will be three parts empty. There's a bit about you in the paper, and a photograph. Not a scrap like you, either."

She flounced out of the room, banging the door. Hateful girl. What did she know about the theatre being full or empty? No one had been able to get a seat who had not put his name down weeks ago, everyone knew that. The weather was not likely to scare off the lucky ones. Where was that bit about her in the paper? She opened the paper and looked it up and down, right through.

Oh, was that all? Three little lines down at the bottom where no one would ever see them. "Miss Maria Delaney, who is appearing in tonight's new play at the Haymarket, is the eldest daughter of . . ." And then a whole lot about Pappy. They might just as well have put Pappy's photograph in the paper instead of hers. Edith was right. It was not like her. Why could not the fools have used the new ones she had had done on purpose? But no. It had to be that idiotic thing of her grinning over her shoulder.

"Miss Maria Delaney, who is appearing in tonight's new play at the Haymarket . . ." Tonight. There was no escape. It had come. It was upon her. She turned to her tray and looked at her grapefruit with distaste. There was not enough sugar, and the marmalade pot was smeared. That was because Truda was away. Truda would be in hospital with an ulcered leg just when she was needed.

There were only two letters on the tray. One was a bill from Selfridge's for some shoes, which she thought she had paid. She was sure she had. The brutes had sent it in again. And the other was from that boring girl who had been on tour with her last summer. "I shall be thinking of you when the great day comes. Some people have all the luck. What's he like? Is he really as exciting as he looks, and is it true he's nearly fifty? It doesn't give his age in Who's Who. . . ."

Not many people knew the address in St. John's Wood. Pappy and Celia had not been there very long. Most people would send their letters and telegrams to the Haymarket. The flowers too. When you came to think of it, the whole business was horribly like having an operation. The telegrams, the flowers. And the long hours of waiting.

She ate some of the grapefruit, but it was very bitter and all mixed up with pith. She spat it out.

She heard shuffling footsteps outside the door, and three fingers tapped in the familiar way.

"Come in," said Maria.

It was Pappy. He wore his old blue dressing gown, and the slippers that Truda had mended again and again. Pappy never bought new clothes. He clung to the things he knew until they were practically unsanitary. There was one old cardigan that was held together with pieces of string.

"Well, my darling," he said.

He came and sat down on the bed and took her hand and kissed it. He had grown much heavier and fatter since the tour in South Africa, and his hair was now quite white. It was as thick as ever, though. It stood up from his powerful head and made him more like a lion than ever. An aging lion.

He held her hand as he sat on the bed, and he took a piece of lump sugar off the tray and chewed it.

"How are you feeling, my darling?" he said.

"Awful," Maria told him.

"I know," he said.

And he smiled and chewed another lump of sugar.

"You've either got it or you haven't," he said. "It's either there at the back of your funny little head, and you'll do what you have to do instinctively, or you'll meander through like sixty per cent of them do, just hanging about, never getting anywhere much."

"How am I to know?" said Maria. "People never tell one the truth, not the real truth. It may be all right tonight, and the notices may be good, and everybody be nice—but I shan't really know."

"You'll know all right," he said, "here." And he tapped his chest. "Inside," he said.

"I feel it's all wrong to be nervous," said Maria. "I feel it's lack of confidence. One ought to go right ahead, never minding."

"Some people do," he said, "but they're the duds. They are the ones that win prizes in school, and you never hear of them again. Go on. Be nervous. Be ill. Be sick down the lavatory pan. It's part of your life from now on. You've got to go through with it. Nothing's worth while if you don't fight for it first, if you haven't a pain in your belly beforehand."

He got up and pottered to the window. His bedroom slippers made a shuffling sound.

"When I first sang in Dublin," he said, "there was a hell of a crowd. A real mixed bunch. And there had been some fuss about the tickets. The wrong people had got the wrong seats. I was so damn nervous beforehand, when I tried to open my mouth my jaw got stuck—I couldn't close it for about five minutes."

He laughed. He moved over to the washstand and fiddled with Maria's tube of tooth paste.

"Then I got angry," he said, "I got angry with myself. What the hell am I frightened of? I said to myself. They're nothing but a lot of micks sitting out there, and if they don't like me I don't like them, and it's just too bad for all of us. So I walked onto the platform and sang."

"Did you sing well?" asked Maria.

He put down the tube of tooth paste. He looked at her and smiled.

"If I had not, we wouldn't be here now," he said, "and you could not be walking onto that stage at the Haymarket tonight. Now get up and take your bath, and don't forget you're a Delaney. Give 'em hell."

And he opened the door and shuffled off down the passage to his room, shouting to André to bring his breakfast.

He'll kiss me tonight and send flowers to the dressing room, thought Maria, but none of that will matter. This is what matters. What he said to me just now.

She got up and went to the bathroom and turned on the hot water, and she emptied into the water all the bath salts that Celia had given her for Christmas.

It's like anointing a corpse before you bury it, she said to herself.

It went on snowing all the morning. The little garden in front of the house was covered. It had a dead, flat look. And everything was silent and still, the queer muffled stillness that comes with snow. You could not hear the traffic in the Finchley Road.

Maria kept wishing Niall would come, but his train was not due until the afternoon. He was leaving school at Easter. This was his last term. Pappy had wangled special leave for him to come up because of the first night. Why could not he come in the morning and not have to wait until the afternoon? She wanted Niall to be with her.

The shoulder strap of her chemise tore when she put it over her head. She looked in the chest of drawers for another and could not find one. She went to the door and shouted for Celia.

"All my underclothes have disappeared," she stormed. "I can't find a thing. You've taken them."

Celia was up and dressed. She was always up before Maria, in case Pappy wanted her for anything, to answer the telephone, to write a letter.

"Nothing's back from the laundry," she said. "It's because Truda isn't here. There's always a muddle. You shall have my best chemise and knickers. The ones Pappy gave me for Christmas."

"You're much fatter than me, they won't fit," grumbled Maria.

"They will fit, they're too small. I was going to give them to you anyway," said Celia.

Her voice was gentle and soothing. She's doing it on purpose, thought Maria. She's being especially nice because of it being my first night, and she knows I'm nervous. For some reason the knowledge of this was irritating. She snatched the chemise and knickers out of Celia's hands. Celia watched her put them on in silence. How lovely Maria looked in them. They fitted perfectly. What it was to be slim and straight . . .

"What are you going to wear tonight?" asked Maria.

Her voice was grumpy. She would not look at Celia.

"My white," said Celia. "It's back from the cleaner's, and it looks rather nice. The trouble is it's shrunk a bit, and when I dance it may give at the back. Do you want just to run through your words? I'll hear them for you."

"No," said Maria. "We did all that yesterday. I'm not going to look at the thing again."

"Is there no rehearsal call today?"

"No, nothing. Oh, *he's* down there, I suppose, messing about with the lights. The rest of us aren't wanted."

"Oughtn't you to send him a telegram?"

"I suppose so. He'll have about five hundred. He doesn't open them anyway. The secretary does all that."

She looked at herself in the glass. Her hair was frightful, but she would wash it after lunch and dry it in front of the dining-room fire. As a matter of fact, she was not going to send him a telegram. She was going to send him some flowers, but she did not want Celia to know, or Pappy. She knew exactly what she was going to send. Anemones, blue and red, in a white bowl. He talked about flowers once at rehearsal, and he said anemones were his favourite flowers. They had some at that florist at the corner of Marylebone Road, she had noticed yesterday. The bowl was extra money, but it did not matter for once. It was extra, too, to have them sent down to the Haymarket.

"Pappy's asked him to the party afterwards," said Celia. "Will he bring that awful wife?"

"She's away. She's in America."

"What a good thing," said Celia.

She wondered just how nervous Maria was, now, at this moment, and whether it would go on getting worse throughout the day or ease off, like a brewing pain. Here was her sister, an actress, about to play her first important part in London, and Celia wanted to talk to her about it and yet she could not; she held back, oddly shy.

Maria went to the wardrobe and pulled down a mackintosh.

"You're surely not going out?" said Celia. "It's snowing hard."

"I shall stifle if I stay here," said Maria. "I must walk, I must move about."

"We shall be alone at lunch," said Celia. "Pappy's going to the Garrick."

"I shan't want much," said Maria. "I'm not hungry."

She went out of the house and round the corner of the avenue into the Finchley Road, and caught a bus to the florist where they had anemones. The title of the play was written in broad black letters on the side of the bus, with his name above it in red. It was a good omen. She must remember to tell Niall.

After she had chosen the anemones with great care, she went to the table in the corner of the shop to write her card. She was not sure what to put. It must not be too familiar. It must not be facetious. The simple thing was always best. She just put his name, and then "With love from Maria." She stuck the card amongst the flowers and went out of the shop. She glanced at her watch. Twelve o'clock. Just over eight hours to go.

They had Irish stew for lunch, and apple charlotte. They finished earlier than usual because of Pappy not being with them. Directly lunch was over, Maria washed her hair and then set it in pins and lay with her back to the dining-room fire.

"Perhaps," she said to Celia casually, yawning a little, "perhaps you could just hear me that bit in the middle of the third act. Just for the words."

Celia read the cues in a flat level voice. Maria answered them, her hands over her eyes. It was all right. She was word-perfect anyway.

"Anywhere else?" asked Celia.

"No, nowhere else."

Celia turned over the pages of the crumpled script. It was marked all over with pencil notes. She looked down at Maria, still lying with her hands over her face. What must it be like for Maria to kiss that man, and have his arms round her, and say all those things that she had to say? Maria never talked about it. She was funny and reserved about things like that. She would say So-and-So had been in a bad temper, or had a hang-over, or had been very funny and amusing, but if you tried to question her about more personal things she was evasive. She did not seem to be interested. She shrugged her shoulders. Perhaps Niall would ask her. Perhaps she would tell Niall.

It was dark very early, about half-past three. It had stopped snowing, but it was cold and bleak outside. Edith came in to draw the curtains.

"It's left off for the moment," she said, dragging the curtains with a jerk, "but there's more to come. And it's ever so mucky underfoot. I just went down to the post and I got drenched."

She stumped out again, leaving a stale current of air behind her.

"Don't they ever wash?" said Maria fiercely. She sat up and stretched herself and began pulling the pins out of her hair. It stood out round her head, short and golden like a halo. Celia put away the script. She had been reading it right through again, from start to finish. She knew it almost as well as Maria.

Suddenly she asked a question. She could not help herself.

"Do you like him?" she said.

"Who?" said Maria.

Celia waved the script in her face.

"Yes, he's awfully nice. I told you," said Maria.

She got up from the floor and straightened her skirt.

"But what's it like, kissing him at rehearsal? Don't you feel awkward?" said Celia.

"I feel awkward if I have to kiss him in the morning," said Maria. "I'm always afraid my breath will smell. It sometimes does, you know, when you're hungry. That's why it's always better after lunch."

"Is it?" said Celia.

But that was not really what she wanted to know.

"Your hair looks lovely," she said instead.

Maria turned and looked at herself in the glass.

"It's queer," she said, "but I don't feel this is happening to me at all. This is some other person going through my day. It's a dreadful feeling. I can't explain it."

They heard the sound of a taxi drawing up outside the house.

"It's Niall," said Maria. "It's Niall, at last."

She ran to the window and pulled the curtain. She banged on the window. He turned, smiling, and waved his hand. He was paying off the driver.

"Go and let him in, quick," said Maria.

Celia went to the front door and opened it. Niall came up the steps, carrying his bag.

"Hullo, funny face," he said, and kissed her.

He was frozen, of course. His hands were like ice, and his hair was all over the place and needed cutting. They went into the dining room together.

"Where on earth have you been?" said Maria angrily. "Why didn't you come sooner?" She did not smile at him at all, nor did she kiss him.

"I went to see Truda," he said. "The hospital is miles away, as you know, and with all this snow it took simply ages."

"Oh, how good of you," said Celia. "Poor Truda, she must have been pleased. How was she?"

"Better," said Niall, "but awfully crotchety. Grumbling at everything. The nurses, the food, the doctors, the other patients. I stayed quite a bit and made her laugh."

"I think it's very selfish of you," said Maria. "You knew it was my day of days, and that I'd be here wanting comfort, and you go off to the other end of London to see Truda. Any time would do for Truda. Now I've only got about two hours before I go down to the theatre."

Niall did not answer. He simply went to the fire and knelt down and held his hands to the flames.

"Truda's sent you a present," he said. "She asked one of the nurses to go specially and buy something during her off time. She told me what it was. It's a horseshoe in white heather. It's gone down to the theatre. She was so pleased. 'Tell Maria I'll be thinking of her all the evening,' she said."

Maria said nothing. She stuck out her underlip and looked sulky.

"I'll go and see about tea," said Celia after a moment.

It was better to leave them together. They knew how to sort themselves out. She went out of the room and upstairs to her bedroom until it should really be time for tea.

Maria knelt down by the fire next to Niall. She rubbed her cheek against his shoulder.

"I feel terrible," she said. "It started in my tummy, and now it's gone to my throat."

"I know," he said, "I feel it too. All over. From the soles of the feet to the back of the neck."

"And every minute," said Maria, "it gets nearer and nearer to the time, and there's nothing to be done about it."

"When I saw the snow this morning," said Niall, "I hoped there'd be an avalanche and it would bury the Haymarket so you couldn't open."

"Did you think that?" said Maria. "So did I. Oh, Niall . . . If I ever marry and have a baby, will you have it for me?"

"It would be one way of getting famous, anyway," said Niall.

He felt in his pocket.

"I didn't really spend all that time with Truda," he said. "I went and bought you a present."

"Oh, Niall . . . Show me, quick."

"It's nothing much," he said. "It's not valuable or anything. I got it with the money Pappy gave me for Christmas. But I hope you'll like it."

He gave her a small package. She undid the string and tore off the paper. It was a little red leather box. Inside the leather box was a ring. The stone was blue. It glistened when she turned it in her hand.

"Niall, darling Niall . . ." she said. It fitted the third finger of her right hand.

"It's nothing much," he said. "It's not worth anything."

"It's worth everything to me," she said. "I shall wear it always. I shall never take it off."

She held out her hand and watched the blue of the stone glisten as she turned the ring. It reminded her of something. Somewhere, sometime, she had seen a ring like that. Then she remembered Mama used to wear a blue ring on her left hand. It was like Mama's ring, only, of course, cheaper. . . .

"I'm glad you like it," said Niall. "Directly I saw it in the shop, I knew I must get it. I knew it was right for you."

"I want you to come with me in the taxi to the theatre," said Maria, "and leave me there at the stage door. Pappy and Celia will come later in the car. Will you do that?"

"Yes, of course," he said, "I meant to do that."

The hours went past too quickly. Tea came, and tea was over, and it was time for Niall to go upstairs and change. Pappy came home about six o'clock. He was very jovial, very merry. He must have had a few drinks at the Garrick.

"The whole world will be there tonight," he told them, "and we're landed with about ten more people for the party afterwards. Celia, you'd better ring up the Green Park. I'm damned if I know who's coming and who isn't. Niall, you'd better wear a buttonhole. André, where's a buttonhole for Niall?"

He lumbered up the stairs, laughing loudly, calling for Maria, calling for everybody in the house. Maria came down from her bedroom with a suitcase. She had her dress in it, for changing afterwards. Celia did not know who looked the whitest, Maria or Niall.

"I think we'd better go," said Maria, her voice tight and rather strained. "I shall feel better down at the theatre. I think we'd better go. Did anyone order a taxi?"

There was no going back now. No returning. The thing had to be faced. It was exactly like an operation. A terrible major operation. And Celia, standing there in the draughty hall, wore the encouraging smile on her face that nurses wore.

"Good-bye, darling—good luck," said Celia.

The taxi was the trolley. The taxi, taking her off to the theatre, was the trolley that carried the corpse.

"Oh, Niall . . ." she said. "Oh, Niall . . ."

He put his arm round her, and the taxi jogged through the slushy streets.

"You must never leave me," she said. "You must never, never leave me."

He held onto her and said nothing.

"Why I'm doing it, I can't think," she said. "It gives no pleasure to me or anyone. It's an absurd thing to do. I hate it."

"You don't hate it, you love it," he said.

"It's not true, I hate it," she said.

She looked out of the window. The streets seemed unfamiliar in the snow.

"Where's he going?" she said. "He's going the wrong way. I shall be late."

"You won't be late," said Niall. "There's heaps of time."

"I must pray," said Maria. "Tell him to go to a church. I must pray. If I don't pray, something dreadful will happen."

Niall thrust his head out of the window.

"Stop at a church," he said, "any church, it doesn't matter where. This young lady wants to get out and pray."

The driver turned round, a moonface of astonishment.

"Anything wrong?" he said.

"No," said Niall. "It's just that she's got to act in about an hour's time. Please find a church."

The man shrugged his shoulders and jerked in the clutch.

He stopped outside St. Martin's in the Fields.

"She'd better go in there," he said. "It's where they hold the memorial services for actors when they die."

"It's an omen," said Niall, "a good one. You must go. I'll wait in the taxi." His teeth were chattering with cold.

Maria got out of the taxi and went up the steps of St. Martin's. She pushed through the doors and went and knelt down in a pew on the left.

"Let it be all right," she said. "Let it be all right."

And she kept saying this over and over again, because there was really nothing else to say.

Then she got up and bobbed to the altar, because it might be a high church, she did not know, and there was a woman in the pew behind looking at her, and she went down the slippery steps to the taxi.

"Feeling better?" said Niall. He looked whiter than ever, and very anxious.

"Much," she said. But she wasn't really. She felt just the same. It was a good thing done, though. Like touching wood. No harm could come of it. . . . In a few moments they were outside the Haymarket.

"We're here," said Niall.

"Yes," she said.

He carried out the suitcase and paid the driver. Pappy had given him the money. Maria had none at all. She had forgotten all about money for a taxi.

"Good-bye," said Maria. She looked at him; she tried to smile.

Suddenly she tore off her glove and showed him her ring.

"You're with me," she said. "I'm safe. You're with me."

And she passed through the stage door and was inside the theatre. Her heart was still beating fast, and her hands were burning, but she felt steadier suddenly, the feeling of panic had gone from her. It was because she was inside the theatre. She was with the others. One of them poked her head round the door. Her face was covered with cold cream, and she had a towel round her head.

"I've got dysentery," she said. "I've lost the whole of my inside. You look wonderful."

Maria knew then that everything was going to be all right. It was what she had asked for in St. Martin's in the Fields. They were all together, the whole lot of them. She was not alone. She was part of them and they were all together.

Suddenly she saw *him* standing in the passage. He was standing by the door looking at her, and whistling under his breath.

"Hullo," he said.

"Hullo," said Maria.

"Come and see my flowers," he said. "It's like a crematorium."

She went to the door of his room. The dresser was unwrapping yet another package. It was some sort of alabaster vase, filled with a gigantic shrub.

"They've been down to Kew," he said, "uprooting something. It doesn't smell at all. Funny. You'd think a thing that size would smell."

She glanced round the room. There were flowers everywhere. And telegrams. Stacks of them. Some of them opened.

Then she saw her bowl of anemones. They were on his dressing table. Just by the looking glass. There were not any other flowers there; only her anemones. He saw her looking at them, but he did not say anything.

"I must go," said Maria.

He looked at her a moment, and she looked back at him, and then she turned and went out of the room.

She went to her own dressing room and found the flowers from the family. The telegrams. The heather horseshoe from Truda. She hung her coat on the door and reached for her dressing gown. Then she saw the parcel. It was long and flat. She felt calm and steady, not excited any more. She opened the parcel, and it was a red leather box. Inside was a gold cigarette case. Her name was written inside the case "Maria." And *his* name, and the date. She sat looking at it for a moment, and then she heard her dresser coming along the passage.

She put the cigarette case hurriedly, furtively, into her evening bag and thrust the bag at the back of the drawer in the table. When the dresser came into the room Maria was bending over Pappy's roses and reading his card. "Good luck, my darling."

"Well," said the dresser, "how are you feeling, dear?"

Maria pretended to start. She looked round as though surprised to see the dresser come into the room.

"Who, me?" she said. "Oh, I'm fine. Everything's going to be all right."

She leant forward and began to cream her face.

Yes, everything was going to be all right. . . .

CHAPTER ELEVEN

NIALL went round to the front of the theatre and stood inside the foyer. He was much too early, of course. There was still an hour to go before the curtain went up. The commissionaire asked him what he was doing and asked for his ticket. He had no ticket. Pappy had the tickets. This involved him in an argument, and he had to explain that his name was Delaney, which he hated doing, because it seemed like showing off. Once Niall told the name, the commissionaire's whole manner changed. He began to talk about Pappy; he had been an admirer of Pappy for years. He began to talk about Mama.

"There's never been anyone like her," he said, "so light on her feet you didn't know she was moving. They talk about the Russian ballet —not in the same street with her. It's all a question of class, you know. The whole thing is class."

He switched from Pappy and Mama to command performances. Niall said nothing and let him ramble on. There was a photograph of Maria on the wall opposite. It was not in the least like the person who had gone to pray in St. Martin's in the Fields and who had clung to him in the taxi. The girl in the photograph had her head thrown back, she smiled seductively, and her lashes were much too long.

"You're here to see your sister, of course," said the commissionaire. "Proud of her, I expect, aren't you?"

"She's not my sister. She's no relation," said Niall suddenly. The man stared at him, nonplussed.

"Well, stepsister, if you like," said Niall. "We're all mixed up. It's rather difficult to explain."

He wished the man would go away, he did not want to talk to him any more. A taxi drove up and stopped. A very old lady got out trailing a feather fan. The commissionaire went to help her. They were beginning to arrive. . . .

As he watched the hands travel round the clock and the foyer gradually fill with excited, chattering people, a sense of claustrophobia came upon Niall and he felt trapped. They buzzed past him and about him, and he tried to flatten himself against the wall. Thank God nobody knew who he was, and he did not have to talk, but the sense of oppression was with him just the same. He was aware of a feeling of acute dislike, almost hatred, towards all these unknown men and women who were filing past him to the stalls. They were like the spectators at an arena in ancient Rome. They had all dined well, and now they had come to watch Maria being torn to pieces by lions. Their eyes were avaricious, their hands were claws. All they wanted to do was to draw blood. . . .

It grew hotter and hotter inside the foyer, and his stiff collar pierced the side of his neck, yet his hands and feet were icy; he was hot and cold in all the wrong places.

How appalling if he fainted. How absolutely frightful if his legs crumpled under him and he heard the girl who sold the programmes say, "There's a young gentleman taken bad—will someone come and give a hand?"

Ten minutes to eight . . . The curtain rang up at eight-fifteen, Maria said, and her entrance was at eight thirty-five. He pulled out his handkerchief and wiped his forehead. Christ! That couple over there were staring at him. Did he know them? Were they friends of Pappy's? Or was it just that they thought the pale-faced boy standing against the wall was going to die?

There was a photographer at the entrance with a flashlight. Every time he clicked the thing there was a fresh buzz of conversation and a little murmur of laughter.

Suddenly Niall saw Pappy with Celia in her white fur coat, pushing through the crowd towards him. Someone said, "There's Delaney," and people were turning to look at Pappy, as they always did, and Pappy was smiling and nodding and waving his hand. He never seemed to be embarrassed. He never seemed to mind. He looked magnificent, towering above everybody else. Celia held Niall's hand. She stared at him, her large eyes anxious.

"Are you all right?" she said. "You look as if you're going to be sick." Pappy came and gripped his shoulder.

"Come on," he said, "let's go to our seats. What a mob. Hullo, how are you?" And he turned again, claimed by some friend, and then by someone else, and all the while the photographer was clicking in the background.

"You must go in alone with Pappy," said Niall to Celia. "It's no use. I can't face it."

Celia looked at him blankly.

"You must come," she said. "Think of Maria. You must come."

"No," said Niall. "I'm going out in the street."

And he pushed his way through the crowd and out into the street and began to walk up the Haymarket to Piccadilly. His shoes were thin and were soon soaked through with the slush, but he did not mind. He would keep walking all the evening, up and down and around the streets, because he could not bear to watch the agony of Maria in the arena.

I'm gutless, he said to himself. That will always be my trouble. I'm absolutely and entirely gutless.

He stood awhile in Piccadilly, looking at the flashing lights and the dark canopy of sky above his head and the dirty falling snow, for it began again, pale soft flakes onto the wet pavement. I remember this, he thought. This has happened before. And he was a child standing in the Place de la Concorde, holding Truda's hand, and the snow was falling just like this, and the taxis swerved and hooted, swerving to right and to left, some making for the bridge across the Seine, the others turning left down the Rue Royal. Frozen water gushed from the mouths of the women in the fountain.

"Come back," said Truda to Maria. "Come back." And Maria was trying to dart across the Place de la Concorde. She looked back, laughing, she wore no hat, and the snow was falling on her hair.

This was Piccadilly, though, and the lights ran up and down the London Pavilion. Eros had a little cap of snow. The snow kept falling. Then it started, the tune in Niall's head. It had nothing to do with Paris or with London. It had nothing to do with lights, or with the Place de la Concorde, or with Piccadilly. It just came, born from nothing and from no one, an echo from the unconscious.

I could get it down if there was a piano, he thought, but there isn't one. Everything's shut. I can't go bursting into the Piccadilly Hotel or somewhere and ask if I can borrow a piano.

He went on walking up and down the streets, getting colder and colder, and the tune was stronger in his head every moment. His head was bursting with the tune. He had forgotten all about Maria. He was not thinking of Maria any more. It was not until he found himself in the Haymarket again, opposite the theatre, that he remembered the play. He looked at his watch. It was a quarter past ten. The play had been running for two hours. The people standing there in the foyer smoking cigarettes must be waiting about during the second interval. The sick feeling of apprehension came upon him once again. If he went in and stood amongst them he might hear them say something terrible about Maria. He felt himself drawn irresistibly towards the theatre. His laggard feet brought him to the doors. He saw the commissionaire standing just by the entrance. He turned his back, he did not want to be seen. It was too late. The commissionaire had recognised him and came forward.

"Your dad's been looking for you," he said. "He's been looking everywhere. He's gone back to his seat now. The curtain's just going up on the third act."

"How's it going?" said Niall, his teeth chattering.

"Lovely," said the commissionaire. "They're just lapping it up. Why don't you go in and join your dad?"

"No, it's all right," said Niall. "I like it outside."

He went back again into the street. He could feel the commissionaire staring at him. He went on walking about in the street until five minutes to eleven, when he judged the play would be over. Then at five minutes to the hour he went and stood outside the doors that led directly onto the street. They were flung open, and he could hear the applause in the far distance. He could not judge the sound. It always seemed to him the same from any theatre. A steady, breaking sound. A sort of roar. It had always sounded the same for as far back as he could remember. Once it had been for Pappy and Mama. Now, please God, it was for Maria. He wondered if always, throughout his life, there would be some part of him somewhere that listenend to applause, and he would be part of it, bound up in it, and yet—as it were —outside, standing in the street the way he was standing now.

The applause died away. Someone must have come forward to make a speech, and then they were clapping again, and then the orchestra started to play "God Save the King." He waited a moment longer. Then the clattering of footsteps began on the side stairs, and voices and laughter and the dark mass of people came swarming into the street.

"Heavens—it's snowing again. We shall never find a taxi," someone said, and a man bumped into him and another woman behind his shoulder, and the cars began moving in a steady stream, with people jumping on the running boards, and he could not hear anyone say a word about Maria.

"Yes, I know," a voice said. "That's what I thought. . . ." And more voices and more laughter. Niall found himself walking towards the main entrance. The mass of people were standing there, waiting for the cars. Two men and a woman stood right on the edge of the pavement.

"I think she's got a curious sort of fascination, but I wouldn't call her lovely," said the woman. "Look, isn't that the car coming now? Wait for it to draw up. I don't want to ruin my shoes."

Silly bitch, thought Niall. Is she talking about Maria? She would be lucky if she had one twentieth part of Maria's looks.

They got into the car. They drove away. Maria could be dying in her dressing room for all they cared.

Two men climbed into the next taxi. They were middle-aged, and they looked tired and bored. They said nothing at all. They were probably critics.

"He's aged rather, don't you think?" said someone. Niall wondered who. Anyway, it did not matter. It was not Maria who had aged.

Still they came on and on, pouring out of the theatre like rats from a sinking ship. And then he found himself clutched by Celia.

"At last," she said. "Where have you been? We thought you must have found a taxi and gone home. Come on quickly. Pappy's gone ahead."

"Where to? What for?"

"Why, around to see Maria, of course. In the dressing room."

"What happened? Was she all right?"

"What happened? Didn't you see any of it, then?"

"No."

"Why, it's wonderful. She's made a huge success. I knew she would. Pappy's in tremendous form. Come on."

Celia was flushed and happy. She dragged at Niall's sleeve. He followed her along the passages to Maria's dressing room. But there were too many people. It was always the same. Far too many people.

"I don't think I'll come," said Niall. "I'll go and wait in the bar."

"Don't be such a wet blanket," said Celia. "There's nothing to worry about now. Everything's all right, and Maria will be so happy."

Maria was standing in the doorway, and Pappy was there, laughing, and several others. Niall did not know any of them, nor did he want to know them or speak to them. He just wanted to make certain that Maria was all right. She had a curious ragged frock on—of course, he remembered, that was the part in the play—and she was smiling up at the man who was talking to Pappy. Niall recognised him. He was laughing too. Everyone was laughing. Everyone was very pleased. Then Pappy turned to talk to someone else, and the man and Maria looked at each other and laughed. It was the laugh of two people who share a secret. The laugh of two people who stand on the brink of an adventure. The adventure had only just begun. Niall understood that look on Maria's face, he understood the expression in her eyes. Although he had never seen her look at anyone in that way before, he knew why she did it, and what it meant, and why she was happy.

She'll always be like that, he thought. I can't stop her. It's all mixed up with her acting. I just have to let it happen.

He looked down at her hand and he saw she was wearing the ring. She was twisting it round her finger as she talked. She did not take it off. She would never take it off, he knew that. She wanted to keep it and hold it, just as she wanted to keep Niall and hold him. We're both of us young, thought Niall, and there may be years and years ahead of us, but she will always go on wearing that ring and we shall always be together. That man there will be dead and gone and forgotten, but we shall be together. This is just an evening that has to be gone through and endured. And there will be other days and other evenings. . . . If he could find a piano somewhere and sit down and play the tune it would be easier. But there was the party at the Green Park, and more people to be faced, and the business of being polite and dancing. The party would get out of control, as Pappy's parties always did, and Pappy would start to sing and no one would get to bed before about four in the morning. And at nine he, Niall, had to catch the train back to school, and still there would have been no time to play that tune on any piano.

Suddenly Maria was beside him, touching his hand.

"It's over," she said. "Oh, Niall, it's over."

The man had gone, but she was still twisting the ring round her finger.

"Part of it's over," said Niall, "and part of it's just begun."

She knew what he meant at once. Her eyes drifted away from him. "Don't say anything," she said.

Then more people came along the passage, and she was caught up with them and hemmed in, laughing and talking, and Niall went on standing and waiting with his back against the wall, wishing he could go away and find a piano and forget everything but the tune.

They must have sat down about twenty-five to supper at the Green Park. Everyone was very gay and merry, and the supper was good, and the waiters kept opening more and more bottles of champagne.

It's like a wedding, thought Niall. Before long Pappy will get up and propose the health of the bride. And the bride will be Maria.

Maria was away down the other end of the table. Once or twice she looked down and waved at Niall, but she was not thinking about him. He danced with Celia once or twice, but nobody else. He did not ask Maria. The band was noisy and the fellow playing the sax thought he was funny, but he was not. You couldn't hear the chap at the piano. The sax drowned him all the time. The very sight of the piano was an added irritant. Niall wanted to turn everybody out of the room and get to it.

"You look awfully cross, what's the matter?"

There was a new woman sitting on his right who had not been there before. It was this woman who had spoken. Her face was familiar, the friendly brown eyes, the rather large mouth, and her hair with the square-cut fringe.

"Pappy sent me down to talk to you," she said. "You don't remember me. I'm Freada."

"Why, yes," he said. "Yes, of course."

She used to live in Paris, she was a friend of Pappy's and Mama's, and she was funny and jolly and kind, and had taken them all to see the Concours Hippique, he remembered now, years ago. She looked the same. That was the queer thing that happened when you grew up. Pappy's friends, who had seemed once so old and tall and out of reach, turned out to be just ordinary people like yourself.

"I haven't seen any of you for about ten years," she said. "You were a funny little chap and very shy. I was in front tonight. Maria was so good. What an attractive creature she's grown into, but so have you all. It makes me feel very old."

She put out her cigarette and lit another. Niall remembered that too. She was one of those people who were always smoking, and she had a long amber holder. She was nice and kind and much too tall.

"You never did like parties, did you?" she said. "I don't blame you. But I like seeing my friends. You've grown very much like your mother; has anyone told you?"

"No," said Niall. Like Mama . . . How strange, how queer . . .

"Pappy tells me you have one more term at school," she said. "What are you going to do when you leave? Play the piano?"

"No," he said. "I play very badly. I'm no good."

"Really," she said, "you surprise me."

Maria had got up and was dancing with the man. She was away and out of sight amongst the other dancers. Niall felt suddenly that Freada, who had been so kind years ago at the Concours Hippique, was an ally and a friend. He remembered how she had brought him a bag of macaroons that day and let him eat the lot, and that when he had wanted to go to the lavatory he had not minded asking her. She had taken it as a matter of course that he would want to go. Queer how you remembered those things through the years.

"I like music more than anything in the world, but I can't play," he said, "not properly, not the way I would want to play. I can only play the sort of stuff they're playing now. I can only think of those sorts of tunes. And it's hell. It's absolute hell."

"Why is it hell?" she said.

"Because it's not what I want," he said. "There's a mass of sound in my head and it won't come out. At least it does come out and it's nothing but a damn silly dance tune."

"I don't see that it should matter," said Freada, "not if the tune is a good one."

"Oh, but it's such bilge," he said. "Who wants to write a dance tune?"

"A lot of people would give their eyes to do it," she said.

"Let them," said Niall. "They can have all mine."

She went on smoking through the long holder, and her eyes were kind. Niall felt she understood.

"As a matter of fact," he said, "I've gone nearly crazy all this evening because of a tune in my head. I want a piano, and I can't get to one because this party will go on half the night. I can't go and turn that fellow off the stand over there."

He laughed. It was such a ridiculous admission. Freada did not

116

seem to think it ridiculous. She accepted it as something quite natural, like wanting to go to the lavatory when he was little, like eating a whole bag of macaroons.

"When did you think of the tune?" she said.

"I was walking round Piccadilly Circus," he said. "I was too nervous to watch the play because of Maria. And suddenly it came—the tune, you know—because of the snow and those electric signs. It made me think of Paris and the fountains in the Place de la Concorde. Not that the tune has anything to do with it. . . . I don't know, I can't explain."

She did not say anything for a moment. The waiter put a plate of ice cream in front of her, but she waved it away. Niall was sorry. He could have eaten it himself.

"Do you remember your mother dancing?" she said suddenly.

"Yes, of course," said Niall.

"Do you remember the dance of the beggar maid in the snow? The lights in the window of a house, and her footsteps in the snow, and the way her hands moved with the falling flakes?" she said.

Niall stared in front of him. Something seemed to click inside his brain. The beggar maid in the snow . . .

"She tried to reach the light in the window," he said slowly. "She tried to reach the light, but she was too weak and too tired and the snow kept falling. I'd forgotten all about it. She didn't do it very often. I think I only saw it about once in my life."

Freada lit another cigarette and put it in the long holder.

"You thought you'd forgotten. You hadn't really," she said. "As a matter of fact, your father wrote the music for the dance of the beggar maid. It was the only thing he ever wrote."

"My father?"

"Yes. I think that's why your mother did not dance it often. The whole affair was a mix-up, you know. Nobody really knows what happened. She never talked about it, not even to her friends. But that's beside the point. The point is that you're a composer and you don't realise it, and I don't care whether it's a polka or a nursery rhyme that comes out of that head of yours, I'd like to hear you play it on the piano."

"Why should you be interested? Why should you care?"

"I was a great friend of your mother's, and I'm devoted to Pappy. And I don't play too badly myself after all."

She turned to him and laughed, very much amused, and Niall felt himself go hot under the collar. How frightful. He had forgotten. Of course, she used to play and sing in cabaret; perhaps she still did. He ought to have known about it. The only thing he had remembered was the Concours Hippique and the bag of macaroons.

"I'm sorry," he said, "I'm awfully sorry."

"Whatever about? The only thing I'm sorry for is that you have to go back to school tomorrow and I shan't be able to hear that tune. Can't you come round to my house in the morning before you go? Number seventeen Gower Street."

"My train leaves at nine o'clock."

"And I'm off to Paris in two days' time. Well, it can't be helped. When you leave school for good we'll do something about it. Tell me more about everything. Is old Truda still alive?"

She was so easy to talk to, one of the easiest people he had ever known, and he was really sorry when she got up and said good-bye.

Down at the other end of the table everyone was laughing very much and making a racket. Pappy was getting tight. When Pappy was tight he was funny. He was funny for about an hour, and then the fun turned to tears. At the moment he was still in the middle of the fun. He began to sing, and it was his joke voice, the one he put on when he imitated the hearty balladmonger type of baritone. He used to make up the words as he went along, and they were always dead right, just the sort of words a hearty baritone would sing. There was always "the surging sweep of the rolling deep," and a bit about it being "grand to be alive with his comrades five," and "the feel of a horse between his thighs." Then, of course, he would let the words run away with him, and they would become more and more vulgar, and the people sitting round him who could hear what he sang became more and more hysterical. And he always laughed himself, which was somehow touching, and made it funnier still.

He was sitting at the end of the table now, leaning back in his chair, with his arm round some woman's shoulders—Niall had no idea whose—and as he sang he shook with laughter and the whole room became aware now of what was happening. The waiters paused, grinning, to watch him, and people looked up from the other tables. The dance band went on with its drum and patter, and the dancers continued dancing, but nobody took any notice of them at all.

Then Pappy suddenly stopped being nonsensical and vulgar, and began to sing in his true voice. And it was "Black Eyes," and he sang the words in Russian. He started very softly, very slowly, the notes coming from deep in his belly, and someone at another table said "Hush . . ." and the band wavered and stopped, and the dancers paused in their dancing. All sound died away, and the conductor of the band held up his hand and made a signal to his pianist, who softly took up the accompaniment, and the pianist followed Pappy, he took up the theme of "Black Eyes." Pappy sat quite still, his massive head thrown back, his arm still round the shoulders of the woman beside him, because he felt comfortable that way. She was something to lean against, and from him came the gentle heart-tearing sound that was his real voice, deep and tender, deeper than anything in the world, so tender and true that it did something to your heart as you listened, and it got you by your throat and you wanted to turn away and cry.

"Black Eyes" ranted by singers everywhere, hammered out on a thousand dance bands and little third-rate orchestras, but when Pappy sang it you felt there had never been another song like it. It was the only song that had ever been written.

When he stopped, everyone was crying, and Pappy was crying too —he was really very tight—and then the band went on playing "Black Eyes," but to quick time so that the people could dance, and Pappy was dancing, too, pushing someone round the floor. He had no idea whom he was pushing, and it could not matter less, but he kept bumping into everybody and roaring with laughter, and Niall heard someone say, "Delaney is absolutely blind."

Celia kept her eyes on him all the time. She wore her anxious face. Niall knew she was not enjoying herself a bit. And Maria was nowhere to be seen. Niall looked everywhere, but he could not see her. He went out into the lounge of the hotel to look for her, but he could not find her.

Quite a lot of people had gone already from their party. Perhaps she had left with them. The man had gone. Perhaps the man had taken her home. . . . Niall felt suddenly that he did not want to stay any longer either. He was sick of the party, he hated the party. He was bored stiff with the whole affair. Somebody would see that Celia and Pappy got home all right. He was not going to stop. The party might go dragging on for hours, with Pappy getting tighter and tighter. Niall went and got his coat, and left the hotel and started walking. There were no buses and no tubes. Perhaps he would pick up a taxi. He had exactly two shillings left in his pocket. The taxi could take him part of the way home. The streets were empty and white and still. Fresh snow lay on the pavements. It was late, it was about a quarter to two. He found a taxi at the top of Bond Street, and when the driver asked him what address, he did not give the name of the house in St. John's Wood. He said, "Seventeen Gower Street."

He knew that there was only one thing at the moment that he wanted to do, and that was to forget about the party and to play his tune on the piano to kind Freada who once, years ago, had given him a bag of macaroons.

If I had drunk some of the champagne I should think I was tight, like Pappy, he said to himself, but I didn't have any. I hate champagne. I feel wide awake, that's all. Queer and strung-up and wide awake.

He had not enough money to get all the way to Gower Street because it would have meant being mean about the tip. The taxi took him part of the way and he walked the rest.

She's probably asleep, he thought. She won't hear the bell.

He could not see any lights, but perhaps there were shutters to the windows. He rang the bell four times, and after the fourth time he heard footsteps coming down the stairs, and someone came and rattled a bolt and chain. The door opened, and Freada stood there. She wore a dressing gown, a sort of red affair, and she had a patchwork quilt round her shoulders. She was still smoking.

"Hullo," she said. "I thought it was a policeman. Have you come to play me the tune? What a good idea. Come in."

She was not angry, nor even surprised. It was most unusual, and such a relief. Even Pappy, who was an unusual person, would have raised hell if someone had rung his bell at two o'clock in the morning.

"Are you hungry?" she said as she led the way up the stairs.

"Yes," said Niall, "as a matter of fact, I am. How did you know?"

"Boys are always hungry," she said.

She switched on a light in a bare untidy drawing room. There were nice pieces of furniture in the room and some good pictures, but it was all in a mess. There were clothes thrown about the place, and a tray on the floor. There was a grand piano in the room. That was the only thing that mattered to Niall.

"Here, have some of this," she said. She spread him a hunk of bread and butter and laid two or three sardines on top. She was still wearing the patchwork quilt. Niall began to laugh.

"What's the matter?" she said.

"You look so funny," said Niall.

"I always do," she answered. "Go on, eat up your sardine sandwich."

The sandwich was very good. When he had finished it he had another. She did not bother about him. She went on pottering about the room, making it more untidy than ever.

"I'm packing," she said. "If I spread everything on the floor I know where I am. Do you want a shirt?"

She threw him a checked shirt from the pile of debris.

"It's a labourer's shirt. I got it in Sardinia, but it's too small for me," she said. "That's the worst of being tall."

"Look out," said Niall, "you're standing on a hat."

She moved her bare feet and bent to pick up the hat. It was an enormous straw affair, the shape of a cartwheel, with two floating streamers.

"Theatrical Garden Party five years ago," she said. "I ran a hoopla stall and everybody kept throwing their rings onto my hat. Do you think Maria would like it?"

"She never wears hats."

"I'll take it to Paris. It would do upside down instead of a dish for fruit, oranges, and things." She threw the hat onto a heap of clothes.

"I can't offer you anything to drink," she said, "unless I make some tea. Want any tea?"

"No, thank you. I'd like some water."

"You'll find some in the bedroom jug. Something's gone wrong with the tap in the kitchen."

He went into her bedroom, picking his way carefully over the clothes spread on the floor. The jug of water on the washstand was full, and the water was quite cold. There did not appear to be a glass, so he drank straight out of the jug.

"Come and play the tune," she called from the drawing room.

He went back into the other room, and she was kneeling on the floor with the patchwork quilt still round her shoulders, examining a silver fox cape.

"Riddled with moths," she said, "but I don't believe anyone would know unless they got very close. I borrowed it from someone and never gave it back. I wonder who."

She sat back on her haunches, thinking, and combing her hair with her cigarette holder, and eating a piece of bread and butter at the same time. Niall sat down at the piano and began to play. He did not feel nervous at all, he was laughing too much.

The piano felt good. It did what he wanted it to do, and even if he made the most frightful noise he knew it would not matter and that Freada would not mind. He forgot she was in the room once he started to play. He was thinking of the tune, and it was coming right. Yes, that was what he meant. Of course that was what he meant. Oh, it was exciting, it was fun. Nothing mattered but this, this crazy exploring for the right note. . . . Got it. Now again, try it again. Shut your eyes and listen for the sound, but you have to feel it in your feet and your finger tips, too, and in the pit of your stomach. That was it. Now he had the whole thing, and it was dance time, it was his old thing of playing against the beat, but the piano alone was no good. You wanted someone with a sax, you wanted someone with a drum.

"You see what I mean?" he said, turning round on the stool. "You see what I mean?"

She was not packing. She was still kneeling on the floor.

"Go on," she said, "don't stop. Do it again."

He went on playing, and it came easier and better. It was a damn good piano, better than any piano he had tried before. Freada got up from the floor and came and stood beside him. She hummed the tune in her deep funny voice, and whistled it, and hummed it again.

"Now play something else," she said. "What else have you made up? Anything, it doesn't matter what."

He remembered bits and pieces of things he had thought of from time to time, but nothing had ever come quite so clearly as the one that had come tonight.

"The trouble is," he said, "I can't write them down. I don't know how it's done."

"That's all right," she said. "I can arrange all that."

He stopped playing. He stared up at her.

"Can you really?" he said. "But are they worth the trouble? I mean, they're nothing to anyone else. I just do it to amuse myself."

She smiled. She put out her hand and patted him on the head.

"Those days are over, then," she said, "because from now on you're going to spend your life amusing other people. What's Pappy's telephone number?"

"What do you want it for?"

"I want to have a talk with him, that's all."

"He'll still be at the party, or if he's home, he'll be in bed and asleep by now. He was awfully tight when I came away."

"He's got to be sober in the morning. Listen, you will have to catch a later train back to school than the one you planned."

"Why?"

"Because you've got to get that tune written down before you leave. If you and I can't do it between us, there are plenty of people I know who can. It's too late now. It's a quarter past three. Now listen, you'll never find a taxi at this hour. You can sleep here on the sofa. I'll put all the clothes on top of you. You can have my patchwork quilt. And we'll ring up Pappy at eight in the morning."

"He won't be awake. He'll be absolutely livid."

"At half-past eight then. At nine. At ten. Come on, you're a growing boy and you must get some sleep. Let's drag the sofa near to the fire and you won't be cold. Want some more sardines?"

"Yes, please."

"Eat them up then while I make your bed."

He finished the loaf of bread and the butter and the sardines, and Freada made up the sofa for him, with blankets and quilts and a pile of her old clothes. It looked terribly uncomfortable, but he did not like to tell her so. It might hurt her feelings, and she had been so sweet, and so funny and so kind.

"There," she said, standing back, her head on one side, surveying her work. "You'll sleep like a newborn baby in a cot. Do you want some pyjamas? I believe there is a pair somewhere. Somebody left them behind once."

She went into the bedroom and came back with a pair of very patched pyjamas.

"Don't know whose they are," she said, "but they've been here for years. They're quite clean. Now sleep well, my pet, and forget your tune for a few hours, and I'll make you some porridge for your breakfast."

She patted his cheek and kissed him and went out of the drawing room and into her own room. He could hear her humming his tune through the door.

He undressed and put on the pyjamas and crawled under the pile of clothes onto the sofa. His feet came up hard on the sofa end. He tucked them up underneath him and sighed and turned out the lamp. The sofa springs had gone in the middle, and there was something hard touching his spine. He did not mind any of it. The trouble was he did not feel sleepy. He had never felt less sleepy in his life. And the tune was still going round in his head, it would not go away. It was sweet of her to say she would arrange about writing it down, but he still did not see how it could be managed when he had to go back to school in the morning. School . . . Oh God, what a waste of time. What a waste of effort. He did not learn a thing. He was in his last term, and so far as learning anything went, it might have been his first. There was no one there who cared a twopenny damn whether he lived or died. He wondered if Pappy and Celia had got back home yet, and Maria. Maria would not be wondering where he was, even if the others were. Maria had too many other things to think about. So many days and weeks stretched ahead for Maria, all of them excit- ing, all of them fun. Weeks of fun and adventure for Maria. Weeks of boredom and monotony for him.

He turned on the sofa, pulling the patchwork quilt round his neck. It smelt queer and strange, like amber. Freada must use amber scent. Smells were awfully important. If you liked the way a person smelt, it meant you liked the person. Pappy had said that once, and Pappy was always right.

There was no fire left in the grate, and in spite of all these clothes it was cold on the sofa, cold and cheerless. The only good thing about the sofa was the quilt smelling of amber scent. If only everything in life could be blotted out except the smell of amber scent, he would be able to sleep. Then he would be peaceful. Then he would be warm. He was getting colder and colder every moment, and the room was getting darker and stranger and more austere. It was like being in a tomb. It was just like being buried in a tomb with the walling closing in upon him. He flung the clothes aside, all except the patchwork quilt, which he held against his face, and the scent of amber was stronger than ever, it was comforting and kind.

He got up from the sofa and felt his way across the dark room to the door. He opened the door and stood in the entrance of her room. He heard her move in the darkness and turn over in her bed, and she said:

"What's the matter? Can't you sleep?"

Niall did not know what to say. He did not know why he had got up from the sofa and come and opened the door. If he told her he could not sleep she would get up and give him aspirin. He hated aspirin. They were no earthly use at all.

"Nothing's the matter," he said. "It's just that—it's awfully lonely in there."

She did not say anything for a moment. It was as though she were lying there thinking in the darkness. She did not turn on the light.

Then she said, "Come on in then. I'll take care of you."

And her voice was deep and kind and understanding, just as it had been years ago when she had given him the bag of macaroons.

CHAPTER TWELVE

PAPPY was very drunk. Now that it was nearly three in the morning and most of the people had gone home and there was nobody left but a few rather stupid women and tired men, Pappy was not funny any longer. He had reached the crying stage. He did not look any different, and he did not slur his words, nor did he fall down. He just cried. His left arm was round Celia's shoulders, and his right arm was round some strange woman who wanted to go home.

"They've all gone and left me," he said, "except this child here. Maria is out in the world, Niall is out in the world, but this child remains. She's the flower of the flock. I've always said so, ever since she was a little child of three years old, wandering about with a finger in her mouth, looking like the infant Samuel. She's the flower of the flock."

The woman's face was set in hard weary lines of boredom. She was longing to go home. She could not catch her husband's eye. If it was her husband. Celia did not know. One never did.

"Maria's all right," said Pappy. "Maria will go to the top; she's got enough of my blood in her to get her to the top. See what happened tonight? Maria's all right. But she doesn't give a damn for anyone but herself." The tears were running down his cheeks. He did not bother to brush them away. He enjoyed the solace, the luxury of grief.

"Watch that boy, Niall," he said, "watch that boy. He's not mine, but I've reared him. Anything that boy does in the future will be due to me. He's my son by adoption. And I feel he is mine. I know every thought that goes on in the back of that boy's head. Watch him. Watch that boy. He's going to startle somebody someday. But he won't startle me. And where is he now? Gone out and left me. Gone off, just like Maria. There's only this child left. The best of the bunch."

He found his handkerchief and blew his nose. Celia could see the woman making frantic signs to the man opposite her.

She looked away. She could not bear for them to guess she saw the signs. The waiters were getting tired and very bored. The headwaiter came again and pushed the bill on a plate, neatly folded, under Pappy's eyes.

"What's this?" said Pappy. "Somebody want my autograph? Who's got a pencil? Anyone got a pencil so that I can sign my autograph?" The waiter coughed. He avoided Celia's eyes.

"It's the bill, Pappy," whispered Celia. "The waiter wants you to pay the bill." A young waiter, standing behind the headwaiter, began to giggle. It was agony.

"We really must be going," said the woman, getting up and pushing back the chair. "It's been a wonderful evening, we have so loved it."

The man opposite understood. He got up too. Celia knew that because of Pappy's being drunk they were afraid they might get stuck with the bill. They must get away quickly, before it could possibly happen.

"They're all leaving," sighed Pappy. "Nobody wants to stay. Soon there'll be nobody left in the whole damn world. They're tricky and they're funny when you have the ready money, but where are they when you're stony broke? I shall have to sign this. I can't pay. I shall have to sign it."

"That will be all right, sir," said the headwaiter smoothly.

"It's been a great evening," said Pappy, "a great evening. Thank you. Thank you all. Wonderful supper. Wonderful service. Thank you."

He rose from his chair and walked slowly and magnificently to the door. "A charming fellow," he said to Celia, "a most charming fellow." He bowed graciously to a couple leaving the room at the same time. "Thank you so much for coming," he said. "We must all get together again very soon. It's been a wonderful evening."

The couple stared in astonishment. They had not been in Pappy's party at all. Celia walked past them, her cheeks flaming, her head held high. She did not have to fetch her fur coat because she had it with her. She stood by the entrance, waiting for Pappy. He was ages in the cloakroom. She thought he would never come. When he did appear he was wearing his coat over his shoulders like a cape, and he had his opera hat tilted on one side. "Where are we going?" he said. "Has some other party been arranged? Are we all meeting somewhere else?"

Celia noticed the porter tried to hide his smile.

"No, Pappy," said Celia, "it's awfully late. We're going home."

"Whatever you say, my darling, whatever you say."

They went out into the street, and the car was parked on the other side. Celia held Pappy's arm and steered him to the car. The snow was thick on the ground. Why had Pappy sent the chauffeur home? He always sent him home. He had this ridiculous conscience about keeping the chauffeur up late. He always made the chauffeur go home to bed. Pappy fumbled for his key. He could not find the key.

" 'I must arise and go now, and go to Innisfree,' " he said. He quoted the whole poem with care and accuracy, and by the time he had finished it he had found the key.

"Get in, my darling," he said, "your little feet will be frozen." Celia climbed into the front seat, and he lowered himself beside her.

" 'Her tiny hand is frozen,' " he sang softly, and pressed the starter button. Nothing happened. He went on pressing it for quite a while. "It's cold," said Celia; "all the snow has made it cold." He did not seem to hear. He went on singing snatches of *La Bohème*. "You'll have to wind the handle, Pappy," said Celia.

" 'Now seems it more than ever rich to die,' " said Pappy, " 'to cease upon the midnight with no pain . . .' "

Very slowly, very carefully, he lowered himself once more from the car and stood outside it in the snow. His coat slipped off his shoulders. "Put your coat on, Pappy," called Celia, "it's very cold. You'll catch a chill."

He waved his hand to her. He went to the front of the car and bent down. He was ages bending down by the front of the car.

There were curious hopeless sounds of a handle that would not turn. After a long while he came back again and peered at her through the window. "We must purchase a new car, my darling," he said. "This one appears to be inefficient."

"Get in and try the starter again," said Celia. "It's only that the engine is cold." In the distance she could see a policeman. He had his back turned to them, but any moment he might walk their way. He would come towards them, and he would see that Pappy was drunk and should not be in charge of a car, and he would do something terrible like taking Pappy to Vine Street, and then it would be in the papers in the morning. "Get back in the car, Pappy," urged Celia, "get back quickly in the car." Once more he lumbered in beside her.

He pushed the starter, and nothing happened.

"I have had playmates, I have had companions,
    In the days of my childhood, in my youthful schooldays,
    All, all are gone, the old familiar faces . . ."

said Pappy. Then he huddled himself in the seat, pulled his hat down over his face, sighed deeply, and composed himself for sleep.

Celia began to cry. Presently she heard footsteps on the pavement. She lowered the window and saw a young man passing by.

"Please," she said, "could you come here a moment?"

The young man stopped. He turned round and came to the window of the car. "Is anything the matter?" he said.

"We can't get the car to start," said Celia, "and my father isn't very well."

The young man looked at Pappy humped in the driver's seat. "I see," he said briskly. "Quite. What do you want me to do? Cope with the car, or cope with your father?"

Celia bit her lip. She could feel the tears welling up in her eyes again. "I don't know," she said. "Whichever you think best."

"I'll tackle the car first," he said.

He went to the bonnet and bent down, as Pappy had done, and in a few moments he had started the car.

He came back, dusting the snow off his hands.

"That's that," he said. "Now if you don't mind climbing into the back seat, I'll push your father into the one you are in now, and I'll drive you home. It seems a pity to wake your father. A little sleep will do him good."

"You're very kind," said Celia. "I don't know how to thank you."

"That's all right," he said cheerfully, "it's all in the day's work. I'm a medical student. I work at St. Thomas's Hospital."

Celia stared out of the window while the young man dealt with Pappy in the front seat. It was too much like trussing up a fowl. The proceedings lacked dignity. Still, if he was a medical student . . .

"There we are, all set," said the young man. "Now, tell me your address." She told him, and he started to drive the car in the direction of home. "Does this sort of thing often happen?" he asked.

"Oh no," said Celia hurriedly, "it's only that we had a party."

"Quite," said the young man.

She dreaded that he would ask her name, because once she told him it would be fatal; he would know who she was and that Pappy was Pappy, and then the news would get round; he would tell his friends at St. Thomas's Hospital that he had spent a most amusing time taking Delaney, drunk as a lord, back to his home in St. John's Wood at half-past three in the morning. He asked no more questions, though. He was very discreet. When they came to the house the young man pulled up the car and Pappy woke up. He sat up and looked about him.

" 'Night's candles are burnt out,' " he said, " 'and jocund day stands tiptoe on the misty mountain tops.' "

"I agree, sir," said the young man, "but how are you going to navigate the steps?"

Pappy stared at him with narrowed eyes.

"Your face is pleasant but unknown to me," he said. "Have we met before?"

"No, sir," said the young man. "I'm a medical student at St. Thomas's Hospital."

"Ah! A butcher," said Pappy. "I know your kind."

"He's been so helpful," began Celia.

"Butchers, all of them," said Pappy firmly. "They can think of nothing but the knife. Is this St. Thomas's?"

"No, sir. I've just brought you home."

"Very civil of you," said Pappy. "I have no desire to be cut to pieces in a hospital. Will you give me a hand out of the car?"

The medical student helped Pappy up the steps of the house. Celia followed with the coat and hat, both of which had fallen in the snow. There was a pause of a moment or two while Pappy searched for his latchkey. "Are you staying with us? I've forgotten," he said to the medical student.

"No, sir. I have to get along back, thank you very much."

"Take the car, my dear fellow, take the car. It's no earthly use to me. I don't know how the damn thing works. Keep it, it's yours." He walked slowly into the hall and switched on the lights. "Where's Truda? Tell Truda to make me some tea."

"Truda's in hospital," said Celia. "I'll make you some tea, Pappy."

"In hospital? Of course." He turned again to the medical student. "You may come across our faithful Truda in the course of your butchery," he said. "She's in one of your morgues. Dear faithful creature, been with us for years. Deal gently with her."

"Yes, sir."

"Always the knife," murmured Pappy, "they can think of nothing but the knife. Butchers, the whole damn tribe."

He wandered into the dining room and stared absently about him. The medical student took Celia's hand.

"Look," he said, "isn't there something more I can do for you? I can't leave you alone with him. Please let me help."

"It's all right," said Celia. "My brother will be upstairs. I can wake him up. It's quite all right. Truly it is."

"I don't like to leave you," he said. "You look so awfully young."

"I'm sixteen," said Celia, "and I always look after Pappy. I'm used to it. Please don't bother about me."

"It's not right," he said, "it's not right at all. I tell you what I'll do, I'll telephone you in the morning. And you must promise to let me know if there is anything I can do."

"Thank you very much."

"I'll telephone you about half-past ten. And I'll put your car away in the garage now."

"How will you get home?"

"Leave that to me. I shall get home all right. Good-bye."

"Good-bye."

Celia shut the front door behind him. She listened for the sound of the car starting up, and then the garage doors being opened, and the car driving in, and then the doors slamming to again. Then nothing more happened. Then he must have gone away. Suddenly she felt very lost and helpless. She went into the dining room. Pappy was still standing in the middle of the room.

"Come upstairs to bed, Pappy," she said.

He frowned. He shook his head. "Now you are going to turn against me," he said. "Now you are going to leave me. You are planning to run away with the butcher from St. Thomas's Hospital."

"No, Pappy," said Celia, "he's gone. Don't be silly. Come along, it's very late, and you must get to bed."

"'How sharper than a serpent's tooth it is to have a thankless child,'" said Pappy. "You are trying to deceive me, my darling."

Celia ran upstairs to fetch Niall. But he was not in his room. His room was just as he had left it before going to the theatre. Niall had not come home. She felt bewildered and frightened, and she did not know what to do. She went along the passage to Maria's room. Perhaps Maria was not in either. Nobody was in. She opened the door of Maria's room and turned on the light. Yes, Maria was back. She was in bed, fast asleep. And there was a note on the dressing table with Celia written on it. She picked it up and read it. "Don't wake me up when you come in," said the note. "I'm dead to the world. And tell Edith not to call me in the morning. And tell everybody to be as quiet as possible." There was another note with Niall written on it. Celia hesitated, then picked it up and read it too. It was shorter than hers. "There's no need to be so po-faced," it said.

Celia looked down at Maria as she lay asleep. She was lying with her face pillowed on her hands, as she used to do when she was little and they shared a room. She's the eldest, thought Celia. She's older than Niall, and older than me, but in a queer way she will always seem the youngest. The ring that Niall had given Maria glistened on her finger. The blue stone had made a little mark against her cheek. There was something else that shone also; it jutted out from under her pillow. Celia bent to look. It was a gold cigarette case. Maria sighed deeply and moved in her sleep. Celia tiptoed from the room and closed the door softly behind her.

She went downstairs again to find Pappy.

"Please come to bed," she said, "please, please, Pappy, come to bed." She took hold of his arm, and he allowed himself to be led upstairs. Once in his room, he sat down heavily on the bed and began to cry.

"You're all going to leave me," he said, "one by one. You'll all go away and leave me."

"I'll never leave you," said Celia, "I promise. Please, Pappy, get undressed and go to bed."

He started to fumble with his evening shoes. "I'm so unhappy," he said, "so dreadfully unhappy, my darling."

"I know," she said, "but you'll be all right in the morning."

She knelt beside him and helped him undo his shoes. She helped him with his coat and waistcoat, and his collar and tie, and his shirt. Further effort was beyond him. He lay down on the bed, rolling his head from side to side. She covered him up with a blanket.

"'Time remembered is grief forgotten,'" he said, "'is grief forgotten . . . is grief forgotten . . .'"

"Yes, Pappy. Sleep now."

"You're so good to me, my darling, so good to me."

He still had hold of her hand, and she did not like to draw it away in case he should begin to cry again. She went on kneeling by the bed. In a moment he was asleep and breathing deeply, like Maria. They were both of them asleep. They had no troubles and no cares. Celia tried to draw her hand away, but he held it fast. She crouched on the floor, her hand in his, and she was so tired she lay her head against the side of the bed and closed her eyes. I shall never get away, she thought. I shall never, never get away. . . . And to console herself, she drew in her mind a picture of immortality. Her people were fairy people, with winged feet and flaxen hair; their kingdom was not of the world, nor of heaven either. Their clothes were more colourful, more glittering, more gold, and they walked forever in the sun. One day I'll draw this for children, she said to herself; one day I'll draw what I mean, and only children will understand. . . . She went on holding Pappy's hand while he slept, and the cold and darkness wrapped themselves about her.

The telephone woke her. She was stiff and numb. At first she could not move. The telephone persisted, and, leaning forward, she reached up to the table by the bed. The clock said half-past eight. She had slept then, after all. She had been sleeping for three hours.

"Who's there?" she whispered.

A woman's voice answered. "Can I speak to Mr. Delaney?"

"He's asleep," whispered Celia. "This is his daughter."

"Is it Celia or Maria?"

"It's Celia." There was a pause, and a murmured conversation the other end. Then, to her surprise, she heard Niall's clear boyish voice take over the telephone.

"Hullo?" he said. "Niall here. I hope Pappy didn't worry about me."

"No," said Celia, "he didn't worry about anyone."

"Good," said Niall. "He's not come to yet, I suppose?"

"No."

"Right. Well, we'll have to telephone you later."

"It's half-past eight, Niall. What about your train?"

"I'm not catching the train. I'm not going back to school. I'm stopping here with Freada."

"With who?"

"With Freada. You remember, she was at the party last night."

"Oh. Oh yes. What do you mean, you're stopping with her?"

"What I say. I'm not going back to school, and I shan't be coming home. We're leaving for Paris in two days' time. I'll ring you later." He clicked the receiver and was gone.

Celia went on holding the receiver in her hand. After a moment the girl on the exchange said, "Number, please." Celia put back the receiver. What on earth was Niall talking about? It must be a practical joke. Of course Freada had been at the party. That tall nice mad-looking woman who used to be a friend of Pappy's and Mama's. But why play practical jokes at half-past eight in the morning? Pappy was fast asleep. Celia could safely leave him now. She was so tired and stiff and cold that she could hardly stand. She could hear Edith downstairs drawing the curtains. She went down to warn her not to call Maria. Then she came upstairs again, to her own room, to dress. Her face looked pinched and yellow in the mirror, and her white evening frock was all crumpled from sitting on the floor. How terrible people looked in the morning, when they still wore evening dress. What could Niall have meant about going to Paris? She was too tired to guess, too tired to care. How nice to spend the day in bed, but with Truda away it would be impossible. Pappy would want her, Maria would want her. Somebody would want her. And anyway, the medical student had said he would telephone. She had her bath and her breakfast, and when she was dressed she went along the passage once more to Pappy's room.

He was awake. He was sitting up in bed in his dressing gown, eating a boiled egg. He looked fit and well, and as if he had been sleeping for twelve hours, instead of five.

"Hullo, my darling," he said. "I've had a series of most amazing dreams. All about some fellow in a hospital trying to cut my gizzard with a carving knife."

Celia sat on the edge of the bed.

134

"I must have drunk too much champagne," said Pappy.

The telephone rang. "Deal with it, my darling," he said, and he went on spooning his boiled egg and dipping his toast in the yoke.

"It's that Freada person," said Celia, handing him the receiver. "She rang up once before, when you were asleep. She wants to talk to you." And for some reason that she could not explain to herself, she slipped off the bed and went towards the door, and opened it, and stood outside in the passage. She felt uneasy, worried. She left Pappy to his conversation and went to see if Maria was awake. Maria was sitting up in bed, surrounded by newspapers.

"At last," said Maria. "I thought you were never coming. They're all good. The *Daily Mail* is damn good. A long bit all to myself. And another special bit in the *Telegraph*. There's only one sniffy one, and that's for the play, so it doesn't matter. Look, you must read them. Come and sit down. What does Pappy say? Has Pappy seen them? Is Pappy pleased?"

"Pappy's only just awake," said Celia. "He's on the telephone."

"Who's he talking to? Someone about the play?"

"No, it's that woman Freada. You know, she used to be in Paris. Niall seems to be with her. I don't understand."

"How can Niall be with her? What do you mean? Niall must have left ages ago. His train went at nine o'clock."

"No," said Celia. "No, he's still in London." She heard Pappy's voice roaring for her down the passage.

"I must go," she said, "Pappy's calling me." Her heart was beating as she ran down the passage. He was still talking on the telephone.

"God damn it," Pappy was shouting, "he's only eighteen. I won't have the boy seduced, I tell you. It's the most monstrous thing I've ever heard in my life. Yes, of course he's clever, of course he's brilliant. I've been telling all these damn-fool schoolmasters that for years. Nobody listens to me. But because the boy is brilliant, it doesn't mean I'm going to deliver him up to you to be seduced. . . . Paris? No, my God, no. A boy of eighteen . . . What do you mean, he's starved? I've never starved him. He eats what he likes. My God, to think that you, one of our oldest friends, should stab me in the back like this. It's nothing more or less than rape, seduction, and stabbing in the back. . . ."

He went on and on, foaming at the mouth with rage, while Celia waited just inside the door. At last he slammed down the receiver.

"What did I tell you?" he said. "It's his father's blood coming out in him after all. His father's rotten French blood. A boy of eighteen, goes off and sleeps with one of my oldest friends."

Celia watched him anxiously. She did not know what to do or what to say.

"I'll have the woman hounded out of England," he said. "I won't allow it. I'll have her hounded out of England."

"Niall said she was going to Paris," said Celia, "and that he was going with her."

"It's his bad blood coming out in him," said Pappy. "I knew it would happen, I always foresaw it. Freada, of all people. Let this be a lesson to you, my darling. Never trust a man or a woman with brown eyes. They always let you down. It's monstrous, it's unforgivable. The Garrick Club shall know of this. I shall tell everyone. I shall tell the world. . . ."

Maria came in the doorway, yawning, her arms above her head. "What on earth's the fuss about? What's the matter?" she said.

"What's the matter?" shouted Pappy. "Niall's the matter. My adopted son. Seduced by one of my oldest friends. God! that I should live to see this day. And you"—he pointed an accusing finger at Maria —"when did you come in last night? When did you get home?"

"Before you did," said Maria. "I was in bed and asleep by half-past twelve."

"Who brought you back?"

"Someone from the theatre."

"Did he kiss you?"

"I really don't see, Pappy——"

"Ha! You don't see. My daughter, brought back at all hours of the night, dumped in the house like a sack of coals, kissed and cheapened, and my adopted son seduced. A fine night, I must say. And there was another fellow, too, hanging about on the doorstep, pretending he was from St. Thomas's Hospital. A fine night for the Delaney family. Have you anything to say?"

No one had anything to say. Everything had been already said.

"Here are the papers," said Maria. "Don't you want to read what they say about the play?"

He reached out a hand for the papers and took them from her without a word. He disappeared with them into the bathroom and slammed the door. Maria shrugged her shoulders.

136

"Really, if he goes on behaving like this I shall have to live somewhere on my own," she said. "It's too absurd. . . . You look awfully tired. What's the matter with you?"

"I didn't get much sleep," Celia said.

"What's the telephone number?" said Maria. "I shall have to ring up and find out what it's all about."

"Whose number?"

"Freada's, of course. I have to speak to Niall."

She went downstairs and shut herself in the morning room, where there was another telephone. She was there a long time. When she came out she looked white and defiant.

"It's true," she said. "He's not going back to school. He's finished with school. He's going to live in Paris with Freada."

"But—will she look after him?" said Celia. "Will he be all right?"

"Of course he'll be all right, don't be so stupid," said Maria, "and he'll have his music. That's the only thing he cares about, his music."

For one brief moment Celia thought that Maria was going to cry. Maria, who despised all crying, who never shed a tear. She looked lost and frightened and utterly forlorn. Then the telephone rang again. Celia went back into the morning room to answer it. When she came back Maria was still standing at the bottom of the stairs. "It's for you," said Celia. "It's—you know."

"Was it the secretary or was he speaking himself?"

"He was speaking himself."

Maria went into the morning room again and shut the door.

Celia walked slowly upstairs. Her head was aching, but she did not want to go to bed. If she went to bed she might miss the telephone call from the medical student. As she turned down the passage Pappy came out of his bathroom with the papers in his hand.

"These are really very good, you know," he said, "very good indeed. All except that little nincompoop in the *Mirror*. I wonder who he is. I'll ring up the editor. I'll get him sacked. Listen to this one in the *Mail*. It's headed: 'Another Delaney Triumph. The Second Generation Gets Away with It.' " He began reading the article aloud, smiling all over his face. He had forgotten all about Niall.

Celia went back to her room and sat and waited. The telephone went on ringing all the morning. But it was never for her. It was always people ringing up to congratulate Maria. When Freada rang at half-past twelve Pappy was still abusive, but not quite so abusive as he had been at half-past ten. He would never forgive her, of course, but it was perfectly true that the boy was wasting his time at school, and if he really had this flair for composing tunes, as Freada insisted, then he had better go to Paris and learn how to write them down. But a boy of eighteen . . . "He may have been a boy last night," said Freada, "but I assure you he's a man this morning."

Monstrous. Disgraceful. But what a story for the Garrick. He went off to lunch at his club in a happy state of indignation. And while Niall sat on the floor of Freada's drawing room in Gower Street eating scrambled eggs with a bent fork, and Maria sat at a corner table at the Savoy overlooking the Embankment and eating oysters à la Baltimore, Celia sat alone in the dining room at St. John's Wood eating prunes and custard and waiting for the telephone to ring. It never did. The medical student had not recognised Pappy after all. And he had forgotten to ask her name.

CHAPTER THIRTEEN

HOW happy were we, when we were young? Perhaps it was all illusion. Perhaps, looking back now, with the forties close upon all three of us, the hours passed then much as they do today, but they took a little longer in the passing. Waking in the morning was an easier thing, we are agreed upon that. Because sleep was heavy. Not the fitful affair it has become. Fifteen years ago we could go to bed, any one of us, at three, at four in the morning, no matter what we had done, and fall like tired puppies onto pillows. Sleep came at once, the deep, forgetful sleep of death. We had our individual ways of lying in our beds. Maria, half turned, her face upon her hand; the other arm above her head, and her right knee bent upwards. Celia upon her back, arms to her side, like a sentry; but with a fold of eiderdown, for comfort, under her chin. Niall slept always like an un-born child. He lay upon his left side, his hands, crossed on his chest, touching his shoulders. His back arched, his knees drawn to his middle.

They say that when we sleep our subconscious selves are revealed, our hidden thoughts and desires are written plain upon our features and our bodies like the tracings of rivers on a map; and no one reads them but the darkness.

These same attitudes are ours today, but we toss and turn more often, hours pass sometimes before we slip away; and when we wake, the birds wake with us, sharply, in a slowly creeping dawn. And traffic, in a city street, has a hungry roar, even at seven in the morning, even at half-past six. Once it would be ten, even eleven in the morning, before we shook ourselves and yawned, and stretched, and the good day opened itself before us like the blank pages of a diary, white and inviting, hungry to be filled.

For Maria, it would be London in the spring. . . .

When the first days of April come, something steals into the air and touches you upon the cheek, and the touch travels downwards to your body, and your body comes alive. The windows are flung open. The sparrows in St. John's Wood chatter, but the little sooty tree on the pavement opposite has a blackbird on its naked branch. Farther down the road there is a house that has almond blossom in the garden. The buds are fat and luscious, ready to burst.

The bath water runs fresh and freely on such a day; it pours from the taps with a great splash of sound, and as it runs you sing above it, you sing so truly that your voice rises above the flow of water. It's funny, Maria would think, soaping herself with a loofah, that in the evening, if you have a bath, your tummy is round and rather full, but in the morning it is flat as a board, and hard.

It's nice to be flat. It's nice to be hard. It's nice to be a person with a figure like this, and not one of those people with great fat behinds that jiggle as they walk, and full of bosoms that have to be braced up with something to keep them as they should be. It's good to have a skin that only needs vanishing cream and powder, and hair that stays put, with just a comb run through it twice a day. Her new frock was green, and a gold clasped belt went with it. There was a gold clip, too, that *he* had given her. This she did not put in the front of her dress until she left the house because Pappy might see it and ask who had given it to her. Truda had seen it once, lying on the dressing table.

"You never bought this with what your management pays you," she said. "Mind you, I'm not asking questions. I'm merely stating a fact."

"It's a bonus," said Maria. "It's what they give you when you've been a clever girl."

"H'm," said Truda, "you'll have plenty of bonuses by the time you retire from the stage, if you go on through life as you've begun."

Ah, Truda was a crotchety old idiot; you never could please Truda. She even grumbled on an April day, saying the spring was bad for her ulcered leg. The spring was not bad for her leg. It was bad for Truda's soul, because Truda was old. . . .

140

Should she wear a hat? No, she would not wear a hat. Even when she did wear a hat, *he* told her to take it off.

What lie now, for today? Yesterday had been a matinee, no need to lie. But one had to think out something for a Thursday. Thursdays were difficult. There was always shopping, but one could not shop all day. A cinema. A cinema with another girl. But then supposing one said a cinema which one had not seen, and Pappy saw it and asked all about it? That was the worst of living at home. The post-mortems on the day. And what were you doing at half-past three if lunch was over at two-thirty and the cinema did not start until five? A flat of one's own, that would be the luxury. But it cost too much money—yet.

"Well, you look like the answer to somebody's prayer," said Pappy as she went in to say good morning. "No hope of your taking your father out to lunch for a change?"

Here it came. "Sorry, Pappy, I've got such a full day. Shopping all the morning, and then lunch with Judy—I promised her weeks ago—and we may do a cinema afterwards, I don't know, it depends on what Judy wants to do. I shan't be home much before half-past six."

"Precious little I see of you, my darling," said Pappy. "Here we are living in the same house, and you sleep in it, but that's about all. Sometimes I wonder if you do sleep in it."

"Oh, don't be silly."

"All right. All right. Go off and enjoy yourself."

And Maria left the room, singing, to show she had a clear conscience, and she ran downstairs before he could ask her any more questions. She tried to sneak out of the house before Celia came from the morning room. Celia had a pen in her mouth, and her preoccupied face. She was busy with Pappy's letters.

"You do look nice," she said. "I love that green. Was it frightfully expensive?"

"Hellish. But I haven't paid yet. I shan't pay until they write that letter saying, 'Madame, we wish to draw your attention . . .'"

"I suppose there's no hope of your lunching with Pappy in London?"

"None at all. Why?"

"Oh, nothing. It's only that he doesn't seem keen to go to the Garrick today; he's at a loose end. Such a lovely day."

"You can go with him."

"Yes . . . I did so awfully want to get on with that drawing. You know, the one I showed you, the lost child standing outside the gate."

"It will be better if you leave it for a day or two. It's a mistake to finish a drawing in one go."

"I don't know. Once I start a thing I like to go on with it. I like to go right ahead until it's finished."

"Well—I can't go with him today. My day is all booked."

Celia looked at her. She knew about it. She did not ask any questions.

"Yes, I see," she said. "Well—have a good time."

She went back into the morning room, with the preoccupied face. Maria was opening the front door when Truda came up from the basement.

"Are you in to lunch?"

"No, I'm not."

"H'm. In to dinner?"

"Yes, I'll be in to dinner."

"Well, be punctual, then. We have it at a quarter to seven especially for you, because of the theatre, so you might have the kindness to be on time. Your Pappy is always on time."

"All right, Truda. Don't nag."

"That's a new dress you're wearing. Pretty."

"Glad you like something of mine, anyway. Good-bye."

She ran down the steps and along the road, and the warm air blew in her face, and the errand boy on the bicycle whistled and grinned. She made a face at him and then looked back, over her shoulder, and it was heaven to be out of the house and away from the family, away from everything, and walking to Regent's Park full of crocuses, yellow, and white, and mauve; with his car waiting for her, and him sitting at the wheel, the car parked in the usual place between St. Dunstan's and the Zoo. The hood would be thrown back today because of the weather. The hood would be thrown back, and there would be lots of rugs in the back, and the picnic things, and as they drove down to the country they would sing, both of them, at the top of their voices. There was no such fun in the world as doing something you knew you should not do, with somebody else who should not be doing it either, on a spring morning with the wind blowing in your hair. And it made it all the more exciting because he was someone older than herself, someone like Pappy, whom people stared at in the street. Instead of driving her to the country he ought to be at a meeting, or at a luncheon, or giving away prizes to a lot of students; and he was doing none of these things, he was sitting beside her in the car. It was this knowledge above all that made her happy inside and made her sing. It was like the old game of Indians that she used to play with Niall and Celia, when she, as Indian Chief, wore a scalp at her belt. She was playing Indians still. . . .

He would talk to her about the theatre, and about his plans.

"When the run of this is over," he would say, "we will do this— and that; you shall play the part of the girl, you're just right for it." "Am I?" she answered. "But wouldn't I be too young? I mean, in the last act, that business when she comes back, much older . . ." "No," he said, "you can do it. You can do anything, if I show you how to do it." He tells me I can do anything, thought Maria; he tells me I can do anything, and I'm only twenty-one.

The car gathered speed and ripped along the hard straight road into the country, passing other cars, and the winds of April were soft and warm and did not mattter; the dust did not matter either, it brought the scent of gorse and broom.

Egg sandwiches tasted good under the sun, so did a cold leg of chicken; and grapes from Fortnum's had a lovely bloom upon them. Even gin and Vermouth drunk straight from the lip of a silver flask tasted better, and more potent, than it did from some old glass; besides, it gurgled down your throat, and you choked, and you had to borrow a handkerchief. Which was fun. Everything was more fun out of doors. No matter if it rained, there were rugs, umbrellas.

> "No," said Robert, "when it pours,
> It is better out of doors."

The line from the child's Strewelpeter came back to her as she lay in the grass hollow when the shower came. And she began to shake with silent laughter, because it was so funny.

"What are you laughing at? What is the matter?" he said. But you could not really say. A man was so touchy and easily offended. He did not understand that laughter rose in you very often, much too often, in a great gulf; and you suddenly thought of the most ridiculous things for no reason at all. His ears, for instance, were keen and pointed, like the china rabbit on the mantelpiece at home, and how was it possible to be serious and intent if you remembered this? Or your thoughts would go shooting off at a tangent: "Damn—I mustn't forget the dentist Friday morning"; or even idly observant, while he would be intent, so that you noticed the branch of a tree hanging overhead and saw that the buds were sprouting and it would be nice to take it back home and put it in water and watch the buds come into leaf. Not always, though. Sometimes you thought of nothing in this world or in heaven either, and the only moment was the moment now, and an earthquake could have opened up the ground and swallowed you and you would not have known, you would not have cared.

There could be no languor like the aftermath of a spring day under the sun. The drive back to London. The passing cars. You had no thoughts and very little feeling, and you did not talk at all. You sat wrapped in a rug like a cocoon. Then the yawn, the jerk into reality, and the growing sound of traffic brought the world too near.

Lighting-up time, and the shops were bright in the suburbs, the people jostled one another on the pavements. Women with shopping baskets, women with prams, lumbering great buses and grinding trams, and a man with one leg advancing with violets on a tray: "Fresh vi'lets—sweet bunch of fresh vi'lets." But they were dusty, they had been on the tray all day. On the top of Hampstead Heath the people still lingered by the pond. Boys with sticks, and girls without coats, calling to barking dogs. One little sailing boat, abandoned by its owner, rocked in the middle of the pond, with sails limp.

Down the hill straggled the people to the underground, weary and fractious, while London lay below, like a vast back cloth on an empty stage.

The car stopped at the routine stopping place in the Finchley Road. "See you presently," he said, touching her face, and then the car gathered speed and went away, and she heard the clock at the corner chime the half-hour. She would just make it in time for dinner.

What a good thing it was, Maria thought, that when you had been making love it did not show. Your face did not turn green, or your hair drop off. God might so easily have made this happen. And then you would be sunk. There would be no hope. Pappy would know. In a way, up to a point, God was on your side. . . .

Pappy was back. The garage doors were shut. If he had been out still, the garage doors would be open. As she let herself in at the front door she saw Edith carrying the tray with glasses and silver

144

into the dining room. Five minutes to spare. The rush to the bath-room, the rush to do the face. And then the inevitable boom-boom of the gong.

"Well, my darling? What sort of a day?"

Celia was an ally. She came to the rescue, always, with what they had been doing themselves, she and Pappy.

"Oh, Maria, you would have laughed; we saw the funniest little old man. . . . Pappy, tell Maria about the little old man." And Pappy, happy to talk, happy to plunge into his own day, would for-get about Maria's, and the dinner, hastily swallowed, that might have been a strain, passed swiftly, safely, with no direct questions, no direct replies.

"Golly—it's half-past seven, I must fly." The kiss on Pappy's fore-head, the smile and the nod to Celia, the shout to Edith to know if the taxi was at the door. Only Truda to put a damper on the day with her glance at Maria's shoes. "Been in the country, haven't you? You've got mud on the heels of your shoes. What a shame to crease your coat like that." "The mud's nothing, and the coat will iron. And for goodness sake, tell that fool of a girl to put my thermos of Ovaltine beside my bed, but hot, not tepid. Good night, Truda."

Down to the theatre, in at the stage door, "Good evening" to the doorkeeper, "Good evening, miss," and up along the passage to her dressing room, with a glance at his closed door. Yes, he was there already, she could hear his voice inside. The languor of the day was shaken off. She was excited now, and fresh, ready for the evening. And it would be exciting, to say to him presently, "Hullo, what a lovely day," in front of the others, as though they were meeting for the first time and had not parted only two hours before. Let's pre-tend. Always the game of let's pretend. And fun, too, just to hint now and again that she knew him rather better than they did, just to say, "Oh well, he said we were going to have an extra matinee anyway." "When? When did he tell you that?" "Oh, I don't know. A day or two ago, at lunch." Then silence. An expressive silence. An unmis-takable hostility. Maria did not care. What did their hostility matter to her?

A tap at the door. Someone said, "It's a wonderful house tonight. They're standing at the back of the circle. My young friend is in front." "Really?" said Maria. "I hope he enjoys it." Who cared about the silly woman's friend?

145

In half an hour she, Maria, would be standing in the wings, waiting for her cue, and she would hear his voice as he stood by the open window on the set—his back was to the audience and he used to make a face at her—and the lines he said, just before, were laugh lines, so that the warm friendly sound of the laughter came flooding up to her as she waited to make her entrance. The warmth and the friendliness used to fill the whole house, it filled the stage, and as she stepped forward she would make a face back at him, at the open window; once more they would be hoodwinking someone. No matter whether it was Pappy, or Truda; or his dreary wife, or his boring secretary; or the rest of the company, or the whole of the audience; they would have thumbed their noses at the world, at life in general, because it had been a spring day in April and Maria was twenty-one and did not care.

For Niall, it would be Paris in midsummer. . . .

The apartment was in rather a drab quarter, off the Avenue de Neuilly, but the rooms were large and had balconies at the long windows, and if it got too hot you shut the shutters. There was a little court inside the entrance, where the concierge lived; there were always things airing inside the court, which was dim and dark and got no light, and cats prowled there and sometimes made a smell, but the smell of garlic was stronger than the smell of cat, and the husband of the concierge, who was bedridden and lay all day propped up with pillows, smoked Caporal tobacco, which nearly killed the garlic.

The apartment was on the fifth floor and looked out over the street, and over the roofs of Paris, while away to the right you could see the tops of the trees in the Bois, and you could see the Avenue de Neuilly rising to the Etoile. The living room was bare but friendly. Freada had turned out the stiff furniture and had bought bits and pieces of her own, things she had collected about her from time to time; like the old Normandy dresser in the corner, and the gate-legged table, and of course the pictures, and the rugs, and the piano. The piano was a Steinway baby grand, and the only thing that mattered, so far as Niall was concerned. The room could have been furnished with bamboo for all he cared.

In the bedroom, which also looked out over the street, there was Freada's bed, large and comfortable, and a hard little divan that she had bought for Niall, because she could not always have Niall in her bed; she said it prevented her from sleeping.

"But I don't kick," argued Niall. "I lie still, I never budge."

"I know, lamb, but I'm aware of you, just the same. I've always had a bed of my own, and I'm not going to change my habits now."

Niall christened his hard divan Sancho Panza. It was just like the Gustave Doré illustrations to *Don Quixote*; the small bed beside the large bed was like the little white pony next to the long yellow steed. He would wake in the morning in Sancho Panza and look across to Freada's bed to see if she was there, but there was never a sleeping, rounded form under the sheets; the sheets would lie limp and crumpled. Freada would be up. Freada was an early riser. He would lie for a little while, blinking, looking at the blue sky through the open window, and listening to the familiar Paris noises, known from childhood, inbred in him, never forgotten.

It was going to be another scorching day. It smelt hot already, the white heat of August; the roses Freada had bought yesterday were limp and drooping in their vase. The woman in the apartment beneath was shaking a mat out of her window. Niall could hear the regular thud-thud of the mat over the balcony. And then she called her little boy playing in the street below, her voice sharp and shrill.

"*Viens vite, Marcel, quand je t'appele.*"

"*Oui, Maman, je viens,*" he answered back, a pretty little boy in the inevitable black pinafore, with a beret on the side of his head. Niall stretched his feet to the end of Sancho Panza. He had grown another inch; his feet dangled over the edge.

"Freada," he called, "Freada, I'm awake."

She came in a few moments, carrying a tray. Although she must have been up for some time, she was not dressed yet. She was still wearing her dressing gown. The breakfast had a goodly smell to it. There were croissants, and two fresh rolls, and twists of very yellow butter, and a jar of honey, and a steaming pot of coffee. There was also a new packet of Toblerone chocolate, and three sucettes on sticks, all of them different colours. He ate all the sucettes, and half the Toblerone, before he started on his breakfast. She sat on the side of her own bed, watching him, while he sat up in Sancho Panza, balancing the tray upon his knees. "I don't know what to do with you," she said, "you'll be eating the furniture next."

147

"I need building up," he said. "You said so, ages ago. I'm much too thin for my age and for my height."

"I said that once, I don't say it now," she answered, and she bent down and kissed the top of his head. "Come on, lazy-bones, eat up your breakfast and then take your shower; you've got to do some work on the piano before you eat again."

"I don't want to work. It's too hot to work. I'll work in the cool of the evening." The soft melting croissant tasted good with the tang of honey. "You'll do nothing of the sort," she answered; "you'll work this morning. And if you behave yourself, like a good boy, we'll have dinner somewhere in Paris and walk back afterwards, after the heat of the day."

The heat of the day . . . Surely no other city in the world threw such a haze of heat from the pavements to the sky. The rail on the balcony blistered to the touch. Niall wore nothing but a pair of workmen's dungarees, with bib and brace, but he was sweating even in them, even in walking from the bedroom to the balcony.

He could have stayed all morning looking down onto the street. The flat, hard sun did not worry him, nor the white haze rising, making a mist round the Tour Eiffel in the distance; he stood on the balcony because the sounds and the smells of Paris came to his ears and his nostrils and lost themselves inside his head and came out again as tunes. The little boy, Marcel, had gone down again from the next apartment and was whipping a top on the pavement, talking to himself; the top kept going in the gutter. A coal cart lumbered along the cobbled street—who wanted coal in August, for heaven's sake?—and the driver called out in his rather angry voice, "Ho, la—ho, la," while the harness bells jingled on the horse's back. Someone in the house next door kept calling, "Germaine? Germaine?" and then a woman came and piled a heap of bedding on the balcony to air. There was a canary singing. The coal cart lumbered away towards the Avenue de Neuilly, where the traffic sounded; the bells of the trams, the high-pitched hooting taxis. An old chiffonnier wandered down the street poking his stick in the gutter, calling his trade in the thin high voice that quavered at the end. In the kitchen Niall could hear Freada talking to the daily cuisinière, who had just returned from market, her morning purchases bulging in her string bag.

There would be fresh Gruyère cheese, and radishes, and a great bowl of salad, presently, for lunch, and possibly foie de veau, fried in butter, with a sprig of garlic. The door from the kitchen opened, and the smell of Freada's Chesterfield cigarettes floated down the passage. She came into the room and stood beside him on the balcony.

"I have not heard that piano yet," she said.

"You're a slave driver," said Niall, "that's what you are. A ranting, ruddy slave driver." He butted his head against her, sniffing the amber, and bit the lobe of her ear.

"You're here to work," she said. "If you don't work I'll send you home. I'll go and buy your ticket this afternoon."

This was a joke between them. Whenever he was more than usually idle she would tell him that she had been on the telephone to Cook's, that Cook's had taken reservations for him on the express to Calais.

"You wouldn't dare," said Niall, "you wouldn't dare." He pulled her round so that she faced him, and he put his hands on her shoulders, and he rubbed his cheek against her hair.

"You can't bully me any longer," he said. "I'll soon be as tall as you. Look, put your feet next to mine."

"Don't stamp on my toes," she said, "there's a corn on the little one. That comes from wearing tight shoes in a heat wave." She pushed him away, and, reaching forward, she pulled the shutters close. "We'll have to keep the room cool somehow," she said.

"It's a fallacy, that business of closing the shutters," said Niall; "they used to do it when we were children. It makes everything much worse."

"It's either that or sitting in the bath all day with the cold tap on my tummy," said Freada. "Don't pull at me, Niall, it's too damn hot."

"It's never too hot," said Niall. She pushed him onto the seat in front of the piano. "Go on, my baby, do what you're told," she said.

He stretched out for a piece of Toblerone chocolate on top of the piano and broke it in two, so that he could have two pieces, one in either cheek, and he laughed and began to play.

"Slave driver," he called over his shoulder, "stinking slave driver."

Once she was out of the room, he did not think about her any more, he thought only of what he wanted from the piano. Freada always cursed him for laziness. He was lazy. He wanted the piano to do the work for him, not the other way about. Freada said nothing was worth doing without effort. Pappy used to say that too. Everyone said it. But when things happened easily, what was the sense in driving yourself, in sweating blood?

"Yes, I know that first song was a winner," said Freada, "but you can't just rest on that. And you must remember that the life of a song hit is short. A couple of months, at best. You've got to work. You've got to do better still."

"I've no ambition," he told her. "Oh yes, if it was real music, then I'd be ambitious all right. But not this nonsense."

And in one hour, two hours, it would come; out of the blue, from nowhere, a song that you could not help singing, a song that did something to your feet and to your hands. It was easy, so damn easy. But it was not work. It was the call of the chiffonnier poking with his stick in the gutter, and the angry coalman saying, "Ho, la," pulling the jingling reins as his horse stumbled on the cobbled stones.

The song hit the ceiling and echoed from the walls; it was fun to do, it was play. But he did not want to write it down. He did not want to have the sweat and toil of writing it down. Why not pay someone else to do that part? And anyway, once he had thought of a song, and played it, and sung it to himself and Freada about fifty times, it was out of his system, he was bored with it, sickened of it, he did not even want to hear it any more. So far as he was concerned, the song was finished. It was like taking a pill, and, the pill having worked, he wanted to pull the plug on it. Finish. Now what next? Anything? No. Just lean over the balcony under the sun. And think about the foie de veau there was going to be for lunch. . . .

"I can't work any more today," he said at half-past one, when he had eaten the last radish; "it's cruelty to animals, and anyway, it's the siesta hour. No one in Paris works in the siesta hour."

"You've done very well," said Freada. "I'll let you off this afternoon. But play the song to me once, just once; because now I'm not an old pro any more, trying to train a pupil. I want to hear your song for sentiment's sake, because I love it, and I love you too."

He went to the piano again and played it for her, and she sat at the table, dropping ash from her Chesterfield cigarette onto the plate where the radishes had been, and the slab of Gruyère cheese, and she shut her eyes and hummed the song in her husky voice that was always a little off key, but it did not matter. As he played and looked at her, he thought suddenly of Maria, and how Maria would sing the song; she would not sit slumped there, in a chair, smoking a cigarette, over the remains of lunch; she would stand straight in the middle of the room and smile. Then something would happen to Maria's shoulders, and her hands would move, and she would say, "I want to dance it. It's no use standing here and listening. I want to dance."

Which was what the song was for, which was why it came like that, out of his head. Not to be sung, not to be echoed in a husky voice by Freada, or by anyone; but to be danced to by two people who moved as one person only, like himself and Maria, in some old back room at the top of a house; not in a restaurant, not in a theatre. He stopped playing and shut down the lid of the piano.

"That's all for today," he said; "they've turned the gas off at the main. Let's go and sleep."

"You can sleep for two hours," said Freada; "after that you must put on a shirt and a pair of pants that hasn't a hole in them. We're meeting people for drinks at five o'clock."

Freada knew too many people, that was the trouble. You always had to be sitting round a table in a café talking to a bunch of people. They were most of them French. And Niall was lazy over French, as lazy as he was about putting sound on paper. Freada was bilingual; she could rattle on for hours, discussing music, songs, the theatre, pictures, anything that came into her head, and her friends sat round closely, laughing, talking, having one drink after another, telling interminable stories about nothing. French people talked too much. They were all wits, they were all raconteurs. Too many sentences started off with "*Je m'en souviens . . .*" and "*Ça me fait penser . . .*" They went on and on. Niall said nothing; he tilted his chair, his eyes half closed, drinking iced beer, and now and again he would frown at Freada, and jerk his head, and sigh heavily, but she never took the slightest notice. She went on talking, biting on her cigarette holder, dropping ash all over the table, and then someone would say something that was funnier than ever, apparently, for there would be a throwing back of heads, a scraping of chairs on the floor of the café, and more laughter, more flow of conversation.

Sometimes, if he was close to Freada, he would kick her under the table, and then she would come to; she would smile across at him and say to her friends, "*Niall s'ennuie*," and everyone would look at him and smile as well, as if he were two years old.

They called him "*L'enfant*," or even "*L'enfant gâte*," and occasionally, worst of all, "*Le p'tit Niall*."

At last they got up and went away, the last of them disappeared, and Niall heaved a great sigh of relief and exasperation.

"Why do you ask them? Why do you do it?"

"But I love talking, I love my friends," said Freada; "besides, that man who came with Raoul this evening has a lot of influence, not only in the musical world in Paris, but in America too. He has contacts everywhere. He can help you a lot."

"I don't care if he has contacts in hell," said Niall, "he's a most deadly bore. And I don't want to be helped."

"Have another beer."

"Don't want another beer."

"What do you want, then?"

What did he want? He looked across at her and wondered. She lit another cigarette from the stub of the last and thrust it in the holder. Why did she have to smoke so much? Why did she allow the coiffeur to put that silly yellow streak on top of her hair? It got yellower and more dried up each time she went, and spoilt her. It made her hair like hay.

As soon as the comparison struck him he felt a pang of remorse. What a beastly thought. How could he have thought of such a thing? Freada was a darling, so good to him, so kind. He loved Freada. He put his hand out to her across the table and kissed it, on sudden impulse. "What do I want? Why, to be by ourselves, of course," he said. She screwed up her face at him, making him laugh; and then she called to the garçon to bring her the bill.

"Come on, then," she said, "we'll walk a little before dinner."

She took his arm and they strolled along the boulevard, slowly, pleasantly, watching the other people, without talking. Even now, with the sun away in the west, and the first lights showing in the cafés, it must be eighty degrees, or near it. No one wore a coat. Nobody wore a hat. The Parisians proper were all away en vacance. These were shopkeepers, out for the evening, to take a breath of air less stifling than they had breathed all day; they were people from the country, from the Midi. Everyone walked languidly, lazily, with a smile; everyone had shiny, greasy faces, and their clothes clung to them damply, and the heat of the boulevard hit them as they walked. The sky turned an amber colour, like Freada's scent, and an amber glow came upon the city, spreading from the west, touching the roofs and the bridges and the spires.

Suddenly the lights went on everywhere, over all the bridges, and the sky was not amber any more, it was purple, like a grape, but the heat still hit you as you walked. The taxis rattled across the bridges, filled to bursting point with heated, sweating adults, and little pale-faced children, tired from a day's outing. The taxis hooted, and screamed, and swerved, and the gendarme blew his whistle violently, and waved his baton. It was like Sullivan, years ago, waving his baton to the orchestra. The lights were going on. The lights were going on in the theatre, the curtain was going up, Mama was going to dance. . . .

"I can't walk any farther, pet, my feet ache," said Freada. Her face was lined and weary; she felt heavy on his arm.

"Please," he begged, "just a little farther. There's a new sound come with the evening, and the lights have brought it. Listen, Freada, listen."

They stood by the bridge, and the lights were reflected in the Seine, making shining hoops of gold, and in the distance the long line of gold travelled up the Champs Elysées to the Etoile. The taxis went past them in a gathering stream, fanning to right and left and centre, and as they passed the warm air lifted and blew in the people's faces, gentle as a fan. Niall could hear something like the beat of a pulse, and it was all part of the screaming taxis and the beckoning lights and the hot pavements and the darkening sky.

"I want to go on walking," he said. "I could walk forever."

"You're young," said Freada, "you can walk alone."

It was no use, the magic was not with them, the magic was away there, up the Champs Elysées, and if you reached the top of the hill by the Etoile it would be gone again, to the heavy scented trees in the heart of the Bois, in the deep trees, in the soft grass. The magic was elusive. You could never touch it. It escaped you always.

"All right," said Niall, "I'll get a taxi."

Now they were just like all the other people, whirling along in a tumbled stream. Hooting, screaming, rattling over the streets. Leaving the magic behind. Letting the magic escape.

"What are you thinking about?" asked Freada.

"Nothing," said Niall.

He sat forward, leaning out of the window, so that the air blew on his face, the warm exciting air, and he could see the long trail of lights, like a winding ribbon, vanish and reappear.

Freada leant back in the taxi and yawned, kicking off her shoes.

"There's only one thing I want," she said, "and that's to plunge my feet into a tepid bath."

Niall did not answer. He nibbled his nails and watched the flickering lights of Paris wink at him and curtsey. He wondered a little sadly whether Freada said this as a gentle hint that he would have to stay put the whole damn night in Sancho Panza.

For Celia it would be any spring, or any summer. . . . Whatever the season, the routine would be the same. Early tea, at half-past eight. She made it herself, on a little spirit stove, because she did not want to put the servants to extra trouble. Her alarm clock would wake her with its shrill impersonal summons, and she reached out her hand to bury it at once beneath the eiderdown. Then she allowed herself five minutes to enjoy the luxury of bed. Five minutes, but no more. Up, to make the tea, to have her bath, to take the morning papers in to Pappy, and to sense his mood and wishes for the day. There was always the little ritual of enquiring how he had slept. "A good night, Pappy?"

"Fair, my darling, fair." And from his tone she would have to gather whether the hours that stretched ahead for both of them held placidity or doom.

"I've had that old pain under the heart again. We had better send for Pleydon."

Then she knew where she was. Then she knew it meant a day at home, very probably in bed, and there would be no hope of going to the art school that morning, or that afternoon.

"Is it bad enough for that?"

"It was so bad at three this morning that I thought I was going to die. That's how bad it was, my darling."

She was on to Pleydon at once. Yes, she was reassured, Pleydon would come round as soon as he could. He had one urgent call to make, but he should be with Mr. Delaney by half-past ten for certain.

"It's all right, Pappy. He'll come. Now, what can I get you?"

"There's a letter there, my darling. We shall have to answer it. From poor old Marcus Guest, living in Majorca. Haven't heard from him for years." Pappy reached across the sheets for his horn-rimmed spectacles. "Read what he says, my darling, read what he says."

Then Celia took the letter—it was closely written, and there were six pages of it, very hard to read. She could hardly understand a word of it; the allusions were to places and to people of whom she had never heard. But Pappy was delighted.

"Poor old Marcus Guest," he kept repeating. "Who would have thought he was still alive? And in Majorca. They say it's very pleasant in Majorca. We ought to try it. It might be good for my voice. Find out about Majorca, my darling. Ring up somebody who can tell us about Majorca."

They passed the time until the doctor came, discussing plans for travel. Yes, there must be trains that went through France. They could take Paris on the way. See Niall. See how Niall was getting on. Perhaps persuade Niall to come with them. Or, better still, not go by train. Go by boat. There were so many shipping lines; they all passed through the Mediterranean. Certainly the best way would be to go by boat. Ah, here was Pleydon. "Pleydon, we are going to Majorca."

"Splendid," said Dr. Pleydon, "do you a world of good. Now let's listen to that chest of yours."

And out came the stethoscope, and the unbuttoning of the pyjama jacket, and the listening, and the putting away of the stethoscope.

"Yes," said Dr. Pleyton, "there may be a little murmur. Nothing much. Nothing to worry about. But you can have a quiet day. Got plenty to read?"

Good-bye to art school. It was the life class today. But never mind. It did not matter.

"Celia will be here," said Pappy. "Celia will look after everything."

She took the doctor to the door and stayed with him a moment in the passage.

"Probably a little flatulence," said Pleydon, "a touch of wind round the heart. But he's big, it's uncomfortable for him. Keep him quiet, and a light diet."

Down to the kitchen. The cook was newish, only been with them for six weeks, and she did not get on with Truda.

"Well, if Mr. Delaney isn't well, I should think something in the fish line would be best," said the cook; "steamed, I could do it steamed, with potatoes lightly boiled."

Truda passed through the kitchen with some sheets over her arm. "Mr. Delaney doesn't care for fish," she snapped.

The cook's mouth tightened. She did not answer. She waited until Truda had gone out of the kitchen and then she spoke. "I'm sorry, Miss Celia," she said, "but really I do my best. I know I haven't been with you long, but if I as much as open my mouth Truda nearly bites my head off. I'm not used to being spoken to in such a way."

"I know," said Celia soothingly, "but you see, she isn't so young as she was, and she's been with us for so long. It's because she's so fond of us that she talks so freely; she knows all our ways."

"It's a funny household," said the cook. "I've never been anywhere before where the dining room wanted a hot dinner at a quarter to seven. It's most unusual."

"I know, it must be trying, but you see, with my sister at the theatre . . ."

"I really think, Miss Celia, that it would be best if you looked for someone else. Someone more suited to your ways."

"Oh, come, don't say that . . ." And on and on, the smoothing down of the cook, with one eye on the pantry door, because André would be hearing it all and take infinite delight in repeating it to Truda. Pappy's bell rang once, twice, urgently. Celia fled upstairs.

"My darling, you know those photograph albums stacked in the morning room?"

"Yes, Pappy."

"I feel like going through them all again. And putting in the mass of odd snapshots that we took in South Africa and got mixed up with the ones from Australia. Will you help me, my darling?"

"Of course I will."

"You haven't got anything else to do?"

"No, oh no . . ."

Down to the morning room, and up with the heavy albums, and down again to look for the forgotten snapshots. They were underneath a pile of books at the back of a cupboard. In the middle of sorting them she remembered that she had given no final orders about the lunch. Back to the kitchen, and to be firm this time and order chicken.

"There's hardly time now, Miss Celia, to get a chicken on."

"Is there anything over?"

"There's that piece of beef we had for lunch yesterday."

"Mince it," said Celia, "mince it, and put a poached egg on top."

She went upstairs again to Pappy. He was up, he was pottering in his dressing gown. "Would you make me some tea, my darling?" he said. "They stew it below. They don't make it like you do."

Along to her bedroom to make the tea, and while she knelt on the floor beside the kettle Truda came in. Her eyes were red. She had been crying.

"It's easy to see when you aren't wanted any more," she said.

Celia jumped up from the floor and put her arms round Truda. "What do you mean? Don't be so silly," she said.

"It will break my heart to leave you," said Truda, "but leave you I must if things go on the way they're going. Nothing I do seems right any more. Ever since I was in hospital with my leg I've felt a kind of coldness, right through the house, from you all, and now my boy is here no longer . . ." The tears rolled down her cheeks.

"Truda, you mustn't say such things, I won't let you," said Celia. And on and on, until the old woman was pacified and went off to put new ribbons in Maria's nightgown.

Maria. Where was Maria? A shout, a wave of the hand, a slam of the front door, Maria was gone. . . .

"Will you have lunch with me, my darling?"

"Yes, Pappy, if you want me to."

"Well, you wouldn't leave me to have it up here all alone?"

Trays. Several trays. Curious how if you had a meal upstairs there had to be so many trays. And André hated carting trays. The old story would be trotted out. He was Mr. Delaney's valet. Mr. Delaney's dresser. He had never been a carrier of trays.

"Eat your mince, Pappy."

"It's cold, my darling, it's stone cold."

"That's because it's such a long way from the kitchen to this floor. I'll send it down to be hotted up again."

"No, my darling, don't bother. I'm not hungry."

He pushed the tray away. And moved his legs under the blankets. There were so many things strewn around. All those heavy albums.

"Take them away, my darling, take them away." Bundle the albums to the floor, straighten the bed.

"Is the room very hot? It seems very hot to me."

"No, I don't think so. It's because you are in bed."

"Open the window, I'm stifling. I'm going to choke."

She flung the window wide, and a stream of cold air blew down across the room. She shivered and moved towards the fireplace.

"Yes, that's better. I think I'll have a little shut-eye. Just for five minutes. Just a little shut-eye. You won't be going out?"

"No, Pappy."

"We'll play bezique, presently, my darling. And then you must get down to answering that letter from old Marcus Guest."

The quiet cold room. The steady, heavy breathing. The albums piled on the floor. And a sheet of blank paper, peeping out from between the pages of one of them. A piece of blank paper, doing nothing at all. Celia took the sheet of paper and balanced it upon one of the albums. She fumbled in her pocket for a pencil. There was no art school today, perhaps no art school tomorrow, but if you had a piece of paper and a pencil you were not entirely lost, not entirely alone. From the open window she could hear the sound of the children in the playground of the council school. They came out always at this time and shouted and called to one another, and skipped with skipping ropes, and hopped, and played. She hoped they would not wake Pappy. He slept on. His mouth a little open. His spectacles on the end of his nose. The children from the council school went on shouting and calling, and their voices were like something from another world. But the faces that she drew were children's faces. And she was happy. And she did not mind.

CHAPTER FOURTEEN

NIALL waited for Maria at the end of the platform of the Gare du Nord. He stood behind the barrier. He was waiting there as the train came in. At once there was a jostle of people and porters, and the usual babble of conversation. And the wrong people streamed past him, through the barrier. Chattering Frenchmen, with voluble wives, and English tourists, and all the sallow individuals of no known nationality who travel forever upon continental trains, biting upon cigars.

Niall's heart thumped under his ribs and he was filled with unbearable anxiety. If Maria did not come, if he had to turn back again, alone . . . She was there. She wore a loose red coat and she carried her hat in her hand. He could see her eyes laughing at him from ten, from twenty yards away. And although she had only two suitcases with her, she was followed by three porters. She was beside him. She put up her face to be kissed.

"You've grown again," she said. "It's not fair. Now you look older than I do, instead of younger."

She took out her handkerchief and rubbed his cheek because she had left lipstick.

"I've only a hundred-franc note," she said. "You must pay the porters."

He had come prepared. He knew how it would be. As they filed through the barrier people turned to look at her and she smiled back at them. She waved to the engine driver, fat and greasy, who laughed down at her from the step of his cab, wiping his hands upon a rag.

"I love him," she said. "I love them all."

"Yes, but not here," said Niall. "Not on the platform."

The anxiety had left him, but the beating heart remained, full, happy, ready to burst. He dealt with the porters, overtipping them with Freada's money. He summoned a taxi, and they bundled in. The driver cocked an eye at Maria and said something to Niall out of the side of his mouth.

"I've forgotten all my French. What did he say?" asked Maria.

"Even if you remembered French," said Niall, "you wouldn't know that one."

"Was it rude?"

"No, complimentary."

"Complimentary to me, or to you?"

"To both of us. He's an understanding man. He has perception."

The taxi swerved away out of the station and, turning a corner sharply, pitched Maria into Niall's arms.

He held her tight and kissed her hair.

"You always smell the same," he said. "Like mustard."

"Why mustard?"

"I don't know. It's not scent. It's just your skin."

She took his hand and measured it with hers.

"That's grown too," she said. "It's cleaner. And you've stopped biting your nails. Did Freada stop you?"

"No one stopped me. I haven't felt like biting them."

"You're happy then. People only bite their nails when they're unhappy. Are you happy?"

"I'm happy now." He bit the tips of her fingers instead of his own. She lay back in his arms and laughed.

"Who are your friends?" he asked.

"I have so many. I don't remember their names."

"Who is number one at the moment?"

"There isn't a number one. If there was I shouldn't be in Paris."

"That's what I thought," said Niall.

"You know what I'm going to do next?" she said.

"You told me, in your letter."

"I want to do all the Barrie parts. I'm good in Barrie."

"Who says so?"

"Barrie."

As the taxi swerved and rattled, she settled herself with greater comfort in Niall's arms, resting her legs across his knees.

160

"The thing is," she said, "people always think I'm ethereal. Wide-eyed and wan. I wonder why."

"Perhaps you don't lie about with them like this," said Niall.

"I do lie about," she said, "from time to time. The trouble is I go off everyone so quickly. I soon get bored."

"Bored with the things they say? Or with the things they do?"

"With the things they do. I never listen to the things they say."

Niall lit a cigarette. No easy matter, in his cramped position.

"It's like music," he said. "After all, there are only eight notes to an octave."

"What about all those sharps and flats?"

"Well, you can play about with them," he said.

"Think of Elgar," she said, " 'Enigma Variations.' And Rachmaninoff, having fun with Paganini."

"You set too high a standard," said Niall. "You must depress your friends."

"I've never had any complaints up to now," said Maria. "Where is the taxi taking us?"

"To your hotel."

"I thought that I was going to stay with you and Freada."

"You can't. There's only one bedroom."

"I see," said Maria. "How very sordid."

She pushed him away and began powdering her nose.

"Why didn't you go on that tour?" asked Niall.

"The wife," said Maria. "No fun for anyone. And anyway, his teeth."

"What about his teeth?"

"They've let him down at last. He's got to have dentures, and he was in a nursing home last week. I sent some lilies."

"Why not a wreath?"

"I thought about a wreath."

"*Finito*, then?"

"*Finito*."

He lifted her wrist and looked at the time on the bracelet watch.

"Well, you've always this," he said. "There's nothing ethereal about this. Did he give it to you for a parting present?"

"No," she said. "He gave it for enigma variations."

When the taxi turned into the Champs Elysées she sat up quickly and leant forward, looking through the window.

"Oh, Niall," she said. "It's us, it's you and me."

Two children were waiting to cross the avenue. The boy wore a blouse, and a beret on his head, and the girl, a little older, tugged at his hand impatiently, her hair blowing about her face.

"You and me," said Maria, "running away from Truda. Why didn't I realise it before? London isn't home. London will never be home."

"That's why I came to Paris," said Niall.

Maria turned from the window and looked at him. Her eyes went dark, without expression, like someone blind.

"Yes," she said, "but you came with the wrong person."

The taxi swerved violently to the right and stopped with a jerk before Maria's hotel.

Back in the apartment off the Avenue de Neuilly, Freada was entertaining Pappy and Celia. They were on their way back to England from a holiday on the Italian lakes. Pappy had not liked the idea of Majorca at all. He had been seized with a sudden fancy for limpid water and, in the distance, mountains that he would not have to climb. Black-muzzled cows in the valleys, with bells round their necks that rang.

"But it rained, Freada, it rained," he said. "The tears of the whole world poured from the dripping sky."

"What did you do?" asked Freada.

"We played bezique," said Pappy.

Celia felt Freada's eyes turned upon hers in sympathy. She looked away. It gave her a funny feeling, sitting in Freada's flat. She was not certain why, but she thought it must be because the flat was small. The one bedroom and Niall's dressing gown hanging on the door.

She tried to think of Freada as a sort of Truda, looking after Niall. But it would not work. "I must be narrow-minded," she said to herself. "I don't mind what Maria does, so why should I mind Niall?"

The flat was very untidy. There were sheets of music lying about, and open books, and shoes kicked in a corner. Perhaps it was the shoes . . . Pappy, who had been so angry once, seemed perfectly at ease. He lay back in one armchair, picking his hollow tooth with his gold toothpick, and discussing Freada's plans.

"Take him about a bit," he said, waving his hand, "take him around the world. Let him play all the capitals of Europe, like his mother did before him, and finish in America. I give my permission."

Celia watched Freada drop ash upon the floor. There was an ash tray on the table which she did not use. It had a bunch of asparagus in it instead, with the ends bitten.

"Niall doesn't want to travel," said Freada. "He has no ambition."

"No ambition?" said Pappy. "No desire to travel? What does he like to do?"

"He likes to eat."

That explains the asparagus tips, thought Celia, and those empty chocolate cartons. She must remember to tell Truda when she got home.

"What else does he like to do?" said Pappy, curious.

But Freada shrugged her shoulders. She fitted another cigarette into her holder.

"He reads," she said, "and sleeps. He sleeps for hours."

"Then all this success, this éclat," said Pappy, "it has not gone to his head? It has not spoilt him?"

"I don't think he knows it has happened," said Freada.

"His mother over again," said Pappy. "She never cared."

"But she took trouble," said Freada, "she worked—heavens how she worked. She had tenacity and drive. Niall has neither. He simply does not care."

Pappy shook his head and whistled.

"That's bad," he said. "That's his French blood."

Celia thought of the blue vein on Niall's hand and wondered if the vein was French. She looked at her own hands, broad and square like Pappy's. Her veins did not show at all.

"Maria's the worker," said Pappy. "Maria's the girl. No slacking with Maria. She starts rehearsing again next week. A chip of the old block. Nothing French about Maria, thank God."

Celia wondered anxiously if there was anything French about Freada. She was bilingual and she lived in France. Pappy could be so tactless.

"I wonder if she has arrived," said Celia, to change the conversation. "The train was due at Calais an hour ago."

"Niall said he would take her straight to the hotel," said Freada. "I suggest you go along down and see if she is there. Niall can come back presently and change."

It was rather like Truda after all, Celia decided. Freada knowing about when Niall should change. She wondered if Freada did his laundry, counted his shirts. Any moment Freada might call Niall "my boy."

Pappy and Celia drove down to the hotel in a taxi.

"I wonder how it goes," said Pappy, curious, "this strange liaison between Niall and Freada. Funny old Freada. I must take her to lunch tomorrow and find out."

"Oh, Pappy, you can't!" said Celia, horrified.

"Whyever not, my darling?"

"Think how embarrassing for Niall," she answered.

"I see no embarrassment," said Pappy. "These things are of importance. They are medical. I look upon Freada as I would look upon a tutor in Oxford, Cambridge, or Heidelberg. She knows her job."

And he began to reckon up the years he had known Freada, casting his mind back to 1912, to 1909.

When they arrived at the hotel the man behind the desk told them that Miss Delaney had arrived and had unpacked and had gone out again, leaving no message. She had been gone for half an hour. The gentleman also. Upstairs in the suite—Pappy never travelled unless he could have a suite—they found disorder. Maria's clothes lay strewn upon every bed. Beds were deranged. Towels were scattered. Talcum powder was spilt upon the floor.

"Disgusting!" said Pappy. "Like an Austrian servant."

Celia began to tidy feverishly. Maria was no longer a chip of the old block.

"They've been drinking, too," said Pappy, examining the tooth glass. "Cognac, judging by the smell. I never knew my daughter drank."

"She doesn't," said Celia, smoothing Pappy's bed. "She always has orangeade. Unless it's a first night, when she has champagne."

"Then it must be Niall," said Pappy. "Someone—and who can it be but Niall?—has been pouring cognac into my tooth glass. I shall attack Freada. Freada is responsible."

He filled the tooth glass with cognac for himself.

"Leave me to change, my darling," he said to Celia. "If Maria chooses to turn this suite into a brothel, she shall answer for it on her return. I will stop her playing Mary Rose. I will wire Barrie tonight."

He began rummaging in the wardrobe for his evening clothes, throwing the suits he did not want onto the floor.

Celia went to her own room to change. There was a note pinned on the pillow: "See you at the cabaret. We're dining out." Celia's dressing-table drawer was open, and her evening bag was missing. Maria must have forgotten to bring her own and had taken Celia's. She had taken Celia's earrings too. The new ones Pappy had bought her in

Milan. Celia began to dress, her heart despondent. She had a feeling that the evening would go wrong. . . .

Niall and Maria were seated side by side on a river boat chugging to St. Cloud. Paris, a haze of beauty, lay behind them. They sat on the top deck eating cherries. They threw the cherry stones onto the heads of people down below. Maria wore Niall's camel coat over her evening dress. The dress was green. Celia's jade earrings matched it to perfection.

"The thing is," she said, "we must never part."

"We never had," said Niall.

"We're parted now," said Maria, "you being in Paris and me in London. It's hateful. I can't bear it. That's why I'm so unhappy."

"Are you unhappy?"

"Terribly," she said.

She spat a cherry stone onto the head of a bald old Frenchman down below. He looked up, ready to explode. When he saw Maria he smiled and bowed. He glanced round to see where there was a ladder leading to the upper deck.

"I get so lonely," she said. "No one ever makes me laugh."

"You won't need to laugh in a few weeks' time," said Niall. "You will be rehearsing."

"That's when I feel the need for laughter most," said Maria.

The river boat chugged along the twisting river to the shadowed trees. Twilight fell upon the quays. The scents and sounds of Paris hummed about them in the air.

"Let's go away," said Niall. "Let's just chuck up everything."

"Where could we go?" said Maria.

"We could go to Mexico," said Niall.

They held hands, staring across the river to the trees.

"Those hats," said Maria, "with pointed crowns. I don't think I like the hats in Mexico."

"You needn't wear a hat. Only the shoes. A special sort of leather, with a smell."

"We can't either of us ride," said Maria. "And in Mexico one has to ride. Mules. And people are always shooting."

She crumpled up the paper bag that had held the cherries, and threw it away into the river.

"The thing is," she said, "I don't think I want to go away. I want to be in London. But for you to be there too."

"The thing is," said Niall, "that I'd rather live in a lighthouse."

"Why a lighthouse?"

"Well, a mill. Or an oasthouse. Or a barge."

Maria sighed and leant back against Niall's shoulder.

"Let's face it, we shall never be together," said Niall.

"We can be together sometimes," said Maria. "From time to time. How much further is it to St. Cloud?"

"I don't know. Why?"

"I only wondered. We must not miss the cabaret, and Freada, and your songs."

Niall laughed and put both arms about her.

"You see," he said, "running away is just pretence with you. St. Cloud is just another Mexico to you."

"We could make it a symbol," said Maria. "Something we always want and never have. Something that is forever out of reach. Isn't there some poem that begins, 'Oh, God, oh, Montreal'? We can say, 'Oh God, St. Cloud.'"

The wind was chilly. She buttoned his camel coat up to her throat.

"I tell you what we can do," she said. "We can have the best of both worlds by driving back to Paris in a taxi through the Bois. The taxi can go slow on purpose. And perhaps the driver will be tactful."

"French drivers never look behind; they've all been trained," said Niall.

"All the same," he added presently, as the taxi drove them through the silent Bois, "I'd rather go to Mexico."

"Beggars can't be choosers," said Maria. "And anyway . . ."

"Anyway, what?"

"Do I still smell of mustard?" asked Maria.

Back in Paris, Celia, Pappy, and Freada dined amid an atmosphere of strain. Pappy was livid. He had taken the trouble to come to visit his stepson, and his stepson had made not the slightest effort to see him. He had paid his daughter's fare from London, he was paying her bill at the hotel, and she had gone out on the streets like a Viennese whore.

All this was said aloud to Freada over dinner.

"I wash my hands of both of them," he said. "Niall is nothing but a pampered pimp. Maria is a slut. Both riddled with bad blood. Both heading for the gutter. Thank God for this child here. Thank God for Celia."

1 6 6

Freada only smiled and went on smoking Chesterfields. Perhaps she was like a tutor after all, thought Celia, an indulgent, understanding tutor.

"They'll turn up," she said. "I was young myself in Paris. Once."

The long meal ended. The session for supper and the cabaret was yet to come. Pappy paid the bill in silence, and they drove, still in silence, to what Pappy chose to term the *bôite-de-nuit*.

"They're all the same, these places," he said glumly. "Haunts of vice. Very different from my day. You've fallen in the world, my dear Freada. Sadly fallen." He shrugged his shoulders, shook his head.

Because of what he said Celia expected to find the bôite-de-nuit a sort of cellar, buried underground. Murky and ill lit. With white-faced, evil people dancing cheek to cheek. She was surprised to walk into a restaurant like the Embassy Club in London. Only smarter. The women exquisitely dressed. Some of them knew Pappy. He smiled and bowed to them. Freada led the way to a table in the corner. Presently a young man with a wasp waist came up to the table and, clicking his heels, bowed low to Celia, asking for a dance. She flushed and glanced at Pappy. He must be a marquis, at least, or a Bourbon prince.

"It's all right," murmured Freada, "it's only the pro. You won't have to talk."

Celia rose to dance, disappointed. Still, it was a kind of compliment. She was blown away in the young man's arms like thistledown. The cabaret came later. There were two turns. A Frenchman who told stories, and then Freada. The Frenchman was very small and very fat. As soon as he walked onto the floor Pappy began to laugh and clap. Pappy was that sort of audience. He always enjoyed himself. Celia could not follow a word the Frenchman said, not because her French was rusty, but because it was not the sort of French she understood. But he must have been terribly vulgar because Pappy laughed so much. He laughed until the tears ran down his cheeks and he gasped for breath. The Frenchman was delighted; his turn had never gone so well before. Then Freada got up from the table and went to the piano. Celia felt herself blushing. It was always embarrassing when someone you knew performed in front of you, in a room, and not upon a stage. They were much too close. Freada was clever. First she did her imitations, and although Celia did not know the people she was imitating—they were French—she knew they must be like, everyone clapped so much.

Then the lights went low and she began to sing Niall's songs.

They had written the words between them; the music, of course, was Niall's. Some were in English, some in French. She had a low, rather husky voice that sometimes went off key, but it did not matter. There was so much warmth and expression to the voice, you did not mind. The songs, which were new to Celia, were not new to the people gathered at the tables. They began to hum, in accompaniment to Freada; softly at first, and then louder, as she swung into the tune and smiled. Celia felt proud and happy, not because of Freada, whom she barely knew, but because the songs belonged to Niall, her brother. They were his possession, like the drawings that belonged to her. She found herself humming under her breath, like the rest of the people, and, glancing at Pappy, she saw that he was humming too. There were tears in his eyes as well, but this time the tears were not champagne. They were tears of pride for Niall, the stepson with the bad French blood. . . .

Outside in the vestibule Niall waited for Maria, who was powdering her nose in the cloakroom. He had hoped they would be late enough to miss the cabaret, but they were still on time. He could hear Freada and the piano. She was guying the last line of the song, which always made a prick of irritation. Better that way, perhaps, he could not judge. And, anyway, who cared? Maria came out of the cloakroom.

"How do I look? All right?" she asked.

"I've seen you look worse," he answered. "Must we really go inside?"

"But of course," she said. "Listen, I hear your song."

They went through the door and stood beside the entrance, watching Freada. The people were singing with her now, and some of them beat time upon the floor. A few heads turned in the direction of Niall and Maria, and Maria hear a murmur, a faint whisper of applause.

She smiled, stepping forward, not conscious that she did so; it was second nature to smile and move when she heard a movement of applause. Then she noticed that the heads were not turned to her at all, they were turned to Niall. People were smiling and pointing at Niall. Freada, turning from the piano, laughing, jerked her head to him, and the murmur from the people came insistent, loud.

"*Le p'tit Niall . . . Le p'tit Niall . . .*" somebody called, and

Maria, alone, ignored, standing against the wall, saw Niall, bored and indifferent, walk across the floor to the piano and, pushing Freada off the seat, sit down and play. Everyone began to clap and laugh, Freada among them, and, leaning against the piano, she sang while Niall played.

Unnoticed, Maria threaded her way among the tables to the far one in the corner where Pappy and Celia sat. She began to apologise, in a low whisper, for being late. "Hush!" Pappy said impatiently. "Listen to Niall." And Maria sat, her hands folded in her lap, twisting Niall's ring on her right finger. She alone amongst the audience did not sing.

Later, when the cabaret was over and they were all sitting round the table having supper, Pappy and Freada deep in technicalities, Maria turned to Niall and said: "You looked awful. I felt quite ashamed. You were the only man in the room who was not dressed."

"Why should I dress?" said Niall. "They would not mind if I wore a vest and hobnailed boots."

"The thing is," she said angrily, "you've got a swollen head. I thought it could never happen, but it has. They would not stand for it in London. You'd be a flop in London."

She shook her head when the waiter offered her champagne.

"Iced water, please," she said.

"You see my point," asked Niall, "about a lighthouse or a barge?"

Maria would not answer. She turned her back on him.

"Did I write and tell you about Lord Wyndham's son?" she said to Celia.

"Yes," said Celia. "You said he was attractive."

"He is. He likes me very much. Not married either."

Out of the corner of her eye Celia saw the wasp-waisted professional dancer approach their table once again. She pushed back her chair in readiness. But the professional did not look at her at all. He bowed low to Maria.

Maria got up from the table, smiling. She floated away with him, talking rapid French. For the first time since the cabaret finished the people at the other tables looked away from Niall and watched Maria.

The earrings suit her, thought Celia sadly, they suit her better than they suit me. I wonder whether she will want me to give them to her.

Beside her, Pappy was talking excitedly to Freada.

"Proud of the children? Of course I'm proud of them," he was saying. "They only bear out what I have always said. Showmanship is in the blood. I don't care if it's a milch cow or a stallion—breeding tells."

Maria circled past their table in the arms of the professional and, looking over her shoulder, she put out her tongue at Niall.

CHAPTER FIFTEEN

THE grandfather clock struck seven. Upstairs there was the sound of bath water running. Charles must be in after all, and wet from his walk, taking a bath. It was ominous that he had gone straight upstairs and had not looked into the drawing room first on his return. This meant that he had not shaken off his mood. And we were still the parasites.

"I'm not looking forward to supper," said Niall. "It's going to be that affair of sitting round the table and nobody saying anything. Except Polly. And she will start one of her conversations: 'Oh, Mummy, I must tell you what the children said when they were undressing.' And it will go on and on."

"It will break the silence," said Celia. "Better for Polly to talk than one of us. And Charles never listens anyway. He's used to it, like a ticking clock."

"I would not mind if the children said something funny, but they never do," said Niall. "Perhaps what they said was funny originally, and then Polly squeezes the humour out of it."

"You're very hard on Polly," said Celia. "She's such a good sort. Really, I don't know how this house would run without her."

"If only we didn't have to eat with her," said Niall. "It brings out the worst in me. I want to pick my teeth and belch."

"You do that anyway," said Maria. "And I agree about feeding with Polly, but what is her alternative? A tray? Where and who carries it? And what is put on it? A leg off our cold chicken?"

"She has that anyway, in the dining room," said Niall.

"Yes," said Maria, "but she does carve it off herself. It would be much more insulting if one cut it and sent it out to her somewhere on her plate, like the dog's dinner. And anyway, it all started in the war, when everyone had high tea at half-past six. People became community-minded."

"I never did," said Niall.

"You didn't have to," said Maria. "So typical of you to fire-watch on some old warehouse where nobody ever went."

"It was very dangerous," said Niall. "Things dropped all round me as I stood alone on that curious-shaped roof. Nobody will ever realise how terribly brave I was. Far braver than Charles, who was doing something with S.H.A.E.F. or whatever it was."

"It wasn't S.H.A.E.F.," said Maria.

"They all sounded the same," said Niall. "Like you and E.N.S.A. People got so used to uniforms and strings of letters that they swallowed anything. I remember telling a woman I was working very hard in S.H.I.T. and she believed me."

Celia got up and began to pat the cushions and tidy the papers. If she did not do it, nobody else would. And Charles hated an untidy room. Maria never seemed to notice, not at Farthings, anyway. Her own flat in London was always spotless, but perhaps that was because it was her own possession. And Farthings belonged to Charles.

"You know, Niall," said Celia, "I believe it's your lack of respect for tradition that has always made Charles a little wary of you."

"I don't know what you mean," said Niall. "I have an immense respect for tradition."

"Yes," said Celia, "but a different sort. When you talk about tradition you think of Queen Elizabeth on horseback making a speech at Greenwich and then wondering whether to send for Essex, or whoever was her person at the time. When Charles speaks of tradition he means the world of today. He means citizenship, doing one's duty, right versus wrong, what this country stands for, all those things."

"How tedious," said Niall.

"There you are," said Celia. "That's just the attitude that Charles detests. No wonder that he calls you a parasite."

"It's not that at all," said Maria, getting up and looking into the mirror over the fireplace. "The whole thing is personal. It's a secret grudge, deep inside Charles. I've always known it and pretended to myself it was not there. Since we are all being so frank this evening, let's admit it."

"Let's admit what?" said Niall.

"Let's admit that Charles has always been jealous of you," said Maria. There was a long silence. The three of us had never faced up to making this admission before; not in so many words.

"Don't let's start playing the truth game, I hate it," said Celia. Maria was usually so reserved. If Maria's reserve broke down, anything might happen. The fat would be in the fire. And directly she thought of this she wondered what she meant. What fat and what fire? It was all too complicated. The day was getting out of hand.

"When did it start?" asked Niall.

"When did what start?"

"The jealousy," said Niall.

Maria had pulled out the lipstick she kept hidden behind the candlestick on the mantelpiece, and was making up her mouth.

"Oh, I don't know," she said. "Very early on. I think—probably—when I went back to the stage again, after Caroline was born. He put it down to you. He thought you influenced me."

"No one has influenced you, ever," said Niall, "and me least of all."

"I know, but he didn't understand that."

"Did he ever say anything about it?" asked Celia.

"No. I just felt it. There was a kind of tension."

"But surely," objected Celia, "he must have always known it was bound to happen. Your wanting to act, I mean. He can't have expected you to settle down in the country like an ordinary person."

"I think he did," said Maria. "I think he got my character all wrong right from the start. I told you before, it was playing Mary Rose that did it. Mary Rose was a country girl. Always hiding up apple trees, and then disappearing on the island. She was a ghost, and Charles fell in love with the ghost."

"What did you fall in love with?" asked Niall.

"As I was being Mary Rose, I fell in love with Simon," said Maria. "And Charles was my idea of Simon. Quiet, dependable, devoted. Besides, at that particular time there was no one much around. And all those flowers."

"Charles was not the only one to send you flowers," said Celia. "People were doing it all the time. There was a rich American who sent you orchids twice a week. What was his name?"

"Hiram Something," said Maria. "He chartered a plane once to take me to Le Touquet, and I was sick all over his coat. He was awfully nice about it."

"Was the week end a success?" asked Niall.

"No. I kept wondering what had happened to the coat. So difficult to clean. And when we flew back on the Sunday night he did not have it with him."

"Perhaps he gave it to the waiter," said Niall, "or to the *valet de chambre*. The valet de chambre, I should think. He would be able to smuggle it away with no questions asked."

"Yes," said Celia. "And being a valet de chambre, he would know the right stuff to get to clean the coat. But anyway, a week end at Le Touquet with Hiram was not the reason why Maria decided to marry Charles. It was not the flowers, nor was it the safe dependability. Nor was it because of Simon and Mary Rose. Maria could have had all those things without marrying. There must have been something very special about Charles to induce her to throw up the theatre for two years and go to live in the country."

"Don't goad the girl," said Niall. "We know perfectly well why she did it. I don't know why you're both being so cagey about it."

Maria put her powder puff back into the vase where it had been hidden since last week end.

"I'm not being cagey," she said. "And if you mean I started Caroline before the wedding, it isn't true. Charles was far too respectable for anything like that. Caroline was born nine months to the day after the marriage. I was just one of those fashionable brides. Getting married was very romantic. Like being unveiled."

"Surely you felt a bit of a hypocrite?" said Celia.

"A hypocrite?" said Maria, turning round from the mirror, indignant. "Not in the slightest. Why on earth should I feel a hypocrite? I had never been married before."

"No, but still . . ."

"It was one of the most exciting moments in my life. That, and then the wedding at St. Margaret's, and going up the aisle on Pappy's arm, white from head to foot. In fact, there was only one bad moment. My shoes were new. I'd ordered them in a fearful hurry, for some reason or other, and the price was on the back. When I knelt down to pray I suddenly remembered that, and I never heard the blessing. I kept thinking, Oh God! Charles's mother will see the price on the back of my shoes."

"Would it have mattered if she had?" asked Niall.

"Yes. She would have known they came from Selfridge's and cost only thirty bob. I could not have borne it."

"Snob," said Niall.

"No," said Celia. "It isn't snob at all. I see Maria's point. Girls are awfully sensitive about things like that. I still am, and I'm no longer a girl, heaven knows. If I buy a dress at Harvey Nichols or somewhere I always cut out the label and leave the back plain. People might think then that the dress came from some very good place or some special dressmaker, and not a store at all."

"But who the hell cares?"

"We care. Women care. It's our personal, rather foolish pride. And anyway, Maria has not told us yet why it was she married Charles."

"She wanted to be the Honourable Mrs. Charles Wyndham," said Niall. "And if you think there was ever any other reason, you have never really known Maria, although Pappy bred the pair of you."

He lit a cigarette and threw the blown match onto the mantelpiece beside Maria's lipstick.

"Is it true?" said Celia doubtfully. "Was that really the reason? I mean, truthfully. As we seem to be taking down our back hair."

Maria's eyes went blank and misty, as they invariably did on the few occasions in her life when she was trapped.

"Yes," she said. "Yes, it's true. But I was in love with him as well."

She looked shamefaced, apologetic, like a little girl caught out in a misdeed.

"After all," she said, "Charles was very good-looking. He still is, in spite of getting rather fat."

"Funny," said Celia, "how one can be related to someone, and brought up with them, and yet one never tumbles to a thing like that. That you should want to be an Honourable. It does not really go with your character."

"Nothing has ever gone with Maria's character," said Niall. "That's what Charles has always found so difficult. She's a chameleon. She changes her personality to suit her mood. That's why she's never bored. It must be lots of fun being somebody different every day. You and I, Celia, have to go on being the same people all the time, for the whole of our lives."

"But the Honourable," Celia persisted, not listening to Niall. "I mean, it's not so very much after all. Had it been a viscount or an earl there would have been something to it."

"It looked very nice written," said Maria wistfully. "The Honourable Mrs. Charles Wyndham. I used to try it out on the back page of my engagement book. And anyway, I did not know any earls or viscounts."

"You could have waited," said Celia. "In your position they would have come along sooner or later."

"I did not want to wait," said Maria. "I wanted to marry Charles."

And she thought of Charles and how he had looked in those days. Slim and straight, without the tendency to stoop that he had now, and without the hint of tummy. His hair fair and crisp. Not pepper-and-salt. The very English texture of skin, rather red, but youthfully red. The skin that went with riding well, and playing polo. And always twice a week in that stall in the fourth row, leaning forward, his hand on his knee, holding his chin, and coming round afterwards and tapping on the door of her dressing room, and going out to supper. Being driven in his car. An Alvis. It had red leather seats, and a grey rug that he used to wrap most carefully round her legs in case she should be cold.

The first time he took her out to supper he told her that his bedside book was Malory's *Morte d'Arthur*.

"And why can't they make a play out of that?" he had said to her. "Why can't some author write the love story of Lancelot and Elaine? You could play Elaine."

"Yes," she had said, "I should love to play Elaine."

And while he retold all the stories of Malory's *Morte d'Arthur*—it took nearly the whole of supper—and she listened and nodded, she was thinking of the wedding she had been to the week before, not at St. Margaret's, but at St. George's, Hanover Square, and the choirboys wore red gowns under their white frilly surplices, and the church was filled with lilies. There was "The Voice That Breathed o'er Eden" and "O Perfect Love."

"It's been dead too long, the age of chivalry," said Charles. "If the flower of my generation had not been blown to bits in the war they would have brought it back again. Now it's too late. So few of us are left."

The bride at St. George's had worn white and silver. When she came down the steps afterwards her veil was thrown back, and people threw confetti. At the reception in Portland Place there were long tables filled with wedding presents. Great solid silver teapots. And trays. And lampshades. The bride and bridegroom stood at the end of a long drawing room to receive their guests. When the bride drove away to her honeymoon she had changed into a blue frock and she had a silver fox fur thrown round her shoulders. "That's a wedding present too," somebody had said to Maria. And the bride waved from the window of the car. She wore very new long white gauntlet gloves. Maria thought of the maid stretching them upstairs and giving them to the bride, with the suède bag, also a present, and she thought of all the tissue paper on the floor. And the bride smiling, not thinking of anything but driving away with the bridegroom in the car.

"The trouble is," Charles had said, "I always think Lancelot was a bit second-rate. The way he carried on with Guinevere. No doubt she led him on. . . . But Parsifal was the best of the bunch. He was the chap who found the Holy Grail."

Maria Delaney . . . Maria Wyndham . . . The Honourable Mrs. Charles Wyndham . . .

Twelve years ago. Twelve years was a long time. And the trouble was that she, Maria, was second-rate like Guinevere, and Charles was still Parsifal, looking for the Holy Grail. Parsifal was upstairs in the bathroom letting the water run away.

"I don't see," said Maria unhappily, twisting Niall's ring, "what I could have done to make it different. If we had the years again. At least I have been honest with Charles. Up to a point."

"What point?" said Niall.

Maria did not answer. There was really nothing she could say.

"You say I'm a chameleon," she said at last. "Perhaps you're right. It's difficult to judge oneself. At least I've never pretended to be a good person. Really good, I mean, like Charles. I've pretended lots of other things, but never that. I'm bad, I'm shallow, I'm immoral, I cheat, I'm selfish, I'm often very stingy and frequently unkind. But I know it all. I don't kid myself that I possess one single quality worth a damn. Isn't that one thing in my favour? If I die tomorrow and there really is a God and I go and stand before Him and say: 'Sir,' or whatever one does say to God, 'here I am, Maria, and I am the lowest form of life,' that would be honest. And honesty counts for something, doesn't it?"

"One doesn't know," said Niall. "That's the frightful thing. One just does not know what goes down well with God. He may think honesty is a form of bragging."

177

"In that case I'm sunk," said Maria.

"I think you're sunk anyway," said Niall.

"I always hope," said Celia, "that one's sins may be forgiven one because of something one did years ago that was kind and one has forgotten. Like the bit in the Bible: 'Anyone who gives a child a cup of cold water in My Name will be forgiven.' "

"I see what you mean," said Maria doubtfully, "but isn't that allegorical? We must all have given the equivalent of cups of water to people. It's just common politeness. If that's all we have to do to be saved, why worry?"

"Think of the unkind things we have forgotten," said Niall. "Those are the ones that will be totted up against us. I sometimes wake up in the early morning and go quite cold thinking of all the things I must have done and can't remember."

"Pappy must have taught you that," said Celia. "Pappy had a fearful theory that when we die we go to a theatre, and we sit down and see the whole of our lives re-enacted before us. And nothing is omitted. Not one single, sordid detail. We have to watch it all."

"Really?" said Maria. "But how just like Pappy."

"It might be rather fun," said Niall. "There are certain things I should like to see all over again."

"Certain things," said Maria, "but not all. How dreadful when the play began to get near to something shaming, and one knew that in a few minutes or so one would see something absolutely—well . . ."

"It depends who one was with," said Niall. "Does one have to go to the theatre alone, or didn't Pappy say?"

"He never said," answered Celia. "Alone, I should imagine. Or perhaps with a few saints and angels. If there are angels."

"Dreary for the angels," said Maria. "Worse than being a dramatic critic. Sitting through somebody's interminable life."

"I'm not so sure," said Niall. "They probably quite enjoy it. And the word goes round if something very special is on. 'I say, old boy, it ought to be pretty lurid tonight. Maria Delaney is on at eight-fifteen.' "

"What nonsense," said Celia. "As if saints and angels are like a lot of beady old men in a club. They would sit quite impassive. Above it all."

"In that case, one wouldn't mind them going," said Maria. "They'd be just a row of dummies."

The door opened and we all three looked self-conscious, as we used to do as children, when the grownups came into the room.

It was Polly. She poked her head round the door. It was one of the habits that infuriated Niall. She never came right into the room.

"The children look such ducks," she said. "They're in bed having their supper. They want you to go up and say good night."

We felt this was fabrication. The children were perfectly happy by themselves. But Polly wanted us to go and see them. See their well-brushed, glossy hair, their shining faces, the red and blue dressing gowns that she had bought at Daniel Neal's.

"All right," said Maria. "We're going up to change anyway."

"I meant to bathe them for you, Polly," said Celia, "but we've all been talking. I forgot it was so late."

"They wondered why you hadn't come," said Polly, "and I told them they mustn't always expect Auntie Celia to run round after them. Auntie Celia likes to talk to Mummy and Uncle Niall."

The head vanished. The door closed. The cheerful footsteps pattered up the stairs.

"That was a nasty crack," said Niall. "A whole world of condemnation in her voice. I believe she had been listening at the door."

"I do feel guilty," said Celia. "It is my thing at week ends to bathe the children. Polly has so much to do."

"I think Polly would be the worst person to have in the stalls at the theatre," said Maria. "After one was dead, I mean. She would stare with stark disapproval at everything I have ever done from the cradle onwards. I can hear her gasp: 'Oh, Mummy. Whatever is Mummy doing now?'"

"It would be an education," said Niall. "It would open new vistas."

"I don't think she would understand half of it," said Celia. "Like taking someone tone-deaf to hear Brahms."

"Nonsense," said Niall. "Polly would have her eyes on sticks."

"Why Brahms?" said Maria.

There was another footstep on the stairs. A heavy one this time. The footsteps paused outside the door of the drawing room and then moved away to the dining room. There was the sound of a bottle being uncorked. Charles was decanting the wine.

"He's still in a bad mood," said Maria. "If he was all right he would have come into the room."

"Not necessarily," whispered Niall. "He always makes such a thing about the wine, and having the right temperature. I hope it's some more of the Château Latour."

"Don't whisper," said Celia, "it makes us look so guilty. After all, nothing has happened. He's only been for a walk."

She glanced hastily round the room. Yes, it was tidy. Niall had dropped the ash on the floor. She rubbed it in the carpet with her foot.

"Come on, let's go and change," she said. "We can't crouch here like criminals."

"I feel rather ill," said Niall. "I have a chill coming on. Maria, can I have a tray in my room?"

"No," said Maria. "If anyone is going to have a tray upstairs it will be me."

"You neither of you need trays," said Celia. "You're both behaving like a couple of children. Maria, surely you are used to coping with a domestic crisis if Niall is not?"

"I'm not used to coping with anything," said Maria. "My path has always been made sweet for me."

"Then it's time you trod on a few thorns," said Celia. She opened the door and listened. There was silence in the dining room. Then the soft, gurgling sound of liquid being poured from a bottle into a glass decanter.

"It's Captain Hook," whispered Niall, "poisoning the medicine."

"No, it's my inside," whispered Maria. "It always does that at rehearsals. At about half-past twelve, when I'm getting hungry."

"It reminds me of that awful time we all went down to Coldhammer to stay with Charles's parents," said Celia, "just after Maria came back from the honeymoon. And Pappy told Lord Wyndham the wine was corked."

"Lady Wyndham though Freada was my mother," said Niall. "The whole thing was disaster from start to finish. Freada left the bathroom tap running. The water came through the ceiling to the room below."

"But of course I remember now," said Maria. "That's when it must have started. That's when it first began."

"When what started?" asked Celia.

"Why, Charles being jealous of Niall," said Maria.

CHAPTER SIXTEEN

WHEN people play the game "Name three or four persons whom you would choose to have with you on a desert island," they never choose the Delaneys. They don't even choose us one by one as individuals. We have earned, not always fairly, we consider, the reputation of being difficult guests. We hate staying in other people's houses. We detest the effort of plunging into a new routine. Houses that are not ours, or where we have staked no claim, are like doctors' houses, like dentists' waiting rooms, like the waiting rooms at stations; we do not belong.

We are unlucky too. We catch the wrong trains and arrive late for dinner. Soufflés are ruined. Or we hire cars and then have to ask if the driver can be put up in the village. All this causes a commotion. We stay up much too late at night, at least Niall does, especially if there is brandy, and in the morning we lie in bed until past twelve. The maids—if there are maids, and in the old days there used to be—never can get into our rooms.

We hate doing the things our host and hostess want us to do. We loathe meeting their friends. Round games, cards, are abhorrent to us, and conversation worst of all. The only possible way of spending a week end in another person's house is to feign illness and hide all day in bed, or else to creep away into the garden.

We are bad at tipping. And our clothes are always wrong. In fact, it is preferable never to stay away unless violently in love. Then, Niall said, it is always worth it, because of creeping along a passage at 3 A.M.

When Maria first married Charles she stayed with him in house parties for about a year, because she was still acting her part of being the Honourable Mrs. Charles Wyndham. But she never really enjoyed it. Not after the first few times of floating downstairs in evening dress. The men always stayed in the dining room far too long, and there would be that interminable business of talking to the women, who, with eager lips, plied her with questions on the theatre. In the daytime the men disappeared with guns, or dogs and horses, and because Maria could neither shoot nor ride, nor do anything at all, she would be left with the women once again. And that, to Maria, was hell.

Celia's problem would be a different one. People, finding her more sympathetic than either Niall or Maria, would pour out to her the story of their lives. "You have no idea what he does to me," and she would find herself involved in another person's troubles, her advice sought, her co-operation demanded, and it would be like a net closing round her from which there was no escape.

Everyone tried hard to behave well, that time at Coldhammer. It was one of those invitations that was given hurriedly, probably without real intention, at Maria's reception. The whole courtship and wedding had been a rush affair; the poor Wyndhams were bewildered, they had really had no time to sort out the Delaney brood. All that had sunk into their confused minds was that their beloved son had decided to marry the lovely, ethereal girl who was playing in the revival of *Mary Rose*, and she happened to be the daughter of Delaney, whose beautiful voice had always brought tears to Lady Wyndham's eyes.

"After all, the fellow is a gentleman," Lord Wyndham must have said.

"And she is such a darling," must have been the echo of his wife.

Lady Wyndham was tall and dignified, like an aristocratic hen, and her gracious manner had a curious frigidity about it, as though she had been dragooned into courtesy from birth. Maria declared that she was easy, and not a bit frightening; but when Maria said this Lady Wyndham had just given her a diamond bracelet and a pair of furs, and Maria was being starry-eyed as Mary Rose. Celia found Lady Wyndham forbidding and intense. She cornered Celia at the wedding reception and began to talk about the Thirty-nine Articles, which Celia, in the first moment of madness, thought was some reference to the objects found in Tutankhamen's tomb. Only later, when she questioned Maria, did she discover that Lady Wyndham's pet hobby horse was Prayer Book reform. Niall insisted that Lady Wyndham was perverted, and kept hidden in some secret closet, known only to herself, a riding whip and spurs.

Lord Wyndham was a bustling, busy little man, a great stickler for time. He was always dragging out a watch, with a huge fob and chain, and consulting the dial, and then comparing it with other clocks and muttering under his breath. He never sat down. He was eternally restless. His day was one long programme with every second filled.

Lady Wyndham called him "Dobbin," which was quite unsuitable. Perhaps it was this that had given Niall the idea about the riding whip and spurs.

"You must come down to Coldhammer directly Charles and Maria return from Scotland," Lady Wyndham said to Pappy, in the maelstrom of the wedding, and Maria, her small face hidden by an enormous bunch of lilies, said, "Yes, Pappy, please," not thinking what she was saying, not considering, in the excitement of the moment, that to see Pappy at Coldhammer would be like wandering in a bishop's rose garden and coming suddenly upon the naked Jove.

Dynamic and robust, Pappy mixed well with kings and queens—especially those in exile—and Italian noblemen and French countesses, and the more bohemian of what was termed London intelligentsia; but with the English "county"—and the Wyndhams were essentially "county"—Pappy seemed out of place. He was unaware of the fact. It was his family who suffered.

"But of course we will come to Coldhammer," said Pappy, who, towering above the other guests at the reception, dwarfed the assembly. "But I insist on sleeping in a four-poster bed. Can you produce one for me? I must sleep in a four-poster bed."

He had cried all through the wedding. Celia, on the return from the vestry, had to support him down the aisle. It might have been Maria's funeral. But now, at the reception, champagne had worked revival. He glowed with love for all. He kissed complete strangers. The remark about the four-poster was a jest to be tossed aside. Lady Wyndham treated it as serious.

"The Queen Anne suite has a four-poster," she said, "but the rooms face north, over the drive. The view from the south is so much better, especially when our *Prunus floribunda* is in flower."

Pappy laid his finger against his nose. Then he bent down to Lady Wyndham's ear.

"Keep your *Prunus floribunda* for others," he said in a loud whisper. "When I visit Coldhammer I expect only my hostess to be in flower."

Lady Wyndham remained unmoved. Not a flicker of understanding passed across her features.

"I am afraid you are no gardener," she said.

"No gardener!" protested Pappy. "Flowers are my passion. All things that grow in nature, my delight. When we were young, my wife and I used to wander barefoot in the meadows, sipping the dew from the lips of buttercups. I shall do it again, at Coldhammer. Celia shall wander with me. We will all wander together. How many of us do you invite? My stepson, Niall? My old love, Freada?"

He waved a vague hand that seemed, in its largesse, to embrace a dozen heads.

"Of course," said Lady Wyndham, "bring whom you wish. We have, at a pinch, put up eighteen. . . ."

A note of doubt crept into her voice. Aversion struggled with civility. As her eyes wandered towards Freada, wearing a more preposterous hat than usual, Niall knew she was trying to place the correct relationship among them all. Was Freada, then, a former wife and Niall her son? Or was everybody illegitimate? No matter. Let it pass. Manners came first. And Charles had married Maria, who at any rate seemed a sweet girl and so unspoilt.

"We shall be delighted," said Lady Wyndham, "to see the whole family. Shan't we, Dobbin?"

Lord Wyndham muttered something unintelligible and pulled out his watch.

"What are they doing?" he said. "They ought to go and change. That's the worst of these things. So much hanging about. Young people always will hang about." He eyed the clock on the wall. "Is that clock right?" Nobody answered.

And it was because of all this that the Delaneys found themselves at Coldhammer.

It was one of those large, imposing houses of indeterminate age, begun possibly before the Tudors and never finished. Wings had been thrown out from time to time. There were flights of steps at the front door, and pillars. The house was separated from the park into which it was plunged by a wide ditch, referred to by the Wyndhams as a "ha-ha." The pleasure grounds lay at the back of the house, southward, beyond a terrace. Maria used to wonder, after the first flush of excitement had died down, what pleasure had ever been obtained from them. There were too many winding paths, raked by assiduous gardeners, and the formal yew hedges, blanketing the view, were clipped every few yards or so into the tortured shapes of cocks. Nothing grew au naturel. Everything was planned. Two roaring lions of stone flanked the terrace on either side, their mouths wide open in a perpetual snarl. Even the spinney, the only possible walk on a wet day, and which looked in the distance like a Rackham drawing, was spoilt in the centre by a lily pond that had no business to be there, beside which squatted a great toad in lead.

"The first thing I can remember in life is that old toad," said Charles, the first time he had taken Maria to Coldhammer, touching it affectionately with his foot. And Maria, pretending to admire it, thought with sudden guilt that it bore an unfortunate, and rather malignant, likeness to Lord Wyndham himself. When Niall came he noticed it at once.

"Old clothes for the country," Pappy said before the visit, "old clothes are always best. A man who goes down to the country in a London suit deserves to be blackballed from his club."

"But not that cardigan darned with my stockings," protested Celia. "And those pyjama trousers have no seat."

"I shall be alone in the four-poster," said Pappy, "unless her ladyship deigns to visit me. What are the odds?"

"A hundred to one against," said Celia. "Unless something happens, like a fire. Pappy, not that tie. It's far too red."

"I must have colour," said Pappy, "colour is all. A red tie with a tweed jacket is correct, my darling. It strikes the casual note. Let us, at all costs, be casual."

He had too much luggage. One suitcase was entirely filled with medicines. Enos, cinnamon, Vapex, Taxel, friar's balsam, even syringes and rubber tubes. "You never know, my darling," said Pappy. "I may be taken ill. I may have to stay at Coldhammer for months, with two nurses, night and day."

"But why, Pappy? We're only going for a night."

"When I pack," said Pappy, "I pack for all eternity."

And he shouted to André to bring up a malacca cane, presented to him once by the Lord Mayor; and a Hawaiian shirt and straw sandals in case of a heat wave. Also a volume of Shakespeare and an unabridged edition of the *Decameron*, illustrated by an unknown Frenchman.

"Old Wyndham might like this," said Pappy. "I ought to take a present to old Wyndham. I paid five pounds for this at Bumpus yesterday."

It was decided to hire a car for the occasion, because everybody could not fit into Pappy's car. Not with the luggage.

And Pappy made the fatal mistake of buying a cap. He was convinced that because he sported a tweed suit he must wear a cap. The cap was new. It looked it. Not only did it look new, it looked common. It gave Pappy the appearance of a giant costermonger on Easter Monday.

"It came from Scott's," said Pappy. "It can't be common."

He planted the cap firmly on his head and took up his stance beside the driver, with an enormous map upon his knees giving none of the roads that mattered, but every bridle path in the immediate Coldhammer country. He argued the course of direction during the full seventy miles of the drive. The fact that his map was eighteenth-century did not fluster him.

If Pappy had brought too much in the way of suitcases, Freada had erred to the opposite extremity and had brought too few.

Her belongings were packed in paper parcels, and she had a sack, like a postman's, thrown over her shoulder, in which was wrapped an evening dress. She and Niall had come over to London for the wedding, intending to stay two nights, and had stayed four weeks, and neither of them had bothered to buy suitcases. It was only when they were ready to start for Coldhammer that Niall had misgivings.

Freada was overdressed. Her long silk frock was striped, increasing her height, and she wore the large picture hat that she had bought for the wedding. White gloves, to the elbow, suggested a royal garden party.

"What's the matter? What's wrong?" she said to Niall.

"I don't know," he said. "I think it's the hat."

She whipped it off. But they had done her hair badly at the hairdresser's. The man had been careless with the dye, and it was much too bright. Niall said nothing, but Freada understood.

"I know," she said, "that's why I've got to wear the hat."

"What about tonight?" said Niall. "When we change for dinner?"

"Tulle," said Freada briefly, "thrown round my head. I can tell Lady Wyndham it's the latest fashion in Paris."

"Whatever happens," said Niall, "we must not let Maria down. We must remember, this is Maria's show."

He began biting his nails. He was nervous. The thought of seeing Maria again as a month-old bride distressed him. Living in Paris, living with Freada, knowing sudden unexpected success with his catch-penny tunes counted as nothing.

The ease of manner that had come to him had vanished. The Niall Delaney who was run after in Paris, and spoilt and petted, was nothing but a boy again with jittery hands.

"We've got to remember," he repeated, "that though all this Coldhammer business seems false as hell to us, it's terribly important to Maria."

"Who says it's false?" said Freada. "I have the greatest respect for English country life. Stop biting your nails."

She walked down the steps to the waiting car, swinging the post-man's bag, and the long white gloves came right above her elbows.

The party had been asked to arrive in time for lunch. Luncheon, Lady Wyndham called it. Luncheon at one-fifteen. "But come about twelve-thirty," she had said in her letter, "which will give you time to settle in."

Because of Pappy's eighteenth-century map, the car took a wrong turning after leaving Hyde Park Corner. There was no question of anybody settling in. The car did not arrive at Coldhammer until five minutes past two. Celia was in agony.

"We must pretend we have lunched," she said. "They will have given us up. We can't possibly ask for lunch now. Maria can get us some biscuits during the afternoon."

"What do you take me for, a hound?" said Pappy, peering round at her from the front seat of the car, his spectacles on his nose. "I haven't driven all this way to eat biscuits. Coldhammer is one of the stately homes of England. I intend to eat, and to eat well, my darling. Ah! What did I tell you?" He leant forward and nudged the driver as the car bumped suddenly in a narrow lane. "This is one of the bridle paths. It's marked quite clearly on the map."

He brandished the map in the air, tremendously excited. Freada opened her eyes and yawned.

"Are we nearly there?" she said. "How wonderful the country smells. We ought to ask Lady Wyndham to let us sleep on the lawn. I wonder if they could produce camp beds."

Niall did not answer. He was feeling sick. He always felt sick in the back of a car. It was one of those wretched things that he had not yet outgrown. Presently the car came to a standstill before a pair of wrought-iron gates. Two columns stood at either side, and on top of the columns a pair of stone griffons rampant.

"This must be it," said Pappy, still following an eighteenth-century coach road on the map. "Look at the griffons, Celia darling. They may be historical. I must ask old Wyndham. Sound the horn, driver."

The driver sounded the horn. He had aged years during the drive of seventy miles. A woman came running from the lodge and opened wide the gates. The car swept through. Pappy bowed to her from the window.

"A nice touch, that," he said. "Probably an old retainer. Been with the Wyndhams for years. Dandled Charles upon her knee. I must find out her name. Always a good thing to know these people's names."

The drive wound across the park towards the house that stood blank and impassive at the far end.

"Adams," said Pappy promptly. "Doric columns."

"Don't you mean Kent?" said Freada.

"Kent and Adams," said Pappy generously.

The car swerved in a circle and drew up before the grey façade. Maria and Charles were waiting, with linked arms, upon the steps. There were far too many dogs, all of different breeds.

Maria broke away from Charles and ran down the steps to open the car. Her natural feelings were too strong for her, after all, and she could not keep up the *Tatler* pose that she had planned. She had been standing on the steps, the dogs grouped about her, for nearly two hours.

"You're terribly late. What happened to you?" she said.

Her voice sounded high-pitched and unnatural, and Niall guessed, from the expression on her face that he knew so well, that she was as nervous as he was himself. Only Pappy remained unperturbed.

"My darling," he said. "My beautiful," and he stepped out of the car, scattering rugs, cushions, walking sticks, and volumes of Shakespeare onto the drive, while the dogs barked furiously.

Charles, with the quiet firm manner of one used to dealing with disciplined men, began explaining to the driver, who was on the verge of a breakdown, the best approach to the garage in the stable yard.

"Leave everything in the car," said Maria, her voice still high. "Vaughan will deal with it. Vaughan knows where it all has to go."

Vaughan was the footman. He stood to attention behind Maria.

"What a disappointment," said Freada, a shade too loud. "I hoped the servants would be powdered. A fine-looking creature all the same."

She stepped out of the car, but, in doing so, her heel caught in a piece of loose rubber on the running board, and she fell full length at the footman's feet, her arms spread wide as in a swallow dive.

"That was effective," said Pappy. "Do it again."

Vaughan and Charles assisted Freada to her feet. Smiling broadly with a cut lip and laddered stockings, she assured them both that to fall on entering a strange house spelt good luck to the owners.

"But your lip is bleeding," said Pappy, his interest quickening. "Where is that case of medicines?"

He turned to the boot of the car to fumble for his luggage.

"I don't think it's much," said Charles, proffering his handkerchief with Raleigh courtesy. "Just a scratch at the corner."

"But, my dear fellow, she might get lockjaw," said Pappy. "Never neglect a scratch. I heard of a man in Sydney who got lockjaw within twenty-four hours. He died in agony, bent backwards like a hoop." In a fever he began throwing the luggage onto the drive. His medicine case was at the bottom. "Ah! I have it," he said. "Iodine. Never travel without iodine. But the lip must be washed first. Charles, where can Freada wash? It is imperative that Freada should wash."

Lord Wyndham advanced to the top of the steps, his watch in his hand.

"Glad to see you. Glad to see you," he muttered, his face set in hard, grim lines. "We feared an accident. Luncheon is just going in. Shall we eat at once? The time is exactly eight and a half minutes past two."

"Let Freada wash afterwards," whispered Celia. "Lockjaw can't act as swiftly as all that. We're keeping everybody waiting."

"I also wish to wash," said Pappy loudly. "Unless I wash now it will mean leaving the luncheon table after the first course."

As the group swept up the steps and past the pillars into the house,

189

Niall glanced back over his shoulder to the car. He saw Vaughan staring at the postman's bag.

It was after half-past two when the party finally settled down into their seats in the large, square dining room. Pappy, on Lady Wyndham's right, talked without ceasing. Celia felt this was a great relief to Lady Wyndham, who wore upon her face the haunted, abstract expression of the hostess who knows that the menu she ordered the day before with confidence has been thrown completely out of gear.

She sat at the head of the table, watching her butler and his assistant hand the dishes, and her guests eating what was before them, much as the uneasy producer of a play watches his team of actors in a rehearsal that has started ill.

Freada, on Lord Wyndham's left, had launched into a discussion on Swedish pewter that was to prove abortive. She had noticed an old tankard on a console table in the far corner of the room, but Lord Wyndham refused to be drawn.

"Swedish?" he muttered. "Possibly. I've no idea. It may be Swedish. Can't say I care very much whether it's Swedish or Japanese. The tankard has always stood there since I was a boy. Probably before."

Niall was watching Maria, who, having recovered her equanimity now that the party was settled, was busy playing the Honourable Mrs. Charles. Because she was the bride she sat, as guest of honour, on Lord Wyndham's right. A Wyndham relative or neighbour, with a sandy, bushy moustache, sat on her left.

"But you're coming to us for Ascot, aren't you?" Maria was saying. "Oh, but you must. We have a box. Leila will be with us, and Bobby Lavington, and we have the Hopton-D'Arcys coming over with their party from Windsor. Did you know that Charles and I are moving into our house at Richmond in two weeks' time? It's Regency. We're mad about it. Father and Mother have been so sweet. We're having some of the lovely stuff from here to help furnish it."

She put out her hand affectionately to Lord Wyndham, who muttered something under his breath. Father and Mother. She called the Wyndhams Father and Mother. "We think it's so right," Maria went on, "to be just on the fringe of London. Then we can see all our friends."

She caught Niall's eye and looked away hurriedly, crumbling a piece of bread. She had done her hair in a new way. It was a little longer than before, caught up and swept behind her ears. And she was thinner in the face. She looked lovelier, Niall thought, than she had ever done; the vague blue of her dress took on the colour of her eyes, and because she knew Niall was watching her she lifted her chin in an arrogant, half-defensive manner and began talking even louder than before about the plans for Ascot. He loved her so much that it hurt, and he could not eat. And he wanted to hit her very, very hard.

Lunch over, at a quarter to four, an intolerable lethargy stole upon the house party, but Pappy, mellow with port and Stilton cheese, announced his firm intention of seeing every inch of Coldhammer, from the attics to the kitchens. "Not forgetting the grounds," he said, waving his hands towards the terrace, "the farmeries, the piggeries, the stillrooms, the venison chambers. I must see all."

"The Home Farm is quite three miles from the house," said Lady Wyndham, her eye searching her husband's, "and there has never been any deer at Coldhammer. I think possibly that, if we put off tea till five, you would have time for a stroll round the pleasure grounds as far as the spinney. That is, unless Dobbin has arranged something else?"

Her glance wavered from her husband towards the butler. A flash of understanding, like a secret code, passed between them. Celia knew that this meant "tea at five," although the words did not frame themselves on Lady Wyndham's lips.

"Too late to follow my arrangements now," snapped Lord Wyndham. "According to my arrangements, we should have done the pleasure grounds by three o'clock. At a quarter to four we were to have driven to see the view from Beacon Hill of the three counties, above Huntsman's Folly."

"Huntsman's Folly? That sounds like folklore and fairies," said Freada. "Can't we visit it tonight, by moonlight? It might be just what you want, Niall, for that ghost dance you were planning."

"It's only a broken piece of wall," said Lady Wyndham. "I don't think it would inspire anyone to dance. Perhaps in the morning, though, if you wish to see the view . . ."

Lord Wyndham compared his watch with the clock on the drawing-room mantelpiece, and Lady Wyndham seized a sunshade. Grim, determined, suffering, with the faces of crusaders, they led us all out onto the terrace, with Pappy in the van wearing his new tweed cap and brandishing his malacca cane.

The day dragged on to evening. The exhaustion of the walk to the spinney and the tour of the house was followed by tea, heavy and indigestible, and the arrival of more guests who had been bidden for this meal only. Pappy, who never touched tea, began to feel the need of stimulant. Celia caught his eye and watched it rove towards the dining room. The question was, how well did he know Charles? Would Charles prove helpful? Or would asking for a whiskey at a quarter to six look odd, coming from the father of the bride? There was a flask upstairs, of course, in case of high emergency, but a pity to touch that too soon. Celia knew all these thoughts were passing through Pappy's mind. She moved over to the window by Maria and pulled her sleeve.

"I know Pappy wants a drink," she whispered. "Is there any hope?" Maria looked anxious.

"It won't go awfully well," she whispered back. "They never have anything here until just before dinner, and then it's always sherry. Didn't he bring his flask?"

"Yes. But he might want that for later."

Maria nodded. "I'll try to get hold of Charles," she said.

Charles was nowhere to be seen. Maria had to go to look for him. Celia's anxiety mounted. Pappy would never hang on until after six. He was like a baby with a bottle. He had to keep to his regular time for his whiskey or his whole system became disorganised.

Presently Charles appeared again with Maria. He went over to Pappy and bent his head in furtive consultation. The two of them left the drawing room together. Celia sighed with relief. There must be a kind of freemasonry among men about these things.

"Your father has not touched his tea," said Lady Wyndham. "He has let it go quite cold. Shall I pour it away and order fresh? Where has he gone?"

"I think Charles is showing him the pictures in the dining room," said Celia.

"There is nothing very good to see in there," said Lady Wyndham. "If it's the Winterhalter he wanted to look at, it's at the head of the stairs, and the light is just wrong for pictures at the moment."

Her duties at the tea tray kept her from pursuit, and soon Pappy came back into the drawing room, bland innocence upon his face.

The dressing gong sounded at a quarter to seven, and with relief the weary guests, and their hosts as well, sought sanctuary within their rooms. Niall flung himself on his bed and lit a cigarette. The need of it at that moment was like cocaine to a drug fiend. He had smoked below, but smoking below was not like smoking alone in an empty room.

Scarcely had he closed his eyes than there came a cautious tap on his door. It was Freada.

"I can't find my clothes," she said. "I've got an enormous bedroom like something at Versailles, but not a sign of any paper parcels or the postman's bag. Dare I ring?"

"Yes," said Niall. "But not in here. You're not supposed to come into my room."

"That's all right," said Freada. "They all think I'm your mother. I'm Pappy's divorced wife. It's terribly confusing, but it serves."

"I think it's rather shocking," said Niall. "Why must you be anything?"

"These people like a tag for everything," said Freada. "Be a lamb and go down to look for the postman's bag. It must be somewhere. I want to have a bath. I have an amazing bathroom, with a step beside the bath. And there are prints by Marcus Stone all round the room. True emblems of the Victorian age. I love this sort of house."

Niall did not have the courage to ring the bell. Nor to question the servants. He finally discovered the postman's bag in the downstairs cloakroom, standing discreetly beside several bags of golf clubs.

As he carried it upstairs Lord Wyndham, dressed for dinner and looking at his watch, came out upon the landing.

"Dinner in fifteen minutes," he muttered. "You have exactly fifteen minutes in which to change. What do you want to do with that sack?"

"It has something in it," said Niall. "It's rather precious."

"Ferrets, did you say?" snapped Lord Wyndham. "We never allow ferrets in the house. Ring for Vaughan. Vaughan will take them."

"No, sir," said Niall, "precious. Something rather precious belonging to—my mother." He bowed his way backwards along the passage. Lord Wyndham stared after him. "Extraordinary youth," he muttered. "Composer . . . Paris. All alike." He hurried down the stairs to compare his watch with the clocks below.

Freada's bathroom was full of steam. She was standing up in the bath, singing loudly, soaping herself all over. She uttered a cry of triumph at the sight of the postman's bag.

193

"Good for you," she said. "Hang it up on the door, pet, will you? The steam will take out the creases. I found the paper parcels. They had all been put in one drawer at the bottom of the wardrobe."

"You'd better buck up," said Niall. "We've only a quarter of an hour left before dinner."

"I'm revelling in this soap," said Freada. "It's Brown Windsor. A good, old-fashioned brand. I shall take it back with me. They'll never miss it. Give my back a scrub, angel, between the shoulder blades."

Niall attacked her with her battered loofah, and she turned on the hot and cold taps together so that the water gushed like fountains.

"Let's have our money's worth of water," said Freada. "I know when we get back to Paris we shall find that damn tap has died on us. The concierge will never think of seeing to it."

"There, will that do for you?" said Niall, shaking his cuffs. "I must go and change. I shall be terribly late."

He went back into Freada's bedroom, wiping his eyes because of the steam. The running water had prevented them both from hearing the tap on the door. Lady Wyndham, in black velvet, stood on the threshold.

"I beg your pardon," she said. "I understood from my maid that there was some misunderstanding about your—your mother's luggage."

"It's all right," swallowed Niall. "I found it."

"Hoi!" shouted Freada from the bath. "Bring me my towel, baby, from the chair, before you go. I've half a mind to pinch that too. The Wyndhams must have towels galore."

Not a muscle moved on the face of Lady Wyndham. But there was a strange, baffled look at the back of her eyes.

"Then your mother has everything she wants?" said Lady Wyndham.

"Yes," said Niall.

"In that case I'll leave you both to dress," said Lady Wyndham. "Your room, as I think you know, is on the other corridor."

She moved away, majestic, forbidding, just as Freada, stark and dripping, pattered with wet feet into the bedroom.

None of the Delaneys was on time for dinner. Even Maria, who should have known better, floated downstairs some ten minutes after the gong had sounded. Her excuse was a new dress from her trousseau that fastened in some curious fashion from the back. And Charles, she said, had clumsy hands and could not hook her up. Niall felt this story to be fabrication. Had he been in Charles's place, Maria would never have been hooked at all. Nor would they have dined. . . .

Pappy, with heightened colour and black tie a trifle crooked, betrayed the fact to his immediate family that the sustenance between tea and dinner had not proved sufficient to carry him through, and he had been forced to have access to his flask. His smile was broad and tolerant. Celia watched him like a young mother uncertain of the behaviour of her child. The fact that she had forgotten to pack her evening shoes did not worry her. Her bedroom slippers were mules and must suffice. So long as Pappy behaved himself, nothing mattered.

Freada made her entry last. Not with intention, because she was without vanity of any sort, but because the winding of the tulle about her hair had taken time. The effect was a little startling and not what she had intended. It was like the flight into Egypt by an indifferent primitive. Lord Wyndham snapped his watch as she arrived.

"Twenty-three and a half minutes after eight," he muttered.

The party filed into the dining room in silence, and Freada, who always lit a cigarette with her soup, lacked the courage to do so for the first time in her life.

It was Pappy whose warm, genial voice, always more Irish in intonation at this hour of the evening than at any other time, broke in above the icy trickle of conversation soon after the fish was served and the champagne had been poured into the glasses.

"I'm sorry to distress you, my dear fellow," he called down the table to his host, "but I have a pronouncement to make. The fact of the matter is your champagne is corked."

There was instant silence.

"Corked? Corked?" said Lord Wyndham. "It should not be corked. It has no business to be corked." The butler hurried to his side in consternation. "Never touch the stuff myself," said Lord Wyndham. "My doctor won't allow it. Who else says the champagne is corked? Charles? What is wrong with the champagne? We must not have it corked."

Everyone tasted the champagne. No one knew what to say. To

agree with Pappy seemed impolite to Lord Wyndham. To disagree made Pappy seem a cad. Fresh bottles were brought. Fresh glasses handed round. We waited in agony while Pappy tasted his.

"I'd say this was corked too," he said, his head a little on one side. "It must be a dud case. You must wire your wine merchant on Monday morning. He has no business to palm you off with corked champagne."

"Take it away," snapped Lord Wyndham to his butler. "We'll drink hock." The glasses were all removed for the second time.

Celia gazed steadfastly at her plate. Niall concentrated upon the silver candlesticks. And Maria, the bride, forgot about being the Honourable Mrs. Charles Wyndham and relapsed once more into her role of Mary Rose. She sat listening to her voices. . . .

"I think a little music would be very soothing," said Lady Wyndham after dinner, a note of real sincerity creeping into her voice, and Niall, fortified by hock, escaped to the piano at the far end of the drawing room. And now, he thought, it really does not matter very much what happens. I can do what I like, play what I like; nobody cares, nobody wants to listen, they all want to forget the agony of dinner. This is really where I come into my own, because my sort of music is like a drug to sap the senses, and old Lord Wyndham with his clicking watch can beat time if he cares to; it will take away the memory of the corked champagne. Lady Wyndham can shut her eyes and think of tomorrow's programme. Pappy can go to sleep. Freada can kick her shoes off under the sofa. Celia can relax. The other people can dance or not as they damn well please, and Maria can hear the songs I write for her that she will never sing.

It was no longer the stiff drawing room at Coldhammer, but any piano in any room where he might be alone. He went on playing, and there was no sound but the sound of Niall's music, which was dance music different from any other. There was something savage about it and something sweet; it was partly foreign and partly sad, and whether you liked it or not, thought Maria, you wanted to dance; you wanted to dance more than anything in the world.

She leant against the piano watching him, and she was not the Honourable Mrs. Charles Wyndham or Mary Rose or any other character she had thought out on the spur of the moment; she was Maria, and Niall knew this as he played, and he laughed because they were together now and he was happy.

196

Celia looked at them both, and then at Pappy, who had fallen asleep in his chair, and suddenly she heard a voice beside her say softly, and with infinite regret: "I would give everything in the world to possess that gift. How lucky he is. He will never know how lucky." It was Charles. And he was staring across the long drawing room at Niall and Maria.

It was close on midnight when we all dispersed to bed. The music had done what the hostess had demanded. Everyone was soothed, except the player. He alone would not sleep with deep content.

"Come and see my room," said Maria, coming out onto the corridor in her nightgown as he was passing by the door on the way to the bathroom. "It's panelled. It has a carved ceiling." She took his hand and pulled him inside the room.

"It's lovely, isn't it?" she said. "Look at that moulding over the fireplace." Niall looked. He cared nothing about moulding.

"Are you happy?" he said.

"Madly," said Maria. She tied a blue ribbon round her hair. "I'm going to have a baby," she said. "You're the first person I've told. Except Charles, of course."

"Are you sure?" said Niall. "It's a bit soon, isn't it? You've only been married a month."

"It must have happened bang off at once, in Scotland," said Maria. "It sometimes does, you know. It's smart, isn't it? Like royalty."

"Why royalty?" said Niall. "Why not a young cat with kittens?"

"I think it's like royalty," said Maria.

She climbed into bed and patted the pillows.

"Does it make you feel any different?" asked Niall.

"No, not really. A bit sick, that's all," said Maria. "And I have funny little blue veins all over my top. Look."

She shook her nightdress off her shoulders, and he saw what she meant. Pale blue veins stood out clearly on her small white breasts.

"How queer," said Niall. "I wonder if that always happens."

"I don't know," said Maria. "It rather spoils them, doesn't it?"

"Yes, I think it does," said Niall.

Just then Charles came into the room from his dressing room. He stood staring, while Maria pulled her nightdress up again with unconcern.

"Niall was just saying good night," said Maria.

"So I see," said Charles.

197

"Good night," said Niall. He went out of the room, shutting the door behind him.

He felt very wide awake and very hungry, but it would be simpler to eat the furniture in his room than to creep downstairs and seek out the mysteries of the Coldhammer larders. It was always possible, of course, that Freada, knowing his habits, had secreted the rolls from dinner in her evening bag and had them hidden at the moment under her pillow. Niall turned along the corridor towards Freada's room, but at the top of the staircase he found his way barred by Lady Wyndham. More formidable than ever in a quilted dressing gown, and grey with fatigue, she was in consultation with two housemaids who carried cloths and pails.

"Your mother left the taps running in the bathroom," she said to Niall. "The water has overflowed, of course, and seeped down into the library below."

"I'm terribly sorry," said Niall. "How very careless of her. Is there anything I can do?"

"Nothing," said Lady Wyndham, "nothing at all. We have done what we can for the moment. The men must see to it in the morning." She disappeared towards her own apartments, followed by the housemaids.

At least one thing is certain, thought Niall as he crept to Freada's door, and that is that none of the Delaneys will be asked again. Except Maria. Maria will go on coming to Coldhammer week after week, month after month, until she dies, a dowager, in that bed.

He did not knock on Freada's door. He went and felt under the pillow. Yes, she had remembered. There were two rolls there and a large banana. He began to unpeel the banana, silently, in the darkness.

"You know what you've done?" he said to Freada.

But she was nearly asleep. She yawned and turned her back.

"I sopped up most of it with my evening dress," she said. "I gave the tulle to the housemaid. She was pleased."

Niall finished his banana.

"Freada."

"What?"

"Does it hurt very much to have a baby?"

"It depends upon the hips," she murmured, heavy with sleep. "They must be wide."

Niall threw the banana skin under the bed and composed himself for sleep. But sleep eluded him. He kept wondering about Maria's hips.

At three in the morning a crash in the corridor brought him to the door. Pappy could not sleep either. Not for the same reason. Disturbed by Lord Wyndham's staircase clock, he had tried to stop it, forcing back the hands, and the pane of glass lay shattered at his feet.

CHAPTER SEVENTEEN

THE nurse had left everything prepared. There was nothing Maria had to do or to find; all was put ready for her. There were four lots of napkins ready folded on the towel horse before the fire, the Harrington squares inside the turkish towel, and new pins to go with each. The feeds were mixed ready in the bottles, and the only thing to be done, said the nurse, was to stand the bottles in hot water for a few minutes, and they would reach the required heat. If Caroline was restless during the afternoon sleep, then she should be allowed a little drop of water in another smaller bottle. But she would not be restless. She always slept. At five o'clock she could lie awake and kick for half an hour or so; she always enjoyed this, it would be good for her limbs. "And I will try to be back soon after ten," said the nurse. "It's just a matter of getting onto that bus, and whether I can see my mother off safely on the train."

And she had gone. Out of reach, out of sight, the heartless, damnable woman, just because she had to see her wretched mother who had been ill, and Maria was left with Caroline for the first time, alone.

Charles was away. It would happen that Charles was away. There was some idiotic dinner near Coldhammer that he had to attend which Maria was certain could not be of the slightest importance; but Charles had firm principles about these things, a promise was a promise, he must never let people down. And he had gone off quite early in the morning in the car. Celia, who should have been available, also begged to be excused.

"I can't come, Maria," she said on the telephone. "I have an appointment that I must keep. Besides, Pappy isn't very well."

"How can you keep an appointment if Pappy isn't well?" protested Maria.

"Because it's quite handy," said Celia. "It's only a matter of taking a taxi to Bloomsbury. But to come out to you at Richmond would take the entire day."

Maria rang off in a temper. It was really very selfish of Celia. If only the nurse had given her longer warning, she could have wired to Truda. Truda could have come from the little cottage where she lived now in retirement at Mill Hill and spent the day. The only thing was that Truda was so crippled with rheumatism, she might have made an excuse as well. Everybody made excuses. Nobody would put themselves out to help Maria. She looked out of her bedroom window and saw with relief that there was no movement within the white pram. The pram was motionless. With any luck the pram would remain motionless until after lunch.

Maria set her hair in pins and looked at the new photographs. Dorothy Wilding had really done them proud. Charles looked a little stiff, and his jaw seemed heavier than it was in reality, but they were the best of herself for a long while, and with Caroline in her arms looking up at her and smiling, the whole effect was really very good. "The Honourable Mrs. Charles Wyndham at home. Mrs. Wyndham was, before her marriage last year, the well-known actress Maria Delaney." Why *was*? Why put her in the past tense? Why insinuate that Maria Delaney did not exist any more? It came as quite a shock to her when she read the lines in the *Tatler*. She had shown them to Charles with irritation.

"Look at this," she said. "Anyone would think that I had given up the stage."

"Haven't you?" he said after a moment or two.

She stared back at him, puzzled.

"Why, what do you mean?" she said.

He was tidying his desk at the time, putting his pens straight, and his letters.

"Nothing," he said. "It does not matter." He went on straightening things, rummaging in pigeonholes.

"Of course I couldn't act when I was having a baby," said Maria, "but people send me plays all the time. People are always ringing up.

Surely you didn't think——" She stopped, because she realised suddenly that she did not know what Charles did think. She had never asked him. It had not occurred to her. Nor had it seemed important.

"The old man is getting rather frail," said Charles. "By rights we ought to be more often down at Coldhammer. I'm not entirely happy about being here at Richmond. There's too much to do down there."

Too much to do . . . That was the agony of Coldhammer. There was nothing to do. Nothing, that was to say, for Maria. It was all right for Charles. It was his home, it was his life, he never seemed to have a moment free when he was there.

"I thought you loved this house," said Maria.

"I do," said Charles. "I love it because I love you, and it's the first home we've had together, and Caroline was born here, but I think we ought to face up to the fact that it's temporary. One of these days my job will be looking after Coldhammer. And you will have to help me."

"You mean when your father dies?" said Maria.

"He may live for many years. That's not quite the point," said Charles. "The point is that he's going to depend on me more and more every year. However much I enjoy fooling around up in London —and to be perfectly candid, I think it's a waste of time, and I despise myself when I do it—I know in my heart that I ought to be at Coldhammer. Not necessarily in the house, but somewhere handy. That house that Lutyens designed—Farthings—on the edge of the estate, would suit us well. I could get hold of it any time. Don't you remember you admired it the other day?"

"Did I?" said Maria vaguely.

And then she had turned away and started talking about something else. The conversation savoured too much of crisis. Crisis was always something to avoid. But sitting alone, this morning, she was reminded of the conversation once again. Richmond was the right distance out of London. Half an hour and she could be at any theatre. Charles picking her up every evening, and they would be home soon after half-past eleven. It was nothing.

Coldhammer was nearly eighty miles from London. To motor up and down from Coldhammer would be out of the question. The train service was rotten. Charles must surely see that, once she started acting again, she would have to be near London. Was it possible that Charles hoped, in his secret heart, that she would not want to act again? Did he picture her enthroned in Farthings, or some other place handy to the estate, doing the things that other wives did, the wives of his friends? Content to order meals, potter about a house, take Caroline for walks when the nurse was out, give little dinners, talk about gardens? Did he expect her, in point of fact, to settle down? That was the word for it. There was no other word. Settle down. Charles hoped to lure her down to Coldhammer to settle down. The house at Richmond was nothing but a bribe, a sop to quiet her. The house at Richmond was part of the process of breaking her in. Right from the start, Charles had never intended the Richmond house to be anything else. She remembered how vague he had always been about the future. She had been vague too. But purposely. Had she been vague because she was afraid? Had she been vague because in her heart she feared that had she said to Charles when they became engaged, "There is no question of my giving up my life for yours," he might have said, "Well, in that case . . ."?

Anyway, better not think about it. Better put it out of her mind. These things, if left alone, would sort themselves out. Charles loved her. She loved Charles. Nothing could go wrong. Besides, she had always got her own way. People and events had a fashion of shaping themselves to suit her. She put away the Dorothy Wilding photographs and picked up the morning paper. There was a paragraph about Niall: "This brilliant young man . . ." And going on to say that everyone would be humming the songs he had written for the new revue due to open in London in two weeks' time. The revue had been a wild success in Paris. "Delaney's stepson, who is half French, has helped to adapt the revue for the English stage. He speaks French like a native." Quite untrue, thought Maria. Niall could jabber very fluently for five minutes with a perfect accent, and then his mind would go blank and he forgot everything. Niall had probably done very little work on the revue, if any. Freada would have done it all.

Niall would have thought of the tunes. Somebody else would have written them down. There was a rehearsal going on probably at this minute. A quarter to twelve. Niall would be playing the piano, making jokes, preventing everybody from doing any work. When the producer got annoyed Niall would become bored and leave them to it, and go upstairs to that funny room at the top and play another piano, all by himself. If the producer telephoned to him to come down he would say that he was not interested, or he was much too busy thinking out another song for the finale, a better one.

"You may get away with that sort of thing in Paris," Maria told him, "but I don't think you will over here. People will say you're insufferable. That you're terribly conceited."

"What if they do?" said Niall. "It doesn't worry me. I don't care a damn about writing songs anyway. I can always go and live in a hut on a cliff."

Because they wanted his songs so badly he was allowed to get away with it. They had given him this room at the top of the theatre, and he lived there. He did as he pleased. Even Freada was not with him. Freada had stayed behind in Paris. . . .

"It's fun," Niall had told Maria. "I like it. If I want anyone here to supper, I ask them. If I don't, I don't. I go out when I please. I come back when I please. Don't you envy me?" And he had looked at her with those queer, penetrating eyes of his that saw too much, and she had turned away, pretending to yawn.

"Why should I envy you? I love living at Richmond."

"Do you?"

"Of course I do. It's wonderful, being married. You ought to try it."

He had laughed at her and had gone on playing the piano.

The paper was right about one thing, anyway. The tunes he had written for this tiresome revue were maddening, insistent; you could not forget them for one single moment. Once you heard them, you went on humming them all the time, throughout the day, until they nearly drove you crazy. The trouble was, thought Maria, that when the time came to dance to them, she would be dancing with Charles. And Charles was a stolid, safe dancer, steering you rather as he might steer a little ship through shoal water, an anxious eye to the bumps of other dancers. Whereas Niall . . . Dancing with Niall had always been like dancing with yourself. You moved, and he followed. Or rather, he moved and you followed. Or was it that you both thought of the same moves at precisely the same moment? And anyway, why think about Niall? Maria sat down at her desk and wrote her letters. There were some bills which she paid with the money Charles allowed her. Then a duty letter to her mother-in-law. Another duty letter to some dull people who had asked Charles and her to stay if they were ever in Norfolk. Why should they ever be in Norfolk? A third letter accepting the invitation to open a bazaar at a village three miles from Coldhammer in the spring.

She did not mind opening a bazaar. It was right for the Honourable

Mrs. Charles Wyndham to open bazaars. The only thing was that in a way it would be more fun, and she could get more amusing people to attend, and certainly more money, if she opened the bazaar as Maria Delaney. Perhaps it was rather disloyal to think that. Perhaps it would be better not to think of it at all. "Dear Vicar," she began, "I shall be delighted to open your bazaar on April fifteenth . . ."

And then it happened. The first wail from the pram.

For a moment or two Maria took no notice. Perhaps it would stop. Perhaps it was only wind. She went on writing, pretending she had not heard. The wail grew louder. And it was not a windy wail. It was the angry, roaring wail of a baby very much awake. Maria heard footsteps on the stairs, followed by a tap on the door.

"Come in," she said. She put on her busy, preoccupied face.

"Please, m'm," said the young housemaid. "Baby is awake."

"That's all right, thank you," said Maria. "I was just going down to her."

She got up from the desk and went downstairs, humming, hoping the housemaid would hear and think to herself, Mrs. Wyndham knows how to manage Baby.

She went to the pram and peered down into the depths.

"Now, now, what is all this about?" she said sternly.

Caroline was red in the face with anger and struggling to raise herself from her pillow. She was a strong child. The nurse said proudly it was most unusual for so young a child to try to raise herself in this way. Why be proud? wondered Maria. Surely it would be more restful for the nurse if Caroline had been a little quiet baby, content and placid on her back.

"Now, now," said Maria. "I can't have this, you know." She lifted up Caroline and patted her back, in case she had wind. The usual hiccough followed. Ah, then it was wind. What a relief. Maria put her back again in the pram and tucked in the rug. Then she went back again into the house. But even as she walked upstairs she could hear that the crying had begun again. She resolved to take no notice. She sat down again to her letters. But it was difficult to concentrate. The crying became louder and louder, with a strange high-pitched violence to the note.

The housemaid tapped once more upon the door. "Baby's off again, m'm," she said.

"I know," said Maria. "There's nothing the matter with her. It's good for her to cry." The housemaid left the room, and Maria could hear her say something to the parlourmaid downstairs.

What was she saying? "Poor little mite," in all probability. Or, "She had no right to have a baby if she don't know how to look after it." Which was very unfair. She did know how to look after the baby. If the housemaid had a baby it would probably be left to cry and cry for hours and nobody would go near it. The crying suddenly stopped. . . .

Caroline was asleep. All was well. But was it? What if Caroline had succeeded in turning herself over and was now lying face downwards in her pillow, suffocated? Headlines. "Actress's Baby Smothered." "Peer's Granddaughter Dies in Pram." There would have to be an inquest, and a coroner asking questions: "Do you mean to say you deliberately left your baby to cry and took no action?" Charles, white-lipped and tense. And the pathetic little coffin with all those daffodils from Coldhammer . . .

Maria left her desk and went downstairs into the garden. The silence from the pram was ominous, terrible. She looked into the pram.

Caroline was lying on her back, staring at the hood. As soon as she saw Maria she began to cry again. Her small face puckered up with loathing. She hated Maria.

This is mother love, thought Maria. This is what Barrie wrote about. This is what I imagined when I took Harry on my knee in *Mary Rose*, and it's all quite different. She looked over her shoulder and saw that the parlourmaid was staring at her from the dining-room window.

"Now, now," said Maria, and, reaching down into the pram, she picked up Caroline and carried her into the house.

"Gladys," she said to the parlourmaid, "as Baby seems restless, I think I had better have my lunch a quarter of an hour earlier than usual. Then I can get it over and attend to her feed."

"Very well, m'm," said Gladys.

But Maria knew Gladys was not deceived. Not for a moment. Gladys guessed that Maria had picked up Caroline and brought her indoors because she did not know what else to do. Maria took Caroline to the nursery. She changed her filthy napkins and put on the first batch of fresh ones. It took ages. Caroline started crying again as soon as she was stretched out on her back, and each time Maria tried to truss her up she kicked and wriggled. Maria jabbed the pin into her own thumb. Why could she not snap the pin with one deft gesture as the nurse did?

She went down for lunch, carrying Caroline in her arms, and she sat eating lunch with Caroline balanced on her left arm, while she fed herself with her right hand and a fork. Caroline cried throughout the meal.

"They're artful, aren't they?" said Gladys. "They know when someone strange has the handling of them." She stood watching in sympathy by the sideboard, her hands behind her back.

"She's hungry, that's all," said Maria coldly. "She will settle directly she has had her two o'clock feed."

The trouble was it was only a quarter past one. The whole of the timetable had been upset. Never mind. The bottle would do the trick. That blessed bottle in the nursery full of Cow-and-Gate.

Maria scraped through her lunch, swallowed down her coffee, and took Caroline up to the nursery once more and heated up the bottle that stood with its fellows on the white trolley. She felt like a bartender preparing a triple gin for some old drunk.

"Make her take it slowly," the nurse had said. "She must work for it. She must not take it all in gulps."

It was all very well for the nurse to talk. How did one make a baby feed slowly? The Cow-and-Gate squirted from the rubber teat into Caroline's mouth like a fountain jet, and if Maria tried to edge the bottle away Caroline screamed and fought like some fearful man with d.t.s. The feed that should have taken twenty minutes was all over in five. And Caroline lay back on Maria's lap, swollen, replete, her lips loose, her eyes closed. She reminded Maria of the old, vagrant women who used to lie asleep after midnight in the alleyway outside the theatre. Maria took her downstairs and put her back in the pram. Then she put on her own coat and walking shoes. "I'm taking Baby for her afternoon walk," she called through to the kitchen. Nobody heard. The three of them were laughing and talking, and the gramophone was on, the gramophone that Charles had given them for Christmas. They were swilling cups of tea. They did not care about her at all. They were enjoying themselves, while she had to take the baby out in the pram.

The air was brisk and cold, but it was fine. And the pram was white with a black hood. It was nicer than other people's prams. Maria walked firmly along the road towards Richmond Park, and it was a pity in a way, she thought, that nobody was there to matter, a friend, or a photographer. It was a waste that no one knew she was there, pushing her baby in a pram. She had just crossed the road and was entering the park gates when it happened. Caroline started to cry again. The patting on the back, the ritual of the morning began again. It had no effect at all. Maria took the pram behind a tree and went into the fearful performance of changing napkins. Caroline cried louder than ever before. Maria tucked her firmly in her rugs and began to walk very rapidly, jerking the pram up and down as she walked. Smothered screams came from beneath the rugs. Because the afternoon was fine there were more people than usual walking in Richmond Park. There were people everywhere. And all of them could hear Caroline crying. As Maria went past them, pushing the pram almost at a run, they turned to look at her, they paused to listen, because of the fearful noise of a baby screaming in a pram. Girls exercising dogs smiled at Maria with pity, and youths on bicycles whizzed past her, laughing.

"Be quiet," hissed Maria in desperation. "Please be quiet." And in panic she turned the pram and went back again out of the park and along the street, and stopped it outside a telephone kiosk at the corner.

She gave the number of the theatre where Niall was rehearsing, and after some delay the stage-door keeper found him.

"What's the matter?" said Niall.

"It's Caroline," said Maria. "The wretched nurse has left me with her, and Charles is away, and she keeps crying and crying. I don't know what to do. I'm speaking from a call box."

"I'll come and fetch you," said Niall at once. "I'll get my car. We'll drive somewhere. The noise of my driving will make her stop."

"Aren't you rehearsing?"

"Yes, but it doesn't matter. Tell me where you are. Describe your call box. It won't take more than twenty-five minutes if I come at once."

"No, come to the end of the road," said Maria. "Wait for me there. I'll have to put the pram in the garden. And I'll fetch another bottle for her. Perhaps the one after lunch wasn't the right temperature."

"Bring all the bottles you can find," said Niall.

Maria stepped out of the telephone box. A policeman at the corner was watching her. Caroline was still crying. Maria turned and pushed the pram in the opposite direction from the policeman. You never knew. It might be against the law to leave a child to cry.

She went back to the house and hid the pram behind a bush in the garden, near the garage. She went upstairs and came down again, carrying two more bottles and another batch of napkins. She felt like a burglar in her own domain. Luckily she met no one. The servants were still downstairs. Immediately she lifted Caroline out of the pram Caroline stopped crying. Maria hid in the garage with the rugs and the bottles and the napkins until she heard the sound of a car at the end of the road brake violently with a screech. That would be Niall. Maria came out of the garage, carrying her belongings, and went down the road to the car.

Niall was dressed oddly. He wore a very old pair of evening trousers and a polo sweater that had moth marks at the neck.

"I came just as I was," he said. "I left them to it. I said I had to take somebody to hospital."

"That's not true," said Maria, climbing into the car with Caroline.

"We can make it true," said Niall. "We can take Caroline to a hospital and leave her in the children's ward for the afternoon."

"Oh no," said Maria, alarmed. "Charles might get to hear. We can't do that. Think of the shame for me."

"Well, what then?"

"I don't know. Just drive."

Niall started the car with a jerk. It was an old Morris that had once belonged to Freada. Niall drove very badly in a series of wild rushes. He either went much too fast, swerving round islands, or crept in the middle of the road like a snail. He never understood the signals of policemen. "That man," he said, "why did he wave me on? What does he mean?"

"I think you apologise," said Maria. "I think you are on the wrong side of the road."

The car zigzagged in and out of traffic. People shouted. And Caroline, who had stopped crying momentarily because of the new movement so different from her pram, began crying again.

"Do you like her?" said Niall.

"Not frightfully. But I shall later, when she can talk."

"She's like Lord Wyndham," said Niall. "I shall give her a wrist watch every birthday, like other godfather's give pearls."

Caroline went on crying, and Niall slowed down the car.

"It's the pace," he said. "She doesn't like the pace. I tell you what. I think we ought to ask advice."

"From whom?"

"From some nice homely woman. There must be a nice homely woman who has had a lot of children who would give us advice," said Niall.

He peered anxiously to right and left, and then, forced onwards by the stream of traffic, he turned the car into a busy thoroughfare, with shops on either side, the pavements thronged with people.

"That woman there, with the basket," said Niall. "She has a cheerful face. How about asking her?" He slowed the car to a standstill, and, reaching over Maria, he lowered the window and called out to the passing woman.

"Excuse me," he said. "Could you come just a moment?"

The woman turned round in surprise. Her face was not quite so cheerful close to as it had seemed in the distance. And she had a cast in one eye.

"This lady doesn't know what to do about the baby," said Niall. "It keeps crying. We wondered whether you would be so terribly kind and help." The woman stared at him, and then down at Maria and the wailing Caroline.

"I beg your pardon?" she said.

"The baby," said Niall. "It goes on and on. It won't stop. And we neither of us know what to do."

The woman turned very red. She thought it was some sort of practical joke.

"You shouldn't try and fool people that way," she said. "There's a policeman over there. Do you want me to call him?"

"No," said Niall. "Of course not. We only wondered . . ."

"It's no use," whispered Maria. "Drive on—drive on."

She bowed haughtily to the woman, who turned away, uttering exclamations of disgust. Niall let in the clutch of the car, and it jerked forward.

"What a beastly woman," he said. "That sort of thing would never happen in France. In France they would offer to mind the baby for the afternoon."

"We're not in France," said Maria. "We're in England. It's typical of the country. All that fuss about prevention of cruelty to children, and yet there's not a soul to help us with Caroline."

"Let's drive to Mill Hill," said Niall, "and leave her with Truda."

"Truda would be angry," said Maria, "and tell Celia, and Celia would tell Pappy, and it would be all over the Garrick in no time. Oh, Niall . . ." She leant against him, and he put his left arm round her and kissed the top of her hair, and the car swerved in all directions.

"We could go on driving westwards forever more," said Niall. "We're heading for Wales at the moment. Welshwomen are probably very good with babies. Shall we go to Wales?"

"I know why mothers leave their babies in shops to be adopted," said Maria. "They can't stand the strain."

"Couldn't we leave Caroline in a shop?" said Niall. "I don't believe Charles would really mind. It would only be his pride. The thing is, no one in their senses would be mad about Caroline, not at this stage. Years later, perhaps, when she's a debutante."

"I wish to God she was a debutante now," said Maria.

"All those trailing feathers," said Niall. "I never can see that anything is gained by it. Stuck in the Mall, hour after hour."

"It's pageantry," said Maria. "I love it. Like being a king's mistress."

"I don't see that it's the slightest bit like being a king's mistress," said Niall. "Driving into the courtyard in a hired Rolls, like you did last year, with Lady Wyndham stuck beside you."

"I adored every minute. . . . Niall?"

"What?"

"I've suddenly thought of something. Let's stop at the next Woolworth's and buy Caroline a comforter."

"What's a comforter?"

"You know, those awful rubber things that common babies have stuck in their mouths."

"Do they make them nowadays?"

"I don't know. We can try."

Niall slowed the Morris to a crawl, looking for Woolworth's, and finally they came to one, and Maria got out of the car and went inside the shop. She returned, her face triumphant.

"Ninepence," she said, "and very good rubber. Red. The girl said her little sister had one at home."

"Where does she live?"

"Who?"

"The little sister. We might take Caroline, and the mother could look after both of them."

"Don't be silly. Now, watch. . . ." Very slowly Maria pushed the comforter into Caroline's mouth. It acted as a sort of gag. Caroline sucked noisily and closed her eyes. The effect was magic. The crying ceased.

"You'd scarcely credit it, would you?" whispered Maria.

"It's rather frightful," said Niall. "Like plugging someone with cocaine. What if it has a terrible effect on Caroline in afterlife?"

"I don't care," said Maria. "Not if it keeps her quiet now."

The sudden peace was wonderful. Calm waters after storm. Niall started the car again, increasing the pace, and Maria leant back against his shoulder.

"How easy it would be," said Niall, "if every time one felt on edge one could just go to Woolworth's and buy a comforter. There must be something psychological about it. I think I shall get one for myself. It's probably what I've wanted all my life."

"I think it would be vicious," said Maria, yawning. "A grown man going around with a bit of rubber in his mouth."

"Why vicious?"

"Well, perhaps not vicious. But putting off . . . Where now?"

"Wherever you like."

Maria considered. She did not want to go back to Richmond. She did not want to carry the now peaceful Caroline upstairs and start the weary routine of the orange juice, the kicking on the cushion, the next feed, the changing of the napkins, and all the things that she was supposed to do. She did not want to play at being the Honourable Mrs. Charles Wyndham all alone at home. The house at Richmond, empty of Charles, empty of everything but wedding presents and the furniture that had come from Coldhammer, seemed suddenly a tie, a millstone round the neck.

She was reminded, curiously and for the first time, of the doll's house that Pappy and Mama had presented to her on her seventh birthday, and with which she had played, enchanted, for a fortnight, letting no one touch it but herself. Then, after one wet day, when she had played with it for a full afternoon, it suddenly bored her, she did not want it any more, and very generously she had given it to Celia. Celia had it still. . . .

"Where are we going?" said Niall.

"Let's go to the theatre," said Maria. "Take me to the theatre. I can watch you rehearse."

The stage-door keeper was an old friend of Maria's. His face was wreathed in smiles as he welcomed her.

"Why, Miss Delaney," he said. "You ought to come to see us more often. You're quite a stranger."

Quite a stranger . . . Why did he say that? Did he mean that people were forgetting her? That already she was slipping from their minds? Niall found some cushions and a rug from the car, and between them they carried Caroline to one of the boxes on the circle level and made up a bed for her on the floor. She was sleeping soundly, the comforter between her lips. Then Niall went down again onto the stage, and Maria went and sat at the back of the dress circle in the dark, because, after all, she had no right to be there; it was cheek to go and watch someone else's rehearsal in a show that was no concern of hers. She had never seen a revue in rehearsal before, and she was glad to find the chaos even greater than the chaos that she knew. So much argument. So many people talking at once. So many bits and pieces that surely never, never could be pulled into one, and every now and then Niall's music, dear and familiar to her because he had played it on the piano, magnified into numbers for the orchestra, and Niall himself, stumbling about in his absurd clothes, getting into everybody's way.

And she wanted to be with them on the stage, not sitting alone there in the circle in the dark, waiting for Caroline to cry.

She wanted to be in a theatre that she knew, where she belonged, in her own sort of play. And for it to be the third week in rehearsal, and knowing her lines, and getting into her stride, and having worked all day—but really all day—and now a little tired, and now her temper rather worn, and snapping "What?" to the producer who called up to her from the stalls. Then quickly regretting it, because, after all, you never knew, you might be fired. But the producer, being also perhaps the actor-manager, and likable, and human, and possibly even lovable, would laugh silently inside himself and call, "Just once through again, Maria darling, if you don't mind." And she would not mind. She would know it had not been right. She would want to do it again. Later, when they broke off, they would go and have a drink together in the pub across the road, and she would talk too much, and he would not mind, and she would be so tired she would want to die. But it would be the right sort of death. The only death . . .

Suddenly she was aware of Niall kneeling beside her in the circle.

"What's the matter?" he whispered. "You're crying."

"I'm not crying," she said. "I never cry."

"They're stopping in a moment," he said. "They always break at six-thirty. You had better come up to my room with Caroline before they know you're here."

She went to the box for Caroline, and Niall carried the rugs and the napkins and the bottles, and led the way upstairs to his curious flat at the top of the theatre.

"Well, what did you think of it?" he said.

"Think of what?" she asked.

"The revue," he said.

"I don't know. I wasn't really watching," said Maria.

He looked at her, but he said nothing. He knew everything, always. He gave her a drink and lit her a cigarette, and she threw it away after a minute or two; she never smoked much. He put her in the armchair —the seat sagged and the springs were broken—and he found another chair for her feet. Caroline was asleep on his bed, wrapped in the rugs. The comforter lolled sideways from her mouth.

"It's nearly seven," sighed Maria. "She has not had a bottle for hours." There were all the napkins too. What should she do with the napkins? She put out her arms to Niall, and he went and knelt beside her. She thought of the Regency drawing room, small, correct, and exquisite, in her house at Richmond. The evening paper, ready beside her chair. The bright fire burning. The maid having tidied and drawn the curtains. Here, in Niall's room at the top of the theatre, the curtains were not yet drawn. The sound of the traffic in Shaftesbury Avenue came to the blank, staring windows, and down on the pavements below them would be hurrying, passing people, some making for the Underground at Piccadilly, others walking to meet their friends and go out upon the town. The lights were going up on all the theatres. The Lyric, the Globe, the Queen's, the Apollo, the Palace. The lights were going up on all the theatres over London.

"The thing is," said Maria, "I shouldn't have married."

"It need not affect you," said Niall. "You can always do two things at once. You always have. Or even three."

"I suppose so," said Maria. "I suppose I can."

They spoke in whispers because of Caroline. If they talked louder Caroline might wake.

"Charles wants to go to live near Coldhammer," said Maria. "What then? I can't go and live at Coldhammer."

"You'll have to have a flat," said Niall, "and go down to Cold-hammer at week ends. It's too far to go up and down every night."

"That's what I thought," said Maria. "But would it work? Would Charles mind? Would it break up our married life?"

"I don't know," said Niall. "I don't know what married people do."

Lights kept flashing from the building opposite, sending streaks of colour into the darkened room. The newsboys at the corner shouted, "Late Night Final! Late Night Final!" The traffic surged below.

"I have to come back," said Maria. "I shall go mad if I don't come back."

"Charles will watch you from a box," said Niall. "He'll be terribly proud of you. He will cut out all your notices and paste them in a book."

"Yes," said Maria, "but he can't spend his life doing that, watching me from a box and pasting things in books."

The telephone started ringing. It was a soft burr-burr. Not a shrill summons. The sound would not wake Caroline, in the drugged sleep that the comforter had given her.

"It often does that," said Niall. "I never answer it. I'm always afraid it might be somebody boring asking me to dinner."

"What if it was me ringing?" said Maria.

"It can't be you tonight. You're here," said Niall.

The telephone went on ringing, and Niall reached for one of Caroline's napkins and threw it over the bell. The shot was a brilliant one. The napkin hung suspended like a shroud.

"We'll have some dinner presently at the Café Royal," said Niall. "They know me there, it's always rather pleasing."

"What about Caroline?"

"We'll take her too. And then I'll drive you home."

The telephone, which had stopped with the throw of the napkin, began again.

"It's a soothing sort of sound," said Niall. "I don't mind it. Does it worry you?" He tucked another cushion under Maria's back.

"No," said Maria, holding out her arms. "Let it ring."

CHAPTER EIGHTEEN

CELIA felt very selfish when she put down the receiver after break-fast. It was the first time she had ever refused doing anything for Maria. She adored the baby. There was nothing she liked better than going over to Richmond and spending a day with the baby. But Pappy's publisher friend at the Garrick had made such a point of her going to see him on this particular day, taking the stories and the drawings, and it would be very discourteous to put him off.

Not that he would mind, not that it would really matter. He was a busy man, and it was just doing her a kindness, because she was Pappy's daughter, that he bothered to see her at all. Only it would be rude not to go. How unfortunate that Maria should have been left without the nurse on this day, of all days. Even if Celia had not made that appointment with the publisher it would be difficult to go over to Richmond. Pappy was not well. He had not been well for nearly a week. He kept complaining of pains. One moment in his head, one moment behind his knee, and the next moment in the small of his back. The doctor said that now he no longer sang he smoked too much. But would smoking too much give a person pains? Pappy had not been down to the club now for several days. He pottered about at home in his dressing gown, and he hated being left alone, even for a few minutes.

"My darling?" he would call. "My darling, where are you?"

"In the morning room, Pappy," and she would cover up the story she was writing with a piece of blotting paper, and hide the pencil drawing underneath a book, because writing and drawing were, to her, private, rather furtive things. If you were suddenly discovered in the midst of them it was like being found in the act of prayer, or the door bursting open in the bathroom.

"Were you working, my darling? I won't interrupt." Pappy would settle himself in the chair by the fire with books and newspapers and letters, but the very fact of his presence did something to the room. She could not concentrate. Instead of being in a world of escape she was back again once more in a world of reality. She was only Pappy's daughter writing fairy tales. She felt self-conscious, cramped. She bit the end of her pencil, trying to recapture the lost mood. Every now and again Pappy coughed or moved, and he rustled the pages of The Times.

"I don't disturb you, do I, my darling?"

"No, Pappy."

And she would lean forward over the table, making a pretence of working, and then after about five minutes or so she would stand up, and stretch, and say, "Well, really, I think that's all for the moment," and gather her things togther, and put them away in a drawer.

"Finished?" said Pappy with relief, dropping The Times. "Yes," she answered.

"I've been wondering about those pills that Pleydon gave me," said Pappy. "I don't think they're suiting me at all. The pains in my head have been much worse the last two days. I wonder if I should have my eyes tested again. It may be my eyes all the time."

"We must go to see an oculist."

"That's what I thought. We will go to someone good. We will find out the name of someone really first-class, my darling."

His eyes followed her as she moved about the room.

"What would I have done," he said, "if you had wanted to be an actress like Maria? Sometimes I wake up in the night and I ask myself, What would I have done?' "

"How silly," said Celia. "It's as silly as if I woke up and wondered what I would have done if you had ever married again, and the pair of us had lived here being bullied by a stranger."

"Impossible, my darling," said Pappy, shaking his head, "impossible. I read an article in some paper the other day about the mute swan. The mute swan mates for life. When the female dies the swan lives disconsolate; he takes no other. I thought to myself as I read it: Ah—that's me. I am the mute swan."

He must have forgotten about Australia, thought Celia, and South Africa, and that time we visited America; there were always women swarming round him like moths; he was not really very mute. Still, she knew what he meant.

"Your little stories and your clever drawings don't take you away from me," said Pappy, "but had you been an actress . . . I tremble to think what would have become of me. I should be in Denville Hall."

"No, you would not," said Celia, "you would be living with me in some sumptuous flat, and I should make more money than Maria."

"Dross," said Pappy, "filthy dross. What is lucre to you and me? Thank God I have not saved a penny. . . . My darling, you must show your little stories to Harrison, and the drawings too. I trust Harrison. His judgment is sound, and the stuff he publishes is good. Not one of the fancy boys. Besides, he will tell the truth to me, he won't beat about the bush. It was I who put him up for the Garrick."

Celia had sent some of her drawings and stories to this James Harrison, following on a lunch he had had with Pappy, and today she was to take any others she could find and be at his office at four o'clock that afternoon. She was worried, though. She wondered what Pappy would do while she was gone.

"I can have a shut-eye, my darling, from two to four," said Pappy, "and then if I feel up to it I can take a little walk. Pleydon said it would not hurt me to walk."

"I don't like your walking alone," said Celia. "You are so vague, you are always thinking of something else. And there's that wretched crossroad where the buses go so fast."

"If it were the summer I could go to Lord's and watch the cricket," said Pappy. "I always enjoy watching cricket. I like sitting in that covered stand next to the pavilion. Looking back, you know, I think I made a mistake in not sending Niall to Eton. He might have been a cricketer. It would have given me great pleasure to have watched Niall playing cricket for Eton."

He was always talking nowadays, thought Celia, of the things he might have done. The houses they should have lived in, the countries they could have visited. It was a pity, he had said only that morning, that he had never taken up swimming really seriously. With his physique, he told Celia, he could easily have swum the Channel. He should have chucked singing directly Mama died and gone in for long-distance swimming. He could have beaten all the experts. He might have swum the Channel twice, from either side. "But why, Pappy?" she asked. "Surely it's much more satisfactory to have done what you have done?"

He shook his head. "My ignorance is profound," he said, "about so many things. Take astrology. I know nothing about astrology. Why all those stars? Why? I ask myself." And there and then she had to ring up Bumpus and find out whether there was a book on stars, a new book, a large book full of plates, and whether Bumpus could send it up in time for lunch by special messenger.

"This will keep me amused, my darling, while you are seeing Harrison," said Pappy. "There is one planet, I never can remember which—Jupiter, I think—that has two moons. They circle about the planet night and day. A wonderful thought. Jupiter, alone amid the darkness, with two moons."

She left him quite happy and contented, propped up in two chairs in the morning room for his afternoon shut-eye, with the volume on stars beside him on the table. The maid was instructed to look in on him once or twice, in case he should need anything, and of course to go to him upon the instant should he ring the bell.

As she took a bus down the Wellington Road as far as Marylebone, where she found a taxi, Celia wondered if Maria had been able to manage Caroline, and her conscience smote her again for having failed Maria in emergency.

"I am tied to the house," Maria had said, "literally tied to the house the livelong day, because of Caroline."

"Only for this once," Celia protested; "that nurse is really very good. She never asks to go out."

"It's the thin edge of the wedge," said Maria. "Now she has started she will always be doing it. It's a great responsibility, being a mother." It was her grumpy, spoilt voice. She did not really mean it. Celia knew the voice so well. In two minutes she would have forgotten all about having asked Celia for the day and would be planning something else. If only Maria lived a little closer Celia could have shared the responsibility of Caroline. It would only mean two children to look after instead of one. Because Pappy was a child. He needed humouring, and coaxing, and taking care of in much the same way as a child.

She even found herself using a special voice to him these days, a gentle, half-teasing banter, a kind of "Come now, what's the matter?"

sort of voice. And if he picked at his food and grumbled, she pretended to take no notice. It was just a child's trick to draw attention. But when he ate well she was careful to remark upon the fact and smile encouragement. "Oh, good, you've managed a whole wing of chicken. That does please me. Would you fancy a tiny scrap more?"

It was strange how a person came full circle. How a man was once a baby and a boy, and then a lover and a father, and now a child again. It was strange that once she had been a little girl, climbing onto Pappy's knee, burying her head into his shoulder, clinging to him for protection, and he had been young, and strong, and like a god. And now it was all over, the purpose of his life. The strength had ebbed away. The man who had lived, and loved, and given the beauty of his voice to millions was weary, and crabbed, and fretful, following with his eyes the daughter he had once protected and carried in his arms. Yes, Pappy had come full circle. He was back again on the road where he had begun. But why? To what end? Would anybody ever know?

The taxi drew up outside the building in the narrow street in Bloomsbury, and Celia, nervous suddenly, uncertain, paid off the driver and, going inside the building, asked at a door marked "Enquiries" for Mr. Harrison. A girl smiled over pince-nez and said Mr. Harrison was expecting her. It was always surprising, and warming, too, when people whom one did not know were kind. Like the girl with the pince-nez. Or bus drivers. Or the fishmonger on the telephone. It made, Celia thought, such a difference to the day.

And Mr. Harrison, when she was shown into the room, rose from his desk at once to greet her, and walked towards her with a smile on his face. She had thought he might be hard and brisk, with a clear-cut decisive manner, like a schoolmaster. But he was fatherly and kind. He pulled forward an armchair for her to sit in, and everything was made easy for her at once because he began to talk about Maria.

"She has not given up the stage, I hope," he said. "It would be a very great loss to all her admirers if she did that."

Celia explained about the baby, and he nodded, he understood, he said he had a nephew who knew Charles.

"Your brother has written the music for this new revue, hasn't he?" he said, and so from Maria they passed to Niall, and all that Niall had achieved during the past years in Paris, and Celia had to explain the muddled relationship among them all, that she was half sister to each, and that Niall and Maria were nothing to do with one another. "They are very close, though," she said; "they understand each other perfectly."

"You are a very talented family, very talented indeed," said Mr. Harrison. He paused after he said this, and he reached for some papers on his desk, and Celia saw her own handwriting on the stories, and the drawings beneath another sheaf of paper.

"Do you remember your mother well?" he said abruptly, reaching for his spectacles, and Celia felt nervous for no reason; he seemed suddenly like the schoolmaster she had feared.

"Yes," she said. "I was between ten and eleven when she died. We have none of us forgotten her. But we don't talk about her much."

"I saw her dance many times," said Mr. Harrison. "She had a quality about her that was entirely individual and that no one, so far as I know, has ever been able to describe. It was not ballet. That was the extraordinary thing. There was no grouping, no set figures. Yet she told a story as she danced, and the dance was the story, and the pathos of the whole world would come suddenly with one movement, with the folding of her hands. She relied on nothing and on no one, not even the music; the music was secondary to the movement. She danced alone. That was the beauty of it, you know. She danced alone." He took off his spectacles and polished them. He seemed quite moved. Celia waited for him to continue. She did not know what to say.

"And you?" he said. "Do you mean to tell me you don't dance?"

Celia smiled nervously. He seemed almost angry with her for some reason. "Oh no," she said, "I can't dance at all. I'm frightfully clumsy, and I've always been too fat. I can do ordinary fox trots, of course, if I get asked to parties, but Niall says I'm heavy and trip against his feet. Niall dances beautifully, and so does Maria."

"Then how is it," said Mr. Harrison, "that you are able to draw like this?" He took one of her drawings from the sheaf of papers on the desk and held it in front of her, in accusation. It was not one that Celia liked very much. It was the one where the child was running from the four winds, and he held his hands up to his ears so that he could not hear the four winds call him. She had tried to make the child stumble as he ran, and she had never thought the stumble was effective. Besides, the background was too vague. The trees were dark, but not dark enough. And anyway, she had finished it in a hurry because of Pappy calling to her, and the mood had gone when she had tried to do something to the trees the following day.

"The little boy is not dancing," said Celia; "he is meant to be running away. He is frightened. It explains it in the story that goes with it. But there are other drawings, better than that."

"I know perfectly well he is not dancing," said Mr. Harrison. "I know he is running away. For how long have you been drawing? Two years? Three years?"

"Oh, longer than that," said Celia. "The fact is, I have always drawn. I've been drawing all my life. It's the only thing I can do."

"The only thing?" said Mr. Harrison. "My dear child, what more do you want? Aren't you satisfied with that?"

He came and stood beside the fireplace, looking down at her.

"I talked just now about your mother," he said, "and a certain quality she possessed. I have not seen that quality before or since, in any other form of art, until this week. Now I have seen it again. In these drawings of yours. Never mind the stories. I don't care a pin about the stories. They are effective, and charming, and will do very well. But these rough drawings of yours are in a class by themselves."

Celia stared up at him, bewildered. How very odd. The drawings had not been difficult to do. But she had taken hours and hours over the stories. What a fearful waste that Mr. Harrison did not think much of the stories.

"You mean," she said, "you think the drawings are the best?"

"I have just told you," he said patiently, "they're in a class by themselves. I don't know anyone today who does that sort of work at all. I am very excited about them, and I hope you are too. You have a great future ahead of you."

It was very kind and very nice, thought Celia, to make such a to-do about her drawings. It would hardly have happened had he not been a friend of Pappy's, and a member of the Garrick, and an old admirer of Mama's.

"Thank you," she said, "thank you very much."

"Don't thank me," he said. "I have done nothing except look at your drawings and show them to an expert, who agreed with my opinion. Now, come on. Have you brought any more with you? What are those things you are carrying in your bag?"

"Well, they are more stories," Celia apologised; "there are only two or three drawings, not awfully good. These stories may be better, though, than the ones you have seen."

He waved them away. He was bored stiff with the stories.

"Let's have a look at the drawings," he said.

He examined them carefully, one by one; he took them to his desk, under the light; he might have been a scientist with a microscope.

"Yes," he said, "these last were done in a hurry, weren't they? You have not taken so much trouble."

"Pappy hasn't been well," said Celia. "I've been rather bothered about Pappy."

"The point is," said Mr. Harrison, "we have not quite enough drawings yet for the book I have in mind. You must do some more work. How long does it take you to finish one of these? Three days, four days?"

"It depends," said Celia. "I can't really work to plan. Because of Pappy." Mr. Harrison brushed Pappy aside, as he had brushed away the stories.

"Don't you worry about your father," he said, "I'll talk to him. He knows what work means. He's been through it himself."

Celia said nothing. It was difficult to explain to Mr. Harrison what it was like at home.

"You see," she said, "I am really in charge. I order the meals and things. And Pappy is not very strong these days. You must have noticed that. I don't get a great deal of time."

"You must make time," said Mr. Harrison; "you can't treat a talent like yours as though it did not matter. I won't allow it."

He was like a schoolmaster, after all. It was just as she had feared. He was now going to make a fuss about her drawings, and write to Pappy, and worry Pappy, and say that time must be set aside for her to work, and everything would become a performance, and a ritual, and be difficult. Drawing would become a burden instead of an escape.

It was nice of Mr. Harrison to take so much trouble, but she wished now she had not come. "Well," she said, getting up from her chair, "it's been most terribly nice of you to take all this trouble, but——"

"Where are you going? What are you doing?" he said. "We have not discussed your contract yet; we have not talked business."

It was after half-past five before she got away. She had to have tea and meet two other men, and they made her sign some terrifying form like a death warrant, promising to give any work that she might do to Mr. Harrison. He insisted, and so did the other men, that the stories were no good without the drawings, and they wanted the other drawings as soon as possible, in four or five weeks' time. She knew she could never do it; she felt trapped. She wondered what would happen if she failed them, now that she had signed the contract. Would they sue her?

Finally she tore herself away, shaking hands twice over, and forgetting, in her haste, to say good-bye to the girl with the pince-nez in Enquiries who had smiled. There was not a taxi to be seen. She had to walk almost as far as Euston before she found a taxi, and then it was close on six o'clock and getting dark. The first thing she noticed when she reached home was that the garage door was open. And the car was not inside. Pappy had not driven the car for several weeks. Not since he had been unwell. Either she had driven him, or he had taken a taxi. She ran up the steps to the house, her heart beating, fumbling for her latchkey. She opened the door and ran inside, calling for the maid.

"Where is Mr. Delaney?" she said. "What has happened?"

The maid looked scared and nervous. "He's gone out, miss," she said. "We couldn't stop him. And we did not know where you were, to let you know."

"How do you mean, he has gone out?"

"He must have fallen asleep, miss, after you went. I went in twice, and he was quite still in his chair, and peaceful. And then, about five o'clock it was, we heard him come out into the hall. I came up from the kitchen, thinking he might want something, and he looked very strange, miss, not like himself at all, very red about the face, and his eyes all queer and staring; I was quite frightened.

" 'I'm going down to the theatre,' he said. 'I'd no idea it was so late.'

"I think he must have been dreaming, miss. He brushed past me and went down the steps to the garage. I heard him start up the car. There was nothing I could do. We've been waiting here, miss, until you came back. 'Perhaps Miss Celia will know where he has gone,' we said."

Celia did not stop to listen to any more. She went into the morning room. The chair was pushed back from the fire, as Pappy had left it. The book about the stars was on the table. It was not even open. There was no clue to tell her where he had gone. No clue at all.

She rang up the Garrick Club. No, said the hall porter, Mr. Delaney had not been to the club today. She telephoned Dr. Pleydon. Dr.

Pleydon was not in. He was not expected before half-past seven. Celia went back to the hall and questioned the maid again.

"What did he say?" she asked. "What were his exact words?"

The maid repeated what she had said before.

"Mr. Delaney said, 'I'm going down to the theatre. I'd no idea it was so late.'"

The theatre. What theatre? Into what dim, dusty labyrinth of the mind was Pappy wandering? Celia telephoned for a taxi and went down again to London, and on the way she tried to explain to the taxi driver what she wished to do. "The car is a Sunbeam," she said, "and I think my father will have tried to park it outside the stage door of a theatre. But I don't know what theatre. It might be almost any theatre."

"Bit of a twister, isn't it?" said the man. "You say any theatre. West End or Hammersmith? What I mean is, there are all sorts, aren't there? Music Hall, Variety, Shaftesbury Avenue, the Strand——"

"The Adelphi," said Celia, "go to the Adelphi."

Was it not at the Adelphi that they had played, that last season, Pappy and Mama? That last London spring season, before Mama died?

The taxi twisted and turned in the stream of traffic, and the driver did not pick his way as he should have done; he took her the longest and most crowded way, right through the centre of Piccadilly Circus, right through the humming heart of London. He cut across no by-streets, but went swinging down the Haymarket, and round Trafalgar Square into the Strand, and when they drew abreast of the Adelphi he stopped the taxi with a jerk and looked back at Celia through the window, saying, "Drawn a blank here, anyway. The theatre's closed." He was right. The doors were closed and barred, and there were no bills posted on the walls. "That's right," the driver said, "the show came off last week, didn't it? A musical."

"I think I will get out, anyway," said Celia. "I'll walk round to the stage door. Perhaps you would wait for me in the street behind."

"It's going to cost you something," said the driver, "trying all the theatres in this way. Why not call in the police?"

But she did not listen to him. She was feeling the barred doors of the closed theatre. They were firmly locked, of course. She turned away and walked up the street at the side and into the alleyway, dark and sinister, where Bill Terris had been murdered. There was no one there at all. The posters of the last play, torn and defaced, stared at her from beside the stage door. A cat came towards her from the shadows. It arched its back, and mewed against her legs, and then prowled away again into the darkness.

She turned back again down the alleyway into the street. The taxi was waiting for her at the corner. The driver had lit a cigarette and sat with his arms folded, watching her. "Any luck?" he said.

"No," said Celia. "Go on waiting for me, please."

He muttered something and set back the flag, and she hurried away once more, along another street, and then another, and all the buildings were the same, dark, blank, and impersonal, and she knew now, of course, that it was not the Adelphi that she wanted at all, but Covent Garden.

There was a policeman standing by the opera house. He flashed his lamp at her as she came across and tried the door of the waiting Sunbeam.

"Are you looking for someone?" he said.

"I am looking for my father," said Celia; "he is not very well, and this is his car. I'm afraid something may have happened to him."

"Are you Miss Delaney?" said the policeman.

"Yes," said Celia, and she was suddenly afraid.

"I was warned to wait here for you, miss," said the policeman, his manner quiet and kind. "The inspector thought one of the family might be along. I'm afraid your father has been taken ill. Loss of memory, they think. They've taken him in an ambulance to the Charing Cross Hospital."

"Thank you," said Celia, "thank you. I understand."

She was calm and steady now, and the feeling of panic had gone from her. Pappy had been found. Pappy was no longer wandering in the streets, lost and lonely, with the dead. He was safe. He was in the Charing Cross Hospital.

"I'll take you round there in the car, miss," said the policeman; "he left the key. He must have been only gone from the car a few minutes when he fell down."

"He fell down?" said Celia.

"Yes, miss. The stage-door keeper at the opera house was standing just across there, by the open door, and saw him fall. He went to him at once. He recognised Mr. Delaney. Then he called for me, and I got the inspector, and we phoned through for the ambulance. Loss of memory, that's what they think it is. But they'll tell you at the hospital."

"I have a taxi waiting round the corner by the Adelphi," said Celia. "I'd better pay him off before we go to the hospital."

"That's all right, miss," said the policeman, "it's all on the way."

For the second time in the day she was struck by the kindness of people. Even the taxi driver, who at first had seemed sullen and unfriendly, was sympathetic when she handed him his change.

"I'm sorry if you've had bad news," he said. "Would you like me to come and wait outside the hospital?"

"No," said Celia, "it's quite all right. Thank you so much. Good night."

As she went into the hospital it was as though the afternoon repeated itself in a strange fashion. Once again she had to go to a room marked "Enquiries," and once again the woman there behind the desk wore pince-nez. But this time she was dressed as a nurse. And she did not smile. She listened, and nodded, and spoke into a telephone.

"That's all right," she said, "they're expecting you." And she rang a bell, and Celia followed another nurse into a lift.

There were many floors, and many corridors, and many nurses, and somewhere in this great building, Celia thought, Pappy lies waiting for me, and he will be alone, and he won't understand. He will think that I have done the thing that I have promised never to do. That I have gone away and left him, and that he does not belong anywhere any more.

They came at last, not to a public ward as she had feared, but to a private room. Pappy was lying on the bed with his eyes closed.

He is dead, of course, she thought. He has been dead for quite a long time. He must have died as soon as he stepped out of the car and looked across at the stage door of Covent Garden.

There was a doctor in the room, and a sister, and another nurse. The doctor wore a white coat. He carried a stethoscope round his neck.

"You are Miss Delaney?" he said. And he looked surprised, a little puzzled. Celia realised then that they must have been expecting Maria. They did not know about her. They had not thought there would be another daughter. "Yes," she said, "I'm the youngest. I live at home with my father."

"I'm afraid you must be prepared for a shock," said the doctor.

"Yes," said Celia. "He's dead, isn't he?"

"No," said the doctor, "but he's had a very severe stroke. He's very ill indeed."

They went and stood together by the bed. They had wrapped Pappy in one of the hospital nightshirts, and it was somehow shocking and rather terrible to see Pappy dressed in this way, not in his own pyjamas, not in his own bed. His breathing was heavy and queer.

"If he must die," said Celia, "I would want him to die at home. He has always been afraid of hospitals. He would not want it to happen here."

They looked at her strangely, the doctor and the nurse, and she wondered if they thought her very rude, very churlish, in saying this; because they were taking a lot of trouble to help Pappy, they had put him here in this bed and were looking after him.

"I appreciate that," said the doctor; "we are all a little bit afraid of hospitals. . . . But your father isn't necessarily going to die, Miss Delaney. His heart is steady. And so is his pulse. He has a magnificent constitution. The point is, that with a case like this it is virtually impossible to forecast what may happen. He might go on like this, with very little change, for weeks, for months."

"Will he be in pain?" said Celia. "That's the only thing that matters. Will he be in pain?"

"No," said the doctor, "no, there should be no pain. But he will be quite helpless. You understand that. He would have to be nursed, day and night, professionally. You have facilities for that at home?"

"Yes," said Celia, "yes, of course."

She said this to reassure the doctor, and in a clear, detached, far-sighted fashion, she thought how she could turn Maria's old room into a room for the nurse, and the nurse and she could share the business of looking after Pappy together. The servants would be distressed because of the extra work, they might even threaten to leave, but then something would have to be arranged. Truda might come perhaps for a few weeks, she might even persuade André to come back again for a little while, and anyway, that new young housemaid was very willing.

Her mind went running on into the future, and she thought how it might be possible, when the warmer weather came, to drag Pappy's bed into the old drawing room on the first floor that they never used;

new curtains would be needed, but they would not be difficult to find, and it would be more cheerful in that room, and quieter too.

The doctor was handing her something in a glass.

"What do you want me to do?" she said. "What's this?"

"Drink it down," he said quietly. "You've had a very great shock, you know." She swallowed down the stuff in the glass, and it did not make her feel better at all. It was bitter, and queer, and her legs were suddenly very weak and stumbly, like cotton wool, and she was tired.

"I would like to ring up my sister," she said.

"Of course," said the doctor, and he led the way out into the corridor, and she was aware of the terrible clean, impersonal smell of hospitals, a smell that belonged to no one, that was part of the building, and the unshaded lights, and the bare scrubbed walls and floors, and had nothing to do with the nurse who walked beside her, or the doctor swinging his stethoscope, or Pappy unconscious in the room where she had left him, or the other sick people lying dumbly in their beds.

The doctor took her to a little room and switched on a light.

"You can telephone from here," he said. "You know the number?"

"Yes," she said, "yes, thank you."

He went out and stood waiting in the passage. And she called the number of Maria's house at Richmond. But it was not Maria who answered. It was Gladys, the parlourmaid.

"Mrs. Wyndham isn't back yet," she said. "She went out this afternoon, taking Baby with her, and we haven't seen anything of her since she went, just after two."

The voice was surprised, a little aggrieved. The voice suggested that the least Mrs. Wyndham might have done was to warn her staff that she expected to be out so long. Celia pressed her hands against her eyes.

"All right," she said, "it does not matter. I'll ring Mrs. Wyndham later."

She put back the receiver and lifted it again. She asked for the number of Niall's room at the theatre. She went on ringing. And surely, she thought with sudden hopelessness and a new kind of dead despair, they can't both be out and away, now at this minute in my life, when I need both of them so much. Surely one of them will come, surely one of them will help me. Because I don't want to go home alone. I don't want to be in the house alone, without Pappy.

The telephone went on ringing. "I'm sorry," the operator said, "there is no reply."

His voice was chill and distant, he was a number at a switchboard, he was not one of the people who were kind.

Celia turned out the light of the little telephone room and fumbled for the handle of the door. She could not find it. Her hands moved over the hard smooth surface of the door. In sudden panic she began to beat against it.

CHAPTER NINETEEN

"WHO wants a bath before supper?" asked Maria.

"Meaning you do," said Niall, "and if anyone else says yes, there won't be enough hot water."

"That," said Maria, "was what I intended to convey."

We all three wandered into the hall. Celia switched off the lights in the drawing room. She left one lamp burning by the fireplace.

"Celia has spinster habits," said Niall, "turning off lights, switching off fires. Knowing what to do with once-cooked food."

"It has nothing to do with being a spinster," said Celia; "it's just the way I'm trained. Not even wartime measures. You forget I had an invalid to look after for three years."

"I had not forgotten," answered Niall; "I prefer not to think about it, that's all."

"You had those nurses to help you," Maria said. "They always seemed very nice. It could not have been very terrible." She led the way upstairs.

"Who said it was terrible?" asked Celia. "I never did."

The various rooms led onto the single corridor. At the far end was a door to the nursery wing.

"Pappy would never have cared for it down here," said Maria, "too much noise. I kept coming back from the theatre to have babies. The noise was bad enough for me."

"It depends on the sort of noise you mean," said Niall, "bombs or babies. Personally, give me bombs every time."

"I agree," said Maria. "I was thinking of the babies." She opened the door of her room and turned on the light. "Anyway," she said, "it was right for Pappy to die in London. He belonged to London more than to any other city. And it was right that he died when he did. Before the world turned drab."

"Who says it's drab?" asked Niall.

"I do," said Maria. "No brightness any more, no life, no fun." She opened her wardrobe door and stared pensively inside.

"It's our age group," said Celia, "that's really the matter. I don't mind reaching mid-thirty, because it does not affect me much one way or the other, but perhaps for you and Niall . . ."

"Nor me," said Niall. "A person can sit staring at a piece of water with a vacant mind at eighty-five. Or sit on a bench and sleep. I've never wanted to do anything else."

Through the door to the children's wing came shouts of laughter.

"They're being vulgar," said Maria.

"That means Polly is downstairs," said Niall.

"Perhaps I ought to go along and see?" said Celia.

Maria shrugged her shoulders. "I'm going to have my bath," she called. "If I am late, tell Charles the reason why." She shut the door.

Niall smiled at Celia. "Well?" he said. "It's been a funny day."

"We haven't achieved anything, have we?" said Celia. "We've come to no conclusions. Perhaps it does not really help, delving into the past. Anyway, I feel the same now as I did then. Even if we are older. Even if the world has turned drab."

"You look the same, too," said Niall, "but perhaps you would, to me. That little grey streak has been in your hair for several years."

"Don't be late for supper," said Celia; "it would be rather awful if I had to face Charles alone."

"I won't be late," said Niall.

He went along to the spare room, whistling under his breath.

"We were very young, we were very merry,
We had ridden back and forth all night upon a ferry . . ."

Niall never knew why he remembered things. Why snatches of verse and odd rhymes and half-finished sentences spoken long ago by forgotten friends should come to him like this at any moment of the day or night. As now, for instance, changing for supper in the spare room at Farthings. He threw off the tweed jacket and hung it on the bedpost. He kicked his heavy shoes into the corner and reached for the pair of American sneakers, then pulled a clean shirt out of his suitcase, and a spotted scarf. He had been too idle to pack a tie. Whenever he came to Farthings for the week end he never bothered to unpack. It was so much simpler to leave his clothes—and he never brought many—folded in the suitcase, instead of tucked away in chests of drawers and wardrobes. This was one of the many things he had learnt from Freada. "Carry what you can upon your back," she used to say; "it all saves time and temper. Have no real possessions. Stake no claim. This is our home, for three, for two nights only. This studio, this lodging house, this unfamiliar room in a hotel."

There had been many of them. Dingy ones, with no *eau coulante*, no *salle de bain*, no *petit déjeuner*, and there, for a brief space, they had belonged. Then better ones, where the femme de chambre asked if she could "*préparer le bain*," and it was always ten francs extra; but the water was steaming hot, and the towel very small, and there would be a bed with a monstrous pouf affair balanced upon the top, embroidered with lace. Once they went a bust and took a suite in a palatial kind of palace in Auvergne, because Freada said she had to take a cure. Why, in the name of Jesus, did Freada have to take a cure?

She got up at eight in the morning and went off to drink the waters or have the waters poured upon her, Niall never really knew which; but he used to lie in bed until she returned in the middle of the day, and he read every one of the works of Maupassant, the book in one hand and a bar of chocolate in the other.

In the afternoon he used to make her climb a mountain. Poor Freada, her ankles always hurt, she hated walking. And he made up frightful scandals about the people staying in the hotel, telling her at meals. She used to kick him under the table and whisper, "Will you please be quiet? We shall be thrown out of here." She pretended to look dignified, but spoilt the dignity by kicking her shoes off under the table, and never finding them again without a scuffle. Then there was that melancholy hotel at Fontainebleau where old maiden ladies stretched themselves upon chaises longues, and Niall had played the piano all day long until they had complained to le *patron*. It was the lady in the chaise longue farthest from the room where the piano stood who made the great complaint. The patron was so apologetic. "You see how it is, monsieur," he said with a charming smile, "but this lady who complains, she has strange notions of morality. To her, all dance music is immoral."

"I agree with her," said Niall, "it is immoral."

"But the point is this, monsieur," explained the patron, "the reason why Madame complains of you is not because of the immorality in itself, but because, so she tells me, you make immorality delicious."

> "We were very young, we were very merry,
> We had ridden back and forth all night upon a ferry . . ."

Well, what was it, for God's sake? Was it a verse in *Punch?* And why now, in the spare room at Farthings? Perhaps it was a fragment snatched from the queer hotchpotch of memories that had flooded in upon him all the day. The wet winter's day, spent in Maria's drawing room. Charles's drawing room. It was not Maria's house, nor Maria's room. Farthings belonged to Charles. It had his stamp upon it. The dining room, with the regimental prints. The staircase, with the family portraits spared from Coldhammer. Even the drawing room, which by courtesy was allowed to be a woman's room, had a sagging seat in the best armchair, which was Charles's chair alone.

What did Charles think about, sitting there alone every evening? Did he read those books upon the shelves? Did he gaze at that picture over the mantelpiece, the water-colour memento of that far-off Scottish honeymoon where he had thought to capture and to hold his elusive Mary Rose? There was a pipe by the side of Charles's chair, and a tobacco jar, and a pile of magazines upon the narrow stool—*Country Life, The Sporting and Dramatic, The Field,* and old back numbers of *The Farmers' Weekly.* What did he do with his life? What was his day? The estate office in the morning, the routine visit to Coldhammer, which still stood empty, bleak, and shuttered, never yet handed back from the Agricultural Committee that had seized upon it for the war. A drive into the market town, a meeting, or several meetings. Drainage schemes, Conservatives, Old Comrades, the church tower. Tea with the children, if he was home in time, Polly presiding with the teapot, and the weekly letter to Caroline at school.

Then what? Dinner in solitude. The empty sofa. No Maria to lie upon the sofa. But if she remembered, if she was doing nothing else, there would be that long-distance call from London when she got back to the flat from the theatre. "Well? What sort of a day?" "So-so, rather busy." His replies mainly "Yes" and "No," while Maria chatted

234

on, spinning out her minutes to ease her conscience. Niall knew. Niall had been too often in the room. Not Charles's room. Maria's.

Well, it was not his business. It had continued in this way for years, with the intervention of the war. Would it not continue to eternity? Or did there come a breaking point?

Niall put on his other jacket and tied his spotted scarf.

The breaking point . . . A man, or a woman either, could take so much, could endure so much, up to a certain testing time, and then . . . What was the answer? Perhaps there was no answer. Certainly there was nothing he could do. Or was there?

It was an odd experience to be hurt by the pain of other people. And Charles had been near to breaking point today. There was still the ritual of the Sunday supper. The day was not yet done. What was it Freada had said once, with her great streak of common sense, her truth, her honesty? "I like that Charles. He is a good man. And she is going to make him suffer horribly."

Niall, angry and irritated at the accusation, denied it hotly at the time.

"Why should she? She loves Charles very much."

Freada had looked at him and smiled. And then she sighed, patting him on the shoulder.

"Your Maria love?" she said. "My poor boy, she doesn't begin to know the meaning of the word. Nor do you."

If Freada really believed that, it meant that Niall and Maria were shallow, without depth? It meant that their emotions were trivial, trifling things, carried to no purpose, shed without a cause? In a sense, he felt it could be true about Maria, but not about himself. Surely, not about himself? It was strangely insulting to be told that you knew nothing about love. Worse than to be accused of lack of humour. If you knew nothing about love, why were you unhappy for no reason? Why that waking in the small hours, with an unquiet spirit, fearful and afraid? Why the dragging despair because of a grey day, because of falling leaves, because of winter? And why the upswing of a riotous mood, the surging zest for folly, that came so swiftly and went again too soon? All this he had hurled at the realistic Freada as he sat upon a bed, drinking cognac out of a tooth glass, angry, reproachful; while she combed her pale dyed hair before the mirror and dropped ash upon the floor. "Oh, those feelings," she said, "you don't take any notice of those. They are due to glands."

All right, then. Everything was due to glands. Laughter at midnight, the colour in a crowd, the sun behind a hill, the smell of water. Shakespeare was glands, and Charlie Chaplin.

He had leant forward excitedly, spilling the cognac; and a letter had fallen out of his pocket from Maria.

"The trouble for you," said Freada, "was that the Almighty went adrift when He made both of you. You ought to have shared the same parents and been twins."

Freada would have agreed with Charles about the parasites. . . .

It was worth while sending a telegram to Freada out in Italy, where she had settled the last few years in that dreary villa on a lake, sending him picture postcards of blue skies and blossoms which never materialised when he stayed with her because it always rained; it was worth sending a telegram to Freada and asking, "Am I a parasite?" She would laugh her deep indulgent laugh and answer, "Yes."

Parasitic upon Freada once; until he had learnt to walk alone and to do without her. Freada, tragicomic, like an unpruned willow waving in the breeze, pretending not to mind, shaking her handkerchief to him from the end of the long platform at the Gare du Nord, in a last gesture of farewell. He had returned to her less and less as the years passed; there had really been nothing to go for any more.

The tragedy of life, thought Niall, brushing his hair with the ebony brush and too few bristles that Pappy had given him on his twenty-first birthday, was not that people died; but that they died, to you. All people died to Niall, except Maria. Therefore, Charles was right. I live and feed upon Maria, thought Niall; in her I have my being, I lie embedded deep in the guts of her, and I can't escape because I don't want to escape, ever . . . ever . . .

Which, when you came to think of it, had quite a Cole Porter touch to it.

Deep in the guts. But the errand boys who liked his tunes would not understand it when they whistled. Nor would the old lady in Fontainebleau who had accused him of making immorality delicious. Well, it was something. To have made immorality delicious to one old, slightly deaf French lady who had always hated dance music was, when all was said and done, no small achievement.

This, dear God, was his contribution to the universe. Take it or leave it. Not for Niall the joys of Paradise, perhaps; but at least not the pangs of Purgatory. A small place, possibly, outside the Golden Gates.

Someone from a newspaper had telephoned him the other day. "Mr. Delaney, we are running a series shortly in our paper, 'What Success Has Done for Me'; can we have your contribution?" No, they could not have his contribution. All success had done for him was to make it impossible to pay his super-tax. "But what is your recipe, Mr. Delaney, for the short road to success?" Mr. Delaney had no recipe.

Success. Well, what did it mean to him? Supposing he had answered the newspaper and spoken the truth? A song burning in his head for two days until he had written it down, when he was purged; when he was free again. Until the next pain came. And the performance was repeated. The disillusion came when the songs were plugged upon the air, moaned by crooners whispered by wailing women, clanged by orchestras, hummed by housemaids; so that what had been once his little private pain became, to put it bluntly, everyone's diarrhoea. Which was cheapening, and intolerable. Negroes offered thousands for the rights to sing his songs. God! The cheques that had rolled in from coloured crooners. Too many cheques, all in one year. Niall had to attend conferences in the city with hard-faced men round desks, all because of some little song that had come into his head one afternoon when lying on his back in the sun. How to escape? Travel. He could always travel.

But where? And with whom? Besides, once he had bought a ticket and found himself a ship, or a plane, there were still things like passports and the customs, the anxiety of wondering who to tip and why. Take a house in Rio? But whom would he invite to stay? If he took a house in Rio the local inhabitants would call. The local inhabitants would invite him to dinner, and he would be forced to pack up and escape again. Mr. Delaney never dines; Mr. Delaney never plays bridge; Mr. Delaney does not care for race horses, for yachts, for glamour girls. What in the name of thunder does Mr. Delaney care for? Damn all, and there you had it. . . . What a waste of time it was to be a man of simple tastes. A shakedown in London, a hut beside the sea. A leaky boat that always needed painting and which, if the truth be known, he could not sail. Turn his back upon the world and give his money to the poor? His back was always turned upon the world, and the poor had most of his money anyhow. It was always possible to become a monk. There would be peace inside a monastery. But what about all the other monks, and all the prayers? Vespers and benediction. He would not mind wearing a robe and sandals and a broad straw hat and taking a fork and digging in a garden; but the business of kneeling at 5 A.M. would get him down. And meditating on Christ's wounds. Though, actually, he could meditate on anything. The abbot, or whoever ran the monastery, would never know. He could lie in his little cell all day and meditate upon Mariâ. But if that was all he would achieve by going into a monastery, why not stay where he was? Ah well—there was always tomorrow. Niall put his change in his pocket. The lucky threepenny bit, the stub of a pencil, the key of the car, the small St. Christopher. And one day, he thought, everything will be worth while, because I shall write a concerto which will fail.

It will be the failure of all time, but shall not mind. It will take months and months of toil, and the labour pains will be intense, but that will be the whole point of the procedure. One day, the concerto . . .

The gong for supper sounded. Niall switched off the bedroom light. Down the passage from the nursery wing came the sound of Maria's children, shouting and laughing.

"We were very young, we were very merry,
    We had ridden back and forth all night upon a ferry . . ."

The question was, what now?

CHAPTER TWENTY

I AM GETTING awfully tired of this old housecoat, thought Maria. But then I say that every week end, and I never do anything about it. It was such a simple matter, too, to walk into a shop and get another. The trouble was that she had got into the habit of not bothering about what she kept at Farthings. Anything would do for Farthings. The same thing applied to the bedroom curtains. Those curtains had been hanging in her bedroom ever since they had come to Farthings. Practically the whole of her married life. Of course during the war it had been impossible to get curtains. But that was not the point. The point was that she was continually buying things for the flat in London, new covers for the chairs, new rugs, bits of china, a lovely mirror only the other day to go over the mantelpiece in the sitting room, and never did she bring anything to Farthings. Niall would say it was psychological. Niall would say the reason she took an interest in the flat was because it was hers alone. She rented it, she paid for it, the whole upkeep of the flat came from the money she earned by her own work; but Farthings belonged to Charles. She was a guest at Farthings. At the flat she was at home. Yet Farthings had been her home, too, at the beginning. They had planned the rooms together, she and Charles. The younger children had been born here, in this bedroom. Once she had planted tulips in the garden. There had been tennis parties on Sunday afternoons. Iced coffee and great jugs of lemonade. Shortbread and scones. She wore a white linen frock that buttoned down the side, and the last four buttons were always left undone, so that her legs could sunburn above the knee.

Then, little by little, the interest that had been seemed to slip away. It was easy to blame everything upon the war. Charles away. Herself away. Farthings a home to both of them in patches. But the war was over; Charles had slipped back into the old routine. And not Maria . . . The trouble was—and she poured some OMY essence into the bath and ran the water, a bath before dinner was essential, even if it was Sunday supper, they must all wait for her, what did it matter?—the trouble was that as one grew older—no, as time passed, as time went on, one's own personal life became more important. Which was another way of saying one became more selfish.

Things were irritating now that were not irritating once. Like rattling doors. Like hard pillows. Like tepid food. Like people who were bores. Bores . . . There were far too many people who were bores. Not Charles, of course. She loved Charles, she loved him very much—but . . . His appearance, for one thing, was not what it had been once. That extra weight. Why did he not do something about that weight? It was not exactly a tummy, but all over. What was more, and this was something she scarcely admitted even to herself, he was slightly deaf. Only one ear. The left one. The war, probably, something to do with guns, but still . . . Men had no business to let themselves get set. Why could they not do exercises before breakfast? Give up potatoes? Stop drinking beer? If she let herself get set, where would she be? Out on her ear . . . Out, my dear. We don't want you. There are plenty of youngsters coming on who can step into your shoes. She stepped into the bath, and it was hot and good, and someone—Polly, she supposed—had put a cake of Morny soap into the bracket.

No, the real bore was her father-in-law, old Lord Wyndham, who simply would not die. He had no business to go on living at eighty-one. Poor old man, he got no enjoyment out of it. It would be so much simpler for him, and for everybody else, if he just faded away. He was so deaf now that he could not even hear the clocks ticking, and as he spent most of his time in a wheeled chair, it could not matter whether it was half-past two or half-past twelve. Coldhammer had been taken over by the Agricultural people during the war and not yet been handed back, and the poor old couple had been living in that dingy dower house, with a few retainers, ever since. The death duties would be appalling, naturally, when he did go. And what with taxation, and servant difficulties, and everything else, she and

Charles would never be able to live at Coldhammer, which, in many ways, was a great relief, because the place was like a morgue. The point was that Charles had given up so much time, and trouble, and thought to dealing with the estate, and with the people, and with the whole district, that he really deserved to be called Lord Wyndham. . . . Maria lathered herself all over with Morny soap, and then leant back in the bath, and relaxed, and closed her eyes.

The smell of Morny soap had made her sick once, before somebody was born. She forgot which child. It was not Caroline. Cigarettes with Caroline. Charles would smoke in the bedroom and then stub it out under her nose with profound remorse. It was a wretched habit, smoking in a bedroom. She had broken him of that in the first year, thank heaven.

But that was something else that happened as one grew older—as time went on. It was such a relief to have a bedroom to oneself. At the flat she could walk about naked if she chose, her face covered in grease, her hair in a turban, whistling, humming, talking to herself, the wireless turned on; she could go to bed at three in the morning if she wanted to, and read or not, just as she pleased, and switch off the light when she felt inclined.

At Farthings they still kept to the routine of twin beds. And Charles liked to settle early; he did not care for the wireless or for the light. She would lie in the darkness, not tired, but wide awake; and she was always aware of the humped back of Charles, asleep. It made an irritation. He might have been any man lying there, a stranger. Actually, a stranger would have made it more exciting. What was the point of having a man in your bedroom if all he could do was to turn his back and sleep? Not that she wanted him to do anything else, but in a way it was an insult. The turned back reminded her of the various other backs that had not been turned. Which was a depressing thought, because it meant she was beginning to live in the past.

Backs That Were Never Turned. The Reminiscences of Maria Delaney . . . No, it was not depressing. It was funny. She must remember to tell Niall after supper, when Charles was out of the room. And Celia, too. Not that Celia mattered, but she was inclined to be governessy. The conversation would lead to an argument which no one but themselves would understand. Maria and Niall.

"I'll tell you who probably did show his back."

"Who?"

"So-and-So."

"You are entirely wrong. He never did. I used to wish he would."

In the war one was always lying huddled against someone's back. That communal thing of dressing gowns in passages. In the first raids one went out from the flat onto a central landing, and everyone took it in turns to make cocoa or tea. Midnight feasts in the dorm. Then with the last raids, the buzz-bombs and the rockets, one just stayed quietly in one's flat and did not make tea at all. One wanted a drink instead. Until the person who had been fire-watching came down the fire escape and in at the back door. The person was usually Niall. Why could he never get a hat that fitted properly? That awful strap. If a bomb had ever struck the building they would have gone to glory. She had once coaxed a little fire in the sitting room and invited Niall to put it out for practice. He had set to work, not a smile on his face, very earnest. The stirrup pump would not function; it made the most fearful rude noises at the bottom of the bucket. And because at that time everyone was nervy and rather highly strung she had not seen the humour of it at all, but had lost her temper. "Do you realise that the population of London are depending on you? That it is this gross sort of inefficiency that may make us lose the war?"

"It's the pump," said Niall, "they've given me a dud pump."

"Nonsense. A bad workman blames his tools."

And they had sat for an hour in silence, while he tried to dismantle the pump. Not a joke. Not a smile. They had hated each other.

The absurd lost intimacy of wartime days and nights . . . How wrong was it, Maria wondered, and whose fault, that the years which had brought so much distress, and loss, and hardship to so many people had brought to her, and to Niall also, nothing but undiminishing success? Perhaps that was one of the things that Charles begrudged them both. Perhaps that was why he had called them parasites. For Maria the war had meant a succession of plays that had run for eighteen months. For Niall it had meant a series of songs that everybody sang. People at home, people in factories; pilots in bombers, going backwards and forwards to Berlin. They whistled and sang them for a fortnight and then forgot them; and then he wrote another one, and they whistled that instead. It was not blood and tears, it was not even sweat. It was the minimum of creative effort, but it worked.

Would it have been better, Maria wondered as the water trickled over her, if she had played in failure after failure; if she had left the stage and driven a tractor in the fields? To have been successful while other people died; to have been a popular actress coining money and applause while other women stood at benches; did Charles, in his secret heart, sometimes despise her?

More hot water, turn on the tap, let it gush, let it flow. If one lay still in a bath for more than five minutes the water became strangely chill. And more OMY essence, so that the scent of it filled the steamy air. Where was she? Yes, the war . . .

There used to be an independence to the day. Never knowing, in the morning, how it would end at eventide. Who would appear. What forgotten friend would come knocking at the door. Plans would be erratic, unfulfilled. Leaving notes, "Back in half an hour," pinned to the front door. Going forth, a basket on the arm, and wearing slacks, to shop in Shepherd Market. Why in slacks? Because, in a sense, it was still pretence. It was Red Indians; it was Cavaliers . . . It was freedom. The freedom of no ties, no set arrangements. The freedom of having no one upon the conscience who might be waiting back at home. The children parked safely in the country. Except for those periodic visits to the dentist when, escorted to and fro by Polly, they descended upon the flat for a breathless morning and were away again, to safety, by three-fifteen. They always came when Maria was dressing, or when she was lying in the bath, as now. It meant leaping from the bath, dripping wet. Snatching a towel and opening the door.

"Darlings! How are you?"

Little peaky faces staring at her, and little beady eyes staring at Mummy's flat, where nobody but Mummy ever stayed. Maria did not mind their beady eyes, but she was bored by Polly.

"Mummy looks very comfortable, doesn't she, children? We would like to be up here keeping Mummy company."

Perhaps they would. But Mummy did not want them.

"Darlings, you would be bored with London. Those horrid sirens going. Much nicer in the country."

The children would potter round the flat, peering into the cupboards, while Maria dragged on her clothes and Polly chatted.

"They need new shoes, and Caroline's coat will never do another summer—it's amazing how they grow. I was thinking if we had time to go into Daniel Neal's, or perhaps Debenham's—a nice catalogue came from Debenham's the other day addressed to you, I opened it, I knew you wouldn't mind—and if we do the dentist afterwards . . . Is that the telephone? Would you like me to answer the telephone for you?"

"No, thank you, I can answer it myself."

Even with this hint, Polly would not leave the room. She stood waiting, wondering who it was that rang up Mummy. . . . Too often it was Niall. Niall back from an expedition to New York. Public relations. So he said. Though what Niall had to do with public relations no one ever found out. He never found out himself.

When Polly was in the room, Maria spoke down the telephone in private code. "Is that Mr. Chichester? This is Miss Delaney here."

Niall, as Mr. Chichester, knew the code signal. He laughed at the other end of the telephone and lowered the voice that had been loud.

"Who's with you? Charles or Polly?"

"My children are up from the country, Mr. Chichester, and my day is very full."

"I suppose that means the dentist. Will they stop the night?"

"Definitely no, Mr. Chichester. Not even if there is fog. Perhaps you can call for me at the theatre, and we can discuss that article of yours in *Women and Beauty* about cooking in the home."

"I should adore to, Miss Delaney. Food is such a problem. I find I miss Indian curry more than anything. . . . Darling, can I stay the night?"

"Where else would you go, Mr. Chichester? And do you remember a dish called Bombay duck? I can't wait for Bombay duck."

"I've forgotten Bombay duck. Does it mean I have to sleep on the floor? The last time I slept on the floor I got lumbago."

"No, that's the way they cook curry in Madras. . . . I must go now, Mr. Chichester. Good-bye."

Back again to childhood, to hiding sweets in cupboards, to doing things that Truda said one must never do. Must there always be someone in the room?

"Is Mummy going to take up cooking lessons?" said Polly brightly.

"Perhaps—perhaps."

And still not dressed, still only in a girdle and a brassière, with her hair beneath a turban, and grease on the face, and the morning's letters yet to open.

DEAR MISS DELANEY,

I have written a three-act play on free love in a nudist colony, and for reasons I cannot understand, it has been turned down by every manager in London. I feel strongly that you, and you, alone, would give just the right quality to the character of Lola . . .

DEAR MISS DELANEY,

I saw you some years ago, in a play whose title I have forgotten, but I have always remembered the smile you gave me when you autographed my album. Since then ill luck has dogged me, I am broken in health, and have just come out of hospital to find my wife has run away with all my savings. If you can see your way to letting me have a temporary loan of three hundred pounds . . .

DEAR MISS DELANEY,

As chairman of the Crookshaven Committee for Fallen Women, I am wondering whether you would be good enough to launch an appeal . . .

Into the wastepaper basket went the lot.

"So I thought I could put a good hem on the bottom," said Polly, "and the dress could do her another winter, but it's the socks that are the trouble. They are through their socks so quickly, and the difficulty I've had in the village to get the shoes soled and heeled. Mr. Gatley is so unobliging; we have to wait our turn now, just like anybody else."

Then a sudden yell. One of the children had fallen down and cut its chin on the edge of the bath. Pandemonium; sticking plaster must be found, where was the sticking plaster? "Mummy needs a new first-aid box. Mummy does not take care of herself properly." Mummy did take care of herself. Mummy was perfectly all right as long as she was left alone.

The dentist, shopping, lunch, shopping again; and the blessed relief of seeing everybody off at the station on the three-fifteen. A pang, for one brief moment, because of the little faces at the window and the waving hands; a queer inexplicable clutch at the heart. Why was Maria not with them? Why did she not look after them? Why did she not behave like other mothers? They were not hers. They did not belong to her. They were Charles's children. Something went wrong from the very start, and it was all her own fault, because she had not thought about them enough, she had not loved them enough; there was always someone else. A play, a person, always something else . . .

A funny lost feeling of despair, turning away from the platform, and pushing through the barrier with those soldiers carrying their kits; what was it all for? Where were they all going? What was Charles doing in the Middle East? Why was she here? All those people pushing through the barriers. All those bewildered, searching faces.

In the theatre there was safety. A deep embedded sense of home, of safety. The dressing room that needed doing up, with the plaster coming off the walls, the dusty ventilator. The crack in the basin. The worn bit of carpet that the rug could not cover. The table and the pots of cream. Someone knocking on the door. "Come in." Charles was forgotten, the children were forgotten, the war and all those strange loose threads of life that parted and dissolved; these could be forgotten too. The only safety lay in the subterfuge. In doing what she had done from the beginning of time. In pretending to be someone else . . . But not only that. In being a gang, a little group together, a ship's crew.

During the performance the rattle of an express train overhead coughed and gasped to its destination. Then the sudden silence. THEY had begun again.

Why did not Niall come and fetch her home afterwards? It was the least he could do, to call for her at the theatre. Try the telephone. No answer from the telephone. Well, then, where was Niall? Supposing, when that last thing burst, it had got to Niall?

"Does anybody know where they had it tonight?"

"Croydon, I think."

Nobody knew. No one was certain. Then another knock at the door. "Come in." And it was Niall. The surge of relief that turned to irritation.

"Where have you been? Why didn't you come before?"

"I was doing something else."

No use, ever, to question Niall. He was a law unto himself.

"I thought you might be in front," she said crossly, cleaning her face.

"I've seen the play four times, and that's about three times too many," answered Niall.

"I was rather good tonight. Quite different from the time you saw me last."

"You're always different. I've never seen you do the same thing twice. Here, take this parcel."

"What is it?"

"A present I bought you in New York, Fifth Avenue. Horribly expensive. It's called a negligee."

"Oh, Niall . . ."

And she was a child again, tearing at the wrappings, flinging tissue paper on the floor; but quickly collecting it again, because tissue paper was difficult to find. Then pulling from the box a flimsy float-ing idiocy, transparent and impractical.

"It must have cost the earth."

"It did."

"Public relations?"

"No, personal. Don't ask me any more. Put it on."

It was such fun to have a present. Why was she such a child about a present?

"How does it look?"

"It looks good."

"It feels good. I shall call it Desire under the Elms."

There were never any taxis to be found. They had to grope their way back to the flat through fog, listening to the onrush of the pant-ing, puffing train above them in the sky. And it was exasperating and queer, irritating and strange, that the person she loved most in the world, even now, was the person she had smacked and bullied as a child. Why reach this point in life and go on clinging to the same little sullen boy? The same familiar eyes, and mouth, and hands? In moments of elation, in moments of despondency, always return to Niall. Always make Niall the whipping boy, the scapegoat to a mood.

"The thing is . . ."

"The thing is what?"

"The thing is, instead of bringing me Desire under the Elms, you should have brought me loads of food in tins. But of course it never entered your head to do that. Gorged as you were with steak."

"What sort of food?"

"Well, hams, and tongues, and chickens' breasts in aspic."

"I did. I left a great parcel of stuff with the hall porter. You'll see directly. But not chickens' breasts. Frankfurters."

"Oh! Oh well . . ."

Pottering in the flat, between the bedroom and the kitchen, one moment she talked to Niall, and the next to the humming kettle.

"Now, don't you dare boil over, I've got my eye on you. . . .

Niall, what are you doing in my linen chest? Leave it alone."

"I've got to find another blanket. What's this thing, plaided, underneath an ironing board, all Scots wha hae wi' Wallace bled?"

"You can't have it. . . . Yes, you can, but don't spill brandy on the bottom."

"I haven't any brandy. I wish I had. The flat is icy. My teeth are chattering."

"Very good for you. Pickled with steam heat . . . Now I've lost the tin opener. Niall, what *have* you got on? You look like a nigger minstrel."

"They are my American pyjamas. Desire under the Dogwood. Don't you admire them?"

"No. That awful liver-coloured stripe . . . Take them off. Wear Scots wha hae instead."

"I thought I might wear Scots wha hae as well."

Another rattling train clattered overhead. Where to? Where from? Better fill the hot-water bottle quickly.

"Are you hungry, Niall?"

"No."

"Will you be hungry later?"

"Yes. Don't worry. If I am I'll bust open one of the tins of frankfurters with a shoehorn. By the way, what *was* Bombay duck?"

"Sharing a compartment in a sleeper. Had you forgotten?"

"Oh, of course. But how does it apply to us tonight?"

"It doesn't. It was just to put off Polly."

The lovely warmth of a scalding cup of tea, and then a bottle in its cover against the toes. The lovely silence when there were no express trains, no rattling doors and windows; only the ticking of the bedside clock, the hands luminous in the darkness, standing at ten to one.

"Niall?"

"What?"

"Did you see that bit in the evening paper about the wife of some old Colonel Noseworthy dying and asking to have 'I've Got You under My Skin' played at her funeral?"

"No."

"Such a good idea. I keep wondering who it was she had got under her skin."

"Old Noseworthy, I suppose. . . . Maria, what are we meant to be doing?"

"I don't know. But whatever it is, it's heaven."

"Well, stop talking, then. . . ."

In the hall at Farthings someone sounded the gong. Maria opened her eyes and sat up, shivering. She reached for the bath plug, and the tepid water ran away gurgling, roaring, outside the bathroom window. She was going to be very late for Sunday supper.

CHAPTER TWENTY-ONE

CELIA shut the door of the children's bedroom behind her. It is true, she said to herself, what we were saying this afternoon; they are different from what we used to be. Our world was one of fantasy. Theirs is reality. They don't pretend. An armchair is always an armchair, to the modern child, never a ship, never a desert island. The patterns on the wall are patterns, not characters whose faces change at dusk. Games like draughts or ludo are games of skill and chance; even as bridge or poker is to an adult. Draughts to us were soldiers, ruthless and malignant; and the crowned king on the back line a puffed-up potentate, jumping with horrible power, backwards and forwards, from square to square. The trouble is, the children have no imagination. They are sweet, and have carefree, honest eyes; but they have not any magic in their day. The magic has all gone. . . .

"Children tucked up, Miss Celia?"

"Yes, Polly. I am so sorry I did not come up to give you a hand with the baths."

"Oh, that's quite all right; I heard you talking in the drawing room, and I thought you must have plenty to discuss. Mrs. Wyndham's looking tired, don't you think?"

"It's only London, Polly. And the rainy weather. And being in a play that is not doing very well."

"I suppose so. Such a pity she doesn't take a long rest and stay down here with Mr. Wyndham and the children."

"It's not easy for an actress to do that, Polly. Besides, it would not suit her."

"The children see so little of her. Caroline writes to Daddy twice a week from school, never to Mummy. I can't help thinking sometimes . . ."

"Yes, well, I must go and tidy, Polly. I shall see you at supper."

No confidences from Polly about Maria. No confidences about Charles, about the children. Too many love affairs she had to straighten and settle, too many private pangs and woes. The Irish night nurse who had lived with them during the final months before Pappy died, she had been the worst. Her endless letters from a married man. Always the flow of someone else's tears.

To live vicariously meant, decided Celia, not to live for other people, but to see life only through their eyes and never through your own. By doing this, of course, she had been spared much pain. At least, she supposed she had. Celia washed her hands in the washbasin in Caroline's bedroom, which had been allotted to her for the week end, and sponged her face. The water was cool. Someone—Maria, no doubt— had drained away the hot to fill her bath; the water was running still. . . . Take love affairs, for instance. If she, Celia, had ever had a love affair, no doubt it would have turned to gall and wormwood, or it would have proved abortive from the start. She would have been one of that sort of women whom men left. "Have you heard about poor Celia? That brute of a man." He would have gone off and deserted her for somebody else's wife. Or else he would have been married himself, like the husband of the Irish nurse, and a Catholic, and unable to be divorced. He and Celia would have met, miserably, week after week, year after year, sitting on a bench in Regent's Park.

"But what are we to do?"

"There is nothing we can do. Maud won't hear of separation." Maud would live forever. Maud would never die. Celia and the man would sit in Regent's Park, talking about Maud's children. She had been spared all that. It was a great relief. Nor, looking back, would there have been time for it. There had been so much to do for Pappy during those helpless years. There had been no time for her drawings and her stories. Much to the exasperation of Mr. Harrison and his firm.

"If you don't do them now, you know, you never will," he said.

"I promise you I shall. Next week, next month, next year." They became tired of her after a while. She did not keep her promises. She was only a half-fledged artist, after all. The quality that had excited

Mr. Harrison and the rest, the quality that had been Mama's, must dwindle away and die. Surely it was more important to make a person happy. It was more important for Pappy, lying helpless in his bed, to watch her with his eyes and say, "My darling, my darling," and to give to him the little comfort that she could; than to sit alone, writing, drawing, creating people who had never lived at all. It was not possible to do both. That was the heart of the matter. She had known it, when she had taken Pappy home from hospital. Either she must give her time to him, for his remaining years, or she must let him go, and turn upon herself and feed her talent.

It was a choice. A simple issue. And she had chosen Pappy.

The thing that people like Mr. Harrison had never understood was that to do this was no sacrifice. It was not unselfishness. She had made her choice of her own free will, because she wished to do it. However demanding Pappy may have been, however tiring, however petulant, he was, in the true and deepest sense, her refuge. He shielded her from action. His was the cloak that covered her. She need not go out into the world, she need not struggle, need not face the things that other people face—because she looked after Pappy.

Let Mr. Harrison and his colleagues go on thinking her a genius hiding from the light of day. By lying hidden, she could not be proven otherwise. She could have done this, she might have done the other, but she could not do either, because of Pappy. Let Maria stand out upon the stage, with the glare upon her. The applause came, but she risked stony silence too; she risked failure. Let Niall write his tunes, and wait for criticism; the tunes might be praised, but they could be damned as well.

Once a person gave his talent to the world, the world put a stamp upon it. The talent was not a personal possession any more. It was something to be traded, bought, and sold. It fetched a high price, or a low one. It was kicked in the common market. Always, forever after, the possessor of the talent must keep a wary eye upon the purchaser. Therefore, if you were sensitive, if you were proud, you turned your back upon the market. You made excuses. Like Celia.

And that is the real reason I looked after Pappy, she thought as she changed her shoes and stockings, because I was afraid of criticism, afraid of failure. Charles was all wrong when he attacked the others. I am the parasite, not they. I preyed on Pappy, while they went into the world. Pappy was dead, but still she made excuses. The war . . .

She could not be expected to draw pictures during the war. There were many more important things to do. Cleaning floors in hospitals. Serving in canteens. Helping in training centres for the blind . . . There had been so many things that a single person, unattached, could do. A single woman, unattached, like Celia. And I did them all, she thought, I never stopped, I was busy all the time, few women worked as hard as I did. But why am I talking to myself like this? What am I trying to prove? The war is over, the war is dead, like Pappy. What, then, do I live for now?

She sat down upon the bed, one stocking in her hand. The wall in front of her was blank. Caroline had no pictures hanging on it. She had taken them with her to boarding school. Why send a little girl to school? She wished to go, said Maria, she was bored at home. Celia could not ask the thing that she wanted. She could not turn to Maria and say, "If Caroline is bored, why not let her come to live with me?" Someone to love, to cherish. A reason for existence. The moment had come, and gone, and now of course it was too late. Caroline was happy at her school, and here was Celia, sitting on Caroline's bed, staring at the blank wall. A blank wall.

It had been a foolish sort of day; that, really, was the trouble. Too much rain. Not going out, not taking exercise. Charles moody and depressed. She pulled on her stocking. Then she turned down her bed and folded the cover. It would save somebody else's doing it later. She laid her nightgown on the pillow, and the woolly bed jacket, and the bed socks, and the rabbit with the torn ear. The rabbit was one of the many things she had salvaged when the furniture went into storage after Pappy died.

"There is so much junk," said Maria, "you can't possibly want a quarter of it. I'd like that desk for the flat, and the round table from the drawing room, and there is a little old rocking chair I've always loved. But don't burden yourself with a mass of stuff. It will only be bombed."

Niall wanted nothing, except some books, and Sargent's drawing of Mama. Celia wanted everything. But how could she keep everything? Where could she put it? Living as she must, from day to day, until the war was over. It hurt so much to throw away familiar things. Even old calendars and Christmas cards. One calendar had hung in the downstairs lavatory the year Maria was married. And Celia had never changed it afterwards, because the picture of apple blossoms in the spring had seemed so right. She had bought little tags in the New Year and stuck them on the bottom. The picture never failed to cheer her, even in moments of depression. And so, when the house was sold, things like the calendar had to be thrown away. Into the wastepaper basket went the apple blossoms. But there were still trunkloads of things that had not been thrown away. Trunkloads of useless objects. Cups and saucers, plates, and coffee urns. Pappy always liked his coffee from that urn. The green vase must be kept. Truda chipped the edge once, when she was filling it, because Niall ran into her, wanting a drink of orange from the pantry. The green vase was a symbol of Niall, aged sixteen. Keep the paper knives, the trays, the old coal scuttle with the brass bands. They were in use once, every day. They served their purpose. They spelt a moment, and a time.

And now, the maisonette at Hampstead, where she had lived for the past year, was filled to overflowing with the things she did not need. But she was glad to have them by her all the same. Like the rabbit with one ear upon her pillow now.

That was another reason, of course, why she had neglected her drawing and her stories. She had been busy moving into the maisonette. "Don't call it maisonette, it sounds so common," said Maria. But what else could it be called? It was a maisonette.

She was only there during the week, because at week ends she always came to Farthings. At least, she had always come to Farthings up till now. She paused, as she buttoned up the mandarin coat Maria had given her, because it was much too big, and why is it, she wondered, that everything today seems so uncertain, like it does on a summer's evening when a storm is brewing, or when one of the children get a temperature and the mind jumps instantly to infantile paralysis?

When she arrived down yesterday, the place was the same, as always. She had caught the usual train on Saturday. Maria had come down in the evening, of course, after the play, with Niall. Celia and Charles and Polly and the children lunched together, as they always lunched on Saturdays. Charles had gone off somewhere in the afternoon, and Celia had walked with Polly and the children. Dinner with Charles was not more quiet than usual. They had switched on the wireless, listened to *Music-hall*, listened to the news. Celia had mended a cushion cover that Maria had torn the week end before. Then she had seen about getting the supper for Maria and Niall, who would arrive hungry. It saved Polly if she did this, and it saved Mrs. Banks; it meant that they need not wait up, but could go to bed. Besides, Celia liked doing it. It had become routine. She cooked better than Mrs. Banks. Made things more tasty, so the others said. Perhaps she had taken too much upon herself by doing these things? Perhaps Charles resented it and was offended?

And suddenly, the things she had taken for granted through the years, like staying at Farthings, like mending cushions for Maria, like darning the socks for the children, became unstable; they were no longer part of her life, and permanent. They would cease to be, like the war, like Pappy. She buttoned the mandarin coat to the chin and powdered her nose. As she looked into the glass she saw the old telltale frown between her brows, and she powdered on top of it, but it would not go.

"Will you stop frowning?" Truda used to say. "It's not right for children of your age to frown."

"Smile, my darling, smile," said Pappy; "you look as though you have the cares of the world upon your shoulders."

But the frown had become ingrained. It would never go. Not now . . . Like the pain in the solar plexus. So often, on and off, during the war, though it had started, really, during the time she was nursing Pappy, she had had the little nagging pain. Nothing intense. Nothing severe. But nagging. It meant indigestion if she ate certain foods. Anyway, those X-ray photographs would prove if there was anything wrong. She would have them next week. But the pain would probably continue, like the frown. . . . Once a woman was over thirty and she was not married, she was sure to have something wrong, some sort of pain, somewhere. . . .

If she went downstairs now, to the drawing room, and made up the fire before the gong sounded, would Charles be there? Would he look at her, thinking: Why must she treat the house as though it belonged to her? Yet the fire would need seeing to, and Polly would be in the kitchen dishing up, with Mrs. Banks. Whatever I do now, thought Celia, will seem like interference; mixing the salad, I've always mixed the salad, nobody else knows how, they will forget the sugar—but Maria ought to do it herself, Maria or Charles. Whatever I do now will seem presumptuous, in my own eyes, if not in anybody else's; the serenity is gone; and Farthings is not a home any longer, it's a house where I am staying as a guest for the week end.

She left her room and went down the back stairs, in case she should meet Charles by the front. In this fashion she could go into the dining room by the other door, and be waiting there, anonymously, with Polly when the gong rang. But the plan was frustrated, because Charles himself was standing in the pantry, with the door open, talking on the telephone. The extension to his study had gone wrong; he had been complaining about it the day before.

Celia drew back into the shadow of the stairs to wait until he had finished. Many times she had herself gone into the pantry to telephone, to the station, perhaps, about trains, or to the garage in the village for a car, and when she lifted the receiver she would hear a voice on the bedroom extension, Maria's voice, talking long-distance to somebody in London, and she would know by the sound of that voice whether the call was business—or something else. Quite often it was something else. Celia would put down the receiver in the pantry and wait, leaning against the sink, until the click in the telephone system on the wall warned her that the call was over. She was reminded of this tonight.

"It's quite definite," Charles was saying. "I made up my mind this afternoon. It's hopeless to go on like this any longer. I shall say so tonight." There was a pause, and then he said, "Yes. The whole outfit. All three of them." Another pause, and then, "Pretty bad all day. But better now. Things are always better when one has the courage to come to a decision."

Turning round, he saw the open pantry door. He lunged at it with his foot. The door swung to and crashed. His voice became a murmur, soft and blurred.

And Celia, crouching against the wall on the back stairs, felt suddenly cold. Something is going to happen. Something none of us has known about is going to happen. The anxiety about her own status as intruder did not matter any more. It swung now to a larger, wider apprehension. She slipped past the pantry into the dining room and, with the colour ebbing from her cheeks, began to mix the salad.

The sound of the gong echoed through the house like a summons.

CHAPTER TWENTY-TWO

THE dining room at Farthings was long and narrow. The table was mahogany, with leaves that lifted at either end, and the chairs were mahogany, too, with straight stiff backs and narrow spindle legs. The carpet was grey, deeper than the soft grey of the walls. There was never a log fire in the dining room, only an electric fire, turned on and off before and after meals, burning with a single bar. Once, in a careless mood, Maria had toasted a kipper before the bar. The oily fat from the smoking kipper splashed and sizzled onto the pure unstained steel of the fire, and in spite of Polly's rubbing with a cloth, the marks had never entirely disappeared.

They remained still, the only stains on the clean and unblemished room. Never a room to dream in, never a room in which to browse and talk. The ritual of the Sunday supper lay spread upon the serving table behind Charles's chair. Soup, in green earthenware pots with little handles, stood upon heated soup plates; these last a tribute to courtesy alone, because the policy was to drink the soup straight from the earthenware pots, thus saving the washing up of extra plates. A cold chicken, garnished about with parsley to make colour; some sausage rolls, the remains of the luncheon joint shrunken in size since midday; these and a vegetable dish filled with baked potatoes wrapped in a napkin were among the more substantial offerings to the feast. There was, of course, the salad. An open tart (fruit of Polly's bottling), and a trifle, and a great slab of blue Danish cheese.

Niall noticed, with relief, that the bottle of claret stood uncorked, but apparently as yet unwarmed, upon the sideboard; he noticed, too, that the bottle of London gin to which he and Maria had helped themselves before going up to change, and which they had left two-thirds full, was now empty. Charles, who waited always for his wine and never mixed a cocktail except for guests, had therefore finished it. Niall glanced at Charles out of the corner of one eye, but Charles, with his back turned, was sharpening the carving knife on steel, preparatory to work upon the chicken. Polly stood at his side, ready to hand the plates. Celia, seated already at the table, was unrolling her napkin from its silver ring. It was the ring she always used, but as she put it down upon the table Niall noticed that she stared at it thoughtfully, as if she posed the ring a question.

The last of the bath water ebbed away down the waste pipe outside the window. Maria could be heard moving in her bedroom overhead. Nobody spoke. Charles continued carving at the chicken. The puppy scratched at the door, and Celia, rising instinctively to let him in, paused halfway, hovering, uncertain, and glanced over her shoulder at the figure carving by the sideboard.

"What about the pup?" she said. "Shall I let him in?"

Charles could not have heard her, for he did not answer; and, looking anxiously and indecisively at Niall, Celia opened the door. The puppy sidled in and, worming its way across the room, crawled beneath the table.

"Who wants the breast?" asked Charles surprisingly.

Now if the three of us had been alone, thought Niall, or if Charles had been Maria, this would be the moment for a merry quip, and the mood for supper set. I always want the breast and get it far too seldom. But not tonight. To quip tonight was but to court disaster. Anyway, it was not for Niall to express a wish. He waited upon Celia.

"I would love a wing if you can spare one, Charles," she said, speaking rather too quickly, her cheeks flushing, "and perhaps a sausage roll. A small one."

It was unlike Charles to carve the second course before he had sat down to his soup. Nothing tonight, though, was as it should be. The ritual was upset. Only Polly remained blank and unaware. She came with the little tray, handing round pots of soup. Yet even she found something was at fault. She paused a moment, her head on one side, like a puzzled sparrow. Then she smiled.

"I have forgotten to turn on *Grand Hotel*," she said.

She handed the last of the soup and, darting to the portable wireless in the corner of the dining room, switched on the knob. The volume was much too loud. A throaty tenor split the air with pain. Niall winced, his eye on Charles. Polly had the sense to turn the knob over to the left, and the tenor subsided, his voice above a whisper. For him, if not for those who listened, the "Temple Bells Were Ringing." Still, the sound drugged feeling and helped to break the silence. The tenor was like another guest to supper, but less effort.

And soup, Niall thought, reveals the character. Celia takes hers out of a spoon, as Truda taught us all three to do, but she does not pour it into her plate; she spoons it from the pot, a wartime custom. Polly takes hers in tiny sips, one finger crooked. Each time she sips she puts the pot down onto the plate, then lifts it up again. In the old days the three of us would have called this mincy manners. Charles, like the man he was, like all the Wyndhams, probably, from the beginning of time, brought up since boyhood to massive great tureens handed by footmen, emptied his soup into a plate, oblivious of the washing up, and spooned it sideways, tipping up his plate. Whereas I, thought Niall, I alone am greedy; and he put his mouth to the pot and drank the soup down in gulps.

The tenor sang "Pale hands I loved" as Maria came at last into the room. She had dressed in a hurry; she wore nothing, Niall knew, under her dressing-gown affair, which was velvet, and the colour of old gold. She wore it every Sunday; that, and a jewelled belt he had brought her once from Paris. He wondered why it was that she always looked lovelier like this, with a comb run through her hair and a smattering of powder, than when she took trouble and dressed formally for grand occasions. He wondered if it was oddity with him, approaching perversion, or the familiarity of years of love and knowledge that made him want her most when a little rumpled as she was now, or drowsy on first waking, or greasy with her hair in pins, her make-up wiped away.

"Oh! Am I late?" she asked, her eyes wide. "I am so sorry." And she sat down in her chair at the end of the table opposite Charles, and her voice was the voice of innocence, of the person who has not heard the gong, who does not know the time of supper. And this, then, decided Niall, is to be the motif for tonight; this is the chosen role; we are all back again to Mary Rose, the ethereal one, the lost child on the island. Whether it works with Charles or not remains to be seen. Because time is all-urgent, time is getting short.

"Supper has always been at eight o'clock," said Charles, "all these years, at your demand. It was at eight tonight."

We are all lined up, thought Niall. We are under starter's orders. The point is, how does Maria eat her soup? Does she sip, or tip? I've never noticed. It probably depends upon the mood. Maria took the green earthenware pot in both her hands. She held the pot lovingly; the warmth of the soup came to her, and she sniffed it, to see what it would be. Then she drank it from the pot, still holding it in both her hands, but she drank slowly, thoughtfully, not in great gulps like Niall. She looked across the table at him and saw him watching her intently with a smile. She smiled back at him, because it was Niall, but puzzled, too, not sure why he was smiling. Had she done something wrong? Or was it the tune? Was there some code significance in the tune that she had not remembered? "Pale hands I loved beside the Shalimar . . ." Where was Shalimar? What lovely, sensuous visions it conjured, anyway, despite the sickly tenor and the honeyed words. A river warm and limpid, the colour of chartreuse. The thing was, why had she never done a tour in India? There was always India. Rajahs, and moonstones, bathing in asses' milk. Women in purdah. Or in suttee. Or in something . . . She looked round the table. The silence was oppressive. Somebody else must grapple with it. Not Maria.

"The children were so funny in the bath, Mummy," said Polly, rising from the table, collecting the pots of soup. "They said, 'I wonder if Mummy and Uncle Niall still have a bath together, like they must have done when they were little, and if Mummy gets angry when the soap goes in her eyes.'" She laughed merrily at the children's jest and waited for comment. What an awfully stupid remark to make just at this moment, thought Celia wretchedly, and how very nearly it is the sort of remark I might have made myself, forgetting, or not minding, with the three of us alone.

"I can't remember, can you," said Niall briskly, "when all three of us last plunged into a bath? Maria was always selfish with the water. She wanted to have it all to herself. But I remember soaping Celia's bottom. It was nice and squidgy, full of dimples. Would you take my soup plate, Polly?"

"Less Than the Dust." So sang the tenor now. And very apropos, to judge from Charles's set expression. Less than the dust beneath his chariot wheels. Niall was less than the dust. Everyone was less than the dust. And Charles, cracking the whip in the chariot, rode above it.

The second course was served without further quotation from the children. Niall was given a long, lean thigh of chicken. Oh well, a thigh could serve its purpose, but would Charles ever warm the claret; would he, which was more important still, ever serve the claret?

Charles was occupied at the moment in handing round the salad. Anyone could hand the salad. The claret was up to Charles. If there was one thing that Niall could not do, it was to pour out the claret in Charles's house. Onto the thigh instead. Do justice to the thigh.

Polly had the wishbone. Later on there would be hell to pay, in all probability, with that same wishbone. She would pick it clean, then hand it to Maria. "Does Mummy want a wish? If Mummy could have her heart's desire, what would Mummy wish?" Danger lay in the wishbone. Why could not Charles have kept it for himself?

Maria had all the breast. She ate it with unconcern. It was wasted on her. Charles ate the other wing. Well, it was his bird, when all was said and done, and he deserved it. Maria looked up after helping herself to salad.

"Aren't we going to have anything to drink?" she said.

Mary Rose it was. But rather a grumpy, pouting Mary Rose. Left in the cherry tree too long by Simon without sustenance.

In the same grim silence Charles approached the sideboard. He poured the claret. No question of warming it now. Celia and Polly both refused, greatly to Niall's relief; Polly with her usual breathless laugh, when offered alcohol: "Oh no, Mr. Wyndham, not for me. I have to face tomorrow."

"So have we all," said Charles.

That was a poser. That was a hit below the belt. Even Mary Rose, her eyes a misty blue and full of dreams, registered interrogation. Niall saw her flash a look across the table at her husband, a wary, doubtful look; then she relapsed once more into her role.

Attack is the best form of defence. Somebody was always saying that. Montgomery or Slim. Niall had heard it on the wireless several times during the war. He wondered if the method would apply tonight. Supposing he leant forward to his host and said, "Look here, what is all this? Where do we stand?" Would Charles stare blankly back at him, nonplussed? The old days were best. The old lost days of duels. A wineglass shivering to fragments. A wine stain down a lace cravat. A hand on the hilt of a sword. Tomorrow? Yes, at dawn. . . . Meanwhile, you did nothing. You attacked the thigh of chicken. You drank your claret and found it much too chill, too sour. A fair communion wine. Charles, groping in the cellarette after his second gin, had passed over the prewar stock from Berry Brothers and had brought out something else. One of those vinegar vintages, marked twelve and six. No matter. Let it go. . . . Celia found a caterpillar in the salad and hid it swiftly under an outside leaf. Mrs. Banks was not so thorough, after all. It was so easy to clean a lettuce if you rinsed it well. Examined every leaf, then rinsed, then shook the whole thing in a clean damp cloth. A good thing the caterpillar had been on her plate and not Maria's. Maria would have said, "Oh God—look at this," and somehow, this evening, that kind of remark would not have been in place.

If only somebody would talk and break the silence; but in an easy way. The children would have helped. The children would have prattled on, unconscious. No one could create an atmosphere when there were children. It was at this moment that the announcer in *Grand Hotel* chose to tell his listeners that the orchestra would play a selection from the dance tunes of Niall Delaney. Polly looked up from her wishbone with a wide, bright smile. "Oh, how nice," she said, "now we shall all be pleased." All, perhaps, but Niall Delaney. Jesus, how ill-timed.

"It's rather hard," said Niall, aloud, "to hear one's mistakes in public. A writer, after all, can forget about them, once he has returned his proofs. Not so the composer of dud songs."

"You mustn't say that, Mr. Niall," said Polly; "you always will belittle yourself. I'm sure you do know, really, how popular they are. You ought to hear Mrs. Banks in the kitchen, washing up. Even her voice can't spoil them! Ah, this is my favourite."

It was everybody else's favourite, too, five years ago. Why bring it back? Why not let it die in the limbo of lost moods? Anyway, the fools were taking it too fast. That awful bouncy rhythm . . . Nine in the morning, it had been, the sun streaming through the window of his room, and so unexpectedly for him at that hour, the energy of all the world on waking; with the song in his head. He had gone to the piano and played the sound of it, and then had rung Maria.

"What is it? What do you want?" Her voice heavy with sleep. She hated the telephone before half-past ten.

"Listen. I want you to hear something."

"No."

"Don't madden me. Listen."

He had played the song half a dozen times, and then lifted the receiver again, and he had known how she was looking, with the turban round her head and the eye pads on her eyes.

"Yes, but it should not do that at the end," she had said; "it should do this." And she sang the last bar so that it went up at the end, instead of down, and of course that was what he had meant all the time.

"You mean like this? Hold on, while I put the telephone on the piano."

He had played it again, going up, as she wanted it; and he sat on the piano stool, laughing, with the receiver tucked between his head and his shoulder, a mad cramped position, like a ventriloquist's dummy, while she hummed the tune down the receiver into his ear.

"Well, now may I go to sleep again?"

"Yes, if you can."

That had been the fun of the mood, for five minutes, for ten minutes, for one hour, perhaps, at most. Then it went. Then it belonged to the crooners. To Mrs. Banks, to Polly . . . He would have liked to get up and switch the wireless off; the business was ill-judged, lacking in taste. It was as though he, Niall, had deliberately told the officials of *Grand Hotel* to play these songs just now, as an insult to Charles. A modern flinging of the gauntlet. I can do this. What can you do?

"Yes," said Charles slowly, "that is my favourite too."

Which, thought Niall, is the sort of thing that makes me want to get up from the table, and go out of the room, and drive to the sea and find my leaky boat and sail it to perdition. Because the look in Charles's eyes as he said that is a thing I can never forget.

"Thank you, Charles," said Niall. And split a baked potato.

Here was the chance, thought Celia. Here was the chance to make everything all right. A bond between us all. Bring Charles into the fold. It was the fault of each one of us, shutting Charles outside. Maria had never realised it. She had not understood. Her mind had always been a child's mind, questing, curious, full of mirrors, reflecting other people. She had not thought about you, Charles, simply because children never think. If the moment could be held, simply by the bond of Niall's music, everything might yet come clear. But Polly blundered in.

"The boy was so funny on the walk this afternoon," she said. "He asked me, 'Polly, when we are grown-up, shall we be clever and famous like Mummy and Uncle Niall?' 'That depends on you,' I told him. 'Little boys don't become famous who bite their nails.'"

"I bit mine to the quick until I was nineteen," said Niall.

"Eighteen," said Maria.

She knew who stopped him, too. She stared at him stonily across the table. And now it's gone, thought Celia, the moment. We have missed the chance. Charles filled his glass with claret and said nothing.

"'Besides,'" continued Polly, "'you don't just become clever and famous by sitting back and doing nothing.' That's what I told the boy. 'Mummy would like to spend more time in her home, with you children and Daddy, but Mummy has to work in London, at the theatre.' And do you know what he said to that? He said, 'She doesn't have to work. She could just be our mummy.' It was really rather sweet."

She sipped her glass of water, crooking her finger, smiling at Maria. I can't make up my mind, thought Niall, whether Polly is a criminal, cunning and dangerous, ripe for the Old Bailey; or just so bloody stupid that it would be kindness to wring her neck and spare the world more pain.

"I think," said Celia bravely, "that the thing to tell the children is this. Being famous is awfully unimportant. What is important is to like the thing you do. Whether it is acting, or composing, or gardening, or being a plumber, you must like the thing you do."

"Does that apply to marriage?" enquired Charles.

Celia had blundered worse than Polly. Niall saw her bite her lip.

"I don't think Polly was discussing marriage, Charles," she said.

"No," said Charles, "but my son and heir obviously was."

It is a pity I'm not a brilliant conversationalist, thought Niall; one of those flamboyant creatures who toss phrases into the air like pancakes, and whip them back and forth across the table. This would be my chance. Steer the conversation into broad wide channels, and from thence into the realm of abstract thought. Every word a gem. Marriage, my dear Charles, is like a feather bed. For some the down, for some the pointed quill. Open up the mattress and the whole thing stinks. . . .

"Is there any breast left?" asked Maria.

"I'm sorry," answered Charles, "you've had it all."

Well, that was one way out of it. And saved the brain much effort.

"What I always mean to do," continued Polly, "is to get a book and write down all the funny things the children say."

"Why get a book when you remember them so well?" asked Niall.

Maria got up from her chair and wandered to the serving table. She dug a fork into the trifle, wrecking the surface. She tasted it, and made a bitter face, and put back the fork belonging to the apple tart. Having spoilt the appearance of the third course, she came back again to the table with an orange. The only orange. She dug her teeth into it, spitting out the skin. If this was a different sort of party, reflected Niall, now would be the moment to start a questionnaire, the kind of questionnaire we play when we're alone. Where is the best place to kiss a person whom you love? It depends upon the person. Must you know them well? Not well enough. Oh well, in that case, probably the neck. Beneath the left ear. And travel downwards. Or, as you became more intimate, upon the ankle. The ankle? Why the ankle? Maria flipped a pip across the table. It hit Niall in the eye. I wish, he thought, that I could tell her what I'm thinking now. It would shatter Mary Rose, and we could laugh.

"I am afraid," said Polly, watching Maria's orange, "that I forgot to put any sherry in the trifle."

Charles rose and began collecting the plates. Niall helped himself to a slab of Danish cheese. Celia took trifle, to spare the offended Polly. Besides, the apple tart would be wanted for tomorrow.

"It's quite a job remembering everything," said Polly, "and really, Mrs. Banks is not much help. She only puts the bare rations on the grocery order. I don't know where we'd be if I didn't put on my thinking cap each Monday."

Monday, thought Niall, was a day to be avoided. Heaven help the world on Mondays.

Charles gave himself neither sweet, nor cheese. He broke off the edge of a biscuit, staring steadily at the silver candlesticks, and then poured out for himself the last of the claret. The dregs. The draught was potent. His face, though heavy nowadays, was usually without great colour, and brown from being mostly out of doors. Now it reddened, and the veins appeared. His hand played with his glass.

"Well?" he said slowly. "And what conclusion did you reach this afternoon?" Nobody answered. Polly glanced up, surprised.

"You've had half a day," he continued, "to consider quietly whether I was right or wrong."

The bravest of the three took up the challenge.

"Right about what?" asked Maria.

265

"Right," said Charles, "about your being parasites."

He lit a cigar and leant back in his chair. Thank the Lord, thought Niall, the dud claret has blurred his feeling. Charles won't suffer while the claret lasts. The announcer on the wireless said good-bye to *Grand Hotel*. The orchestra played themselves out and vanished.

"Does anybody want the serial?" asked Polly. Charles waved his hand. Like a well-trained hound, she understood his signal. She got up and switched the wireless off.

"I don't know that we discussed it," said Maria, biting her orange; "we talked of so many other things. We always do."

"We had a curious afternoon," said Niall; "we all three of us plunged back into the past. We remembered lots of things we thought forgotten. Or, if not forgotten, buried."

"Once upon a time," said Charles, "in my official position as magistrate to this district, I was obliged to attend an exhumation. The opening of the grave was unattractive. And the body smelt."

"The smells of unknown people, dead or alive, are never attractive," said Niall, "but one's own smell, and the smell of those you love, can have a curious charm. And a certain value, too. I think we found it so this afternoon."

Charles drew at his cigar. Niall lit a cigarette. Celia listened to her own anxious, beating heart. Maria ate her orange.

"Indeed," said Charles, "and what value did you extract from your dead past?"

"Only what I've always suspected," said Niall, "that you travel full circle, like the world upon its axis, and return to the same place from where you started. It's very simple."

"Yes," said Celia, "I feel that too. But there's more to it than that. There's a reason why we have to do it. Even if we do come back to the starting place, we've acquired something on the way. A sort of knowledge. A sense of understanding."

"I think you are both quite wrong," said Maria. "I don't feel that at all. I am not back where I started from, I have reached some other place. And I have got there through my own effort, and my own will. There is no going back. There is only going forward."

"Really?" said Charles. "And may one ask, to what?"

Polly, who had glanced from one to the other of us with a bright yet bewildered look, snatched at her chance to join the conversation.

"We all hope Mummy will go forward to another big success when her present play comes off," she said; "that is what Mummy hopes too."

Pleased with her discretion, she began to stack the plates upon the tray, ready for clearing. It was close to her moment for departure. Sunday supper, yes; but, tactfully, she left when Mrs. Banks opened the door and handed in the tray of coffee. Daddy and Mummy liked their coffee to themselves. And Mrs. Banks liked help with the dirty dishes.

"Success," said Niall, "really did not come into our discussion. Like fame, as Celia said just now, it's so very unimportant. Too often it can be a millstone round the neck. Success stories, too, in our particular walk of life, are always very boring. Once anyone is launched, there is no story. Maria's success story would be lists of plays. My own, a string of tunes. They could not matter less."

"What, then, in your opinion, does matter?" enquired Charles.

"I don't know," said Niall, "and I never have. I wish to God I did."

Mrs. Banks opened the door and stood motionless, bearing the tray of coffee. Polly took it from her. The door closed again.

"I will tell you what matters," said Charles; "it matters to have principles, to have standards, to have ideals. It matters to have faith, and a belief. It matters very much if you love a woman, and a woman loves a man, and you marry, and you breed children, and you share each other's lives, and you grow old together, and you lie buried in the same grave. It matters even more if the man loves the wrong woman, and the woman loves the wrong man, and the two come from different worlds that just won't mix, that won't turn into one world, belonging to both. Because when that happens, a man goes adrift and is lost, and his ideals and illusions and traditions get lost too. There is nothing much to live for any more. So he chucks his hand in. He says to himself: Why bother? The woman I love does not believe in any of the things that I believe in. Therefore, I may as well stop believing in them too. I also can lower standards."

He took the cup of coffee that Polly had placed beside him, and stirred it with the spoon. There was no need to stir. There was no sugar in the coffee.

"Please, Charles," said Celia, "don't talk like that. I can't bear to hear you talk like that."

"I could not bear it," said Charles, "when I began to think like that. Which was quite some little while ago. I'm used to it now."

"Charles," said Niall, "I'm bad at putting points across, but I think you have the whole thing out of focus, out of line. You talk of different worlds. Our world, Maria's and mine, is different from yours, and always has been; but only on the surface. We have our traditions too. We have our standards. But we look at them from another angle. Just as a Frenchman, say, sees things another way from a Dutchman, from an Italian. It does not mean that the two don't mix. Don't get along together."

"I quite agree," said Charles, "but as I have never asked a Frenchman, or a Dutchman, or an Italian to share my life with me, you evade the point at issue."

"What is the point at issue?" asked Maria.

"I think," said Polly, standing by the door, "if you don't mind, that I will say good night now and go along and help Mrs. Banks with the washing up." She flashed a smile at us and went.

"The point at issue," answered Charles, "is whether you give, in life, or whether you take. If you take, there comes a time when you suck the giver dry, just as you, Maria, at this minute have sucked the last of that orange. And the outlook, for the taker, becomes grim. The outlook for the giver is equally grim, because he has practically no feeling left. But he has enough determination to decide one thing. And that is not to waste the little feeling that remains."

The ash from his cigar fell in the coffee saucer. It lay in a spot of liquid and turned soggy brown.

"Quite frankly," said Maria, "I don't know what you mean."

"I mean," said Charles, "that we have all come to a parting of the ways."

"Have you had too much claret?" asked Maria.

Not enough, thought Niall. Charles has not had enough. If there could have been but half a bottle more, Charles would not suffer. Nobody need suffer. We would only have thick heads tomorrow morning. Whereas now . . .

"No," said Charles, "I have only had enough to loosen the tongue, which happens to have been tied too many years. This afternoon, while you three were raking up the past, I came to a decision. Quite a simple one. People take it every day. But as it will affect the three of you, you may as well be told."

"I came to a decision too," said Niall swiftly; "we possibly all three did, in our various ways. You asked me just now what mattered in life.

I lied when I said I did not know. It matters to write good music. I have never done it yet, I probably never will. But I want to try. I want to go away and try. So whatever you were deciding on your walk in the rain, you can safely count me out of your calculations. I shan't be here, Charles. It will mean one parasite the less."

Charles did not answer. He pulled slowly at his cigar.

"I feel very apologetic," said Celia, "for coming so often at week ends. Somehow, after Pappy died, I began to look upon it as my home. Especially in the war. And being with the children. It made such a difference, knowing children. But now I'm really settling down into those rooms at Hampstead, it will be different, quite different. I'm going to do what I've never had time to do before. I'm going to write. I'm going to draw."

Charles went on gazing at the silver candlesticks.

"Business was down again last week," said Maria; "I very much doubt if the play will go on running into the spring. It's years, isn't it, since we took a holiday together? It's quite absurd, but there are lots of places I've never even seen. We could go away, Charles, when the play comes off. Would you like that? Would it make you happy?"

Charles laid his cigar down on his plate and folded his dinner napkin.

"A very charming suggestion," he said. "The only thing wrong with it is that it comes too late."

Too late for the concerto, too late to write good music and not bad? Too late to draw, too late to put those stories into print? Too late to make a home, to settle down, to love the children?

"Tomorrow," said Charles, "I propose doing the business through the right channels. Getting a lawyer to write you a proper letter."

"A letter?" said Maria. "A letter about what?"

"A letter asking you to give me a divorce," said Charles.

We none of us spoke. We stared at Charles, perplexed. That was the voice I did not hear, thought Celia, the voice at the other end of the line. That was what made me uneasy, that was what made me afraid. That and the way he pushed the pantry door with his foot.

Too late, thought Niall, too late for Charles as well. And he knows it. The parasites have done their work.

"Divorce you?" said Maria. "What do you mean, divorce you? I don't want to divorce you. I love you very much."

"That is too bad, isn't it?" said Charles. "You should have told me so more often. No use telling me now, when it does not interest me to listen. You see, I happen to be in love with someone else."

Niall looked across the table at Maria. She was no longer Mary Rose, she was no longer anyone. She was the little girl who, nearly thirty years before, had stood at the back of the stalls and watched Mama upon the stage. She had watched Mama, and then turned to the mirrors on the wall, and the gestures that she copied were borrowed, not her own; the hands were the hands of another, so was the smile, so were the dancing feet. The eyes were the eyes of a child who lived in a world of fantasy, of masks, and faces, and scarlet hanging curtains; a child who, when she was shown real life, became bewildered, frightened, lost.

"No," said Maria. "No . . ."

She got up, and stood looking at Charles, with her hands clasped. The part of an injured wife was one she had never played.

CHAPTER TWENTY–THREE

CELIA had left her gloves and her library book in the doctor's waiting room. She went back to fetch them after the consultation. The woman with the little boy was no longer there. She must have been going to see one of the other doctors whose names were written on the brass plates of the front door. A man was sitting at the table instead, glancing through the pages of *The Sphere*. His face was grey and haggard. Perhaps he is very ill, thought Celia, perhaps he is going to be told something far worse than I was told. That is why he does not really read the pages of *The Sphere*, but flicks them over, two by two, with a queer impatient gesture. And none of the people who come to this room know why the others suffer. Or what they think. Or why they come. She picked up her gloves from the table, and her library book, and left the room. The secretary-receptionist stood in a white coat by the open front door. "It has turned colder," she said.

"Yes," said Celia.

"A treacherous time of year," said the secretary. "Good afternoon."

The front door slammed. Celia walked down the steps and turned to the left up Harley Street. It was colder, as the woman said. The wind came in little gusts. It was a day to be inside somewhere, cosseted and loved; by a warm fireside, with the clatter of friendly cups and saucers, a sleepy cat licking its paws, a cyclamen in a pot on a window sill putting forth new buds.

"Well, what happened? Put your feet up, tell me everything." But one had not got that sort of friend. She turned down Wigmore Street towards the Times Book Club. Fibroids. Lots of women had fibroids. It was quite a common thing. The operation nowadays, as the doctor said, was nothing out of the ordinary. She would be much better after it; she would not know herself. Take it easy at first, a few weeks' rest, and then ready for anything. No, she was not scared at all of the operation. Just the knowledge that she would never be able to have children. It was so foolish, so idiotic to mind. There was no question of her getting married, she was not in love, never had been in love, and she was not likely to meet anyone now; nor did she want to fall in love, nor had she any desire to marry.

"Were you contemplating marriage?" the doctor asked.

"No, oh no."

"Well, then, you have nobody but yourself to consider?"

"No one at all."

"Your general health is very good, you know. And I assure you there is nothing whatever to worry about. I'd be frank and tell you if there was."

"I'm not worried. Truly."

"All right. Splendid. Then it's just a question of fixing the time and the place. And the surgeon."

No children, though. Never. No possibility, once one had the operation. Today one was a woman, capable of bearing children. But not in a few weeks' time. . . . In a few weeks' time one would be a sort of shell. No more than a shell. That woman, there, walking ahead of Celia along Wigmore Street, she may have had the operation too. She looked heavy, set. On the other hand, she might be married with several children. So it would not matter. She had the look of a married woman. A stolid vicar's wife, up from the country. She was hesitating now; she crossed the road to Debenham's and stared into a window. She made up her mind; she went inside. One would never know whether the woman had had the operation that one must have oneself.

Celia pushed through the swing door of the Times Book Club and walked upstairs to the library. She went to the table of her initial letter. The usual girl was in her place. The one with platinum hair.

"Good afternoon, Miss Delaney."

"Good afternoon."

And suddenly Celia had an impulse to tell the girl about the operation. To say, "I have got to have my insides out, which means I can never have children." What would the platinum girl say? Would she say, "Oh dear, I am so sorry," and her expression of sympathy bring a warmth to the heart, so that one could walk out of the Times Book Club, happier, more reconciled? Or would she stare in embarrassment and, glancing down at the finger on Celia's hand, see that Celia was not married? So that it could not matter? So why should Celia care?

"I have that biography you were asking for, Miss Delaney."

"Oh, thank you." But Celia did not feel like a biography.

"You haven't any short stories? Good ones that are easy just to pick up and put down again?"

Idiotic phrase. What did she mean? She meant what the man was doing to *The Sphere* in the waiting room in Harley Street.

"Nothing much, I'm afraid, in the way of short stories. But there's a nice bright new novel out, a first novel, that has had very good reviews."

"Can I see?"

The platinum girl handed the novel up over the desk.

"Is it light?"

"Oh yes, quite light. Very easy reading."

"Very well. I'll take it."

The novel was published by the firm of which Mr. Harrison was managing director. The novel was written by some woman who had the time to write. She had signed a contract, honoured it, lived up to it. Unlike Celia. If Celia had only applied herself, if there had not been Pappy to nurse, if there had not been the war, there would be people coming up to the table here and saying to the platinum girl, "Any new stories out by Celia Delaney?" It was only a question of going back to the rooms in Hampstead, of sitting down, of making time. No amount of operations could prevent her doing that. A sick person could always think. A sick person could scribble in bed. Prop up a drawing board in bed.

"Would you like to take the biography too? I kept it especially for you."

"All right, thank you. All right, I will."

The biography and the new light novel were handed together over the table.

"I saw your sister's play the other night."

"Did you? Did you like it?"

"I didn't think much of the play, but I loved her. She is wonderful, isn't she? Not a bit alike, are you?"

"No. No, we aren't really. You see, we are only half sisters."

"Oh, that accounts for it, perhaps. Well, I would go and see her again, any day. And so would my boy friend. He was mad about her. I was quite jealous!"

The platinum girl had a ring on her finger. Celia noticed it for the first time.

"I did not know you were engaged."

"Yes. Been engaged for nearly a year. Going to be married at Easter. The library won't see me any more after that."

"Have you got a house?"

"Yes, of course."

But Celia could not go on talking to the platinum girl because some man in a bowler hat and glasses, who had been getting impatient, pushed forward with his library book, and there was someone else waiting behind him.

"Good afternoon."

"Good afternoon."

Down the stairs of the library, and out across the street, and the gusty wind colder than ever, blowing down the back of her neck. It was true, then, that personal selfish anxiety swamped every other feeling. The visit to Harley Street had coloured the day. Not once, since leaving the consulting room, had Celia thought about Maria.

"You're not a bit alike, are you?"

"No. No, we are only half sisters."

But we must be alike, because we both have Pappy's blood in our veins. We have his strength, his vigour, his tenacity of life. At least, Maria has. That was why she stood for one moment only, looking at Charles across the table, with those frightened eyes. One moment only. Then she pulled herself together and said, "How stupid of me. I'm so sorry. I ought to have known. Who is it, by the way?"

And when Charles told her, Maria answered, "Oh! Oh, her . . . Yes. I see. There couldn't really be anybody else, could there? I mean, not living quietly as you do, down here."

After which she began to clear away the coffee cups as Polly might have done. No one knew what she was thinking about, or what went on inside. Niall got up then and went out of the room; he did not say good night to anyone. Celia helped Maria with the remaining plates. Charles went on smoking his cigar. And Celia thought that if words could be taken back and swallowed, if the hands of the clock could be turned and moved backwards to the morning hours, if the day could begin again and all of them have one more chance, then none of that need have happened. Charles would not have gone out upon his walk and taken his decision. He would not have spoken down the telephone. The day would have ended in another fashion. "Is there anything I can do?" she had said to Maria, putting the cups and saucers on the sideboard. Her voice an undertone, as when someone was ill, with a temperature; the same urgent need to help the person in pain, to fetch hot milk, water bottles, blankets.

"You? No, darling, nothing."

Maria, who never cleared away but left the debris for other people, took the tray through the door into the pantry. Maria, who never called Celia darling, only Niall, smiled over her shoulder and was gone. Then Celia had done the unforgivable. She had meddled. She had turned back into the dining room to speak to Charles.

"Please don't make this final," she had said. "I know things have not been easy for you, ever. But you knew that when you married Maria, didn't you? You knew her life could never be quite the same as yours. And then the war. The war did fearful things to so many people. Please, Charles, don't break everything up. Think of the children."

It was useless, though. It was talking to a man one had never really known. A man whose life, whose thoughts, whose actions were things one could not claim to understand.

"I must ask you, Celia," he said, "not to interfere. It is really no concern of yours, is it?"

No, it was no concern of hers. The marriage of Maria, the children, the house where she had stayed, the home she had so often shared. No concern at all. They did not need her help. Maria would face the future on her own. There was nothing Celia could do. Nothing at all. And going back to London the next day, by the usual train, was somehow like going back to the house in St. John's Wood after Pappy died. There was the same sense of aftermath. A moment in time had ended. Somewhere, in the deep earth, a body lay buried. A life.

The children, from the drive, had waved farewell. "See you next week end." But Celia would never go again. Not now.

Here she was, she thought, crossing Vere Street into the back entrance of Marshall's, shaken out of security because of fibroids and the threat of operation, while Maria had to face the destruction of married life. Here was Celia mourning the loss of children never born while Maria would lose children who really lived. That was what divorce would mean. Charles, though technically the guilty party, would want to have the children. The children belonged to Farthings, to Coldhammer. Visits to the flat, yes. The excursion to the theatre. To see Mummy act. But not often. The visits less and less. And it was so much nicer living in the country, with Daddy, and Polly, and what would they call the new mother? By her Christian name, in all probability. That was the modern way. Everyone would settle down. Everyone would jog along.

"Hi. Has anyone sent Auntie Celia a Christmas present?"

"No. Oh! Must we? I mean, we needn't, need we, now?"

"We never see her. Why should we?"

Someone prodded Celia in the back, and she moved on, apologising. It was very full in Marshall's. She had been blocking the gangway, by the steps going down into the haberdashery. She could not remember what it was she had come to buy. Was it some shoes? Yes, it was shoes. But the shoe department was already full of people. And women were sitting about on chairs with sad, despondent faces, and useless stockinged feet, waiting for the attention that never came

"I'm sorry, madam. We're very busy this afternnon. Come back later."

On again then, moving with the throng towards the lift. Upstairs. Had any of these women had the operation? That woman there, with the ugly hat, her mauve lips clashing with the trimming, had she got fibroids? Even if she had, it did not matter. That broad band on her ungloved hand proclaimed her married. She probably had a little boy at school in Sunningdale.

"I'm going down to see David on Saturday."

"What fun. A picnic lunch?"

"Yes, if it is fine. Then football afterwards. David's playing." The woman stepped out of the lift and went towards the underwear.

"Going up? Going up? Any more going up, please?"

One may as well go somewhere. One may as well wander through Marshall's because there was something depressing in the thought of getting into the Bond Street tube, and changing at Tottenham Court Road for the Edgware line to Hampstead, and then walking home to empty rooms.

Baby linen. Cots. Pram covers. Little lawn frocks with smocking on them. Rattles. She remembered coming here with Maria before Caroline was born. Maria had ordered a complete layette, and put it down to Lady Wyndham.

"She can pay for everything," said Maria, "except the pram. I shall make Pappy give me the pram."

Celia had chosen a large blue shawl. She had changed it afterwards for pink, Caroline being a girl. There was a shawl on the counter now, not such good quality, though, nowadays. She fingered the shawl, her mind with Caroline at school. What would happen to Caroline?

"Are you looking for shawls, madam? This has just come in. They get snapped up very easily. The demand is so great."

"Is it?"

"Oh yes, madam. We have not had this quality since before the war. Was it for a first baby, madam?"

"No. Oh no . . . I was only looking."

The woman's interest waned. Celia moved away. Not for a first baby. Not for any baby. No pram rugs, smocks, or rattles. What would the woman say if Celia looked into her bored grey eyes and said, "I have got fibroids. I can't ever have a baby"? Would she summon a tag end of courtesy and answer back, "I'm very sorry, madam, I'm sure"? Or would she look startled, and whisper to the assistant farther down the counter, and the assistant call for the head of the department? "We are afraid there is a lady here, not very well." Better, for all concerned, to move away. . . .

"Going up, please?"

Why had Niall driven away on Sunday night without saying good-bye to anyone? Why had he just got into his car and gone?

"You're not very alike are you?"

"No. No, he's only my half brother."

But we must be alike, because we both have Mama's blood in our veins. Mama's singleness of purpose, her concentration, her love of solitude. At least, Niall had. That was why Niall had left Farthings Sunday night and driven to the sea, probably, to his boat; so that the things that hurt, the people he loved, should not come between him and his music. So that he could be by himself, with the sounds in his head, untouched, uninterrupted; in the same way that Mama had danced alone. Was that why he had gone? Or was it because he thought: This is my fault. This is all our faults. The three of us have murdered Charles.

Ladies' Rest Room. On the left . . . That was thoughtful of the people in control of Marshall's. There must be so many women like herself with fibroids. With a slight headache. With tired feet. With a little nagging pain. And there they were, sitting on chairs round the wall, for all the world as if they were back again in the doctor's consulting room. Women with parcels. Women without parcels.

Two with heads together, chattering. Happy enough. They did not mind. Fibroids were nothing. One woman sat at a table, writing swiftly, on sheet after sheet of note paper. "My own darling, this is to tell you that the thing we feared is true. I shall have to have the operation. I know what this will mean in both our lives. . . ."

Well, at least that was something she was spared. One did not have to go home to write a letter. One did not have to telephone a lover. One did not have a husband waiting by the fire.

"What happened? What did the fellow say?"

Celia went on sitting in the rest room at Marshall's, and the truth is, she told herself, that I am making a stupid fuss about all this, I am taking it all too seriously, I am behaving as if I were going to die, and it's just because the doctor said there could never be a baby, and I was not going to have a baby anyway. I was never going to have one. And there would have been a tragedy if I had. It would have died. Or been a trouble to me, all its life. A weak character. Sponging on me. Borrowing money. Marrying the wrong woman. My daughter-in-law would have disliked me. She would never have stayed with me.

"We'd better go and stay with the old girl."

"Oh no! Not again. It's such a bore."

The cloakroom attendant came up to Celia.

"Excuse me, madam, but we are closing now. It's just on five-thirty."

"Sorry. Thank you."

Down in the lift with all the other people. All the other people swarming to the swing doors.

"Taxi, madam?"

And why not? Surely the extravagance of a taxi, for this day, at least. But the embarrassing thing was that Celia had no change to give the commissionaire. The taxi was waiting, and she had ten shillings only for the taxi. Not so much as a sixpence for the commissionaire.

She got in, too shamefaced to explain. He slammed the door. He waved the taxi on. The ash tray by the window was full of the stubs of cigarettes. One stub was smoking still. The end was stained with lipstick. Who could she have been, that other occupant, who had given place to Celia? Someone happy, someone gay, someone going to a party? A woman going to a lover? A mother going to meet her son? The strange romance of taxis. Moments of madness, moments of farewell. But perhaps the woman was just another spinster like herself with fibroids. A nervier type of woman who drew ease from cigarettes.

She was glad the taxi went through Regent's Park, instead of the more familiar route of the Finchley Road. The desolate shattered houses of St. John's Wood were very hard to bear. There were no windows in the house where she had lived with Pappy, and the plaster had come away from all the walls. The gate hung crooked, the railings were torn away. She could not bear to pass it nowadays.

She had ventured once with Niall a few years back. The rooms were gaping and horrible. She hoped always that Pappy, if afterlife were true, if he peered down upon the world with Mama from some private paradise, would not be permitted by God to see the house.

He would surely blame Celia and not the war for its destruction. "But, my darling, what has happened? What have you done?"

Up the hill to Hampstead. To the left, by Church Row, and right again. Just a bit farther on, please. There, the house at the corner. Anyway, no matter if it was a maisonette, it was her own, her place of sanctuary. The window boxes would be gay with hyacinths in the spring. And the side steps were her own. It was her own front door. Apple green and cheerful. And the name, "The Studio."

She never quite got over the surprise of the key turning in the lock, and admitting her, to her own dwelling. It seemed so easy. Such a simple thing. It was good to be back. It was good to see her own familiar things. The chairs, the desk, the pictures, even one or two of her own drawings, framed, upon the walls.

Celia knelt down and lit the fire, and as she waited for it to burn, she read her letters. There were two of them.

The typewritten one she opened first. It was curious, after all this time, and on this day of all days, that she should have a letter from the firm of publishers. From the new director who had taken on after Mr. Harrison had retired.

DEAR MISS DELANEY,

Do you remember meeting me, many years ago, on a certain memorable occasion, when you visited the office? As you possibly know, I am now managing director in place of James Harrison, and I am writing to know if there is any chance of your fulfilling your old contract with us or, better still, signing a new one, now that the war is over. You know what a high opinion my predecessor had of your work, especially of your drawings, an opinion which I share in equal measure. He and I always felt that if you could only bring yourself to give that talent to us, and to the world in general, you could bring even greater lustre to the Delaney name than it has at present. I do ask you to think most seriously about this. Please let me hear from you in the near future.

Kindest regards,
Yours sincerely,

Like Mr. Harrison of many years ago, it was really very kind. And this time she would not fail them. This time she would not disappoint them. She would look at the stories and the drawings this very evening, tomorrow morning, tomorrow afternoon. And she would start to plan her life, from now on, with this end in view. Never mind the fibroids and the operation. They did not count. She opened her other letter. It was from Caroline at school.

DEAREST AUNTIE CELIA,

Mummy came to see me yesterday and told me about her and Daddy. She said I wasn't to tell anyone at school. I know two girls whose parents have been divorced. It doesn't seem to make much difference. The only thing is, it's not much fun at Farthings in the holidays, there's nothing to do, and I don't like riding as much as the others, so I wondered if I could come to stay with you? That is, if you could have me. I should simply love to come. I must fly now, the bell for prep has gone.

Lots of Love,
Caroline

Celia sat back before the fire and read the letter through again. Twice, three times. Her heart beat faster, and a strange feeling came into her throat. Absurd, almost as though she were going to cry. Caroline wanted to come and stay with her. Without being asked. Without being prompted by anyone, by Charles, by Maria. Caroline wanted to come and stay with her, with Celia.

But of course she should come. She should always come. Next holiday. Every holiday. The little room, next to her own, upstairs. Turn the little room into a room for Caroline. Furnish it as Caroline wished. They would go for walks on the Heath together; she would buy Caroline a dog. Celia would keep the dog while Caroline was at school. There were many things that she and Caroline could do together. Museums, theatres—and Caroline could draw quite nicely; she might teach Caroline to draw. She had a pretty little voice, too, which might develop as she grew older. She could take Caroline to singing lessons. Now she came to think of it, there had always been something about Caroline that reminded her of Pappy. A look in the eyes, and the way she carried her head. She was tall, too, for her age.

There was no doubt about it, Caroline was exactly like Pappy. Affectionate, too, needing sympathy, attention, love. Celia would give her all that. Nothing mattered but that the child should be happy. Nothing in the world.

Celia piled more logs onto the fire and threw the letter from the publisher into the blaze. She would answer it sometime. She would do something about it sometime. There was no hurry, though. No hurry now. There were more important things to do. There were so many plans to make for Caroline. For Caroline.

CHAPTER TWENTY-FOUR

WHATEVER happens, thought Maria, nobody must know that I feel anything, that I mind. Not even Celia, not even Niall. They must all think that the divorce is an amicable, straightforward thing, suited to us both, because the division of life between London and the country has become a nuisance and a bore. I find I cannot give the time I would like to Charles and the house and the children; better to part.

And although it breaks Charles's heart to do so, he sees the force of it, he sees that it is better for us both. When he marries this other woman, he does so, not because she is particularly attractive or because he has fallen in love with her, but because her ways are suited to the country, she is good with horses, dogs; and anyway, it was from her that we bought that pony for the children. I remember thinking at the time that she had sly eyes. Auburn hair, too, which means that later on she will run to fat, and the skin that goes with auburn hair smells. Charles can't have discovered that yet. He will in time. The point is that everyone must think it is a pity. Divorce is always a pity, especially when there are children, and when two people have been married for some time.

But they were never really suited to one another. He was too quiet, too dull, his whole interest bound up in that estate. How could he ever hope to hold her? She was much too elusive. No one would ever hold her.

That must be the line to put across. And what is more, thought

Maria, I shall soon believe it myself; I am beginning to believe it myself already, because whatever I pretend in my mind, to myself, always comes true. That is where I am lucky. That is where God is always on my side. So that the lonely feeling that I have now, lying in the dark here, with the wireless turned on and the eye pads over my eyes, won't last; it never does. It will go, like toothache; and just as I forget after an aching tooth what the pain was like, so shall I forget this pain, this shock of emptiness. It was nearly midnight, and when midnight came, the programme on the wireless was over for the day, there was nothing more to hear. Even the foreign stations became silent, became dead.

Then, thought Maria, then it won't be so good. Then it won't be so funny. Because round and round in my head will travel images of Charles through the years. Here was where I made my first mistake. There, the second. This moment was a foolish one. I could have given way with better grace. That moment was sheer folly, it need never have occurred.

If only I had thought a little deeper. If I had only taken two ounces more of trouble. No, not two ounces, one. This is what Pappy meant. This is the punishment. It does not come in afterlife, the day of reckoning. It comes at midnight, now, alone in the dark with the wireless silent. There is no need for me to sit through a film of my life, I know it all too well. God is the clever one. God knows all the answers. So He does to me the one thing I never dreamt could happen. He does to me the thing I have done to others. He makes me look a fool. Poor Maria, her husband has left her for another woman. Someone younger than herself. Poor Maria.

Think of all the women throughout the world left by their husbands. A dreary, forsaken crew. Solitary, plain, and dull. I am now one of them. I belong to the crew. The cleverness of God . . . If I could be self-righteous, but I cannot. If I could say with the rest of the forsaken wretches, "I gave Charles everything in the world and this is his return," but I cannot. Because I gave him nothing. It serves me right. I have not one leg to stand on. All the clichés describe my situation now. Paid back in my own coin. Do unto others as I would they should do unto me. Now I know what it means. Now I know what that woman felt like years ago. And I thought her such a bore. Such a po-faced, dreary bore. I never dared ring him on the telephone in case she answered, which she often did. I used to joke about it.

I'm sorry. God in heaven, I am sorry. Forgive me, now, as I lie here in the dark. Would it be any good if I went tomorrow and sought her out? "I did not realise how unhappy I must have made you once. Now I know. Now I understand." But I don't know where she lives. And now I come to think of it I have a frightful feeling she is dead. That I saw last year in *The Times* that she was dead. If she is dead, perhaps she can see me now. Perhaps she gloats in heaven. Forgive us our trespasses as we forgive them that trespass against us.

But I don't forgive the red-haired woman near Coldhammer. I hate her. So the woman in heaven won't forgive me. It's a vicious circle. . . . Why is not Niall here to comfort me? I shall never forgive him, never. The one most desperate moment in my whole life when I need Niall, and he is not here. The thing is, I have to sleep. If I don't go to sleep I shall look like hell in the morning. One comfort, there is no matinee. But *Home Life* are coming to photograph the flat, I've just remembered. Let them come. I can go out. Where can I go? I don't want to see anyone, or talk to anyone. I have got to get over this by myself. It's only toothache, and the pain will go. It has to go. . . .

"Head a little to the left, Miss Delaney, please. That's better. Quite still. Hold it. Right."

The man pressed the bulb, exploded the flash, and smiled.

"Now, how would it be if we had you in that chair? With the photograph of your husband and your children in the background, on the table? Would you try it? And shall we have your profile this time? Yes . . . Very nice, I like that. I like it very much."

He turned aside, murmuring something to his assistant, who did something to the screen. The man himself dragged a sofa out of the way. Then he rearranged the flowers. Go on, thought Maria, wreck the whole place, I don't mind. Break the furniture. Smash the crockery. What happens today will have to be wiped off the slate anyway. God! I'm tired.

"Now, smile, please, Miss Delaney. Wonderful. Keep it. Hold it."

The thing is, these men will be here all day. What shall I do for lunch? I was going to boil an egg in the kitchen. I can't do that if they are here. I must pretend I have an appointment. I shall pretend I am lunching at the Ritz. I would not mind lunching at the Ritz, anyway, but I can't go there alone.

"Miss Delaney, could you now relax upon the sofa and take up a play? You read plays often, I suppose, with an eye to production?"

"I do indeed."

"That's just what we want. What would you wear, now? A negligee?"

"I'd wear anything. Can't I keep on this frock? It's such a bore to change."

"It would please the readers of *Home Life* if they could see you in a negligee. Something quite casual, of course."

You idiotic man, what do you suppose I should wear? Black satin and sequins, with ospreys in my hair? I know what I'll do. I'll have no lunch; it won't matter, it will be good for my figure. I shall have no lunch, and I shall drive down and see Caroline at school. She's mine. She belongs to me. I shall tell Caroline what has happened. She is old enough to understand. I shall tell Caroline before Charles has a chance.

"Husband and children well, Miss Delaney?"

"Yes, wonderful."

"Getting quite big now, I suppose?"

"Yes. They grow up quickly."

"Fine place, Coldhammer. I should very much like to have some pictures of you there."

"It hasn't been handed back yet. We're not living there, you know."

"Oh. Oh, I see. Now, lie full length, please, Miss Delaney. One hand drooping over the sofa edge. Yes, very characteristic."

Characteristic of what, for God's sweet sake? Anyone would think I spend my whole life lolling about on sofas. Get on with it. Get on.

"Play doing well, Miss Delaney?"

"Fair. It's a bad time of year."

It was not. It was the best. He would not know, the fool.

"It's the dreamy parts the public like you in best, you know, Miss Delaney. Not-quite-of-the-world, if you understand. Spiritual, I suppose you'd call it. That's the impression you always give. Something far away and spiritual. Now, chin up just a little. . . . Hold it. . . . Thank you."

This really is the end. I refuse to do any more.

"I have a luncheon appointment at the Ritz at one o'clock."

"Oh dear. We would have loved to have one or two of you in the bedroom. Could you come back after lunch?"

"Quite impossible. I have a full afternoon ahead."

"What a pity . . . Still, we must take one or two interiors without you. Have you any pets, Miss Delaney? I see no pets."

"I have no pets."

"Readers always like to see their favourites fondling a pet. So homely. Never mind. We can say your pets are in the country."

My pets are all in the country, fondled by a woman with red hair, if you must know. If you want to know. A woman with red hair, who smells.

"Thank you so much, Miss Delaney. You have been extremely patient. Don't worry about the apartment. We will tidy up."

"Don't forget to send me the proofs to pass."

"Of course, Miss Delaney. Of course."

With smiles, with gestures, they bowed Miss Delaney out of her own flat; from the window they watched her climb into a taxi, three minutes late for her luncheon at the Ritz. The taxi took Miss Delaney to her own garage behind the block of flats. And with no luncheon inside her Miss Delaney drove to the country to see Caroline at school. An hour to the school, south out of London.

Too much traffic, too many tram lines, and I am not quite certain what to say when I get there, because I suddenly realise I don't know Caroline well. Beyond saying "Darling" and giving her presents, I don't know her at all. What was I doing when I was her age? I was pretending to be someone else. I was making faces in the looking glass. I was teasing Niall. . . . Why must this thin woman look at me with so much surprise.

"Oh? It's Mrs. Wyndham. We were not expecting you."

"No. I happened to be passing. Can I see Caroline, please?"

"She's playing net ball at the moment. . . . But still . . . Jean dear, would you run along to number-two ground and tell Caroline Wyndham that her mother has come to see her?"

"Yes, Miss Oliver."

A child with round eyes bounced away.

"Parents usually come on Saturdays or Sundays, unless, of course, they give warning. These are the new photographs. Would you care to see them? Taken on Founders' Day. Such a pity you could not come. Caroline was so disappointed. . . . Yes, she told me. A matinee. These things do interfere so with private life, don't they? You must be very torn, I always feel. . . . Yes, the entire school, staff and all. Let me see, there is Caroline, sitting cross-legged in the front. We always make the younger ones sit down."

Rows and rows of girls, all exactly alike, and Maria would never have found Caroline if Miss Oliver had not pointed her out. Is that my child?

"Yes, she seems very happy. She's in 3-A, you know. They are a cheery little crowd in 3-A. Would you care to walk down to the playing field to meet Caroline?"

As a matter of fact, I would rather get into the car again and drive back to London. Because I did not sleep last night, and I have had no lunch. God only knows why I am here at all.

"Thank you, Miss Oliver, I will. Such a lovely day. So wonderful to get into the country, even for half an hour."

I must do my stuff and smile. I must leave behind me my expected aura of charm. It is not a lovely day, either. It is cold. And I am wearing the wrong shoes. They will get stuck in all that idiotic crazy paving. Here comes a panting, overheated little girl in a brief blue skirt. And it is Caroline.

"Hullo, Mummy."

"Hullo, darling."

"Is Daddy with you?"

"No. I've come alone."

"Oh."

And what do I do now? And where do I go? Somewhere along this walk.

"I'm afraid I've come on a bad day."

"Well, actually, any weekday is bad. You see, we're practising at the moment for the inter-form trophy at the end of term. We play for the number of points. So our form, which is 3-A, has an equal chance of winning the cup as the sixth form has. Because although of course they would beat us in actual play, they might be down in the finals on the number of points."

"Yes, I see."

I don't of course. It's Greek. It's meaningless.

"Are you good, darling? Do you play well?"

"Oh heavens, no. I'm ghastly. Do you want to watch?"

"Not frightfully. The thing is——"

"Perhaps you'd rather see the art display in Botticelli?"

"The what?"

"The art display. Botticelli is the name we give to the sixth-form studio. It's behind the chapel. Some people have done very good drawings."

"What I'd really like to do, darling, is to go somewhere."

"Oh yes, of course. I'll take you upstairs."

Lists on walls. And strange girls scurrying past. Scrubbed stairs the worn linoleum. Why not put broad arrows on their backs and have done with it? And that roaring, gushing plug, with the cistern leaking. Somebody ought to be told about it. The matron.

"Is this your bed? It looks very hard."

"It's all right."

Seven beds in rows, all of them the same. With hard, blunt pillows.

"How's Daddy?"

"Very well." Now was the moment. I sit down on the bed, and I powder my nose and I am quite casual, I am not bitter at all.

"The fact is, darling—and that is what I came to tell you; you will probably hear from Daddy yourself—he wants a divorce."

"Oh."

I don't know what I expected her to do. Perhaps I thought she might look frightened, or she might cry, or she might put her arms round me, which I would have liked, and it would be the start of something I have never had.

"Yes. We have not quarrelled or anything like that. It's just that he has to be in the country and I have to be in London, and it's not really fair on either of us. Things would really work out better if we were independent."

"It won't make any difference, then?"

"No, no, not really. Except that I shan't live at Farthings any more."

"You are never there much, anyway."

"No."

"Shall we come and stay with you in London?"

"Of course. Whenever you want."

"There's not much room at the flat, though, is there? I'd much rather go and stay with Auntie Celia."

"Would you?" But why the pain? Why the sudden emptiness?

"The girl who sleeps in that bed has parents who are divorced. And her mother married again. She has a stepfather."

"Well, as a matter of fact, I think you will probably have a stepmother. I believe Daddy may marry again."

288

"Carrots, I suppose."

"What?"

"We always call her Carrots. She taught us to ride, you know. Last summer. She and Daddy are great friends. Oh, that's all right. I don't mind Carrots. She's very jolly. Will you marry someone too?"

"No . . . No, I don't want to marry anyone."

"What about the man in your play? He's rather nice."

"He's married. . . . Besides, I don't want to."

"When will Daddy marry Carrots?"

"I don't know. It has not been discussed. We're not divorced yet."

"No, of course not. Can I tell them here?"

"No. Certainly not. It's—it's a private sort of thing."

I ought to be intensely relieved that Caroline is taking it like this, but I am not. I'm shocked. I'm bewildered. I don't understand. . . . If Pappy and Mama had been divorced it would have meant the end of the world. And Mama was not my mother. Pappy and Mama . . .

"Are you going to stay for tea, Mummy?"

"No, I don't think so. I have to be in the theatre, anyway, by six."

"I shall write to Auntie Celia and ask if I can go and stay next holiday."

"Yes, darling, of course."

Down the scrubbed stairs, and through the hall full of lists, and out of the front door to the waiting car.

"Good-bye, darling, I'm sorry if I made you miss the game."

"It's all right, Mummy. I'll dash now. There's still another half-hour left." Caroline waved, and before Maria had turned the car, she was running out of sight behind the great brick building.

This is one of those terrible moments when I want to cry. I don't cry often, I'm not the crying kind. Celia was always crying as a child. But now it would be a relief. Now it is the only thing in the world that I want to do. For someone else to take over this wheel and drive the car, so that I could lie back against the seat and cry. I won't let myself, though. Because it would show on my face and in my eyes. And I have to be in the theatre by six o'clock. So instead of crying I shall sing. Very loudly and completely out of tune. This is why Niall wrote his songs. So that, when I faced my Waterloo, I could sing.

But perhaps it would be better if I went into a church and prayed.

I might be converted. I might leave the stage altogether and go about the world doing good. Strength through prayer. Strength through joy. No, that was Hitler. Well, strength through something. There is a church at the corner. Perhaps it is a symbol, like looking in the Bible before a first night. Shall I park the car and go into the church and pray? I will.

The church was dark and gloomy. It could not have been built very long. No atmosphere at all. Maria sat down in a pew and waited. Perhaps if she waited long enough something would happen. A dove come from the air. A feeling of peace descend upon her. And she would be able to walk out of the church consoled, refreshed, ready to face the future. Perhaps a priest would come, a dear, kind old priest with white hair and calm, grey eyes. It would help, surely, to talk to some kind old priest. They had so much experience of the world, of suffering, of lost, unhappy people. Maria waited, but there was not any dove. She could hear the sound of schoolboys in the distance playing football, laughing. Presently the door behind her opened. She looked over her shoulder, and yes, it must be the vicar of the church. But he was not old. He was youthful, he wore glasses. He walked briskly up the aisle towards the vestry, looking neither to right nor left. And his shoes squeaked. . . .

It was no good. He would never convert anyone. Nor would the church. The whole thing was just a waste of time. Back to the car . . .

Well, I can always have my hair done. Lucien will give me a cup of tea and some biscuits. A cup of tea is really what I need. I can sit in that cubicle, pretending to look at an old *Tatler*, and Lucien will burble on; I don't have to listen. I can close my eyes and think of nothing. Or try to think of nothing. Lucien is the answer. The burbling patter of Lucien is more refreshing than the patter of a priest. They are probably the same, at heart. Niall would say there is no difference.

"Good afternoon, madame. What a pleasant surprise."

"I'm exhausted, Lucien. I have had a terrible day."

Hairdressers were like doctors: they had the same smooth manner, and they asked no questions. They smiled. They understood.

Lucien waved Maria to her usual chair, in her usual cubicle, and there was even a new bottle of bath essence sitting before the mirror, wrapped in cellophane, the bottle itself a shining, glittering green. The name upon it, Venetian Balm, temptation in itself. Like the sweets when I was a child, thought Maria, sweets wrapped in gilded paper; they always made me better if I was angry, if I was tired.

"Lucien, if I told you I was on the verge of suicide, that I was contemplating throwing myself under a tram, that the whole world had turned sour upon me, and the people that I love don't love me any more—what would you suggest as panacea?"

Lucien looked at her with narrowed eyes, his head a little on one side.

"How about a facial, madame?" he said.

It was a minute to six when Maria pushed through the stage door.

"Good evening, Bob."

"Good evening, Miss Delaney."

The stage-door keeper half rose from the chair in his cubbyhole.

"A telephone call for you a few minutes ago, miss. Mr. Wyndham, from the country."

"Did he leave any message?"

"He asked if you would ring him as soon as you got in."

"Switch the extension plug through to my room, Bob, please."

"Yes, Miss Delaney."

Maria ran down the stairs to her dressing room. Charles had telephoned. That meant that everything was all right, that he had been thinking things over, and he realised now that the whole business of divorce was out of the question. Charles was ringing up to apologise. Perhaps he had suffered today as much as she had. In which case there must be no reproaches, no post-mortems. Start afresh. Begin again.

She went into her room and threw her coat onto the divan.

"I'll call you when I'm ready," she told her dresser. She seized the telephone on the corner table and asked for trunks. They were slow to answer. After a moment or two the operator said, "The lines are engaged to trunks. We'll call you later." Maria put on her dressing gown and tied her hair up with a handkerchief. She began to cream her face.

I wonder if Charles will want to come up to London tomorrow for the reconciliation. It was a bad day, a matinee, but if he comes early to the flat, we could lunch; and possibly he would find something to do during the day, and he could then stay the night. It would be quite a good idea if he stayed the night. I won't go down to Farthings, though, for the week end if that red-haired woman is in the neighbourhood. He will have to get rid of her. I really can't swallow her. It would be too much.

Her face wiped clean of all powder and foundation, smooth and fresh like a little girl before a bath, Maria knelt once more beside the telephone.

"Can't you get trunks? It's very urgent."

At last the answering response, "Trunk number, please," and then the rather high-pitched ring of the Farthings call.

But it was not Charles who answered, it was Polly.

"I want Mr. Wyndham."

"He left about five minutes ago. He couldn't wait any longer. Oh dear, such a day, Mummy."

"Why? What's happened?"

"A message from the Dower House soon after lunch. Would Daddy go over right away? Lord Wyndham had had a heart attack. I was to have taken the children to tea in the afternoon, but of course that was out of the question. Daddy came back here at five, and he has sent for the specialist from London, who is on his way now; that's why Daddy had to go back again and couldn't wait for your call, but he told me—of course not in front of the children—that he didn't think there was much hope, and that Lord Wyndham would probably die during the night. Isn't it awful? Poor Granny."

"Did Mr. Wyndham leave any sort of message for me?"

"No. Just that I was to tell you what had happened, and to warn you that he feared it was the end."

"Yes. It sounds like the end."

"Do you want to speak to the chldren?"

"No, Polly. Not now. Good-bye."

It was the end all right. When a poor old man was over eighty, he did not survive a major heart attack. The clock that had been running down for the last ten years would stop at last.

Charles would be Lord Wyndham in the morning. And the red-haired woman whom Caroline called Carrots would be Lady Wyndham in a few months' time. And God, thought Maria, must be having a pretty good field day over my affairs today. He must be fairly splitting his sides over the joke. "Let's think of something else to shake Maria. Come on, St. Peter and the rest of you boys, what can we do next? What about a rotten egg from the back of the pit to-night? Slap between the eyes. That will learn her."

All right. All right, said Maria. Two can play at that game, my friends. And what was it that Pappy said to me all those years ago, before my very first big part in London? "Nothing is worth while if you don't fight back." Other things, too, he used to say, which I did not listen to at the time, but if I think about them now they will come back.

"Never truckle under, my darling. Never pull a poor mouth. The duds truckle under. The duds pull poor mouths. Stick your chin out. And when everything else fails, there's always your work. Not work with a capital W, my darling. Not art with a big A. Leave art to the high-brows; believe me, it's their only consolation, and if they put the letter f before it, they'd be dead on the nail every time. No, do the work you feel in your bones you have to do, because it's the only damn thing you can do, the only thing you understand. Sometimes you will be happy. Sometimes you will know despair. But don't ever whine. Delaneys don't whine. Just go ahead and do your tricks. . . ."

All right, Pappy. You were always closer to Celia than you were to me, because I was generally thinking about something else; but now, at this moment, I feel as if you were beside me in the room. I can see your funny blue eyes, like mine, looking down at me from the photograph on the wall; and your nose is a bit cockeyed, too, like mine is, and your hair stands up from your head in the same way, but what Niall always calls my mobile mouth must have come from that mother in Vienna whom I never saw, who beguiled you, Pappy, when you ought to have known better. All I hope is that she does not start to let me down. Not at this particular moment in my existence. She has been on my side up till now.

"Come in."

"There's a gentleman to see you, Miss Delaney," said the dresser. "A French gentleman. A Mr. Laforge."

"A Mr. What? Tell him to go away. You know I never seen anyone before a performance."

"He's very persistent. He has a play for you to read. He says you used to know his father."

"That's a very old one. Tell him I've heard that one before."

"He flew over from Paris this afternoon. He says his play is coming on in Paris very shortly, and he has done the translation himself, and he wants to do a London production over here at the same time."

"I bet he does. Why pick on me?"

"Because you used to know his father."

Well, for heaven's sake. On with the make-up.

"What does he look like?"

"Rather nice. Fair. Looks as if he had been sun bathing somewhere."

"Draw the curtains and I'll shout through them. Tell him he can only stay two minutes."

The thing is, that if I am going to spend the rest of my life reading plays by unknown Frenchmen, it's a pretty poor outlook.

"How do you do? Who's your father?"

Sounds like Harry Tate. Perhaps that's my ultimate answer. Vaudeville.

"How do you do, Miss Delaney? My father sends you his very best respects. His name is Michel Laforge, and he knew you years and years ago in Brittany."

Michel . . . Brittany . . . What an extraordinary coincidence. Because wasn't I thinking about Brittany on Sunday afternoon at Farthings?

"Why, of course. I remember your father very well. How is your father?"

"The same as ever, Miss Delaney. He hasn't aged at all."

He must be a rollicking fifty-five if he's a day. I wonder if he still lies about on rocks, looking for starfish, and seducing little girls.

"What is this play you want me to read?"

"A play of the dix-neuvième siècle, Miss Delaney. Lovely music, lovely décor, and only you could play the part of the duchess."

"A duchess? I have to be a duchess, do I?"

"Yes, Miss Delaney. A very lovely, very wicked duchess."

Well, I suppose I can always be a duchess. I have never been a duchess yet. And a wicked duchess would be more amusing than a good one.

"What does your duchess do?"

"She has five men at her feet."

"Why only five?"

"I could always add a sixth, if you desire it."

Where's my other dressing gown, the blue one? Somebody else now knocking at the door. People treat my room like a public bar.

"Who is it?"

The stage-door man's voice: "A telegram, Miss Delaney."

"All right. Put it on the table."

Lucien has mucked up my hair. Why that curl over the right ear? Always so much better when I do the thing myself. Draw back the curtains.

"How do you do again, Mr. Laforge?"

Not bad-looking, after all. Better than Michel, as I remember him. But rather young. Hardly out of the egg.

"So you want me to be a duchess?"

"Wouldn't you like to be a duchess?"

Yes, I would. I would not mind at all. I'll be the Queen of Sheba or the bad girl in a brothel, if the play is any good and it amuses me.

"Are you doing anything for supper, Mr. Laforge?"

"No."

"Come back, then, after the performance. You shall take me out to supper, and we will talk about your play. Now run along."

He went. He vanished. And the back of his head was really rather nice. The stage manager's voice came through the loud-speaker.

"Quarter of an hour, please."

The dresser pointed towards the telegram on the table.

"You haven't read your telegram, Miss Delaney."

"I never read telegrams before a performance. Don't you know that by this time? My Pappy never did. Nor do I. It brings bad luck."

Maria stood before the mirror; she fastened the belt round her dress.

"Do you remember the song of the Miller of Dee?" she said.

"What was it?" asked the dresser.

Maria laughed and patted a curl into place.

> "I care for nobody, no, not I,
> If nobody cares for me."

The dresser smiled. "You're in very good form tonight, aren't you?" she said.

"I always am," answered Maria. "Every night."

The muffled murmur of the audience, chattering as they took their seats, crackled through the loud-speaker on the walls.

CHAPTER TWENTY-FIVE

WHEN Niall left the dining room at Farthings he went straight up to his room and threw his remaining things into his suitcase, and then he went down again and out of the house, and round the corner of the drive to the garage. He had enough petrol to take him to the coast. It had always been a convenient thing that Farthings was placed strategically between London and the place where he kept his ramshackle boat.

Now it was more than convenient. It meant salvation of the spirit. Always an indifferent driver of a car, Niall became worse through the years, because he became progressively more vague. He never noticed signs and symbols, "Turn Left" or "One-Way Street." He shot traffic lights, not with intention, but because momentarily he would confuse green with red; or alternatively he would stay waiting, over-time, when the colours changed, so that only the infuriated hooting of drivers in the rear, behind him, would startle him from a temporary dream into instant, and often fatal, action. It was a miracle to Maria, to Celia, to all who knew him, that he had never yet been warned or summoned.

It was for this reason, knowing his deficiencies as a driver in the turmoil of daytime traffic, that Niall liked to drive by night. He was safe by night. No one could oppose him. Driving by night had glamour, like Dick Turpin on Black Bess. Doing anything by night was always better than doing anything by day. A song composed at three in the morning was often better than one composed at three in the afternoon. A walk by moonlight made a walk by day seem drab. How good a kipper tasted in the small hours, how potent a hunk of cheese. What energy flowed from the body to the brain, what power, what quicksilver. Whereas the late mornings and the afternoons were created surely for siesta. For lying in the sun. For sleeping behind drawn curtains. For leaving the spirit fallow.

As Niall drove through the silent country roads on his way to the coast, he planned, with characteristic calm, the days to come.

At the moment there was nothing he could do to help Maria. In the immediate future she would swing north and south, east and west, like a weathercock to the winds of thought that blew upon her.

There would be the mood of anger, the mood of resignation. The mood of gay defiance, the mood of the hurt child. When she had worked through the whole gamut of emotion, she would begin again, perhaps, in another key. Some fresh interest would come along to blow her to another compass point. Nothing, the gods be praised, would hurt for long.

Maria's mind was like her body in that it would not scar. A sudden flare-up in her side, some years before, had been diagnosed as a grumbling appendix, and the appendix was removed. The wound healed in about three weeks. In three months nothing showed upon her body but a thin, white line. Whereas with other women, purple weals, and blotches. How often, too, the performance of bearing children tore the guts out of a woman. Not Maria.

It was almost as if Maria was favoured by the gods, and she had been permitted through her life to get away with everything. Had she committed murder, she would never have been caught. Nor would her conscience trouble her. Even if the day of reckoning should come, and it was possible that day was dawning now, her guardian angel would see to it that the day was not too long. The day could be turned to good account. It was true, Niall decided, that the Almighty loved a sinner. He loved no one else. The good, the gentle, the uncomplaining, the self-sacrificing had a raw deal every time. He washed His hands of them. And somewhere Niall had read that the only happy creatures in the world were idiots. Statistics proved it. Psychologists swore to it. Children borne into the world with vacant minds, children with small eyes and blubbing lips, overflowed—so doctors said—with joy, with happiness. They adored everything they saw, from eggs to earthworms. From parents to parasites. To parasites . . . Here we are, then, mused

Niall as he banked a corner; back to parasites. So what does it all prove? That the Mind who controls the universe has the mind of the idiot child, and has a tender spot for parasites. Blessed are the parasites, for they shall inherit the earth. The parasites shall grow rich, and multiply. Theirs is the kingdom of heaven . . . It wanted an hour still to midnight when he reached the saltings. The clock in the village, hidden by the elms, struck eleven. He had made good time. He swung off to the left, and followed the narrow, rutty lane that finished abruptly by the water's edge.

The tide was low, the mudbanks were exposed, and the tall, green rushes that shivered in the months of summer stood bleached and still under the winter sky. The night was dark, the air nippy-cold.

Niall left the car, unlit, drawn to the far side of the road; and, taking the suitcase that held his few possessions, he walked down a muddy path that ran parallel to the mud flats. He came to a rough wooden pontoon jutting into the water.

The tide was still ebbing; he could hear the water suck away from the mud, and it ran fast, swirling round the post of the pontoon. There was a small dinghy tied to the handrail by the post. Niall lowered the suitcase into the dinghy and climbed in after it.

He began to row downstream. It was less cold upon the water than on the land. As he dipped his hand to try the temperature, it struck warm, without the chill he had expected. The paddles creaked in the rowlocks, and the sound echoed in the still quiet air, sharply persistent. There were other boats moored on the right bank of the stream, in deep water below the flats. Niall passed them one by one, muffled shapes in the darkness, lying to rusty chains, left by their owners for the winter months until the spring.

His own boat was the last one of the line. He pulled alongside and, shipping the paddles of the dinghy, climbed into the narrow cockpit and made fast. He took the key from its hiding place in the locker, and opened up the hatch into the cabin. The smell of the cabin was warm and friendly; it held none of the musty dankness of disuse. He struck a match and lit the lamp suspended from the mast. Then, kneeling beside the little bogey stove, he lit the fire. This done, he stood up, humpbacked, because the boat lacked full head room for his height, and, pottering about the small, confined cabin, set things to rights.

As usual, he was hungry. A tongue, sent by an unknown admirer of his songs from Illinois, and not yet acknowledged, made easy eating;

so did a tin of still more dubious origin marked "Halibut, tasty on toast." The toast was not forthcoming, but biscuits from Illinois, wrapped in cellophane, served the same purpose. There were figs with Christmas greetings from a "Buddy in Baltimore" who rang no bell, and find of all finds, a jar of ginger. He poured the ginger syrup into a glass and laced it well with brandy, then, after stirring, warmed the brew in a saucepan on the bogey stove. The mixture tasted like the smell of gorse on a hot day and had a curiously lightening effect, a carefree soporific influence, so that Niall, kicking off his shoes onto the bunk, felt as a bumblebee would feel who emerged, limp-winged and dizzy, from the belly of a foxglove.

He propped two pillows behind his head and, reaching for his notebook, stretched himself full length upon the bunk and began to rough out the plan of the concerto. It was irritating to find, after two hours of work, that the theme predominate, which should be classic, stark, and plain, linking the three movements all together, eluded discipline. The imp who fed his brain and who crouched in a cell of matter, tongue in cheek, would not be harnessed to solemnity. Dignity and poise swung into melody, and the melody itself, unfettered, uncontrolled, soared to a silly, sensuous ecstasy. At first Niall blamed the ginger syrup and the brandy; he blamed the drive, he blamed the winter air, he blamed the pull downstream upon the limpid water. Then he sat up and threw the notes aside.

It was no use. Why beat the brain to feats it could not do? Accept the status in the underworld of sound; leave magic to musicians. Lisp in numbers when the numbers came. To hell with the concerto.

He tucked the blankets round him, and with his hands upon his shoulders, his knees drawn to his chin, he slept as he had always slept, like an infant still unborn.

The next day passed in work, in idleness. In flashes of inspiration. In moments of apathy.

He ate. He drank. He smoked. He walked along the flats. He pulled about the creek. He painted one quarter of his boat a dusty grey. This is the only answer, then, to be alone. This is the ultimate reply. Dependent upon no soul but your own self. Dependent upon the sounds that flood the mind. Creator of your world, your universe.

That night, with the labour pains of a schoolboy in examination, he wrote down clearly, in a fair, round hand, the score of the elusive melody that had haunted him all day.

No mighty composition this, no grand concerto; only another fragment for a fortnight, to be whistled by an errand boy and drummed upon the air. But he had written it down without the piano's aid, which, for Niall, was great achievement. When it was all over and the work was done, the aftermath set in. He felt bleak and strangely lonely. And he wanted Maria. . . . But Maria was many miles away in travail, with her own sins and her own omissions, and the thought of Maria lying in the cramped bunk of his small ship made him laugh aloud.

She had consented to sail once with him for a day. Her one sail and her last. Knowing even less of sailing than he did himself, she accused him violently of pulling the wrong ropes. They became becalmed and he, and not Maria, was sick. The wind, when it did come, came from the wrong quarter and, scudding out to sea, they were just lost to land until a motorboat, large and complacent, ran beside them in the lopping swell and took them in tow. Maria lost a favourite cardigan outboard. She also lost her shoes. Niall, cold and wet, caught a chill. They drove back to Farthings in silence, and Charles, when informed of the fiasco, shrugged his shoulders, saying to his wife, "What else did you expect?"

Celia was an easier boat companion. Handy in a galley. Useful in swabbing decks, but always with an eye to tragedy. "I don't like the look of that dark cloud." "How about turning back while it's still fine?" "Is that a rock I see in the distance, or a poor dead dog?"

She put a damper on adventure. No, it was by far better to sail a boat alone.

The day after he had written the song dawned fair and fine, with a good sailing breeze offshore. Niall pulled up the river to the pontoon, and walked back along the path to where he had left the car, two nights before. It was as he had left it by the side of the lane. He got in and set off for the village. He bought bread and a few provisions, and then he went to the post office and wrote out a telegram. After he had written it he spoke to the girl behind the barrier. She was young and pretty, and he smiled.

"I want you to do something for me," said Niall.

"What is it?" she asked.

"I'm going for a sail," he said, "and I don't know when I shall be back. It depends upon the wind, the state of my boat, and ultimately upon my mood. I want you to keep this telegram until, shall we say, five o'clock this afternoon. If I am back by then I will come and retrieve the telegram and possibly send another one instead, depending, as I have said before, upon my mood. If I am not back—then you may send the telegram, this one here, to that name and address."

The girl looked doubtful and pursed her mouth.

"It's against regulations," she said. "I don't think I can."

"Many things in life," said Niall, "are against regulations. Haven't you discovered that yet?"

The girl blushed.

"It would be against regulations," said Niall, "if, when I came back, I asked you to have supper with me on my boat. But if the supper was good enough you might accept."

"I'm not that sort of girl," she answered.

"A pity," said Niall, "because that sort of girl has fun."

She read through the telegram again. "What time do you want me to send it off?" she said.

"If I'm not back," said Niall, "send it at five o'clock."

"O.K.," she said, and turned her back on him.

Niall read through the telegram again, and paid his money.

It was addressed to Maria Delaney, and then the name of the theatre, London: "Darling, I love you. I'm going for a sail. I have written you a song. If you get this telegram it will mean one of two things. Either I have reached the shores of France or the boat has sunk. I love you again. Niall."

Then, whistling his own tune, he climbed back again into the car, with a loaf of bread, some carrots, and a few potatoes.

It took him quite two hours to get his ship under way, because as he hauled his mainsail the rope became entangled in a block and hung suspended, like a man in chains. In some sailing book that he had read in an idle moment, Niall recollected that a sail, when it did this, was known as scandalised. The name was apt. Scandalised it was. Shamefaced and shy, the sail swung about in the wind, and Niall was forced to climb the mast to get it down, after which the process was repeated, without the scandal. Then the dinghy had to be left upon the buoy, always a difficult manoeuvre. The chain invariably seemed too heavy for the small boat, and weighed it down, bows deep in the water.

Alone, adrift, and launched upon the tide—ebbing, thank God—Niall seized the tiller and broke the jib. The little headsail was reluctant and wrapped itself, protecting, round the stay.

301

Niall was obliged to leave the tiller and climb over the deck to free it. By the time he returned to the tiller, his ship was heading for the mud. He swung her downstream in the nick of time.

What a lamentable figure he must cut from the nearby shore, he thought, and how angry Maria would be.

His course down-river to the sea passed without incident. The ship moved with the wind and tide, and nothing stopped her. Niall would not have known how to stop her had he wished.

Outside, the wind was fresh; but the sun shone and the sea was calm. One of those cold bright days of winter when the land slipped by unnoticed, and the sharp line of the horizon was like a pencil drawing, firm and clear. Niall steered his ship on what seemed to him a favourable course, the smudge of a distant steamer. Forgetting that it moved even as his own ship moved, he lashed the helm in a knot that came undone, and went below to cook himself a luncheon.

Some of the Illinois tongue heated in a frying pan, with chipped potatoes and diced carrots, made a passable meal. His lunch cooked to his liking, Niall climbed with it to the cockpit, and sat eating from the frying pan, one hand on the tiller. The land astern of him was a soft, grey blur, but this did not worry Niall because the sea was smooth. A gull followed him doubtfully, hovering in mid-air, and Niall threw scraps of frazzled tongue to appease his greed. When the tongue was finished, he threw a carrot top. The gull swallowed it and choked; then flew away, screaming, like a vulture, skimming the water with its wings.

Niall went below and fetched a cushion, and, propping it on the combing under his head, he stretched himself out in the cockpit, with one leg over the tiller, and closed his eyes. This, then, was the peak.

In London, in Paris, in New York, men were in offices, seated at desks, ringing bells, speaking on the telephone; men were pouring out of Undergrounds, swarming up bus ladders, standing behind shop counters, hewing rocks in mines. Men were fighting, quarrelling, drinking, making love; men were arguing about money, politics, religion.

Everywhere, all over the world, men were in a ferment somewhere, about something. They had anxiety. They were troubled. Even the people whom he loved had turmoil of the spirit. Maria and Charles had to make up their minds about the future. Celia had to make up her mind about herself. The problem "What now?" stared them in the face.

For Niall, it did not matter. Nothing mattered. He was alone upon the sea. And he had written a song. He was at peace.

If he wished, he need never return. The boat could sail forever. The wind was fair, the water still, and somewhere across that grey expanse of sea was the coast of France; the smells, the sounds of France. What Pappy used to call, in moments of emotion, "Niall's low French blood" still simmered in his veins, if lazily, if now a little slow. England was only home through force of circumstances, because of events, because it happened that way, because of Maria.

Easy enough to sail to France. To send a telegram to Maria from France. "I am here. You come too."

The trouble with Maria, she liked her comforts. She wanted beds and bath essence. Crepe de chine against the skin. And well-cooked food. She would not want to lie with him like this, her head upon a combing, her legs over a tiller. Besides, she had ambition.

Maria, he considered, would live to a grand old age. She would become a legend. White-haired and ruthless, she would shake a crutch at ninety-nine and put the fear of God into all who knew her. And when she died, she would die surprised, indignant. "Death? Not if I know it. There's still so much to do."

Celia would accept the end with patience. Letters would be filed, the bills paid, the things unpacked from the laundry and put away. Otherwise such a nuisance for people who found the body. But she would have her little, anxious frown between the brows. "What should one say to God, if He should be there?"

Niall laughed and stretched himself and yawned. He wondered if it would be a good idea to finish the brandy and the ginger syrup. He stared idly down into the cabin. It was then he noticed, for the first time, the long trickle of water on the cabin floor. He stared at it, puzzled. There was nothing to upset. No spray had come in through the ports, and anyway, the ports were closed. No rain had settled in the bilges, because no rain had fallen for the past two days. Why, then, the water on the cabin floor? Niall went down below to inspect the trickle closer.

He put his fingers in the liquid. It was salt. He looked about him for a screw driver to lift up the floor board. He found one at last at the back of a locker. The search had taken time, and when he knelt down to lift the board, the trickle had become a stream.

He jerked up the board with his screw driver, and he saw that the bilges were full of water, salt like the stream upon the floor. In some part of the boat, whether forward or aft, he had no notion where, a leak had sprung. He supposed that it must be a bad leak because of the rate at which the water was entering the boat.

He wondered what to do. He took up more floor boards, with the idea of finding the leak and plugging it with something, but when he did this the water came up more quickly and lapped over his feet.

He hastily put back the boards, so that the water became a stream again. But the trouble was that it became an ever-widening stream.

He remembered vaguely a phrase from boyhood books, "All hands to the pumps," and he knew there was a pump in the locker aft of the cockpit. He found the pump. It was rusty; he had not used it for some time. He assembled it clumsily and placed the nozzle in the socket on the deck. It made a curious hissing sound, like the pump on a child's bicycle that would not work. It felt much too light. He took it out of the nozzle and examined it. The rubber washer round the base had perished, and there was a hole that should have had a screw inside it, but the screw was missing. The pump, in fact, was useless. Nor had he a bailer, he had left the bailer in the dinghy at the moorings. There was an old jug below that would have to serve instead. He went below again to get the jug, but by now the water covered the boards of the floor. He started bailing the water with the jug. After five minutes of this, kneeling, with cramped back, and throwing the water from the porthole, he realised that he was making little if no impression on the rising stream. To bail was wasted effort. He went up again on deck.

The wind, if anything, had lightened; the sea was slaty-smooth. There was no steamer smoke now on the horizon, and no sign of any ship. The land lay astern, about seven miles distant. Even the gull had gone. Niall sat down in the cockpit once again and watched the water rising on the cabin floor.

His first reaction was relief to be alone. He had not the responsibility of a second person. But swiftly upon this thought came a feeling of melancholy, of sadness. It would have been nice, at such a moment, to talk aloud. Someone like Charles would have been invaluable. Men who had fought in wars, who ran estates, who were efficient, would be sure to know how to cope with a leaking boat. Charles would have found the leak. Charles, if he had not found the leak, would have known how to make a raft. He would have busied himself lashing boards together. Niall did not know how to do any of these things. He only knew how to write songs. Thinking of his song, he looked down again into the cabin, and he saw that the notebook in which he had written down the score had fallen from the ledge beside his bunk and was now floating, face downwards, in the rising stream. Already it was brown and sodden. He rescued it and brought it back, and kept it beside him on the cockpit seat. There was something sinister and inevitable about the swishing water in the cabin, and he closed the hatch, so that he need not watch it rise. He set a course for land, but now that the breeze had fallen away, the ship had very little way under her and hardly moved. The sails lapped softly, scandalised no longer, it was true, but ill at ease. Niall had never installed an engine in the boat because he had always known that he could not make an engine work. He was glad the wind did not come in gusts to rattle him. Had it done so, the odds were that something would have carried away, some rope, some shroud, some vital piece of tackle.

He was glad, too, that the sea was still so smooth. To swim about for hours in rough water would have frightened him, made him catch his breath and choke and lose his head. Whereas in the water that lay about him now, he need not even swim; he could lie upon his back and float.

One thing, at any rate, was certain. Maria would get his telegram.

As Niall sat in the cockpit, waiting, and watching the sun go down upon the land, he found himself thinking, not of Maria, not of the songs he had written, not even of the lost faded image of Mama; but of Truda. He thought of kind, comforting old Truda, and of her broad, safe lap. He thought of the grey stuff dress she used to wear and of how he had rubbed his face against it as a little boy.

And it seemed to him, sitting there in the cockpit, alone upon the sea, that the sea itself was calm and comforting, even as Truda had been long ago. The sea was another Truda, upon which he could cast himself when the time came, without anguish, without fear.

F   73-226
Du Maurier, Daphne

     The Parasites.

DATE DUE

| MAR 25 |
| APR 30 |
| MAY 29 |
| JUN 24 |
| AUG |
| APR 2 |
| SEP |
| JUL |
| NO0 |

F
DuMaurier, Daphne   73-226
AUTHOR
           The Parasites.
TITLE

DATE DUE	BORROWER'S NAME
MAR 25	Judy Long
APR 30	Jessie Ricker
MAY 29	Lucille Burgel
JUN 21	Marie Kemmer
AUG 7	Dar
APR 30	